# Praise for
## *New York Times* be[illegible]
## Carla N[illegible]



"When it comes to rom[illegible]
suspense, nobody deliver[illegible]
—Jayne Ann [illegible]

"Fans of romantic suspens[illegible] be charmed."
—*Publishers Weekly* on *The Angel*

"Suspense, romance and the rocky Maine coast—
what more could a reader ask?
*The Harbor* has it all."
—Tess Gerritsen

"Neggers keeps the reader guessing 'whodunit'
to the end of her intriguing novel."
—*Publishers Weekly* on *The Widow*

"Neggers has created yet another
well-matched pair of characters and given them
a crackerjack mystery to solve—
complete with a seriously creepy villain."
—*Romantic Times BOOKreviews* on *Abandon*

"[Neggers's] skill at creating colorful characters
and deliciously twisted story lines
makes this an addictive read."
—*Publishers Weekly* on *Stonebrook Cottage*

"A keen ear for dialogue
and a sure hand with multidimensional
characterizations are Neggers' greatest gifts as a
storyteller.... By turns creepy and amusing."
—*Romantic Times BOOKreviews* on *Breakwater*

"Carla Neggers is one of the most distinctive,
talented writers of our genre."
—Debbie Macomber

*Also by CARLA NEGGERS*

TEMPTING FATE
THE ANGEL
ABANDON
CUT AND RUN
THE WIDOW
BREAKWATER
DARK SKY
THE RAPIDS
NIGHT'S LANDING
COLD RIDGE
ON THE EDGE
"Shelter Island"
THE HARBOR
STONEBROOK COTTAGE
THE CABIN
THE CARRIAGE HOUSE
THE WATERFALL
ON FIRE
KISS THE MOON
CLAIM THE CROWN

*And coming March 2009*

BETRAYALS

# CARLA NEGGERS

# COLD PURSUIT

ISBN-13: 978-0-7783-2553-6
ISBN-10: 0-7783-2553-9

COLD PURSUIT



www.MIRABooks.com

**Printed in U.S.A.**

To my brother-in-law Bill Ochs

## ACKNOWLEDGMENTS

Special thanks to Lieutenant Jocelyn Stohl of the Vermont State Police and to Susan Bayley and Kenneth Thibodeaux of the White River Junction (Vermont) Veterans Affairs Medical Center for your help, as well as for the remarkable work you do. Once again I want to thank Paul Hudson—judge, scholar, friend and a Vermonter with deep roots in this incredibly beautiful part of our country.

And, as always, many thanks to Joe, Kate, Conor and Zack. We do have fun together!

# *Prologue*

Drew Cameron slipped and went down on one knee in the heavy, wet spring snow, but he forced himself back up again, propelled by a sense of urgency he had never known before.

*Not Elijah.*

*Please, God. Not my son....*

Drew took another step, then another, pushing against the fierce wind. Sleet cut into his face and pelted onto the snow-covered trees and juts of granite on the steep terrain. The mid-April storm was worse than was forecasted. In the valley, daffodils were starting to pop up out of the ground. It was mud season in Vermont. If anything, he'd worried about causing more erosion on the trails, still wet from the melting winter snows.

He hadn't bothered strapping a pair of snowshoes onto his pack in case conditions warranted—a mistake, he realized now.

But he refused to turn back.

He had gone off the main trail hours ago, but he knew every inch of Cameron Mountain. By now, the snow would have covered any footprints he'd left. If anything happened to him, he'd be lucky if searchers found his body for his family to bury.

"I don't care." He spoke in a ragged whisper. "Take me."

*Take me instead of my son.*

How many fathers through the millennia had cried out those same words?

Drew coughed and spat, catching his breath as he came to a lull in the upward sweep of the mountain. The summit was another thousand feet up, but he had no intention of going that far. In all his seventy-seven years, he had never operated on such blind instinct. He couldn't stop himself—he had to be here, now, at this moment, asking questions, searching for answers.

He wasn't an emotional man, but he couldn't shake the fear that had gripped him since dawn.

He couldn't shake the images.

The certainty.

*I'm an old man.*

*Let me die in my son's place.*

As he eased among a dense grove of tall spruce trees, their branches drooping under the weight of the clinging, wet snow, he saw young men huddled, battling an unseen enemy.

He saw their blood oozing into the ground of the faraway land where they fought.

He heard their moans of pain amid the rapid, nonstop gunfire.

*An ambush...*

The vision wasn't born of books and movies, and it wasn't a nightmare to be chased off with daylight and coffee. It was real. Every second of it. Drew didn't understand how the vision of his son in battle had come to him, but he trusted it—believed it.

It wasn't a premonition. The attack on Elijah's position wasn't imminent—it was happening now.

Drew stood up straight, out of the worst of the wind. The

ice had abruptly changed back to snow. Fat flakes fell silently in the white landscape, but he saw, as clearly as if he were there, the bright stars of the moonless Afghan night. Elijah never talked about his secret missions. He had joined the army at nineteen, without discussing his decision with anyone—not his two brothers, his sister, his friends.

Definitely not his father.

But there were reasons for that.

"Dear God," Drew whispered, "let me make up for what I did to him. Please. Give me that chance."

For fifteen years he had convinced himself he had done the right thing when he had kicked Elijah out of the house and sent Jo Harper back to her family. Even now, Drew accepted that he'd had no other choice.

That didn't mean he didn't have regrets.

A.J., Sean and Rose would forgive him if he died on the mountain he loved, but they'd never forgive him if their brother was killed. That Elijah had chosen to become a soldier and accepted the risks that came with it wouldn't soften his siblings from holding their father responsible for driving him away from the only place he'd ever truly wanted to be.

Drew scooped up snow into his waterproof glove and formed it into a smooth ball. Two weeks ago he had held in his palms a dozen fragrant pink blossoms that had fallen from Washington's famous cherry trees, even as Jo Harper, in her early thirties now, had scrutinized him, obviously wondering if he was half out of his mind.

He hadn't gone into his other reasons for coming to Washington. It seemed crazy now. Crazier even than his reasons for seeking out Jo. More visions emerged, as clear and real as the one of his son in battle—Elijah, the boy Jo had loved, now a man.

Drew dropped the snowball into a drift.

Maybe he *was* half out of his mind.

He noticed footprints—fresh ones—slowly disappearing in the falling snow. He went very still. He wasn't so disoriented and preoccupied that he'd gone in circles.

No, he thought. They weren't his prints.

Someone was up here with him.

Drew crept past the spruce and, just ahead, saw the little house he had spent most of last fall building. He hadn't bothered with permits—he figured he'd get slapped with a fine one of these days, but he didn't care. He hadn't meant for the project to get away from him the way it had. After years of searching, he had finally found the cellar hole of the original Cameron house on Cameron Mountain. He had started by clearing out some trees and fixing up the rock foundation, and next thing he knew he was drawing up plans for a simple post-and-beam structure—more shed than house, really. When he finished it, he meant to present it as a surprise to his family, perhaps their last surprise from him.

The closest trail was up the remote north side of the mountain from a seldom-used old logging road. His great-great-grandfather would have taken that route two hundred years ago. Few even knew about it anymore, and it was impassable for most of the winter.

Drew stopped, held his breath.

There…voices.

"We have to think through every detail of every assignment." A man's voice. Arrogant, deliberate. "We can't go off half-cocked. We have to plan."

"You plan." It was a woman this time, impatient. "I'll take action."

"This is business. We're being paid to do a job. It's not some adventure to keep you in adrenaline rushes. Just because you don't need the money—"

"I *want* the money. That's enough for me."

"You've never killed anyone," the man said quietly.

A slight pause. "How do you know?"

The door to Drew's little house opened, but he didn't look at who stood on the threshold. Instead he gazed up into the falling snow, letting one flake after another melt on his face. Now he understood his visions. He understood why he was here on Cameron Mountain at this moment.

It was meant to be. He was a father who would get his wish.

His son would live.

*Elijah will come home.*

# One

*Seven months later*

A red-tailed hawk swooped down from Cameron Mountain and out over the small lake, gray and quiet in the mid-November gloom, as if to warn Jo Harper she wasn't alone—but she had already figured that out.

She glanced down the private dirt road she shared with Elijah Cameron.

Yep. He was still coming.

Ignoring the tug of pain in her left side, she reached into the trunk of her car for a cardboard box filled with food and supplies she'd grabbed out of her apartment. She thought of the other places she could have exiled herself. New Zealand, for example. The south of France. Costa Rica. It didn't have to be Vermont. Black Falls. Her picturesque hometown in the heart of the Green Mountains.

It was summer in New Zealand, she thought as she lifted the box on her uninjured hip and noted that it was barely four o'clock and yet almost dark. The long, dark winter nights were upon northern New England. She'd left Washington early in order to arrive in Vermont while it was still daylight.

Using her elbow, she shut the trunk. Three brown-spotted bananas on top of the overflowing box hadn't fared well on the long trip north, but she hadn't wanted to leave them to rot in her microscopic Georgetown apartment. She didn't know when she'd be back at her job with the Secret Service. Technically, she was just taking some time off. But everyone knew she'd been all but ordered to clear out of town for a bit.

Jo knew it, too.

Elijah seemed to be carrying a vase of flowers, but that didn't make sense.

Flowers? Elijah?

Even from fifty yards away, he looked as sexy, rugged and forbidden as ever. She hadn't realized he was home from the army. Not that her family in Black Falls would have told her, especially this week—because then she really might have chucked it all and bought a one-way ticket to New Zealand.

Elijah had built a house on the wooded hillside adjoining the thirty acres and its dozen, one-room, falling-down cabins he and his brothers and sister had every reason to expect to inherit one day. Instead, Drew Cameron had left the property to Jo. The shock of his death from hypothermia in an April snowstorm had only been compounded by that one detail in his last will and testament.

None of the Cameron siblings was more taken aback than Jo was herself by their father's inexplicable act of generosity.

And yet…

She pushed the uncomfortable memory of her last encounter with Drew Cameron out of her mind. She didn't want to go there. Not now, not especially with Elijah ambling her way.

She watched the hawk glide back toward her and disappear into the woods and hills above the cabins.

Cameron land.

There was no wind, but the air was brisk and chilly—she'd gotten used to Washington's warmer climate. She'd had to pull on her black fleece jacket when she'd crossed the Vermont border. She hadn't expected to be back in Black Falls until Thanksgiving, and then only for a short visit with her family.

But here she was, and who knew for how long?

The brightly colored leaves of October had fallen, just the rusts and maroons of dying oak leaves clinging to branches among the hemlocks, pines and spruces along the dot of a glacial lake. Jo noticed a battered dark green wooden canoe in the grayish frost-killed grass down by the lake. It was on her property, but it wasn't her canoe. No doubt it belonged to a Cameron—probably the one walking down the road with the flowers.

She carried her box across the weeds and dead pine needles that passed for a yard. Elijah kept coming. She saw no sign of a limp—her sister, Beth, had e-mailed her in April after news hit town that Elijah, a Special Forces soldier, had been wounded, badly, in Afghanistan.

It was the day after Devin Shay, a Black Falls High School senior, had found Drew Cameron dead on the mountain named for his ancestors.

Jo stopped at the front door—the only door—to the largest of the dilapidated cabins. It was set up on blocks and had moss growing on its roof, which couldn't be good, and its board-and-batten exterior needed a fresh coat of dark brown paint.

But it was the closest to the lake and the best of the lot. Most of the cabins probably should have been condemned years ago. A.J., the eldest Cameron, supposedly had drawn up plans for expanding Black Falls Lodge down to the lake, never expecting the land wouldn't one day be his.

Elijah left the dirt road and walked toward her as if he didn't have a care in the world. He wore a canvas jacket, close-fitting jeans and a navy blue Red Sox cap, and Jo noted the dark stubble of beard on his square Cameron jaw. If possible, he was even more appealing than he had been at nineteen, when he had whisked her off for three nights and four days in the very cabins she had just inherited.

She had never loved anyone the way she had Elijah Cameron.

But that was a long time ago.

He came up to the doorstep with his vase of flowers. They were all lilies—Asiatic lilies in varying shades of cream, apricot and copper.

Jo settled the box onto her right hip. She could have stayed with her sister or brother or in her old room growing up, but she'd opted for space, quiet and solitude. She'd always loved the lake. While she was doing damage control on her career, she figured she could also consider her options for what to do with her lakefront property.

Elijah barely contained a smile. "Rough week, Agent Harper?"

It wasn't looking to get better anytime soon. "Hello, Elijah."

"Jo."

"I didn't see you—"

"Not a chance. You're a Secret Service agent who protects the lives of important people. You spotted me before you took the key out of your ignition."

She sighed. "You're not going to make this easy, are you?"

His eyes, the same deep blue that had captivated her as a teenager, sparked with humor. "No, ma'am. It's too good."

"No one else is making this easy. No reason you should." She nodded to the enormous vase of lilies he carried in the crook of one arm. "Taking up flower arranging, Elijah?"

"Penny dropped them off earlier. She didn't want to leave them out in the open. They're for you."

Penny Hodges owned the only flower shop in Black Falls and had always had a soft spot for Elijah. She and his mother had been best friends. Drew used to accuse both women of coddling his second-born son and had seen himself as the only one willing to impose discipline on him.

Ancient history, Jo thought, and now both Elijah's parents were gone.

"Who're they from?" she asked.

"What makes you think I know?"

"You looked at the card."

"Ah. Well." He sniffed an apricot-colored lily. "So I did. Are you armed?"

"Elijah—"

"It can be dangerous, having a badass Secret Service agent next door."

Just her luck that Elijah would be the first person she ran into in Black Falls. Despite the ordeals of the past seven months—his father's death, his own near death—he looked fit, as muscular and as physical as ever. But Jo didn't fool herself. Elijah Cameron wasn't the same small-town Vermont boy who had stolen her heart and soul as a teenager.

And she wasn't the same small-town girl.

"If the flowers are a gag gift from one of my colleagues,

you can dump them in the lake. Paddle your canoe out to a deep spot and give them the heave-ho."

"They're from your new best friend in Washington."

Charlie Neal, Jo thought. That little bastard had the gall to send her flowers.

She contained her reaction and said tightly, "Take them inside if you would. My hands aren't exactly free."

Elijah tugged open the rickety screen door. "Did you pick this cabin for old times' sake?"

It was the cabin where they'd made love night and day after her high-school graduation. He had graduated the year before and spent the year working at Black Falls Lodge—long before A.J. took it over—and avoiding arrest by Jo's father, the local police chief.

"This one has the best heat," Jo said, neutral.

"It also has bats. I see them flying in and out at dusk."

"It's too cold now for bats."

"They're snug in their beds up in your rafters," he said, entering the cabin.

Jo stepped inside and set her box on the rough wood floor next to her duffel bag, which she'd already hauled from her car. She wasn't that sure what all she'd packed. Frustrated, aggravated, anxious to get out of Washington as fast as she could, she'd tossed together clothes, reading material and leftovers with little thought to what she'd need.

Elijah put the flowers on the small drop-leaf table near the window overlooking the lake. Three of her colleagues who'd stayed in the cabins in October had referred to the decor as early junkyard, but they'd enjoyed the setting—the woods, the lake, the hills. They'd hiked, fished, gone canoeing, read books in the quiet.

That was before Jo's bad week. She doubted any of her fellow Secret Service agents would head to Vermont anytime soon, even if she did fix up the cabins.

She avoided looking at the iron four-poster bed in the alcove—it was the same bed she and Elijah had found so useful fifteen years ago.

"How long are you planning to stay?" he asked.

"Until the dust settles in Washington."

Jo bent down and grabbed the bananas from the top of her box. How long *would* she be here? As she stood up straight again, she tried not to wince in front of Elijah, a matter of personal pride, but she knew she'd failed.

"Still hurting?" he asked with no detectable amusement or sarcasm.

"Not really."

"Baking soda and water might help."

*Now* she detected a note of amusement and sarcasm. "Thanks. I'm fine."

She had heard every conceivable homemade remedy in the past seventy-two hours, ever since she'd fallen victim to a prank orchestrated by the sixteen-year-old son of the vice president of the United States. Charles Preston Neal was a notorious handful. He had invited his cousins and friends over to the madhouse that was the vice president's residence for an elaborate simulated firefight with realistic-looking fake weapons. Jo was assigned to Marissa Neal, the eldest of Charlie's four older sisters, who lived nearby and was there for a visit.

Five minutes into their firefight, Charlie had pointed at his cousin Conor, who was about to shoot, and yelled, "I think it's a real gun!"

Jo had reacted instantly, jumping into action to save Charlie and his friends from possible injury or death. But the "weapon" turned out to be another of the authentic-looking toy pistols and rifles in the boys' extensive arsenal. She'd intercepted a barrage of airsoft pellets zipping toward Charlie and took the dozens of tiny, fake rounds meant for him.

Trying to live down the spray of pinprick welts on her left arm, side and hip would have been bad enough, but Charlie had collapsed in hysterical laughter, and that was it. Jo pulled him up by the ear and gave him an uncensored piece of her mind.

*That* was what one of his cousins or friends—no one knew which one—had secretly captured on video and put on the Internet.

Hence, today's drive up to Vermont.

Vice President Neal had mandated the boys all take a police-sanctioned safety course if they were to have any more simulated battles in the backyard, and he'd personally sat them down at the kitchen table and had them write notes of apology to Jo. There was no telling how many of them were in on the prank, but Charlie clearly was the ringleader.

But the damage was done. The video was out there forever, with Secret Service Special Agent Jo Harper grabbing the vice president's son by the ear and giving him a piece of her mind.

Not one of the finer moments in her career.

Marissa Neal was sympathetic, having fallen victim to her brother's pranks herself. Jo's quick action a few weeks earlier had saved Marissa from severe burns and possibly death when a gas stove had exploded in a cabin she and friends had rented in the Shenandoah Mountains. A simple accident. It wasn't publicized, much less splashed over the Internet.

"Dyeing your hair these days, Jo?"

She frowned at Elijah. "What?"

"I like the copper," he said, then nodded to the flowers. "That must explain Charlie's choice of colors for your lilies. They go with your hair."

"He has an IQ of a hundred and eighty. He knows how to manipulate people."

"Maybe he has a crush on you."

"I doubt that."

The youngest of five and the only son of a busy, popular vice president, Charlie was also desperate to be noticed, desperate to matter. As a Secret Service agent, and one not directly assigned to him, Jo couldn't let that be her concern—but she couldn't help but notice, either.

He was also fair-haired, good-looking, exceptionally bright and surprisingly unworldly given his wealthy, high-profile family background.

Elijah pushed open the screen door and glanced back at her. "You really can't tell a toy gun from a real one?"

"Go ahead, Elijah, have your fun. Yes, I can tell. That's not why I got hit." She set the bananas on the two-foot cracked Formica counter in the bare-bones kitchen area. They'd be mush by morning. "It doesn't matter. Charlie and the rest of those kids are all safe."

"You did your job," Elijah said.

"That's the way I look at it."

His eyes stayed on her for a fraction longer than she found comfortable. "Didn't know I was back, did you?"

"No."

She returned to the box and saw that she'd made a mistake in packing the three cartons of yogurt she'd had in her fridge.

They were squished now, and ten hours in her trunk couldn't have been good for their contents.

Thinking about yogurt gone bad wasn't enough to distract her from the man standing in the doorway.

"I heard you were wounded," she said, raising her gaze to him. "You're okay now?"

"Never better."

His response was classic Elijah. Jo had never met anyone more resilient. Most of his years as a Special Forces soldier were clouded in mystery and the subject of much speculation in Black Falls. Even with her high-level security clearances, Jo doubted she could find out the specifics of the April firefight. She'd heard that a bullet had nicked his femoral artery, a highly dangerous injury. He could have easily bled to death.

According to her sister, he was evacuated to Landstuhl Regional Medical Center in southern Germany, and only when he was out of danger had his family informed him of his father's death. Beth had heard the story straight from Rose Cameron, Elijah's younger sister, who had flown to Germany to be with her brother.

"But he already knew," Beth had said. "No one had to tell him."

Jo suspected that one look at Rose's face probably had been enough for Elijah to figure out the bad news for himself.

"I'm sorry about your father." She ran a finger along the delicate edge of a dark maroon lily. "I had no idea he planned to leave me this place. I never asked him for anything, Elijah. Ever. He didn't owe me."

His expression was unreadable. "That doesn't seem to be how he saw it, does it?"

She resisted comment. To get into a discussion about Drew

Cameron now, after her long day and lousy week, in the very cabin in which he had discovered her and Elijah as teenagers and changed the course of their lives, made no sense.

"Thanks for delivering the flowers," she said.

"Anytime. And relax. Give yourself time to heal." He grinned suddenly. "I hear those airsoft pellets sting like hell."

"Funny, Elijah."

"You haven't seen the video, have you?"

"No, and I don't intend to." A colleague had brought his personal laptop to her desk to show her two-minute video, but his battery had run out. Her one stroke of luck all week, as far as she was concerned. "You have?"

"A.J. and I had a couple of beers the other night and watched it start to finish at least three times."

"You did not."

"Okay. Six times."

The screen door creaked shut as he headed out, laughing.

After he left, Jo checked the card tucked among the lilies.

*Thank you for your willingness to save my life.*
*Someday I'll make amends. Charles P. Neal.*

She sighed and told herself she was glad there hadn't been a real gun. No one had been seriously hurt that day. The rest didn't matter.

On her drive north, Jo had tried to be optimistic and thought of the various ways that being in Black Falls would do her good. She could go for runs in the fresh, crisp northern New England air. She could watch the last of the leaves fall off the trees. Wait for the first real snow. Watch the birds migrate for warmer climates.

Listen for bats in the rafters and avoid her nearest neighbor.

She got busy unpacking before she could change her mind and load up her car again and head to Montreal or Buffalo—anywhere, she thought, that would put her more than a couple hundred yards from Elijah Cameron.

Ten minutes later, Jo was already bored with unpacking. She opened a bottle of merlot, poured herself a glass and took it outside, crossing the dirt road and heading down to the lake.

She stood on a rounded boulder and sipped her wine. The sky was almost dark now. The air was frosty, and the landscape had the stark, empty feel of November, so different from the warm spring afternoon when she'd walked among the cherry blossoms with Drew Cameron.

She hadn't told anyone—family, friends, colleagues or, most of all, Drew Cameron's three sons and daughter—about the strange visit two weeks before his death.

She could see him now as they'd walked along the Tidal Basin. He'd surprised her when he'd shown up at her apartment and asked her to go with him to see the cherry blossoms. He was alone—A.J. was working nonstop at the lodge, Elijah was deployed to parts unknown, Sean was in southern California making money and Rose was off with her search dogs, picking through the remains of a string of Midwestern tornadoes.

The brown flannel shirt Drew wore was too warm for early April in Washington, but he hadn't seemed to notice. Surrounded by the stunning pale pink blossoms, the hard-bitten man Jo had once blamed for helping to ruin her life had startled her further by asking if she was okay these days.

"You've never married, Jo," he'd said.

"I'm only thirty-three." She'd laughed. "There's still time."

"I guess things are different now. Elijah's never married, either, but I don't think he ever expected to live this long. I'm not saying he has a death wish or anything. He's just being practical." Drew had paused, his face lined with deep wrinkles as much from a life spent mostly outdoors in the mountains he loved as from age. "We Camerons are a practical lot."

Uncomfortable with his seriousness, Jo had gone for another lighthearted remark. "I don't know that moving to Vermont in the middle of the Revolutionary War was all that practical. Then staying there. Your ancestors could have cleared out and joined the westward expansion." She'd caught a falling cherry blossom in a palm and smiled at him. "Taken a flatboat to Ohio or something."

"Harpers got to Vermont before any Camerons did."

"Not all of us Harpers stayed," she said.

"True. Jo, there are days…" He'd hesitated and gazed up at the cherry trees and the cloudless sky. It was one of those rare, glorious early-spring afternoons in the nation's capital. Finally, he'd shifted back to Jo, with tears in his eyes. "I wake up on cold mornings and see the grandchildren you and Elijah should have had. They're as clear to me as you are right now. They line up in front of my bed and look at me as if I did something wrong."

Jo had needed a moment to collect herself. She hadn't expected such words—such an image—to come from Drew Cameron. But she'd sensed his pain, his age, and however much she'd hated him in the past, blamed him for the way he'd humiliated her at eighteen, she couldn't hate him then. "Don't torture yourself," she'd said quietly. "I'm happy. Elijah's happy—"

"I keep dreaming I'm going to lose him."

"Mr. Cameron…Drew…"

"I wake up in a cold sweat, Jo. My heart pounds and I can't go back to sleep. I know he's going to die over there. I don't know what he's doing, exactly—he tells me what he can. But it's dangerous. And he's not going to survive."

Jo had crushed the cherry blossoms in her palms and dropped them on the walk. Drew Cameron wasn't a worrier. She doubted there was a Cameron ever born who was. They were action oriented and forward looking. They didn't brood—they didn't dwell on those things they couldn't do anything about.

Like keeping a son at war safe from harm.

Jo was unable to fathom Elijah dying young. He would always be the devil-may-care teenager she'd promised to love forever.

Except it hadn't worked out that way.

"It's natural to worry," she'd told his father, "especially given the nature of Elijah's work."

"I'd give my life for Elijah," Drew had said simply.

"He knows that. Come on. Let's look at the cherry blossoms."

"Jo…"

She had never seen him—maybe any Cameron—so openly emotional, but every instinct she had told her why he had come to see her. She'd stopped, staring out at the Tidal Basin as she spoke. "You did what you thought was right when you broke up Elijah and me and kicked him out of your house. There's nothing for either of us to forgive."

"Will you still think that if he's killed?"

"Have faith."

They'd continued their cherry-blossom tour in near silence,

and Jo couldn't help but imagine what the children the usually stolid man next to her claimed to have seen looked like. How many of them were there? Were they boys, girls—a mix?

Did they have Elijah's deep blue eyes?

She hadn't been able to bring herself to ask Drew to describe them.

She'd fallen for a bad boy and a Cameron all those years ago, and he'd left her for the army. There was no going back.

When Jo received word of Drew's death on Cameron Mountain and Elijah's narrow escape in Afghanistan, she had thought back to that eerie conversation among the cherry blossoms and wondered if, somehow, Drew had gotten his wish—if he had, at least in his own mind, exchanged his life for his son's.

It wasn't a conversation she intended ever to have with Elijah or any Cameron.

Recent evidence to the contrary, she did know that some things needed to be left unsaid.

She jumped down from her rock and decided to resume unpacking.

But when she returned to the cabin, she dug out her cell phone and checked the signal. *Weak.* She tried her boss's direct line, anyway.

Deputy Special Agent in Charge Mark Francona picked up on the second ring and sighed. "What?"

"I'm in Vermont," Jo said. "How long do I get to stay in exile?"

"Who is this?"

"Jo Harper."

"Jo who?"

*Click.*

Despite his enormous responsibilities and straight-as-an-arrow professionalism, her boss had a peculiar sense of humor.

On the other hand, maybe he was being serious.

Jo flipped her cell phone shut and dropped onto the ratty couch. She stared up at a dusty picture of a trout on the cheap wood paneling above the old propane heater.

Maybe, in his own way, Francona was trying to tell her that the sand was running out of the hourglass on her Secret Service career, and she'd be stuck in Black Falls forever.

# Two

Elijah grabbed a neatly split, perfectly dried log from the two cords of wood he'd had delivered at the top of his driveway. He felt no pain or even residual stiffness in his right thigh where he'd been shot. He had tied on a tourniquet himself that long, bad night to stem the bleeding and keep on fighting.

He hadn't expected to live. The Special Forces medic who'd treated him, and later his doctors, had said it was a miracle he hadn't bled to death.

He didn't believe in miracles.

A sudden cold wind blew up from the lake. Even if it took until midnight, he wanted to get the wood stacked tonight.

His help, in the form of two teenagers, apparently had deserted him.

It was dark now, the pines and naked birches and maples on his hillside black silhouettes against the star-sprinkled night sky.

Jo had gone back inside with her glass of wine or whatever it was she'd stood on her rock drinking.

Through the trees, he saw a light come on in her rat heap of a cabin.

Having the Secret Service next door was a complication he didn't need when he was on the hunt for answers, but Elijah figured he didn't have much choice in the matter—and at least Jo was easier to look at than the three agents who'd stayed in the cabins a few weeks ago when he'd just arrived back home.

It wasn't until last week, on a solitary hike up Cameron Mountain, that he'd flat-out decided he didn't have the full story behind his father's death in April.

Just as he was starting to push for answers, Jo had to get herself into trouble in Washington and turn up on the lake.

Elijah grabbed more logs. He'd switched on the lights in the lower level of his home, but even so, it was a dark night. He pictured Jo at ten, freckle-faced and full of mischief, scrambling up a tall oak on the lakeshore to cut the rope to his tire swing. He'd sailed out over the water. By the time he swam back to shore, she'd lit out. He never did catch up with her.

He pictured her skinny-dipping in an isolated cove on a chilly fall night at fifteen. He remembered her mortification when he'd stumbled onto her. Then her anger as she'd pelted him with a rock.

Those turquoise eyes of hers.

And he pictured her at eighteen, whispering to him in the moonlight. "I love you, Elijah. I'll love you forever."

She'd long since come to her senses.

He'd been a sucker for Jo Harper for as long as he could remember.

He took his load of logs to the lean-to he'd built on the front lower level of his house, under the deck, and lined them up side by side. When he'd bought his five hillside acres three years ago, he hadn't even considered that it didn't have any lake frontage. He'd expected the adjoining acreage to stay in the family. He'd worked on his place whenever he could get back to Black Falls, clearing the land, building his post-and-beam house. It was nothing fancy, but he was satisfied with the results.

As he returned to his woodpile, he heard a rustling in the fallen leaves up on the steep, rocky trail from Black Falls Lodge. In another two seconds, Devin Shay burst from the shadows and trees, panting and out of breath. "Hey, Elijah."

So his help hadn't deserted him entirely after all. "You're late," Elijah said. "Grab a log. Where's your girlfriend?"

"Right behind me. She's not— We're not…" Devin shuffled over to the heap of cordwood. "Nora and I are just friends."

"It's dark. Does she have a flashlight?" Devin didn't, but Nora Asher hadn't grown up in Black Falls and couldn't know every rock and root on the lodge trail.

"There's nothing in the dark that's not there in the light." Devin grabbed a log in each hand. He was lanky and surly—and trouble. "Isn't that what you always say, Elijah?"

The kid wasn't being funny, Elijah decided. He was being a jerk.

Seven months ago, Devin had found the frozen body of Elijah's father on the north side of Cameron Mountain. It was three days after he'd disappeared. Rose had been up on the mountain with her search dog. A.J. and his wife, Lauren, were out there. Sean had flown in from southern California. The Vermont State Police search-and-rescue team had launched an official search. But it was a high-school senior who'd located Drew Cameron. The autopsy indicated he'd died of hypothermia.

He had, literally, collapsed in the snow and gone to sleep.

Devin seemed chastened when Elijah didn't respond. "Nora's right behind me," he said.

"I'm here, I'm here," she called cheerfully, bounding out from the trail. "Don't be mad, Elijah. I told Devin not to wait for me. Sorry I'm late."

Elijah eyed the two of them, both eighteen, both insecure and unreliable. But any similarities ended there. Nora was short and a little overweight, attractive with her dark, curly hair and big smile. She'd had her pick of colleges after graduating from her expensive Washington, D.C., prep school in May, but she'd dropped out of Dartmouth College over in New Hampshire six weeks ago and moved to Black Falls to get a job and experience "real life" for a year. That she was living rent free in a guesthouse on an expensive Vermont country estate owned by family friends didn't seem to interfere with her concept of "real life."

Nora set to work on the wood. "Come on, Devin," she said. "Let's get this done."

Devin hung back, watching her as if he couldn't imagine what was so great about stacking wood. He had been in the back of a cruiser a few times, particularly since graduating—barely—in June. Elijah had gotten into plenty of scrapes at that age. Jo's father, the local police chief, hadn't cut him any slack, and not just because of Jo, or because Elijah was a Cameron, or because he deserved it. "I'm trying to save you from yourself, son," Chief Harper would say as he'd slapped on the handcuffs.

Wes Harper was retired now. The new chief didn't have the same connections to the town he served. If Devin stepped too far out of line, he'd be up on charges. His weakness seemed to be standing up to bullies, which Elijah could appreciate—but he was also convinced that Devin hadn't told everything he knew about what had happened on the mountain that spring.

*"Devin,"* Nora said, impatient. "Come *on*."

Finally he sighed, glowered at Elijah and got to work.

Devin stacked the logs quickly and ably, automatically crisscrossing them to keep them from toppling over, but Nora had to think, pause, figure out just how to arrange the logs in her arms, how many she could manage at a time, how to unload them without dropping one on her foot. She was enthusiastic, Elijah saw, but inexperienced. She'd been like that in an all-day winter hiking class A.J. had talked him into teaching at the lodge a week ago—eager, naive and yet also a little snotty.

Elijah lost patience after fifteen minutes. "Go on. I'll finish."

They didn't argue with him. He fetched a flashlight off his deck steps and handed it to Devin for the hike back to the lodge. "I can drive you up there if you want."

"We prefer to walk," Nora said before Devin could answer. She brushed bits of bark and sawdust off the sleeves of her expensive jacket. "I love the Vermont night sky. The stars are so bright."

Devin shrugged. "I never noticed." He nodded toward Jo's cabin through the bare trees. "Is some new Secret Service agent here?"

Elijah kept his expression neutral. "Jo Harper."

Nora looked startled, and Devin grinned, his first show of humor since arriving. "Did she get fired?"

"The Secret Service equivalent of being sent to her room."

"Beth says Jo's such a good shot now, she can take the eyes out of a crow."

"Good to know."

"What about you, Elijah? Are you that good a shot?"

He didn't answer. Devin was being a jerk again.

"A lot of people in town think you're still special ops."

"People can think what they want to think."

Nora seemed to go a little pale. "I hate war," she said. "Sorry. I just do."

Elijah picked up several good-size pieces of dried bark that had come off some of the logs and would work well as kindling. "Understood."

She blushed. "I didn't mean— I just..." She dropped whatever she meant to say and turned to Devin. "I'm ready if you are."

Elijah paid them in cash, and as they returned to the hillside trail, Devin flipped on the flashlight, directing the beam of light at the ground. "See you, Elijah. We'll get here on time if you ever have any more work for us."

After they left, Elijah walked down to the lake in the dark, the ground familiar to him, the clean, cold air welcome after breathing in wood particles. He heard an owl in the woods off to his left, and to his right, he saw a bat against the starlit sky, beelining for Jo's cabin. He couldn't resist a smile. Whether the bat went into the cabin or not, he couldn't tell.

So many nights in faraway places, he had imagined himself as he was now, on the edge of the lake on a biting fall night. Sometimes Jo would be there with him. Not always, but when she was, he would see her clearly—the sharp angles of her face, the spray of freckles on her cheeks and nose, the spark of her eyes. He would hear her laugh and be soothed by her smile. He hadn't considered it a vision or a fantasy. Just Jo being with him out here on the lake.

He'd often wondered if she ever thought about him and had hoped she didn't.

He turned away from the lake. Jo's cabin was dark now.

His father had only bought the lakefront property a few years ago, after finally wearing down old Pete Harper, the original owner, an eccentric ninety-year-old cousin of Jo's grandfather, who had since died.

Elijah returned to his woodpile. He'd gone out to his father's grave in his first days back home. Still recuperating in Germany, he'd missed the funeral. As he'd stared at the simple stone marker, he'd understood, at least in his own mind, that whatever had occurred on Cameron Mountain last April still required a reckoning. Answers. Justice, even.

He knew himself, and he wouldn't stop until he had a clear picture of everything that had happened in Black Falls that spring.

His father would expect no less of him.

But Jo Harper was back in town, and as Elijah reached for another log, he debated which was the bigger problem—that she was as pretty as ever, or that she was a federal agent with a gun and the power of arrest.

Not that it mattered. Either way, Jo had never been one to break rules.

Except, of course, with him.

# *Three*

Thomas Asher folded the *Washington Post* and set it to the side of his table with a chuckle of amusement after reading a rip-roaring, tongue-in-cheek op-ed on the Jo Harper incident. It focused on her and the vice president's beloved, unruly family—the point being, how could anyone expect the Secret Service to keep track of such incorrigible rascals?

The furor over Jo's encounter with Charlie Neal should have abated by now, but it went on because politicians and media hounds wanted it to.

And because there was that video, of course.

To Thomas—and to most people, he had no doubt—Jo came across as a competent professional who hadn't lost control but had simply, finally, done what the vice president or his wife should have done a long time ago: take their one and only son by the ear and read him the riot act.

Thomas settled back in his upholstered chair. The restaurant was on the first floor of an elegant, historic hotel a few blocks from Lafayette Park and the White House. He'd walked from his office where he worked as a political scientist for a respected think tank. Alex Bruni had called late yesterday afternoon to ask Thomas to breakfast. Of course, Alex was late. It was an annoyance, but not a surprise.

Thomas thought about Jo again. He suspected she was finished in the Secret Service, if only because it prized anonymity and discretion and both had gotten away from her after Charlie Neal's prank.

Unfair, perhaps, but he was secretly glad. She was capable of doing more with her life than working for the Secret Service. An elitist position on his part, he supposed, but an honest one. He'd met Jo in February on a long weekend in Vermont with his daughter. The trip was against his better judgment, but Nora, then a high-school senior, had pleaded with him to go. He was still licking his wounds after his wife—his *ex*-wife—had married Alex, one of Thomas's closest friends, and Nora was desperate to find a way for them to make peace with each other. She'd wanted beautiful Black Falls, Vermont, to be their common ground. It wasn't that simple, of course, but Thomas would do anything for his daughter. They'd gone snowshoeing in an apple orchard one morning, and he'd spotted an attractive woman battling her way up an icy, treacherous incline—Jo Harper, as it turned out. He remembered his surprise at discovering she was not only a Black Falls native but a federal agent with an impeccable reputation.

When he returned to Washington, he'd debated asking Jo out, but she hadn't shown an interest in a romantic relationship. In the end, he hadn't risked more rejection.

Now he realized his hesitation had worked in his favor. In April, when he'd gone back to Black Falls with his daughter, a lovely woman had asked to share his table at a bustling, popular village café. She'd introduced herself as Melanie

Kendall and said she was taking a few days to get away from New York and her work as a self-employed interior decorator.

Thomas's life hadn't been the same since. With Melanie, he finally understood how dull and routine his first marriage had become. He wouldn't have ended it if Carolyn hadn't made the first move, but now, in retrospect, he could see how tedious their relationship must have become for her, too.

His waiter had left him a heavy silver pot of strong coffee and a small, chilled silver pitcher of cream—Thomas knew he should request low-fat milk, but he didn't. *Go with the real stuff.* He was, after all, meeting the man who'd stolen Carolyn from him, and passing on cream in his coffee struck him as something that Alex would seize upon as a sign of weakness.

When he'd called yesterday Alex claimed he wanted to discuss Nora, but Thomas couldn't imagine that Alex really cared that she'd dropped out of Dartmouth and moved to Black Falls to work in a café. The same café, in fact, where Thomas had met Melanie seven months ago.

He suspected Alex's motives for inviting him to breakfast weren't that simple—nothing with Alex ever was.

And everything, Thomas thought with a fresh surge of annoyance, was always on Alex's terms. When to meet. Where. What they'd discuss. But not only would Thomas do anything for his daughter, he also had to admit he was curious about what else was on Alex's mind—something, certainly. He had called instead of e-mailed and insisted on speaking directly to Thomas, refusing to leave a message with his secretary.

"We need to talk about Nora and Vermont," Alex had said. "It's complicated. I'll explain when I see you."

Alex had obviously assumed Thomas would drop everything and show up, which was exactly what he'd done. He'd also kept their meeting to himself, not out of paranoia, he told himself, but habit and discretion.

And because it was Alex. He had recently ended a stint as the U.S. ambassador to Great Britain. Speculation about what he'd do next was rampant. Persistent rumors put him in consideration for a very high-level appointment, possibly even Secretary of State. Washington thrived on gossip and scandal, turning the innocent into the sensational. Alex Bruni was born knowing how to play such games; Thomas had never quite learned.

He opened up another section of the *Post,* flipped through it, studied the ads, read the commentaries and drank his coffee.

Ten minutes ticked by. Where the hell was Alex?

Thomas glanced at his watch. *Fifteen minutes late.* Any lingering amusement over the op-ed on Jo faded. Although he'd cleared his calendar for the entire morning, he was a busy man—as busy in his own way as Alex. But Thomas knew better than to compare himself to Alex, a lesson learned twenty years ago when he and his ambitious, overachieving friend were law students at Yale—long before Alex had taken up with his best friend's wife.

In spite of that blinding act of betrayal, Thomas couldn't hate Alex, and there was no gain to such negativity and strong emotion, anyway. Alexander Bruni was a respected diplomat on everyone in Washington's short list of "good people to know."

And if his longtime friend had any fresh insights into what to do about Nora and her behavior, Thomas was willing to listen. He was convinced the combination of the early northern New England winter and limited funds would nip her sense of romance and adventure about life in Vermont in the bud. Alex and her mother had decided to help Nora out with cash and a car, a source of friction, but Thomas doubted it was what had prompted Alex to arrange this meeting. At least Carolyn, an expert on emerging markets, was in Hong Kong at a conference and wouldn't be there.

Thomas's newspaper moved, startling him, until he realized he'd put it on top of his cell phone, which was set on vibrate. He picked up the phone, flipped it open and saw that he had a text message.

*Melanie.*

Not Nora, of course. His daughter had stopped most communications with him after he had cut off her funds. He hadn't been harsh—he'd hardly had a chance to say a word before she'd hung up on him. Nora was, technically, an adult. She'd made her decision to quit college on her own and only informed him, her mother and Alex after she'd already moved to Black Falls and gotten a job.

Thomas found his way to the text message and smiled as he saw that, indeed, it was from his fiancée.

Dinner set...c u tonite. Luv u. Mel.

After two tries, he managed to type in his reply.

Great. Love you, too.

He'd never get used to text-message shorthand, but Melanie was young, hip, beautiful and had no trouble whatsoever. She'd never have a YouTube moment like Jo or stick him with a fait accompli like his daughter.

A shriek jerked him half out of his chair.

More screams penetrated the quiet of the elegant dining room, and he leaped to his feet, his napkin falling onto the floor as his fellow diners responded in kind.

"Oh my God!" A woman's voice, panicked, came from the adjoining lobby. "That car just ran him over! Call 911."

"Get the license plate," a man yelled. "Run…run, damn it!"

Thomas heard more urgent comments, orders, questions, exclamations. Once he was assured of his own safety—the hotel wasn't under attack—he grabbed his cell phone and briefcase and joined a dozen or so people rushing from the restaurant to the lobby, where all the commotion was occurring.

A car accident? A hit-and-run?

In the glittering lobby, doormen and bystanders scurried, yelling, motioning wildly as they tried to come to terms with some kind of emergency outside on the sidewalk.

Thomas felt his step falter. He stood next to a polished round table with a massive vase of fresh flowers as its centerpiece and peered through the revolving doors.

People had gathered in front of the body of a man sprawled on the edge of the busy street. Thomas made out shiny black loafers and dark gray pants, but the man's upper body was screened by two men crouched at his side, obviously trying to help.

*I need to see his face….*

But Thomas's eyes fixed on a briefcase that lay, intact, on the sidewalk.

Bile rose in his throat. His heart pounded. *No.*

The scarred leather…the broken buckle…

"Alex," he whispered. "No, no. No…please."

A young woman with a long, tangled ponytail caught her

breath in front of him. He'd noticed her burst into the lobby through the revolving door. She carried a messenger bag and wore bike shorts and shoes. "Do you know him?" she asked, gesturing outside at the street.

"I beg your pardon?"

"The guy who was hit—I can't believe it." Her entire body was shaking, her lips quivering as she held back tears. "This car came out of nowhere and just mowed him down. He went flying. I…" She seemed to gag.

Thomas pushed back his own panic. "Are you going to be ill?"

She shook her head. "I'm okay. I just want to get out of here. I heard people calling the police, and someone else must have seen—" She broke off abruptly, squinted tightly as if to gather her thoughts. "The car never stopped or hesitated. It was horrible."

"You should wait and talk to the police—"

"Yeah. Yeah, sure. I'll just go deliver this package upstairs first." Clearly in shock, she clutched the strap to her bag. "It's supposed to be there in five minutes. Not that anyone will care if it's late given the circumstances. I just don't know what else to do."

"The victim—he's dead?"

Her face paled to a grayish white. "There's no hope. He wasn't a friend, was he?"

Thomas thought quickly. Alex wouldn't have mentioned the breakfast to anyone. It wasn't a secret, but why give people a reason to chatter? He was a regular diner at the hotel. No one would question his presence outside its doors.

"No," Thomas told the young messenger. "He's not a friend. I'm just in shock. What a terrible thing."

"Pretty awful."

"Maybe the driver didn't realize—"

"Oh, no. It was deliberate. I mean, that's what it looked like to me. I'm sure there were other witnesses."

"I'm so sorry you had to see such a thing." Thomas tried to give her what he hoped was a reassuring look. "If you'll excuse me, I have a meeting I must get to."

"Right. I'll get this package upstairs. It's so weird, to be flying down the street on my bike one minute, thinking this was the most important thing in the world, and then…" She blew out a breath. "Whatever. I have to go. Have a good meeting."

She rushed toward the escalators, and Thomas fought back a choking sob.

*Alex is dead. There's nothing I can do now.*

In Thomas's place, Alex would protect himself, without question. He would protect Carolyn, protect Nora, protect his adult children from his first marriage. As difficult as he could be, Alex did care about the people he loved.

*As do I.*

Nora and even Carolyn, whom Thomas still cared about despite her betrayal, didn't need the scandal, questions and scrutiny that his presence at the hotel would spark. The headlines screeching about this morning's tragedy would be horrendous enough without mention of how the great Ambassador Bruni had been on his way to have breakfast with the longtime friend whose ex-wife was now his widow.

No, Thomas thought. He wouldn't put any of them through such an ordeal.

Best just to melt into the crowd, go back to his office and pretend he knew nothing about why Alex was on his way into the hotel on that particular morning.

Thomas had lied to the young messenger. He had no meeting he needed to get to. His only meeting was his breakfast with Alexander Bruni, which had just been cruelly canceled.

# *Four*

Melanie Kendall vomited in the ladies' room of an upscale restaurant several blocks north of the hotel where Alexander Bruni had just been killed in what police were already describing as a suspicious hit-and-run.

Suspicious, indeed.

She had resisted the impulse to peek down the street as she'd rushed past on foot, her car—the one that had struck Bruni—safely abandoned in a nearby garage, along with her wig and the black poncho she'd worn. She'd discarded them in a trash can, avoiding any surveillance cameras.

Everything had been carefully planned, although not by her. She wasn't a planner. At least not of murders. A beautiful decorating scheme—that she could plan.

But she could execute a murder with precision and daring, and that, she'd discovered, was a rare skill. Five kills in seven months. Murder investigations in London, San Diego, New York and now Washington, D.C. Her first kill had been declared an accidental death, but that, apparently, was what the client had wanted. Melanie didn't know the specifics.

*Not my job,* she thought as she gave one last dry heave. She wasn't repulsed by killing. Vomiting was simply her release after all the excitement.

No one was in the ladies' room with her, but Melanie didn't care. She knew how to puke without making a sound. She flushed the toilet, let the stall door shut behind her and splashed her face with cold water in the spotless shiny black sink, then took a thin, folded towel from a neat pile on the granite counter and patted her skin dry.

In the mirror, her reflection looked fine. Her eyes were a little bloodshot, but they'd clear up in a few minutes.

They always did.

She was small—tiny, really—with long, straight dark hair that she could make elegant or informal with just a quick twist or a flip. Her fiancé, Thomas Asher, the incongruous man of her dreams, had once told her that his first wife had always agonized over her hair.

His first wife being Carolyn Asher Bruni, now Alex Bruni's widow.

Being a decent man, Thomas would probably feel bad for Carolyn, but Melanie couldn't help that.

She adjusted her expensive jeans and made sure she would blend in with the upscale, professional crowd at the restaurant. Now wasn't the time to draw attention to herself. Thomas liked her natural flair for clothes, too, and how she always dressed appropriately for whatever she was doing, whether business or pleasure.

She liked thinking about him. Saying his name to herself. That she was fifteen years younger than he was—she was just thirty—blew Thomas away. She knew he saw her as sophisticated, worldly, well read and yet completely charming.

Not as a killer.

Melanie tossed the towel into a wicker basket and returned to her two-person table in the main dining room. It wasn't quite eleven yet. Breakfast was still being served. She picked up her menu, smiling at the waiter. "I'll have the oatmeal with fresh berries on the side—and coffee. Low-fat milk, please."

"Of course, ma'am."

She hated being called ma'am. But she noticed Kyle Rigby making his way toward her and told the waiter, "Make that two coffees, and add a muffin. What kind do you have today?"

"Raspberry and—"

"Whatever. Anything. Warm it up, will you?"

He retreated as Kyle dropped into the chair opposite her. She hadn't been this close to him in over a week. With his very short silver-streaked hair and broad shoulders, he looked more like a high-priced Washington lobbyist in his expensive tan suit than a thug. A killer.

She might be a killer, too, Melanie thought, but she wasn't a thug.

And she was giving up killing. She had no regrets about her life over most of the last year, but she was moving on. It was time. Ever since she was a little girl on Long Island, she'd envisioned marrying a man like Thomas. Quiet, intelligent, privileged—a true blue blood, as her mother, who had always wanted Melanie to marry well, would say.

Melanie wanted nothing more than to be a real, old-money Virginia lady, attending luncheons, hosting teas and benefits, sitting on charity boards. Carolyn had been uninterested in any of those traditions. His daughter was hopeless in that regard. Melanie looked forward to them.

But first she had to finish her business with Kyle, preferably before people started hanging their Christmas wreaths. As she'd donned her blond wig earlier that morning, Melanie had considered how little she knew about him. His real name, where he'd grown up, if he had family. Whether he was poor or middle-class or rich. Whether his father had beat him or his mother had loved him. If he had brothers and sisters, if they all were thugs or killers.

She supposed she hadn't wanted to know. He had come into her life eight months ago, when she'd caught him about to shoot a would-be decorating client, a rich, scummy defense attorney she knew would never pay her on time. She could have stopped Kyle. She could have called the police, distracted him, done *something,* but even as she'd stood there in near shock, he'd known she wouldn't do anything. She'd never killed anyone or witnessed someone being killed, but she'd been mesmerized as Kyle had smiled at her then fired. She'd never felt so alive. With her would-be client's body still warm on the living-room floor, Kyle had swept her into an upstairs bedroom and made love to her. Every second of that night was burned into her soul.

Never, ever would she have such an experience again.

He'd made her help him clean up the scene. The body wasn't discovered until four days later. The police still had no leads. The dead lawyer hadn't noted anywhere that he'd had an appointment with an interior decorator about redoing his sunroom. Fingerprints and DNA weren't an issue for Melanie. She was Ms. Perfect. She'd never had so much as a speeding ticket.

As little as she knew about Kyle, here they were, she thought—partners, lovers. Their months together had been an adventure she would never forget, but whatever he did after she made her exit was his problem. She'd be planning the last details of her wedding and honeymoon.

She didn't like the smug look he gave her from across the small table. It reminded her of the night they'd met. She often wondered what he'd have done if she hadn't reacted as she had, but that didn't bear thinking about right now.

She placed her cloth napkin on her lap. "Someone could see us," she said, her throat still raw from puking.

"If you're expecting paparazzi, forget it." Kyle lifted his own napkin, his nails, she noticed, neatly buffed and filed. He had the biggest hands she'd ever seen, but in his suit and cuff links, he managed to blend in with the Washington types. "No one in Washington cares you're marrying Thomas Asher."

"A prominent ambassador was just killed a few blocks from here."

"Really? Did he have a heart attack?"

"When the car hit him, maybe."

Melanie couldn't hold back a smile. It seemed to erupt from deep inside her, along with a giddy excitement. She always felt this way after taking risks. There was nothing like it. The mix of power, relief, fear, guilt, energy—the tension that existed among such contradictory emotions.

Indescribable, really.

Kyle didn't smile back. He was doing a job, and it was serious business for him. He didn't have the imagination to understand the psychological addiction of killing, the emotional draw—the satisfaction that went beyond a paycheck. Melanie liked money. But money wasn't why she'd become a paid assassin.

"I'm not letting you screw up a good thing for me." He sat

back and gave her a grim look. "You should never have gotten involved with Thomas Asher. You should have at least told me when you did."

He'd found out two weeks ago when he'd come to Washington to discuss the Bruni hit. "I didn't know we'd be given Alex Bruni as a target." Melanie kept her voice low, but she was careful not to sound defensive. "We're partners, Kyle, but you don't own me. You and I are together *maybe* a week, at most two weeks, a month. You don't live in Washington. I'm not even sure where you *do* live. I'm entitled to have a life."

"Not with someone you met in Black Falls, Vermont."

She ignored him. "Thomas could have seen me this morning," she said.

Kyle shook his head. "No, he couldn't have, and it wouldn't have mattered. Your disguise was good. Your timing was perfect. You did exactly what you were supposed to do."

"Your plan worked," Melanie said, hoping flattery would distract him from how annoyed he was about her relationship with Thomas.

"Yes, it did."

There was no pride, no sense of accomplishment, where there should have been. She never could have pulled off such a hit by herself—she wasn't the planner Kyle was. Calculating the details of running a prominent ambassador over in broad daylight was where his limited imagination kicked into action and combined with his logical, lethal mind. He'd left nothing to chance. The hit-and-run death of Alex Bruni was pure choreography.

But thanks to her relationship with Thomas, she'd known

Bruni would be at the hotel that morning, thus making the final choice of the time and place to kill him that much simpler.

"There was a messenger," she said in a near whisper. "A young woman on a bicycle—I almost ran her over, too."

"She didn't see anything that can identify either of us."

He was so calm. So certain, so reassuring. Melanie felt a twitch of desire and knew it would become more urgent—it always did after a successful mission. Very soon the twitch would become an ache that would take over her body, her mind, every fiber of her being. She wouldn't be able to think about anything else until it was satisfied.

"Kyle..."

He was like a rock. "Meet me at my hotel in an hour. Room 257."

She glanced around the restaurant. "If we're seen together—"

"I'm one of your decorating clients. Nothing more."

Melanie hesitated. "Kyle...why did we kill Alex Bruni?"

"He had enemies. One of them wanted him dead enough to pay to make it happen."

The equation was always so simple and direct for him. "I don't like it that Bruni vacationed in Black Falls. He knew Drew Cameron. I don't understand why we killed him, either. Who wanted Bruni dead? Who hired us? It wasn't his wife—his ex-wife?" *Or Thomas. It couldn't have been Thomas.*

"You know as much as I do."

Melanie doubted that. Kyle dealt with their employers. Their transactions were conducted entirely over the Internet—no names, no faces. Just codes and passwords. He claimed even he didn't know who paid them to kill people, who served as the middleman between them and the enemies of their targets. She executed her part of Kyle's plan and asked no questions. She was paid well and accepted that nothing short of perfection was expected of her.

But soon none of that would be of any concern to her. "I haven't changed my mind," she said. "I'm still retiring."

"Sure."

"I'm willing to give up the thrills for what Thomas can offer me."

"No, you're not."

His sarcasm—his certainty—bothered her. "You don't know me. You think you do, but you don't. Ever since I was a little girl, I've wanted to marry a man like Thomas."

"One with a trust fund."

"You don't understand. I'm talking about my destiny."

"Doesn't matter right now, does it?"

He leaned toward her, and his eyes narrowed into slits, making him look more like the coldhearted killer he was. Part of Melanie expected the handful of well-dressed Washington elites at some of the other tables to notice and quietly exit the restaurant. But no one paid any attention to her or to Kyle.

"We still have work to do," he said.

Her stomach lurched. She'd hoped he'd just used the threat as leverage to get her to focus on the Bruni hit, but his mind didn't work that way. From the moment they'd met in the middle of the murder of her client, Melanie had been drawn to his straightforward simplicity.

She nodded, picked up her coffee, her hands steady now. She'd pushed back any irritation—any desire, even, at least for the moment. "Yes. I know."

*Nora Asher.*

Melanie's future stepdaughter was a spoiled, headstrong

college dropout who was asking too many questions—questions that cut too close to the truth for Kyle's comfort. Or hers. Nora hadn't put together what she'd gathered on Melanie into a coherent whole that posed a danger to her or to Kyle—or their employers—but it could happen. With Bruni's death, Nora could become emboldened, frightened, perhaps more determined.

And that was a problem.

"Nora's just jealous of me. Thomas unconsciously looked to her for reassurance after Carolyn left him for Alex. Nora got used to being needed. There's no reason to think she's discovered anything that would get us in trouble."

"She's a time bomb."

Melanie said nothing.

"Jo Harper is in Black Falls," Kyle said.

"She's from there."

"Perfect cover. Send the hometown girl back to Vermont in damage-control mode and let her nose around." He got to his feet. "One hour." He eyed Melanie without a hint of a smile. "Enjoy your oatmeal."

The desire returned stronger than that first tingle. Melanie trembled, hot now. Her waiter set a bowl of steaming, steel-cut oatmeal and a smaller bowl of fat, perfect blueberries and raspberries in front of her.

She smiled, thanked him, even as she thought she would melt.

"Your friend's not staying?" he asked.

"No. Just leave the muffin, anyway."

He set the plate on the table and retreated.

Melanie smelled the muffin's sweetness, felt the steam from it.

*One hour.*

Using her fingers, she lifted a plump blueberry to her lips. She wouldn't let anyone or anything spoil her life with Thomas. Not his daughter—and not Kyle Rigby.

He walked past the restaurant window without making eye contact with her.

"Don't get in my way," Melanie whispered.

It was as if her partner in killing heard her through the window. He paused suddenly, took a half step back and smirked at her.

She pretended not to see him and ate the blueberry.

# *Five*

Jo unzipped her fleece jacket as she entered the breakfast-lunch café that her sister owned with two of her friends. They called it Three Sisters, in honor of their tight friendship. It was located across from the village green on the first floor of a graceful 1835 brick house owned by Sean Cameron, arguably the most charming of the Cameron siblings. Not, Jo thought, that it took that much to be more charming than A.J. or Elijah—or even Rose. And since Sean was a multimillionaire developer in southern California these days, Jo suspected he was as exacting in his own way as his siblings, just with smoother edges.

The café wasn't crowded. It was late for breakfast and early for lunch. Jo was meeting her sister there after their five-mile run that morning, Beth griping every inch of the way. They'd gone along the lake road past Elijah's house, then doubled back out to the main road. Jo had enjoyed the run. Her airsoft welts had calmed down and didn't ache as much, and she and Beth had encountered deer, wild turkeys, squirrels, chipmunks, crows, chickadees and one woodpecker.

She nodded to Scott Thorne, a state trooper Beth was dating, as he added cream to his coffee-to-go, but he pretended not to see her as he headed for a riverside table on the back wall. So she called to him. "Hey, Scott."

He sighed. "Jo."

Her sister rolled her eyes as she slipped on an apron in dark evergreen—the café's signature color—behind the glass case. She was a paramedic as well as co-owner of the café, two years younger and slightly taller than Jo, and the copper highlights in her dark hair were natural. "Don't pick on Scott," she said cheerfully. "What's your pleasure, Agent Harper?"

Jo surveyed the tempting array of treats and pointed at a plate of buttermilk-currant scones. "I want one of those. I know I should go for the nuts-and-seeds bread, but we ran five miles this morning."

"*You* ran five miles. I slogged."

But when she reached into the case, Beth grabbed two scones—one for Jo, one for herself—and set them on small evergreen-colored plates. Jo got mugs and filled them at the coffee bar.

They joined Scott at his table overlooking the river. He was in uniform, and Jo recognized the prestigious silver ram's horns insignia that identified him as a member of the Vermont State Police search-and-rescue team. He gave Jo a quick glance, then got up and addressed Beth. "I have to run."

Beth didn't look the least bit offended. "Dominique's making leek-and-goat-cheese tarts," she said, referring to Dominique Belair, one of the three "sisters." Beth grinned. "I can snag one for dinner—"

"That's okay," Scott said with the barest flicker of a smile. "I'll see you later, though."

Once he was back on the street, Jo sighed. "Looks as if I ran off your trooper boyfriend."

"Scott," Beth said. "His name is Scott. I guess he could have been nicer to you, huh?"

"Nah. He did what I'd have done in his position—be polite and scoot."

"He'll like you once things settle down with you and that Internet flap. But he really is good-looking, isn't he?"

"Very. I think I saw dimples when he smiled at you."

"Don't tell him he has dimples. He'll never warm up to you."

Jo laughed, relishing her sister's company. How long had it been since they'd had lazy days to spend together? "Fresh scones, hot coffee and a nice view. Life in exile's not too bad."

Beth snorted. "For you. It's killing me. Canoeing in the cold yesterday, a five-mile run in the cold this morning." She gave an exaggerated stretch of her lower back. "A three-mile run would have been fine with me. *No* run would have been fine. I don't need to be in shape to leap tall buildings and run after bad guys. Then again, at the rate you're going, before long neither will you."

Jo broke open her scone, which was filled with tiny dried currants. "Fair point."

"I'm just saying." Beth dipped her knife into a small pot of Vermont-made butter and slathered it on her scone. "You like this kid, Charlie, don't you?"

"Charlie counts on people liking him."

"Maybe he was looking for attention with that prank of his. Big family, father's the vice president—you Secret Service types everywhere. It can't be all that easy to stand out."

"Not my problem. He and his friends and bazillion cousins are okay. That's really all that matters."

"Even if you lose your job?"

"Even if."

"That's very Secret Service of you, video or no video."

"I'll survive. There are other jobs for someone who can leap tall buildings and run after bad guys." Jo smiled at her sister. "The Vermont State Police might take me."

Beth almost spit out her coffee. "Scott would just die, wouldn't he?"

A muffled sob back toward the glass case drew their attention, and they both turned as Nora Asher burst from the café kitchen, whipping off a dark green apron and charging for the front door.

Jo started to get up, but Beth shook her head, subtly pointing as Devin Shay quietly came out from the kitchen, hesitated, then followed Nora outside.

"What was that all about?" Jo asked.

"Devin's in over his head with that girl." Beth sat back, still and serious now. "He's in over his head with a lot of things these days. He's had a rough time since he found Drew Cameron. That was a tough one, Jo, I have to tell you. Drew was a father figure to Devin. He almost didn't graduate. He's been in and out of trouble ever since—nothing too bad, but it could turn bad fast."

"Does he have any plans to go to college?"

"Talks about community college, but he can't plan what to have for supper much less what he's going to do six months from now."

Jo looked out at the street, but she couldn't see the two teenagers. "How long have he and Nora been seeing each other?"

"A month, maybe. She's only been in town six or seven weeks. She's a hard worker, but she's using Devin—not consciously, I'm sure. She's just caught up in the romance of living in Vermont."

"Mountains, moose, maple syrup, pretty cows."

Beth barely cracked a smile. "She likes the idea of hooking up with a 'native' Vermonter. Devin didn't climb off a Norman Rockwell painting. I didn't, either."

"What's he see in Nora?"

"Everything he isn't."

Jo drank more of her coffee and watched the sun dance on the clear, copper water in the shallow river. She remembered Drew fussing about why Sean had wanted to buy the gracious old house in the first place, never mind why he hung on to it. The three friends—Beth, Dominique and Hannah, Devin's older sister—had applied their talent, vision and energy into creating their cozy, very popular café. They'd sanded, painted, scrubbed, added cottage-style furniture and come up with a varied, appealing menu. Dominique was responsible for most of the food, Hannah for keeping the books and managing the staff, and Beth for maintenance and comfort food.

Finally Jo shifted back to her sister. "What else?"

Beth drummed her fingers on the table. She'd finished her scone and most of her coffee and seemed ready to jump up and get out of there. While Jo was off chipping away at a career in the Secret Service, Beth had stayed in Vermont, gone to college, worked—but Jo wasn't fooled. Her sister had the same restless energy as she, but Beth funneled hers into her life in Black Falls.

"Beth…"

"It's nothing. Never mind. Have you figured out what to do with your cabins yet?"

Jo went along with the change in subject. "Besides hope for a fire? No."

"What about your neighbor?"

"Elijah? I haven't seen much of him."

"He's at a loose end. You're at a loose end." Beth shook her head. "A soldier and a federal agent with nothing to do. My definition of dangerous."

Jo smiled. "We can't get into too much trouble out on our quiet Vermont lake."

Her sister was serious again. "He should be dead, Jo. He tied a tourniquet on his leg and expected to fight until his last breath and save his men. Instead—he lived."

"He says he's fully recovered."

"He probably is. Physically, at least. He's lucky. You've had advance medical training as a Secret Service agent—you know how dangerous femoral artery injuries are. I can't imagine one in the middle of a firefight in the remote mountains of Afghanistan. It's a miracle he lived. An absolute miracle."

"Was anyone else injured?"

"Rose tried to pry what she could out of him and his doctors. It's not much. He was part of a joint special operations team that came under attack. A Navy SEAL was killed. Another was grievously wounded. Elijah spent a month in the hospital. He did rehab and supposedly got some kind of staff assignment for a while. Now he's home."

"Permanently?"

"Who knows? There are lots of rumors about Elijah, as you can imagine. Including that he's not satisfied with the official explanation of his father's death. Scott helped with the search."

"Tough time."

Beth nodded. "The worst. It's not Elijah's fault his father died, but in my opinion, he's looking to assuage his own guilt for not being here. Of course, that wasn't his fault, either."

"Maybe he has legitimate unanswered questions."

"And maybe his questions have no answers. Uh-oh. Speak of the devil." Beth pushed back her chair and made a face. "He's all yours, Jo."

Jo glanced back toward the street and saw that, in fact, Elijah had arrived at the café. She grinned at her sister. "Chicken."

"You bet. He scares me when he comes in here and orders a scone. Can you imagine, Elijah Cameron sitting down with a scone and butter?"

"You're bad, Beth. Honestly."

Her sister laughed. "Scott would agree with you. I'll have to tell him you two have common ground after all." She got to her feet and gathered up her plate and mug. "My hamstrings are on fire. I need at least a day's rest before we go for another run."

"It felt good, running up here instead of in the city—"

"And running with your out-of-shape sister instead of all your buff Secret Service friends."

"You're not that out of shape, Beth."

"Ha," she said as she dumped her plate and mug in a dishpan on a side table and scooted out, passing Elijah on his way in. No Red Sox cap today—the sun caught the ends of his close-cropped tawny hair, reminding Jo, somehow, of him at nineteen. But she knew it would be a mistake to fall back on old habits.

Plus, he was obviously in some kind of cantankerous, rotten Cameron mood.

He didn't say a word to Beth, then ignored Jo, or maybe didn't notice her, and headed straight for the glass case, where Hannah Shay was unloading cookies from a big metal sheet onto an evergreen plate. She had on a frumpy skirt, and her fair hair was pulled back in a simple ponytail that emphasized the delicate bone structure of her face.

She gave Elijah a cool look. “What can I get you? The cookies are still warm. I have peanut butter, chocolate chip—”

“Is Devin here?”

More coolness. “No, Elijah, he’s not.”

“Where is he?”

“I’m sorry.” Hannah tucked the empty tray under one arm. “I don’t have time to talk. I have to study.”

She set the tray on the spotless counter, peeled off her apron and walked calmly out from behind the case. Whatever was going on between her and Elijah, Hannah, Jo thought, had herself under control. She always did. She was in her late twenties but seemed older, perhaps because of the hard life she’d led. She’d grown up in an isolated hollow just outside Black Falls, a different Vermont from the one Jo had known. After her mother died, Hannah took over as guardian to her two younger brothers, Devin and Toby, who were just ten and eleven at the time. Their father had abandoned the family over and over before finally running his car into a tree and killing himself not long after Toby was born. In addition to running the café with Beth and Dominique, Hannah was putting herself through law school. Most people in town had learned not to underestimate her.

“It’s good to see you, Jo,” Hannah said graciously. “Dominique makes amazing scones, doesn’t she?”

“She does. Nice to see you, too, Hannah.”

Hannah didn’t make a gibe about Charlie Neal and the video, but that wasn’t her style. Instead of going out the front entrance, she left through a side door that opened into the house’s center hall and headed up the curving stairs to the apartment she shared with her brothers.

Elijah made a move toward the door. He had on his canvas jacket, jeans and scarred hiking boots, and he looked as if he wanted to punch a fist through the nearest wall. Not that he was angry at Hannah. Something else, Jo thought.

She cupped her coffee mug in both hands. "Hannah doesn't want to talk to you."

He walked over to her table and helped himself to a chunk of her scone. The intensity of a moment ago seemed to have vanished. "I figured you for raw eggs and wheat germ in a blender."

"Everything in moderation," Jo said. "Beth and I ran this morning."

"Did you? I just saw you stretching in your undies down by the lake."

"Don't get your hopes up. Those were my yoga clothes."

He winked at her. "Looked like undies to me."

The man was hunting trouble. "Don't you have a job?"

"I stay busy. I saw you on your roof yesterday. Checking for bats?"

"Rot. I don't want leaks."

"If a bat gets in, you can scream. I'll come rescue you."

She bit off a sigh and set down her mug. "I can't believe I almost eloped with you."

"Sure you can." The intensity was back, not quite contained behind his winks and teasing. "What's the matter, Jo, don't you have a sexy bad boy waiting for you back in Washington?"

"A straitlaced FBI agent. He follows the rules. We just started seeing each other."

"Bet he loves your video."

She didn't respond and wished she hadn't let Elijah goad

her down this road. He'd always known what buttons to push with her—physically, emotionally.

There *was* a straitlaced FBI agent. But they weren't going anywhere together, and they both knew it.

Elijah narrowed his deep blue eyes on her. "Ah." He looked amused now. "You don't know what he thinks of your video. He doesn't return your calls, does he?"

"I haven't called him."

"Want me to—"

"Do nothing, Elijah. I want you to do nothing."

"If I were in your shoes," he said, "I'd make up a strait-laced FBI agent just in case having an old flame next door became a distraction. Isn't that the big thing with the Secret Service—prevention?"

"We do pretty well with snipers, too."

It wasn't something she should have said, but it had no effect whatsoever on Elijah. He grinned at her; it wasn't a pleasant grin. "See you, Agent Harper. Do more yoga. Go back up on the roof. I like watching the wild turkeys, but you're prettier, even armed."

She resisted shooting him as he headed out. Once the door shut behind him, she counted to three, breathed, then set her mug and plate in the dishpan. She didn't know whether to blame her run, boredom or what for letting herself get into a sexually charged verbal sparring match with an out-of-work ex-soldier or whatever Elijah was these days.

Ex-lover. He would always be that to her.

She pushed a flood of memories aside and quickly ducked into the center hall. She didn't hear anything from upstairs and resisted going up and knocking on Hannah's door. Only pure nosiness made her want to find out what was going on between Hannah and Elijah.

Instead, she zipped up her fleece jacket and stepped outside. The village of Black Falls was located in a narrow river valley in the heart of the Green Mountains that ran up the middle of Vermont. Its attractive main street was lined with renovated old houses—clapboard, brick, stone—that were often the subject of Vermont postcards. Most had been converted into shops and businesses.

Across the street, the midday sun peeked through the naked trees on the sliver of a town green and sparkled on brightly colored fallen leaves. Not a bad place to be, Jo thought, even with Elijah in town. She felt some of the tension of being around him ease. She enjoyed the chance to spend time with her family. They'd all had spaghetti up at her parents' place last night.

But she still had an afternoon to kill and wasn't used to being at a loose end.

As she reached her car, her cell phone rang. Service was spotty in the nooks and crannies of south-central Vermont, but she had a decent signal.

"Jo…thank God."

She recognized Thomas Asher's strangled voice. "Thomas? What's—"

"There's been an accident." He gulped in a breath and rushed forward, his words coming fast. "I don't know. Maybe it wasn't an accident. The police… I can't think… I…"

"Whoa, Thomas, slow down. Start from the beginning. Who's hurt?"

"Alex. Alex Bruni. Jo—he's dead. I can't believe it. He was hit by a car outside a hotel across from his office. He… The police say he was killed instantly. It was a hit-and-run. The driver took off."

"Does Nora know?"

"Yes. I called and told her." He sounded slightly calmer now that he had delivered the news. "I don't know how much she heard or didn't hear—we didn't have a good connection. Jo, could I ask you to check on her? Would you mind? Nora doesn't know many people up there. I'd feel better if you could—" His voice cracked. "I'm in shock. Alex and I have been…we were friends for more than twenty years."

"Thomas, do you have any reason to suspect Nora is in any danger?"

"No! No, no, she's not in danger. I'm just worried about her emotional state. She and Alex didn't get along that well, but she's close to her mother. Carolyn will get the first flight she can out of Hong Kong, but it'll take a while."

"Have you been in touch with the police?"

"What?"

"The police. If Ambassador Bruni was killed in a hit-and-run—"

"Right, of course." He seemed to have trouble focusing. "The police are investigating. I don't know the details, Jo. I was here at my office working on a presentation when I heard."

"How did you find out?"

"Alex's secretary called me. So that I could tell Nora before she heard it on the news." He was breathless, obviously shaken. "I didn't have to tell Carolyn. Thank heaven for that. I think the police told her. I spoke to her, of course—I assured her I'd take care of Nora. Jo…"

"I'll check on her right now, Thomas. I'm sorry about Ambassador Bruni."

"I knew him longer than Carolyn. People wonder why

we stayed friends after they got together, but there was never a question…" He sobbed openly. "I can't believe he's gone."

"How did Nora take the news?" Jo asked, trying to cut through his grief.

"Hard to tell. She stayed calm, but it's such a shock. I just want to be sure she's okay. She's so young, Jo—she should be at college, with professors and counselors and friends."

"Do you want her to make arrangements to get back to Washington?"

"I don't know. A funeral is on hold for now, pending the—the autopsy…." He seemed to drift off, then added quietly, "It's hard to think about the future."

"Then don't. Think about what you need to do right now. Are you alone?"

"Melanie's on her way."

The fiancée. Jo pulled her car door open. "That's good."

"We'll come up there if we need to. Nora and I—we used to be so close. I wish you'd known us then. She doesn't communicate with me the way she used to. Remember being eighteen?"

Staying on the lake next to Elijah, she'd been remembering being eighteen a lot. But she wasn't going there. "Why did Nora quit school? Was there a precipitating incident—a crisis, anything?"

"I think it was pure impulse. She loves Vermont, or at least the idea of it." Thomas's tone cooled noticeably. "Her decision to take a break from college has nothing to do with Alex's death."

"All right. I'll get back to you as soon as I've laid eyes on her."

"I haven't even asked how you are," he said quietly.

"I just had a warm scone and coffee at the café where I understand you and Melanie met."

"Ah." He seemed to try to sound cheerful. "The Three Sisters Café of Black Falls, Vermont, has the best scones anywhere." But he choked up with emotion. "Jo..."

"I know, Thomas. I'm so sorry. I'll go look in on Nora now."

"Thank you."

He hung up, and Jo climbed into her car and stuck the key in the ignition. Her head felt pinched, tight. Had Nora talked to her father before she'd fled the café? Was that why she was so upset? Had Devin known her stepfather was dead?

Had Elijah known?

She debated, then dialed several law enforcement friends in Washington. No one picked up. A cell signal wasn't the problem this time. "From hero to goat," she muttered. She wasn't offended. She relented and tried her boss.

Francona picked up on the first ring. "Thought you'd be in a canoe."

"Ambassador Bruni's stepdaughter lives in Black Falls. She just took off from the café where she works—"

"Three Sisters on Main Street. I've got the Web site up now." He paused and added, "Quaint."

"The owners aren't sisters."

"Beth Harper's your sister."

Jo didn't respond.

"I'm surprised the lakes up there aren't all frozen. Do you own a canoe?"

Yesterday, she and Beth had appropriated the canoe left on her property. Elijah's, no doubt. "Actually, no."

"Borrow one. Rent one. Whatever."

Jo sighed. "Did a report on Bruni just cross your desk? Is that why you had the café Web site up?"

"Wear a life vest."

He disconnected.

Mark Francona was difficult and exacting on a good day. Today, Jo thought, wasn't a good day.

She drove up along the town green and crossed the covered bridge over the river, heading up a hill toward the country estate where Nora Asher lived.

*"I'd give my life for Elijah."*

Jo gripped the wheel and pushed back the image of Drew Cameron on their walk among the cherry blossoms. She didn't know anything that would connect their unsettling conversation and his death two weeks later, much less Alexander Bruni's death a few hours ago.

But something was wrong in Black Falls, she thought, and had been for some time.

# *Six*

Fighting tears, Nora set her backpack on the gray-painted wood floor of the small porch of the stone guesthouse she'd moved into after she'd quit college. She'd wanted to rent her own apartment—to really be independent—but when Lowell and Vivian Whittaker, the couple who owned the guesthouse, offered to let her live there in exchange for odd jobs, her parents had bullied her into agreeing. The Whittakers were closer friends with Alex and her mom than with her dad, but he'd jumped right in with them. They'd all provided practical reasons why living in the guesthouse made sense, but she knew they just didn't think she could make it on her own. But the guesthouse was working out okay. It was cute, and the Whittakers weren't in Black Falls that much and mostly left her alone.

Nora didn't care about any of that right now. She held a breath to keep herself from crying.

*Alex is dead.*

"Don't think about it," she told herself out loud.

She noticed a tear had dropped onto the checklist Elijah

had insisted each student in his wilderness-skills class come up with of what to take on a winter hike. She had everything on her list. Map, compass, food, shelter, knife, matches, clothes, a whistle, water, water-purification tablets. A lot of the stuff was new and it was all good quality.

*You'll be fine.*

She squatted to zip up a small outer compartment on her backpack. Her head spun. She couldn't make it stop. "Alex is dead," she whispered. "I can't believe he's dead."

She was so scared. She couldn't see straight. She didn't know what to do.

Her hands trembled and already felt frozen, but she wasn't even that cold yet. She had packed gloves—she'd shown them to Elijah to make sure they would work for winter conditions, and he'd given his approval. He wasn't as cocky as she'd expected a Special Forces soldier to be. He was just super-competent and professional. Everyone in Black Falls that she met said no one knew the mountains better than Elijah.

Nora wished she could be that confident—that good—one day.

She sniffled, refusing to cry outright. She'd been so excited about moving to Black Falls, and now her life there was just a big mess. She loved her apartment, and the Whittakers' estate—a classic Vermont gentleman's farm—was so beautiful. The guesthouse, once a separate property, was nestled at the bottom of a sloping, manicured lawn that swept up to a huge charcoal-gray, black-shuttered farmhouse.

Nora hadn't told the Whittakers, who'd arrived in Black Falls a couple of days ago, about Alex. She didn't plan to tell them, either. Alex had met them on a trip to Vermont last October. He'd been a regular guest at the Camerons' lodge for several years and came up one weekend while her mom was on a business trip. He and the Whittakers had hit it off, and they'd invited him to stay with them and to bring his fiancée and her daughter. Nora fell in love with Black Falls. She came up twice after that with Alex and her mother. Then the Whittakers insisted she bring her father one weekend. Just the two of them. He was reluctant at first, but Nora talked him into it. They'd had such a great time together. She'd fantasized about all of them coming to Vermont one day—her, her dad, her mom, Alex. She thought Lowell and Vivian understood.

If only, though, she hadn't told them she and her father were heading north in April to look at colleges. They'd immediately invited them to stay at their place in Black Falls. If they hadn't—if they'd just stayed in another town—he never would have met Melanie Kendall.

*It's my fault he met that bitch.*

"Nora."

She jumped, but stifled a scream when she saw it was Devin on the stone walk in front of the guesthouse. She straightened, sniffled back her tears. "Devin, what are you doing here? You startled me."

"Sorry." He looked almost forlorn. "I just want to talk."

"There's nothing to talk about. Really."

A pair of mallards floated in a small man-made pond behind him. The banks of the pond were planted with weeping willows and rhododendrons. Everything about the estate was beautifully done, carefully planned. As much as she wanted her own apartment, Nora loved being there, having her own space and being surrounded by wilderness. She'd hated living in a dorm.

Devin nodded to her pack. "Are you going somewhere?"

"Maybe. I don't know. I wanted to see how all the stuff I've been collecting since the class I took with Elijah would fit into my backpack."

"Looks heavy."

"I can manage."

"Nora, what's going on?"

There was no irritation or frustration in his tone. Obviously he didn't know about Alex, and she couldn't bring herself to repeat out loud what her father had told her.

*"I have terrible news, Nora. Alex has been killed...."*

It wasn't a mistake. Her dad wouldn't have called her unless he was positive.

Alex was dead.

*My mom's a widow.*

Devin took an audible breath. "Nora...please. Talk to me."

She wanted to believe in him. Until that morning, she had. She'd never met anyone steadier or more reliable than Devin. People in Black Falls didn't understand that about him. They thought he was just a dumb, screwed-up kid from a bad family.

Nora didn't want to be the one to prove them right.

She let her pack lean against her knee. "You stole money from me, Devin."

He didn't respond. He looked hurt, and that made her want to cry even more.

"If you needed money, you could have asked me." All the starch had gone out of her. "I'd never refuse you. Even if I don't have much to spare—"

"I didn't steal from you."

Even now, reeling, frightened, confused, Nora wanted to find a way it *couldn't* have been him. Devin was her best friend in Black Falls. He understood how she felt about her father's odious fiancée and didn't tell her she was just jealous.

Something was off about Melanie. Nora couldn't pinpoint what it was, but she didn't like her, didn't trust her and was convinced the feeling was mutual on Melanie's part. She'd gotten Devin to help her. They'd essentially been doing their own background check on Melanie—something Nora's father probably should have done himself.

"Nora, are you running from me?"

She shook her head. "I don't care about the money." Her voice was hoarse, barely a whisper. She gave a fake little smile. "I just need some space to clear my head."

She hoisted up her pack. It was expensive and brand-new—it even smelled new. Her mother had actually loved the idea of her taking a wilderness-skills class and told Nora to put the backpack on her credit card. Elijah had a simple beat-up pack he'd had for years. He'd probably taken it on hundreds of hikes. It wasn't an army-issue pack—Nora knew that much. They'd all talked behind his back in class about what he must have done as a soldier. Supposedly he could speak the different languages of Afghanistan and knew the culture, the people, as well as how to handle himself in a firefight.

Elijah's class had consisted of her and six other students just as green and eager and stupid as she was. She was the youngest, though. That had made her feel a little less self-conscious. The women in the class all thought Elijah was sexy. Nora did, too, but thinking that way made her feel disloyal to Devin, even if they were just friends. Elijah was a total stud and very serious about the information he was giving, but it was so obvious to Nora that she and her classmates were nothing like the soldiers he was used to in the military. But he was so thorough, and that was a good thing. Otherwise she'd have tossed a sundress or something equally useless into her pack, because she was so crazed she couldn't *think*.

"Nora," Devin said, his voice tortured. "Come on—"

"I have to go."

She shivered as if she were already on Cameron Mountain. She'd left her cell phone in the kitchen because it was a way for someone to track her.

And she didn't want to be tracked. Every instinct she had told her to get up on the mountain and disappear, even if it violated the basic tenets of safe hiking. Don't hike alone. Leave her route with someone. Tell someone how long she expected to be gone. Nora didn't care. She didn't want anyone to find her unless she wanted to be found—unless she knew exactly who was looking for her and why. She'd been planning this trip for days. She'd meant to ask Devin to go with her—but forget that now. She wanted to get away from everyone.

Devin took another step toward her. "Did your dad find out you were snooping into Melanie's background?"

"No, I don't think so. And I'm not that concerned if he does. He should have checked her out himself. He's too trusting."

"Are they on their way up here? Is that why you're doing this?"

"No, they're not on their way. Devin, please." Her head was still spinning, and she didn't want to start crying in front of him. "I just— Devin, the money…" She hadn't wanted to get into it with him. He'd come to the café knowing something was wrong, and she'd refused to talk to him. She blinked back tears now and hoisted her pack onto one shoulder. Devin was right—it *was* heavy. "I'm missing a hundred dollars," she said.

"And you think I stole it?"

She looked away.

"Was it in your wallet?"

"My kitchen." She nodded back toward the front door of the guesthouse. It was divided into two side-by-side apartments—she'd had her pick and chosen the one with the better view of the pond and surrounding hills, so gorgeous when the leaves were turning. She'd never been afraid there. Not once, until today. "I keep a hundred dollars in cash for emergencies, and it's gone."

"Where? A drawer, the freezer?"

"Under a pot of parsley in the window. I check it every morning. I checked it yesterday morning, and it was there. I checked it this morning, and it was gone."

"There's no sign anyone broke in?"

"No. I worked late yesterday, then went on a bike ride."

"You don't lock your doors," Devin said. "Anyone could have walked in."

"I don't want to discuss it."

She marched down the steps with her backpack and brushed past him, her throat tight, tears spilling down her cheeks. Her mother had probably called by now. Nora had turned off her cell phone. She didn't want to talk to her. She couldn't bear her mother's grief—couldn't handle having her mother dump on her to make herself feel better. Nora had talked to a friend whose father was a psychologist, and her friend had said that was what her mother did.

It still seemed selfish and wrong not to talk to her mother when her husband had just been killed. She and Alex had truly loved each other.

Nora continued down the stone path toward the gravel turnaround where she'd parked. The main entrance to the estate was a quarter-mile up the road. The air was chilly, but she had all the right clothes. She was a little afraid of staying up on the mountain at night this time of year. Elijah had lectured the class about the dangers of hypothermia.

That was how his father had died in April, right before *her* father fell for the bitch Melanie over scones at the Three Sisters Café.

Nora heard Devin behind her. Part of her wanted to run up to the Whittakers and let them take care of her.

Maybe Alex was right and she was just a wimp.

Of course, he hadn't said "wimp." He was the big diplomat, after all. He'd just had a talk with her about accepting herself, understanding her limitations, pushing herself in areas where she could excel instead of setting herself up for failure.

In other words, she was a wimp.

She'd never liked him that much. Even when he and her dad were friends—before he'd married her mom—she'd thought he was a jerk. When she'd mentioned her class with Elijah, Alex had laughed and said he'd like to see her down at the local army recruiting office. Normally she'd have laughed, too, and pretended she wasn't hurt, but instead she'd summoned up the guts to tell him he was making fun of her and she didn't appreciate it. He'd gotten this shocked look and said he just meant to tease her, not to demean her. He'd seemed so genuine, so serious, that for about two seconds Nora had believed he wanted a real relationship with her, one that meant something.

Now he was dead.

*Murdered…*

She wondered if her father was as upset by Alex's death as her mother was. Everyone had thought her dad would hate Alex, but he didn't.

No one would think about how she felt. The in-the-way stepdaughter.

It was all so surreal.

She picked up her pace, already debating whether she needed *everything* in her pack. It was *so* heavy. She felt a sudden, blinding anger toward her father for telling her about Alex the way he had, calling her on her cell phone, just blurting out that he was dead. Deep down, though, she knew there was no easy way to give someone such news. She could imagine how awful it must have been for Devin when he'd found Drew Cameron. He'd hiked up the north side of the mountain alone and had been forced to leave Drew's body up there in the snow while he hiked down again, got back to his truck and drove out to where he could get a cell signal and call for help. At least he hadn't actually been the one to give the Camerons the terrible news. The state police had done that part. And Drew Cameron's death had been an accident. As much as she didn't like Alex, it sickened Nora to think that someone could have run him over on purpose.

*My dad, for one.*

"No!"

Devin rushed to her side, and she realized she'd screamed. "I'm okay," she said quickly, not looking at him. How could she even think such a thing? Her father could never kill anyone. That he could fall for a woman as horrible as Melanie didn't mean he was capable of running over the friend who'd stolen his first wife from him.

Her father *loved* Melanie, and that gave him even less reason to kill Alex.

Her dad couldn't possibly be a suspect.

"You're freaking me out," Devin said.

Nora pushed ahead of him out to the gravel turnaround. "Sorry. I have a lot on my mind."

"Did something else happen, besides realizing your money's missing? Did Melanie find out we're checking her out?"

"No, nothing like that."

*Melanie already knows I hate her. She knows.*

Nora set her pack down next to the car Alex had bought for her against her father's wishes. It was a used Subaru; it wasn't as if he'd given her a brand-new, expensive car. As irritating and demeaning as he could be, Alex hadn't wanted her riding her bicycle on the hills and narrow roads of Black Falls, or hitchhiking, or relying on friends. In his own way, he'd tried to help her, even if his primary purpose was to keep her from bugging him. He would tell her that he worked so hard because he was dedicated to making the world a better place. How could she complain about him not coming to her high-school graduation ceremony when he was off saving the world?

She was aware of Devin watching her, but refused to look back at him. If she could have sprouted wings and flown away, she would have.

With a steadier hand, she opened up the front passenger door. She cried openly now, picturing Alex running across a busy Washington street, oblivious to the car coming at him, unaware that he was in the last moments of his life. He'd have been wearing a suit—he always wore suits in Washington. He'd have had his briefcase with him. Had he held on to it, or had it gone flying?

What had gone through his mind? Had he thought about his wife, his ex-wife, his children?

Had he thought about his stepdaughter up in Vermont?

Had he thought about anything?

Nora hefted her backpack onto the seat and shut the door hard. She knew she couldn't bring herself to tell Devin about Alex. She just couldn't do it.

She turned to him and said softly, "I know you're not a thief. I'll be okay. We both will."

"Stay, Nora. Don't do this."

"Just find out what you can about Melanie. Clients, travels—especially since April when she met my father."

Melanie had been in Black Falls when Drew Cameron went missing. Now Alex was dead in Washington.

She was bad luck.

"I'll do what I can," Devin said. "Where will I find you?"

Nora pretended not to hear him and got into her car. She'd drive out to Black Falls Lodge and park at a trailhead. She had a good map and, even with the short days, she still had several hours of daylight to hike before she had to worry about pitching her tent.

In another minute, she was backing out onto the quiet road. She had time to get a good way out into the woods, away from everyone before dark. She could think, and she wouldn't screw anything up for anyone. She wouldn't say something stupid, like her father had good reason to want Alex Bruni dead.

*He didn't. He and Alex were friends.*

And she'd be safe on the mountain.

Safe from whoever had killed Alex, because every instinct she had told her she wasn't safe now.

She had to trust herself.

She had to run.

# Seven

Thirty minutes after he'd left the Three Sisters Café, Elijah twirled the stem of a bright red leaf he'd scooped off the pile of leaves Vivian Whittaker had heaped up on the front lawn of her Vermont country home. Her husband, Lowell, was in the house, collecting himself, she'd said, after hearing about Alex Bruni's death. She'd told Elijah the news in a clipped, straightforward manner, never pausing her raking. He'd run into the Whittakers a few times since his return home, but he only knew them to nod to on the street.

He'd stopped at the guesthouse first. No Nora, no Devin. Then he'd spotted Vivian raking leaves and walked up to find out if she'd seen either of the teenagers.

A.J. had called while Jo and her sister were still on their run. Devin hadn't shown up for work at the lodge. Money was missing. Elijah had headed out to see what he could learn. He hadn't considered that Nora's stepfather would be killed in Washington.

Vivian raked a patch of grass with such force she took up

dirt along with the last of the fallen leaves. She was a tall, thin, fair woman in her mid-forties. A trust-fund type, according to Sean, who knew such things. Her family's money came from a New York-based investment bank. Lowell was some kind of money type himself, although not as rich as his wife. Even as well-off as Elijah's younger brother Sean was, the Whittakers had to be, by far, the wealthiest landowners in Black Falls. For as long as Elijah could remember, the "farm" on the rolling hills above the river had been owned by out-of-staters.

"It's colder than I expected today," Vivian said, not looking at him. "I'm glad I wore gloves. They're just garden gloves, but they keep my hands warm enough."

Elijah thought it was a fine November day. The cool air felt good to him. Helped him get his head together. He figured Jo couldn't have known about Bruni back at the café, not because he didn't think she could control her emotions, but because she wouldn't have continued to sit there eating a scone and looking at the river. Given the kind of week she'd had—given the type of person she was— she'd latch on to news of a dead ambassador whose stepdaughter was in Black Falls. No question in Elijah's mind.

She'd probably found out by now. He wasn't sure how long he had before she turned up. If she didn't have a reason, she'd think of one. He wasn't about to break any laws, but he was accustomed to a certain level of autonomy and wanted to do things his own way. Go from there. He wanted to find Devin and confront him about the missing money.

He didn't need a Secret Service agent throwing up roadblocks.

And he hadn't anticipated Nora's stepfather turning up dead.

But he saw tears glisten in Vivian's eyes and reminded

himself the woman had just lost a friend. "I'm sorry about Ambassador Bruni," he said.

She quickly brought herself back under control. "Yes. Well. It's unfortunate. I only hope his death turns out to be a horrible accident. The idea of someone targeting him is beyond my comprehension. He was such a good man."

"Who told you?"

"Lowell spoke to Thomas Asher, Nora's father." She dipped her rake under a sugar maple, one of a half dozen that dotted the lawn, and scraped the tines over exposed roots. "He called while we were out here working in the yard and left a message. Lowell listened to it. He said it was obvious from Thomas's tone that something was wrong. He had already spoken to Nora and given her the dreadful news by the time Lowell reached him.

Then Nora knew about her stepfather's death.

"The police are investigating, of course," Vivian said, briskly raking her fresh batch of leaves over to the pile. "Alex dedicated himself to diplomacy and public service. It's difficult to believe he had enemies."

"Do you know where Nora is now?" Elijah asked.

"You just missed her." A gust of wind whipped up leaves and lifted Vivian's fine, pale blond bangs back from her forehead. She paused, breathing hard from her manic raking. "I waved her down as she was leaving. I was raking at the end of the driveway. I didn't know about Alex at that point. Lowell had just gone inside. Nora was clearly upset, but I didn't think much of it. She said she was going on a camping trip."

"What kind of camping trip?"

Vivian stood her rake up on end and picked bits of leaves and debris from the tines. "She didn't go into detail—an overnight trip, though. I assume she'll be gone a couple of nights. She obviously didn't want to talk, and I didn't push her for details. She assured me she knows what she's doing."

Elijah settled back on his heels. Knowing what to do wasn't the same as doing it, and Nora had just taken an emotional hit with her stepfather's death. "Did she leave her route with you?"

Vivian shook her head. "Not with me. I urged her to tell someone exactly where she was going and how long she planned to be out. I also warned her not to hike alone. She's an adult. Lowell and I enjoy having her here, but we can only do so much."

"You mentioned she was upset."

"Visibly so, yes. If I'd realized Alex had been killed, I'd have discouraged her from going anywhere." She squinted out at the vista of mountains, her mouth compressed as she inhaled through her nose. "If Alex was run over on purpose, that's murder. That's rather frightening, isn't it?"

"Did you know him well?" Elijah asked.

"We met him here in Black Falls a year ago, not long after we bought this place. We've had him and Carolyn up here several times. I can't even imagine what she's going through." Vivian flipped her rakc back over and dragged a few stray leaves to her pile. "I doubt the police will want to talk to us, but I suppose they could."

Down across the lawn, Elijah noticed Jo's car pull between the stone posts that marked the entrance to the Whittakers' long, paved driveway.

Vivian followed his gaze but didn't comment on Jo's arrival. "You didn't come out here because of poor Alex. You weren't aware of his death until I told you just now. Is there something I can help you with?"

"I'm looking for Devin Shay."

"Devin? I haven't seen him, but he and Nora have been spending a lot of time together." She paused, leaning on her rake. "Do you mind if I ask why you're looking for him?"

Jo parked along a hedge of arbor vitae, got out of her car and fired a look straight at Elijah. He decided he'd be smart to keep in mind that she had ten years as a Secret Service agent under her belt. A few days ago, she'd willingly dived in front of what could have been real bullets heading for the son of the vice president. They hadn't been, and that was damn funny—but the rest wasn't.

She was a serious professional with a serious job, and that was something Elijah did understand.

With one eye on Jo marching toward them, he said, "If you run into Devin, tell him I want to talk to him."

Vivian gave him a distant smile. "Is that an order, Elijah?" But she hesitated, shivering, not from the cold, he thought, so much as the shock of her friend's sudden, violent death. "I worry about Nora. She's so young. She and Devin both look up to you, Elijah. You know that, don't you? You're the black-ops soldier—our own Rambo in the heart of the Green Mountains."

He couldn't tell if she was being sarcastic or sincere, but either way, he had no intention of responding. "Did Nora give any indication Devin was joining her on her hike?"

"No, she didn't." Vivian nodded to her four-foot-by-four-foot pile of leaves. "I planned to have Nora bag up these leaves. That's part of the deal we have. She stays at the guesthouse in exchange for doing odd jobs like bagging leaves, washing screens and gassing up the cars. It was her father's idea. Of course, Lowell and I never ask her to do anything that conflicts with our yard or cleaning services. We don't want to take work away from them."

Elijah started to respond, but Jo came around a sugar maple, most of its fallen leaves in Vivian's pile. "I'm sorry about Ambassador Bruni," she said simply, her expression grim as she addressed Vivian. "I know you were friends."

"Yes. Thank you. We're all sorry." Vivian laid her rake onto the mound of leaves. "I can't believe this." She shook her head. "Whether it was an accident or deliberate, it's ridiculous for such a man to die that way."

"Nora's father asked me to check on her," Jo said.

Elijah's brow went up. Thomas Asher and Jo knew each other?

Vivian said, "I just told Elijah that Nora's gone on a camping trip." She winced and did a neck roll, then stretched her shoulders back. "I'm so stiff, but I wouldn't give up raking leaves for the world. I love November in Vermont, how the landscape opens up with all the leaves off the trees."

If her comment struck Jo as odd, Elijah couldn't tell. It did him.

Lowell Whittaker pushed a wheelbarrow down from the house. He was the picture of a contented country gentleman in his barn jacket and wellies. He looked a lot like his wife—tall, thin, fair. But he was quieter, more cerebral, more likely to wrap his head around a friend's sudden death by taking a few moments to himself than by madly raking.

"Agent Harper, Sergeant Cameron—Jo, Elijah. It's good to see you both, although I wish it were under less difficult circumstances." Lowell set the wheelbarrow down and smiled sadly. "Don't you have an urge to forget everything and take a running leap into the leaves? I can see the two of you jumping in leaves as kids."

"It was something to do," Jo said, but her voice was tight, her mind obviously on the hit-and-run of the Whittakers' friend in Washington.

"I adore Vermont," Lowell said. "What a wonderful place to grow up."

Elijah tossed his leaf onto the pile. He figured Jo had started plotting how to get out of Vermont at about the age of five, but she didn't meet his eye, and he wondered if she was remembering how as kids they'd all taken turns jumping out of a maple tree in the Harper yard into huge piles of leaves. Elijah had pushed Jo out of the tree a few times, but he'd never hurt her. That, he thought, hadn't come until much later.

She stuck to the issue at hand. "Does Nora have friends here she could be meeting up with? Anyone from college, anyone she's met in town—friends from high school who've visited?"

Lowell reached into the pile of leaves and grabbed as many as he could in both arms. Several escaped, but he let them go as he dumped the rest in his wheelbarrow. "Nora and Devin Shay seem to get along," he said thoughtfully. "She likes your sister and the two other women she works for at the café. They're older, of course, but if Nora was upset and wanted to talk to someone, I think she'd turn to them."

Vivian peeled off her garden gloves with sudden energy. "She might just want to be alone after getting such awful news. I can understand that. I didn't realize you and Thomas were friends. I'm so pleased that he and Melanie have decided to get married. Have you met her?"

"Not yet, no," Jo said.

"She's lovely," Vivian said. "Lowell and I don't know Thomas as well as we do Carolyn and Alex, but..." She bit back tears. "I let myself forget for a split second."

"Alex was a good man," Lowell said quietly, as if he was giving a eulogy. "Smart, driven—it's hard to believe all that energy of his is gone now. He'll be missed."

Vivian nodded. "We enjoyed his visits here. He and Carolyn were wonderful together. Such bright, intelligent, gifted people." She smiled awkwardly, tears shining in her pale eyes. "I can see Alex now down at the pond. He wasn't one for relaxation, but he enjoyed watching the ducks."

"Come, dear," Lowell said softly, taking his wife's gloves and placing them atop the leaves in the wheelbarrow. "We haven't had lunch. Let's take a break and forget about work for the rest of the afternoon. Elijah, Jo—if there's anything we can do, please don't hesitate to ask."

Vivian turned stiffly to them. "We have no reason to be concerned for Nora's physical safety. She's an experienced day hiker and has been eager to try out the skills she learned in your class, Elijah. Of course, she should have delayed this trip under the circumstances, but the fight-or-flight response can be very powerful after such a shock."

The wind picked up again, blowing leaves out of the wheelbarrow. Vivian seemed to force herself to resist going after them and continued about the characteristics of fight-or-flight syndrome, which Elijah took as his cue to leave.

He headed back down to the guesthouse. The sky was clear and a deep blue above the gray landscape.

It'd be cold tonight. If Nora Asher wasn't prepared, she'd be in trouble.

And if Devin had gone with her?

Elijah shook off the thought. If Devin had any sense, he would be back at the lodge doing his job and working out terms with A.J. for any money he'd "borrowed." But he was eighteen and smitten, and that didn't make it easy, as Elijah knew from personal experience, to have any sense.

A few minutes after he reached the duck pond, Elijah saw Jo coming down the lawn at a fast clip. She'd always been able to move quickly. How many times had he given up the chase when she'd provoked him as a kid and he'd gone after her?

Finally, at nineteen, he'd caught her. Held her. Loved her. Vowed never to let her go, never to disappoint her, never to hurt her—but he'd done them all.

He wasn't one to look back, but Jo being in town was messing with his head.

She didn't slow her pace until she stood next to him and grabbed him by the upper arm. "What the hell's going on?"

Elijah felt her fingers digging though his canvas jacket into the muscles of his arm. Her eyes were steady, focused—not shining with the sincerity of the eighteen-year-old whose heart he broke but with the determination of the dedicated, experienced federal agent she was now.

Time to get his head screwed back on straight. Fifteen years had passed since he'd left Jo in Black Falls and headed to basic training. He'd covered a lot of ground since then.

His father was dead, and now Alex Bruni was dead.

Elijah reminded himself he had a job to do.

"Jo," he said calmly, not at all nastily, "I'm not some nut who's threatened the vice president's family."

She didn't release him. If anything, she tightened her grip. "No, you're the Special Forces soldier who doesn't know what comes next in his life."

"I'm the guy who could get your hand off me if I wanted to."

"You don't want to."

He grinned suddenly. "No, actually, I don't."

That got her, and she let go. "Fifteen years in the army turned you into a real wiseass."

"Your nose is red. Been crying?"

She sighed. "You don't let up, do you? It's the cold. I'm not used to it anymore. Did you know Ambassador Bruni?"

He shook his head. "I know he stayed at the lodge a few times. Not much impresses A.J., but an ambassador checking in got his attention. Then Bruni and the Whittakers became friends. What about you? Did you know him?"

"Not really, no. I'm not sure I was ever in town the same time he was. Elijah, the Whittakers said Nora took a wilderness-skills class you taught at the lodge. A.J. must have blackmailed you into that one, but never mind. It's supposed to get into the low twenties tonight. Is she prepared to handle a hike in these conditions?"

"She bought all the right equipment, and I taught her what to do."

"But she's never actually pitched a tent on a frigid mountain." Jo stated the obvious, then bent and picked up a small stone, rubbing it between her fingers. "I tried calling her cell phone, but I just got her voice mail."

"Her father's worried?"

"Wouldn't you be?"

Elijah picked up his own stone, immediately skipping it out across the cold, quiet water, away from the two ducks on the far shore. It skipped once, twice, three times. "What's with you and Nora's father?"

"Thomas? Nothing, really. We ran into each other cross-country skiing in February and realized we're both from Washington." She continued rubbing her stone, as if it might suddenly produce a genie and grant her three wishes. "We stayed in touch."

"He's from a prominent Virginia family."

"Yes, he's quite the gentleman."

"Ah. No wonder you two didn't stick. You like your bad boys."

She ignored him and tried skipping her stone across the pond, but it went straight in. "I never have gotten the hang of skipping stones. You must have shown me how to do it a million times." Using the toe of her running shoe, she scraped another stone free from the dirt. "Just to set the record straight, there was never anything between Thomas and me."

"So you didn't hit the self-destruct button because he got engaged?"

"I fell for a prank and intercepted a barrage of airsoft pellets. If I'd wanted to self-destruct, I could have picked a more efficient way than getting nailed with a fake gun." She scooped up her stone and rubbed the dirt off it. "Elijah, if what you're up to has anything to do with Ambassador Bruni's death, I need to know."

"Why?"

She narrowed a look at him and didn't answer.

He asked, "Have you checked with your friends in Washington about what happened this morning?"

He noted a thinning of her lips as she curved her arm, reared back and tried again, flinging her stone with ferocity if not much finesse. It skipped once. An improvement. But she still didn't meet his eye.

Elijah put two and two together. "You tried checking with friends. No one took your call."

"It's not that simple." She rubbed her hands together, brushing off the dirt from her rocks. "Elijah, people in town say you're not satisfied with the official explanation of your father's death. If you have reason to suspect it wasn't an accident—"

"I'm just here skipping stones."

She steadied her gaze on him. "Take whatever questions you have to the police, Elijah. Let them get the answers."

Her words hit him in all the wrong places. He picked up another stone and shot it across the water, getting close enough to the ducks for them to move toward the opposite bank.

He turned to Jo, looked her straight in the eye. "Maybe I'll buy your dad a cup of coffee and tell him I'm thinking about sleeping with you again."

She shoved her hands into the pockets of her fleece jacket. "Go ahead, Elijah. Give me your best shot. I'm not a besotted teenager anymore."

"Not a teenager, Jo. Still besotted."

"Ha. Don't you wish." But he thought he heard just the slightest catch in her voice. She glanced around at the stone guesthouse, which, like everything on the estate, was bucolic, perfect. "Nora's sense of trust must have taken a hit when her mother had an affair and then married one of her father's best friends."

"It couldn't have helped when her father didn't do anything about it."

"Like what, shoot him?"

"He was passive." Elijah started up the slight incline to a

stone walk. He'd parked his truck in the turnaround on the side of the road. Time to get out of there, before he really did something he regretted. But he turned back to Jo and finished his thought. "Nora needed to see him stand up for himself. He didn't have to fight. He could have forgiven her mother and Bruni. Instead he weaseled out of doing anything."

Jo cocked her head back and gave him a knowing look. "Elijah. It wasn't the same for us—fifteen years ago we were kids."

"I should have fought for you, Jo," he said suddenly, not exactly sure where the words came from. "Think of what might have been if I had. Even if I'd ended up in the army and you in the Secret Service—"

"We'd have split up in six months."

"That's not what you believe."

"Forgiving yourself is a lot harder than forgiving someone else."

He took two steps back to her and touched her hair, silky under his cold fingers. "Jo. Don't. You didn't do anything you need to forgive yourself for."

"Neither did you."

He leaned toward her, kissed her lightly on the lips. "Yes, I did," he said, then dropped his hand from her hair and pulled back before he went further. Being around her was firing him up in ways that were dangerous—intrusive. He needed to stay focused on his own mission, not get mixed up with a Secret Service agent angling to get back to Washington as fast as she could.

"Elijah," she said. "We can't—"

He cut her off. "Nora's bumping up against the difference between reality and fantasy. Sometimes that's no damn fun."

"Are you going to tell me what you're doing out here?"

He shrugged. "Following you."

"You're a lousy liar. You didn't follow me. You got here first."

"I'm clairvoyant. I knew you'd be here. See you later, Jo."

She reached for him but seemed to think better of grabbing him by the arm again. She tilted her head back, scrutinizing him with those deep, suspicious turquoise eyes. "What's going on, Elijah?"

"Nothing that concerns you, Agent Harper."

He thought he saw a twitch of irritation at one corner of her mouth. "Tell me about Devin Shay," she said. "Why are you looking for him?"

"If you want to show me your badge and interrogate me, have at it. You can even slap on handcuffs and haul me off somewhere. It won't be the first time a Harper's nailed my ass. Otherwise, I've got things to do and places to go. I'm sorry about Ambassador Bruni, but I didn't know him."

She looked as if she was, in fact, debating showing him her badge, slapping him in handcuffs and finding a hot light somewhere to interrogate him. "Where are you going now?"

Elijah didn't answer. Jo had always hated being ignored, and from the rock she threw at him, he guessed that hadn't changed. She missed him by two yards. He grinned back at her. "Your arm still sucks."

"I missed on purpose."

"Right."

"I should have gone into exile in New Zealand after all. Having me here after what you've been through in Afghanistan and your father's death isn't helping."

"It's better than your Secret Service friends. That last

bunch was scary. Big hairy guys. No yoga pants." Elijah laughed as she threw another rock and missed him again. "See you back at the lake, Agent Harper."

Maybe it was the sun or his imagination—or not enough to do—but he thought he saw her give a hint of a smile as he climbed into his truck.

There was no chance she wouldn't follow him. She was a Harper, and there hadn't been one born who knew when to give up.

Elijah drove up to the high, open ridge above the village of Black Falls. Old, graceful maple trees and stone walls lined the narrow road. He found a spot with passable cell service and called Ryan Taylor, a Navy SEAL who'd fought and bled with him in Afghanistan. Everyone called him Grit, which made sense once people met him.

Grit didn't appreciate chitchat, so Elijah got straight to the point. "Hit-and-run of Alexander Bruni this morning. What do you know?"

"It's a big deal," Grit said in his smooth north Florida accent. "No national security implications at this point. No ID of car or driver. No consistent witness reports—it's not as if people stand around on the streets waiting for a car to hit someone. By the time it happens, it's over."

"All right." Elijah wasn't surprised that Grit was on top of the situation, even if Grit himself was, at least apparently, still in rehab seven months after the firefight that had left him without his lower left leg. But Grit wasn't accustomed to telling anyone what all he did in a day. "That's what's known. What's suspected?"

"It was a hit."

"Why?" Elijah asked.

"Rich, powerful, well-connected men don't get run over by accident. I haven't heard any talk, in case you're wondering. Bruni's been in this town too long not to have enemies. Hell, he married his best friend's wife. You heard about that?"

"I did."

"Figured," Grit said. "He leaves her and two grown sons by his first wife. There's also a college-age stepdaughter."

"What, have you been searching the Internet on this guy?"

"Not hard to find stuff. Obits are all over the place already. Gives me something to do."

"You could go to the theater."

Grit didn't respond for a half beat. "I could. I like the theater. What's your interest in Bruni?"

"His stepdaughter dropped out of college and is living in Black Falls."

"Ah."

"See what else you can find out about Bruni's death. Unless you decide to go to the theater after all."

Grit had hung up.

Elijah started up his truck again, Cameron Mountain looming out across a wide, grassy field. He imagined his father up there in a sudden April snowstorm. Thomas Asher had been in Black Falls then with his daughter.

Now Nora's stepfather was dead.

And Jo had met Bruni and knew Thomas Asher, the betrayed friend, and she was in town.

Elijah tightened his grip on the wheel, still feeling the softness of her lips. He considered putting the question of Jo Harper to Grit Taylor next. Grit had contacts in Washington. He could ask about Elijah's Secret Service-agent neighbor.

Not a good idea, he decided, heading down the road toward Black Falls Lodge. He doubted Devin was back at work. If Devin knew Nora was up on the mountain, coping by herself with her stepfather's sudden, suspicious death, he'd go look for her. It would be a simple equation for him. Nora was upset. He'd want to be there for her.

Elijah figured he'd get up on the mountain and see if he could pick up either teenager's trail. Alone. Without the Secret Service.

He'd tell A.J. that Jo was on his heels. A.J. was stubborn and closemouthed by nature, and he'd never been one of Jo Harper's biggest fans.

His brother would stall her and buy Elijah time to handle the situation his way.

# *Eight*

When she was twelve, Jo had fantasized that Black Falls Lodge was straight out of *The Sound of Music* and one day she might meet her own Captain Von Trapp there. Then Elijah told her *The Sound of Music* gave him dry heaves, which ended that bit of fun.

The Von Trapp family had settled in Stowe, farther to the north, and started a resort that was still one of the most beautiful and popular in Vermont. Black Falls Lodge wasn't as big an operation, but its location along an open ridge, with stunning views of the endless mountains, was nothing short of breathtaking—enough, Jo thought, to get Elijah's kiss out of her mind. On the drive up to the lodge, she'd decided it'd been inevitable. Now that it was out of the way, she could concentrate on other things.

Like what was going on with the Camerons.

She parked next to Elijah's truck and soaked in the scenery as she got out of her car. The air was colder, the breeze stiffer. She crossed the parking lot on the edge of a wide meadow that, in spring and summer, would be afire with wildflowers.

Evergreens and rust-colored oak leaves provided color in the otherwise bare, gray landscape.

A corner of the lake was visible down in the hollow below. Her red-tailed hawk was patrolling the graying sky.

It was the slow season—even the mountain bikers weren't out. The leaf peepers had gone home, and the cross-country skiers and snowshoers hadn't arrived yet. Snow was in the forecast, but it was still early for winter recreation.

The lodge would do a good business over Thanksgiving, but it was quiet now. The property consisted of the original rustic-style lodge, a new recreational building with an indoor pool, racquetball court and health club, a half-dozen separate cottages and a shop that sold and rented bicycles, cross-country skis, snowshoes, canoes and kayaks—never mind that the lodge wasn't on a lake or river frontage.

Jo followed a stone walk to the back of the lodge and stepped up onto a terrace, its tables and chairs unoccupied on the chilly November afternoon. Drew Cameron had pulled together parcels of land to reclaim Cameron Mountain and get Black Falls Lodge started, but what it was today was A.J.'s doing—his hard work, and his dream, now shared by his wife, Lauren, who, according to Beth, had talked A.J. into agreeing to build a top-notch spa on the premises.

A.J. came out onto the terrace from the French doors that led into the lodge's main dining room. His hair was a shade darker than Elijah's, and he was a little shorter—but he had the Cameron blue eyes. They all did, including Rose.

"It's been a long time, Jo," he said, kissing her on the cheek. "How are you?"

She was immediately suspicious. "Did Elijah tell you to stall me?"

He grinned at her. "You two. Nothing ever changes." He nodded toward the doors. "Come inside."

Jo didn't budge. "What's he up to, A.J.?"

"It's cold out here, and I'm not wearing a coat. You're used to Washington temperatures." He motioned for her to go in ahead of him. "Let's go inside and talk in front of the fire."

Definitely he was stalling, but Jo acquiesced and went ahead of him into the dining room. It, too, was unoccupied. A.J. led her down the hall to the lobby, where, indeed, a fire crackled in the massive stone fireplace. The furnishings were sturdy, done in mountain colors—dark green, burgundy, brown. A huge stuffed moose—fake, not real—stood in a corner.

Jo welcomed the warmth of the fire, but she remained on her feet. She hadn't run into A.J. since learning his father had left her the lakefront property. If he was bitter about his father's will, he didn't let it show as he reached for a black-iron poker. "I heard you were in town," he said.

"I figured you had. That's Elijah's truck I'm parked next to, isn't it?"

"You know it is."

"He's here, then."

It wasn't a question, but A.J. shrugged. "Looks that way."

She recognized the flicker of stubbornness in his eyes. When Camerons didn't want to talk, they didn't. They were independent, tight-knit and honest, but that didn't mean they played by the rules.

"Okay. So is he in here somewhere? Is he preparing another wilderness-skills class? Hiking? Teaching your little ones to light fires with their fingernails? What?"

A.J. seemed to realize she was being only half sarcastic. The other half was totally serious. He pulled back the screen on the fire. "You got yourself into a mess in Washington. I hope you're not here looking for ways to restore your reputation."

"I'm not worried about my reputation. Where's Elijah?"

"You were always relentless, Jo. I actually liked that about you—"

"But it's bugging you right now, isn't it?"

He gave her a grudging smile. "It's not helping. Elijah didn't take to teaching, by the way. One class was enough for him." The fire made A.J.'s eyes seem darker. "I heard about Alex Bruni. That's a hard one, Jo. Lauren and I enjoyed having him here. We weren't friends, but he loved being in Black Falls. I hate the thought that someone could have killed him."

"I'm sorry, A.J."

"I haven't seen Nora Asher, if that's why you're here."

"What about Devin Shay?"

A short pause. "He's not here."

"What does he do for you? Sweep floors and that sort of thing, or does he get out on the mountain, work on trails—what?"

"Maintenance."

A.J. obviously didn't like being asked questions. Jo was undeterred. "As in digging holes and moving big rocks, or something he could turn into a career?"

"That's between Devin and me."

None of her business, in other words.

He lifted a burning log with his poker, the fire popping, rekindled flames rising up. "You should relax, Jo." He pulled the poker from the fire and set the screen back in place. "Sit here by the fire. Find a good book to read. Have you had lunch? There's apple pie in the dining room. Feel free to help yourself to anything in the kitchen. As you can see, we don't have a crowd."

The Whittakers had invited her to lunch, but she wasn't hungry. She reined in her impatience, reminding herself that, for all intents and purposes, she was the outsider here. "What's going on, A.J.?"

"Nothing that involves Ambassador Bruni's death or concerns the Secret Service."

"That you know of," she said.

He didn't respond. If any Cameron had reason to resent her, it was A.J., who was responsible for keeping the lodge competitive, an attractive option to visitors to Vermont. Direct access to the lake would help. She hadn't gotten so far as to think about selling or leasing her property, let alone broaching the subject with him.

"Is there anything I should know about your father's death?" she asked bluntly.

A.J. gave her a steady look. "It was a tragedy."

"I know that, A.J."

"Do you, Jo?" He turned back to the fire, staring at the hot, glowing coals. "You must have wished him a rough passing."

"No. Not ever. Even at my most brokenhearted and angriest, I understood that he did what any father who cared about a son like Elijah would have done—at least any father with guts."

"He cared about you, too," A.J. said quietly.

She nodded. "Yes, I know that now. I didn't at the time. Elijah did well in the army, despite the hardships he faced. And things worked out for me. I'm happy."

"Are you?" A.J. gave her a brief glance, then looked back at the fire. "Elijah always wanted to come back to Vermont. Assuming he lived. Not you. You wanted out of Black Falls, Jo, and you got out."

"You make living here sound like a prison sentence."

"Isn't that what you thought?"

"For five minutes at seventeen, maybe. Not anymore."

"Elijah didn't want to hem you in."

"Hem me in? A.J., it's been fifteen years. Elijah and I went our separate ways a long time ago."

A.J. moved back from the fire. "I think he always envisioned you being here when he got home. One way or the other."

"That's romantic B.S., and you know it."

He grinned. "You're tough as nails."

But she felt Elijah's mouth on hers, saw the spark of desire in his eyes…a kind of soul-deep longing that she knew was mostly her imagination at work. She warned herself against reading too much—anything—into an impulsive kiss.

She stiffened, refocused on why she'd come up to the lodge. "Why is Elijah looking for Devin?"

"Okay, I give up," A.J. said, not particularly harshly. "Elijah's on the falls trail. Go ahead. Try to catch up with him if you want."

"You figure you've bought him enough time."

"No, Jo." He gave her a small grin. "I figure Elijah can handle you."

"Before I leave here today, A.J., you and your brother are going to level with me about what's going on."

"Don't get lost."

Jo left through the front entrance. The wind went right through her fleece jacket, and she almost reconsidered the pie, the book and the fire. Hunching her shoulders against the cold, she walked over to the edge of the road. The lodge trails were part of a network of recreational trails on state, federal and private land. Nora Asher could go for miles—days—if she wanted to. She'd started out a few hours ago. Who knew where she could be now?

Cameron Mountain rose up above the open fields across the quiet road. Jo hadn't spent much time up here in recent years—and she'd repressed a lot of memories, since most of them involved Elijah.

She heard laughter behind her and turned, seeing Lauren, A.J.'s wife of five years, who was businesslike but not as flinty as her husband, and their four-year-old son and two-year-old daughter. The little ones were running in circles on the grass, the wind catching the ends of their blond hair, their cheeks rosy red as they squealed in delight.

They made an abrupt ninety-degree turn and bolted back toward the lodge. In an instant, Jo saw why, as A.J. walked out and scooped up his children.

She felt a tug of emotion she didn't expect.

*"I wake up on cold mornings and see the grandchildren you and Elijah should have had..."*

Jo got out of there, quickly crossing the road, making her way onto a beaten-down grass path that would take her through the field and out to the falls trail. She wasn't equipped for a full-fledged hike in the mountains, but she'd do her best to pick up Elijah's trail.

# *Nine*

Ryan "Grit" Taylor stood in front of the hotel where Alexander Bruni had met his end six hours ago. Cabs, limos, delivery trucks and regular cars packed the street now, but Grit knew the cops hadn't all disappeared once they'd released the scene. He didn't see them, but there was no question they were there. The D.C. police, the FBI, maybe even a Diplomatic Security Service or Secret Service agent or two.

An ambassador getting run down on a Washington street was a big deal.

Television reporters had set up a little ways past the revolving doors for live shots and were on the lookout for anyone who'd been there that morning.

Bruni had been run over on a bad spot on a bad street. Grit had been out there for ten minutes, and with the traffic, the distracted tourists, he decided it was not out of the realm of possibility for Bruni to have been hit by accident. A busy man with a lot on his mind crosses the street without looking, and—that's it. He's done.

Leaving the scene was another matter. That didn't look good.

Moose Ferrerra, a fellow Navy SEAL, materialized next to Grit. *"The Grim Reaper comes for you fast or slow. Either way, he always wins."*

"I know, Moose," Grit said. "I know."

Moose didn't respond. He looked the same as he had thirteen years ago on his first day of SEAL training. Fresh, young, eager, cocky. Nothing like he had in April when the Grim Reaper had swooped down on their position in eastern Afghanistan.

A hellish mountain pass, newly opened after the harsh winter. A helicopter with mechanical trouble. Heavily armed, pissed-off bad guys.

Not a great combo.

Grit and Moose and the rest of their SEAL team had joined up with a Special Forces unit to take out a series of enemy weapons caches. Everything went fine until the SEAL exfiltration. The Green Berets stayed behind to protect friendly local villagers, who'd helped pinpoint the caches, from retaliation and continue their work.

The helicopter ran into problems almost immediately and was forced to make a hard landing in an enemy hot spot.

Moose was shot first. Then Grit. Then Elijah Cameron and his guys came to their aid.

Elijah was shot.

It had been a long night.

Grit was convinced that the Grim Reaper had come for him, not Moose, and he still didn't know why things hadn't worked out the way they'd been meant to. He only knew that he should have died that night. It wasn't superstition or pessimism or depression—it was dead-on certainty.

He *knew* he should be dead.

And he wasn't grateful he'd survived. Most days, he wished he hadn't.

Which annoyed the hell out of Moose. *"My friend, you need to get an attitude of gratitude."*

Moose's voice. Clear as a bell. He was right, too. As always.

Grit watched Washington types go through the revolving doors into the hotel lobby. It was too early for happy hour, but he had learned, since Elijah's call, that the hotel was a favorite for meetings, from multi-day conventions to an afternoon workshop on how to sell mortgages.

Bruni had likely been on his way to some sort of power breakfast in the hotel dining room. Or maybe breakfast by himself. Never mind that he was an ambassador, he had to eat.

Grit stepped out of the way for a brisk woman pushing a baby in a stroller the size of a VW Bug. She didn't make eye contact with him. Neither did her cute, slobbering, bald-headed bambino.

They disappeared around the corner, and Grit sighed. His left foot hurt.

*"You don't have a left foot,"* Moose said.

"I know I don't."

After seven months, Grit hadn't forgotten that he'd lost his lower left leg, but his left foot *did,* in fact, hurt. Phantom pain, he'd learned, was a common and very real phenomenon. It had to do with how nerves in the residual limb communicated to the brain. His doctors and physical therapists at Bethesda had explained how it all worked in careful detail. Grit had learned more about the nerves, muscles and workings of legs than he'd ever imagined knowing. He'd made good progress; he wasn't back to his preinjury mobility, but he had confidence, which he hadn't had in the beginning, that he'd get there.

He was on his second prosthesis. He'd probably need another one or two in the coming months as his leg adapted and toughened and adjusted to the mechanics of prosthetic use.

Since he hadn't died in that mountain pass, he figured he might as well get on with living. Not that he was grateful.

Moose was the one who'd urged the Special Forces medic to cut off Grit's leg. "Don't listen to Grit. Don't let him die. Just do your duty."

That transtibial—below-the-knee—field amputation had probably saved Grit's life.

A short woman with ultrablack dyed hair emerged from a knot of reporters and walked up to Grit. She had bloodred nails and wore a denim jacket over a black dress and flat gold shoes that he figured cost more than he earned in a week. Maybe a month.

She took a lipstick out of a gigantic black handbag and looked sideways at him as she opened it up. She had big, lavender eyes. Grit put her at somewhere between fifty and a hundred. Whatever her age, she was still a knockout.

She dabbed her mouth with the lipstick. As far as he could see, it was the same color as her lips. What was the point?

"You're not a reporter," she said with a trace of a Southern accent, not unlike his own. "What are you doing hanging around out here?"

He figured he didn't have to answer her question. "Who are you?"

"I'm a reporter. Myrtle Smith."

Grit had never heard of her. "Nice to meet you, Ms. Smith."

"Myrtle's fine, but if you make fun of my name or tell me you have an aunt Myrtle—" she smiled "—I'll cut off your balls."

She weighed maybe a hundred pounds. But she could have

a sharp little knife in that big handbag. Grit realized his foot wasn't hurting anymore. "I do have an aunt Myrtle. She's my great-aunt. My grandmother's older sister."

"What's your grandmother's name?"

"Vasselona."

"I like that. Your name?"

He debated telling her. "Ryan Taylor."

"Mind if I call you Ryan?"

"Most people call me Grit."

She gave him a frank once-over. He was dark and wiry, his hair almost as black as hers, and he had on jeans and a plain gray sweatshirt. "I can see why." She shoved her lipstick back in her handbag. "Well, Grit, what are you up to?"

He didn't answer.

"Not a talker, are you? Okay. I'll talk. The police are looking for eyewitnesses to the hit-and-run this morning. No one's come forward yet."

A beefy doorman opened up the back door of a black limo that had pulled up to the hotel. Myrtle watched who got out but didn't react. Just a businessman, no bodyguards, no Secret Service. Not anyone high up in law enforcement.

Grit figured something about him had sparked Myrtle's interest.

*"It's those dreamy black eyes of yours,"* Moose said.

"Shut up," Grit said calmly. Moose had always had a sense of humor.

Myrtle frowned. "What did you say?"

Grit ignored her question. Moose wasn't easy to explain to people. "What else do you have on Ambassador Bruni's death?"

"Police want to know if he was meeting someone here at the hotel or just was on his way to breakfast by himself.

There's nothing on his calendar. His office is across the street and up a few doors."

"Lots of talk about where he'd end up next."

"Yes. Did you know Ambassador Bruni, Grit?"

"No, ma'am."

She didn't look offended that he'd called her ma'am. "I hear he could be difficult." She opened her handbag again, fished out a business card and handed it to him. "That's how to reach me if you want to talk."

"About what, Myrtle?"

"Life, death, the virtues of Southern peach cobbler. Whatever you want."

She eased off down the street. The doormen all watched her. The beefy one came and stood next to Grit. "That accident this morning's killing business today. Maybe the reporters will come in for a drink when they're done. Bottom-feeders."

"Don't like reporters?"

"Nope."

He didn't look as if he liked many people. Grit didn't mind.

"It's not as if that bastard died in the service of anyone but himself," the doorman said.

"Not a popular guy?"

"I hate to speak ill of the dead, but, no, he wasn't popular, at least not with me. He was in here a few times a week. Most days he was a Class A prick."

"A mean bastard, huh?"

"Entitled. I'll take a mean scrapper any day over some trust-fund jackass who thinks he can push people around. They're not all like that—we get some damn fine trust-fund types in here. Bruni wasn't one of them."

"Think someone ran him over on purpose?"

"I suppose someone else could have. But no, that's not what I think. I think he just stepped in front of a car and got hit."

"The car took off."

"I missed the whole thing, myself, but the way I hear it, the driver might not have realized what happened. Just one of those freak things."

"I run over a mouse, I know it. Anyone else around when Bruni got hit?"

"Lots of people."

"Anyone stand out?"

"No. Not really." The doorman nodded down the street. "You know Myrtle Smith?"

"We just met. Who is she?"

"Old warhorse reporter. You're not from here, are you?"

"No, sir."

"Myrtle's down on her luck these days. I heard she hasn't worked in a couple months, but she's got money in the bank, so no worries." The doorman squinted at Grit, then said quietly, "And no one's been shooting at her lately. Thank you for your service."

Grit didn't ask how he knew. "It's my privilege to serve."

"It's tough, losing a leg in the line of duty."

Not everyone could tell he wore a prosthesis, even after just seven months. "How do you know I didn't just get hit by a bus?"

"I know."

Grit had a feeling the doorman was a bit of a prick himself.

*"He does know,"* Moose said. *"He was in Vietnam. He lost friends in the Central Highlands."*

"Enough, Moose."

The doorman frowned. "Beg your pardon?"

Grit didn't answer and headed up to the corner. Old Myrtle

was nowhere in sight. He felt the humidity even in the chilly air. He decided he didn't like November in Washington. It'd be worse in Vermont. He hoped Elijah figured things out before he'd have to get up there to help him.

Moose sighed next to him. *"It can snow in Vermont in November."*

Yes, it could.

Grit had never liked snow.

# Ten

Elijah dipped onto a narrow, seldom-used spur off the falls trail and picked up his pace, not because he'd caught a glimpse of Jo below him—although he had—but because he'd spotted Devin up by a hemlock, about thirty yards away.

Jo wouldn't catch up unless Elijah wanted her to or he fell flat on his face on the steep, rocky trail, which was possible given his mood. He didn't know if she'd seen him, if A.J. had ratted him out or if some Secret Service instinct had kicked in, but she seemed to have a fair idea of where he was.

Maybe she'd spotted Devin, too.

Hiking straight up to the summit of Cameron Mountain and back down again could be done in a day. The main trails were well marked and well maintained. But leave them, either for a less popular trail or to go off-trail altogether, and even experienced hikers could end up lost in the miles of woods, cliffs, hollows, streams and steep, unforgiving terrain. In his first days back home, Elijah had fetched a pair of lost honeymooners from Boston off the mountain. They were in one of the few spots with cell phone service and were able to call the lodge for help.

He'd tried calling Devin's cell phone but didn't get an answer.

Elijah adjusted his daypack, which he kept in his truck at all times, and hoofed it up a near-vertical incline of rock. At the top, the trail leveled off for about three feet then switchbacked on up the mountain.

Devin was directly above him, climbing over a spruce tree that wind or an ice storm had dropped across the trail. The densely wooded hillside was littered with fallen trees.

"Hold up, Devin," Elijah said calmly. "I want to talk to you."

He stood up, gripping a thick walking stick, breathing hard. "Leave me alone, okay? Just go back and stack some more wood."

"Wood's stacked. What are you doing up here?"

Devin ignored him, wiped his brow with his sleeve and continued on his way.

Seeing how the shortest distance between two points was a straight line, Elijah left the trail and pushed uphill through dead leaves, pine needles and rocks, emerging on the other side of the fallen spruce.

Devin faltered for a half beat, looking uncertain, then pivoted and kept going.

"You're wearing the wrong clothes," Elijah said. "You're not carrying a pack. That means you have no water. You're asking for dehydration and hypothermia."

Devin glanced back, sullen, his ball cap low over his eyes. "Did my sister sic you on me?"

"I'm here on my own, but if she'd asked me to find you, it'd be because she's worried."

"Hannah worries too much."

"Maybe so, but she has good reason—"

"Not on my account."

Elijah climbed over the fallen spruce, mindful of dead, sharp branches and sticky pitch. Seven months ago, picturing himself out here had kept him going through grief and rehab—and anger. "Are you on your way to meet Nora?" he asked Devin. "Her stepfather was killed this morning in Washington. She took off suddenly. If you've talked to her you could help reassure the people who care about her."

"And who would that be?" Devin spun around and glared bitterly down the trail at Elijah. "Her father doesn't care about her. Her mother, either. They're into their own lives—they don't care about Nora. And her stepfather. She didn't tell me about the hit-and-run. Hannah did. I'm sorry he got killed, but he never wanted anything to do with Nora."

"Is that from your own observations, or what she told you?"

"Doesn't matter."

"It's easy to feel alienated when you're trying to figure out your life."

"Go to hell, Elijah."

He'd have responded the same way at eighteen. "Nora isn't used to being out here the way you are."

"She just wants to clear her head and to practice what you taught her. I tried to tell her the same stuff you did in that class, but she had to hear it from you." He raised his chin. "The big Green Beret."

Elijah let that one go. "Any idea what route she took? There are a lot of ways she can get lost or into trouble out here. Does she have a cell phone, GPS?"

"I don't know. She didn't tell me her plans."

"Is she avoiding you, Devin?"

"Get off my case, Elijah. I know you and A.J. think I'm no damn good. Tough."

"If you don't know where Nora is, then hike back to the lodge with me. Let's sit down with A.J. and figure things out."

"You go back to the lodge."

Elijah felt like wringing Devin's neck. "Why are you so combative?"

"I don't like being under the Cameron microscope. I found your father's body, and what thanks do I get?"

"Did you expect thanks, Devin?"

He paled slightly, seemed to realize he'd gone too far.

"For two cents," Elijah said, "I'd throw you off this damn mountain. Hell, I'd do it for free. If you see Nora, let her know that she's not alone."

"She is alone." Devin stood in the middle of the trail, his cheeks red with the cold and emotion as he hooked his walking stick under one arm. "We're all alone when it comes right down to it."

Elijah couldn't argue with him on that score. "You're a lot of fun these days."

"I'm a realist."

"Devin, if you need a hand—"

"I don't need anything."

"Money's missing from the lodge," Elijah said quietly.

Devin stared down into the dense evergreens and seemed to take a moment to collect himself. "I don't steal," he said. "Not from anyone."

"You're short one day, cash is sitting right there…"

"I didn't take anything from A.J. or the lodge. If either of you had any evidence against me, you'd call the police."

"Not necessarily."

"How stupid do you think I am?" He spun back onto the trail, set his walking stick on a soft spot and moved forward. "Camerons don't do favors for anyone but themselves."

Elijah stayed within ten feet of Devin, and he wondered how fast Jo was gaining on them. He still didn't want to talk about missing money in front of her. "What about Nora? She's used to having money. She's probably had quite a wake-up call being on her own."

"She doesn't steal, either."

"Think you might impress her if you had some extra cash to toss around?"

Devin humped it up a rock face in the middle of the trail. Short of wrestling him to the ground, Elijah had little choice but to let him go. "Take your time," he said. "Don't trip on a root or a rock and split your head open. I'm not going to follow you. If you want to talk to me, you know where to find me. Anytime. Day or night."

No response.

"Where will you be if I want to talk to you?"

Devin raised his middle finger without so much as a pause in his step or a backward glance down the trail.

Message received, Elijah thought.

He started back down the trail, not taking his shortcut this time. A cool breeze floated through the trees, bringing with it the acidic smell of the pines and spruces. He could camp up here for the night. He didn't have to go back.

But Jo would be gaining on him. He kept going, rounding the hairpin turn, then dropping off the thick roots of a giant spruce tree, landing in front of her. "Agent Harper," he said amiably. "Nice day for a hike, but watch out for wet spots this time of year. We don't want to contribute to trail erosion."

She wasn't breathing all that hard for someone who'd hiked up the mountain as rapidly as she had. She looked past him. "Where's Devin headed?"

"He didn't say. Why? He hasn't done anything to alert the Secret Service, has he?"

Jo ignored his bantering tone. "What about Nora Asher?"

"I haven't seen her."

"Has Devin?"

"Didn't say."

"Is he meeting her?"

"Likewise, he didn't say." Elijah noticed the color high in Jo's cheeks—wind, exertion, irritation. A sense of purpose. "Getting banished to Vermont must be rough when you have an ambassador turn up dead in Washington. Nora taking off into the woods by itself isn't a big deal, but it reminds you that you have nothing to do. So you turn it into something—"

"Elijah."

"So intense, Jo." He grinned at her. "Damn, but you have pretty eyes. The copper highlights bring out the turquoise."

"Elijah, we can do this nice, or I can shoot you. Which will it be?"

"You're not supposed to talk like that. You're a professional."

"No witnesses."

"You didn't think there were witnesses at the Neals', either."

"No, I didn't care if there were. There's a difference."

Jo did have a way about her. Elijah jumped lightly onto a flat, gray rock. A breeze rustled through the trees. "Devin's not a bad kid, and if Nora's decided to try winter camping, for whatever reason, she knows what to do."

"A lot of people who know what to do end up in trouble up here."

His father, for one.

Jo seemed to read his mind and took a sharp breath. "Elijah, I'm sorry."

"Forget it. You just stated a fact. I understand Nora's father is worried about her, but she's got a good head start on us. Even if we find her, we'll probably run out of daylight before we can get her off the mountain. I'm prepared to spend the night up here. You're not."

"She is?"

He shrugged. "If she packed the gear she showed me, absolutely."

"Devin?"

"He's a natural. Give him a jackknife, and he could survive Antarctica." But Elijah saw that Jo wasn't going to respond to his humor, and he said, "I'm not worried about Devin. Let's get moving before we end up in trouble ourselves." He nodded down the trail. "You walk point. I'd rather look at your butt than have you look at mine."

"Elijah..."

"You're blushing, Agent Harper. I thought I'd never see the day. Even fifteen years ago when we were—"

"Right now, Elijah, I'm looking for a good spot to hide your body."

She tried to pull off a scowl but couldn't do it, and he laughed, appreciating that she hadn't let mention of his father's death stop her from reacting exactly the way he'd expected, the way he'd wanted her to—sharp-tongued, feisty, smart.

She lifted a foot onto a knee-high boulder and stretched her calf muscles, and he couldn't help but notice the curve of her hip. "You're wearing jeans," he said. "Jeans aren't good in the cold."

"I'm aware of that, and, if you'll notice, you're also in jeans."

He patted the strap of his daypack. "But I have a change of clothes. Not carrying any water, either?"

She didn't answer and dropped her foot back to the trail.

"I have more than enough water to share," Elijah said.

"Thank you. I'll let you know if I get thirsty."

"When was the last time you were up here on your own?"

"Years," she said, and left it at that as she about-faced and plunged back down the trail.

Her butt really wasn't hard to look at, Elijah noted. It never had been.

She stopped abruptly and turned to him. "I want to know what you and A.J. aren't telling me."

He stepped down next to her. "I don't know about A.J., but I'm debating the wisdom of telling you that you have mud splattered on your left thigh."

"I'm serious."

"Honest, Jo. It's about three inches below where you got plastered with airsoft pellets."

"You don't have a clue where I got hit."

"I do. It was on the video. The kid who put it up on the Internet had these red arrows point to where you got nailed."

She sighed. "I'm never living this one down, am I?"

"Probably not."

"Listen, Elijah." She was calmer now, not so combative. "I figure you and A.J. aren't telling me what Devin did or what you suspect him of having done because you want to give him a chance to make good on it. Am I right?"

He didn't answer.

"I am right," she said.

"You're a Harper. You do love being right."

It wasn't the nicest thing to say, but she ignored him and put her hands on her slim hips. She was serious now. She looked out at the woods. "Your father knew this mountain better than anyone, except maybe you. He had a full pack. He was prepared—"

"No snowshoes."

"The snow wasn't that deep. He managed to get up the mountain in boots. His pack was located a few yards from where he died. That's significant, Elijah. You know that. People suffering from hypothermia can become disoriented and exercise poor judgment."

"We don't know what happened."

Jo scrutinized him as only she could. Finally, she said, "You don't believe his death was an accident."

"Doesn't matter what I think."

"Maybe he fell and dropped his pack before he began to suffer the effects of hypothermia," she said. "He was experienced—he'd rescued enough people off the mountain to know he was at risk under those conditions. At the first sign of trouble, if he were able, he'd have dug into his pack for more clothes, pulled out whatever he had for emergency shelter—"

"Two trash bags."

She nodded. "That'd work, but he never used them, did he?"

"No." Elijah slipped his pack off his shoulder, got out his water bottle, uncapped it and took a long drink as he eyed Jo. "Do you want me to throw you over my shoulder and carry you down this mountain, or do you want to keep moving?"

"I don't know. Throwing me over your shoulder could be fun."

"Jo."

She grinned at him, her eyes sparking, but she got moving.

He recapped his water bottle and followed her at an easy pace. She put some distance between them, and he lost her on a steep downward turn. When he rounded it, she was there, planted in the middle of the trail with both hands up to block him.

"An ambush," he said, amused, ignoring her intense look. "I think you tried this when you were twelve and I just picked you up and moved you."

She was having none of it. "Listen to me, Elijah," she said, her voice tight, low, as she placed her hands on his chest, pushed him back on his heels. "Even if your father had used everything he had with him, he still might have succumbed to hypothermia eventually. You know that. But whatever happened, he's gone. Nora and Devin aren't. If you have information to suggest either of them is in trouble—"

"I don't. If I did, I'd tell the local police."

She took his gibe without visible reaction. She nodded. "I believe you."

"Do you?" As she started to take a step back from him, he caught her hands into his and heard her intake of breath as he drew her closer to him. Her fingers were cold, but there was nothing cold about her expression. Her lips parted, and she didn't avert her eyes as he stared into them, let himself say what was on his mind. "We could be at the falls in twenty minutes. We could go swimming. The water's freezing, but we could forget everything for a little while." He smiled, aching to kiss her, to make love to her again. "Hell of an image, isn't it?"

"How out of control are you, Elijah?"

He lifted her hands to his lips and kissed her fingertips. "Not out of control at all." He winked as he released her. "Otherwise, sweet pea, we'd be peeling off our clothes at the falls right now."

"You would. Not me. My skinny-dipping days are over." She tucked her hands into fists at her sides and was serious again. "Elijah, Devin isn't you at eighteen. It's not your job to save him."

Her comment rubbed him in all the wrong ways. He eased past her on the trail, then stopped, looking up at her. In the already fading afternoon light, her eyes were dark, her skin pale. "It would be a mistake to think you know me."

"Is that supposed to make me shake in my boots?" Her reaction wasn't at all what he'd expected. She walked down to him. "Because it doesn't. I appreciate your military service, Elijah, and I'm sorry you got shot, and I'm sorry your father died—and I'm sorry he left me the lakefront property instead of you all. But you don't scare me."

"Damn, Jo, you're a pain. No wonder Charlie Neal arranged to have you shot in the ass. For the record, you scare the hell out of me."

"Will you stop?"

"No, I'm serious. When you were fifteen…holy hell. You were scary even then. I can see those turquoise eyes of yours flashing at me when you wanted to stop me dead in my tracks. By the time you were eighteen, how was I supposed to resist?"

"You didn't even try, as I recall. You pursued me like there was no tomorrow."

"Fun, wasn't it?"

"Memorable." She shivered against a sudden gust of wind and looked out at the view through the bare trees. "Eighteen didn't feel as young then as it does now." She glanced sideways at him and smiled. "No wonder my father looked for ways to arrest you. I've often thought it was just as well your father was the one who discovered us."

"Were you rebelling, falling for me?"

She didn't hesitate. "Not even a little." But her federal-agent discipline kicked in as she started back down the trail. "Maybe Devin decided to forget Nora and go home. He could be taking another trail off the mountain. He still lives with his sister, doesn't he?"

"A.J. lets him stay at the lodge."

"You mean Lauren does."

"That would be another way of putting it, yes."

"Maybe we should knock on his door."

Elijah nodded. "Fine. We'll knock on his door."

# *Eleven*

The wind cut through Jo's jeans as she crossed the open field and the quiet road to the lodge, picturesque under the lavender-streaked graying sky. It was late afternoon, but already getting dark. She was tempted to head for the stone fireplace and warm up, but Elijah had gone ahead of her and didn't even pause at the lodge entrance. Without so much as a glance back at her, he walked straight down to the shop, located in a small building tucked among evergreens.

Jo caught up with him. "What if I'd tripped in the field and broken a leg?"

He still didn't look back at her. "I'd know."

"Ah. Eyes behind your head. Keen situational awareness. The experienced soldier—"

"Nope." Now he glanced behind him, his eyes almost navy in the fast-fading light. "I just know you're not one to go quietly."

They came to the shop. It was closed, but a sign in the window directed customers to the lodge. An arrangement of cornstalks, pumpkins and vibrant yellow, white and rust-colored mums cheered its front door—undoubtedly Lauren's doing, Jo thought. Pre-Lauren, A.J. had left the spot bare.

Elijah reached into the mums and produced a key.

"The first place I'd look is the mums," Jo said behind him.

"Tell A.J."

He unlocked the door and pushed it open. Some of his intensity had abated since she'd intercepted him on the mountain, but he was still a man with a mission. She could just leave him to it, but she knew she wouldn't. Her gut as well as the facts told her that whatever was going on between Devin Shay and the Cameron brothers was mixed up somehow with Nora Asher's sudden decision to bolt for the mountains. She might have been planning a camping trip, and her stepfather's death might have triggered her decision to leave when she did, but Jo remembered Nora's tearful departure from the café that morning, Devin following helplessly behind her. Thomas hadn't reached her at that point to tell her about Alex Bruni's death.

Something was up, and Jo wanted to know what.

But she didn't fool herself. She wanted to know because of Elijah, too.

She followed him into the tidy one-room shop. It offered a limited but carefully selected range of outdoor equipment and gear, from the brightly colored kayaks that hung from the ceiling to the racks of mountain bikes, snowshoes, cross-country skis and backpacks. Jo squeezed past a display of hats and gloves that reminded her of the deficiencies in her Vermont wardrobe. She hadn't packed for traipsing after mountain man Elijah. She debated helping herself to a pair of wool socks, but instead she filled a triangular paper cup from the watercooler.

Elijah headed straight to the wooden stairs.

Jo took two gulps of water and followed him up the stairs. She considered saying something about his butt, which looked extremely fine to her, but decided she'd been reckless enough with him for one day.

She stayed behind Elijah as he knocked on a closed door at the top of the stairs. But there was no answer. No surprise, but Jo noticed his hesitation, the tension in his hand as he held it to the door. "Tempted to break in?" she asked calmly.

"I don't need to. A.J. has the key."

"Same difference, Elijah. If Devin—"

"Easy, Agent Harper." He lowered his fist back to his side and turned from the door, face-to-face with her and very close. "You're getting all excited thinking about slapping me in handcuffs." He was obviously enjoying himself. "Another time, sweet pea."

"You used to call me sweet pea at eighteen. I don't think I liked it then, either."

"You loved it," he said with a grin, brushing past her and trotting back down the stairs.

Jo crushed her paper water cup and followed him at a more deliberate pace, her thighs feeling her five-mile run with Beth that morning and her fast trek up and down a decent chunk of Cameron Mountain. Her left side ached from her airsoft bruises—a well-timed reminder of why she was in Vermont in the first place.

Elijah dipped behind the counter and disappeared through an open door into a small back room. Jo tossed her paper cup in a trash can, again thinking about the virtues of a trip to New Zealand. Elijah had fifteen years of military experience that had honed his natural skills as a leader and an independent thinker, but even before he'd joined the army, he'd had a remarkably positive mental attitude. All the Camerons did. They weren't brooders. She wasn't afraid of Elijah going off half-cocked, but that didn't mean he'd do things her way. The past seven months had dealt him a tough hand.

He came out of the back room and set a gray metal box on the counter, then opened it up. "A.J. keeps petty cash in here." He flipped the box around, allowing Jo to see inside. Index cards, a few dollar bills and change. Then he said, "Three hundred dollars in fives, tens and twenties is unaccounted for."

"You mean it's been stolen."

"Borrowed, stolen—it's gone. A.J. noticed first thing this morning. Normally he doesn't check the box every day, especially this time of year when it's slow, but lately he has been."

"Because you asked him to keep an eye on Devin. You think he hasn't told you everything he knows about your father's death."

"He hasn't," Elijah said. "He skipped work this morning, too. A.J. called me. I checked the café first. Then I headed out to the Whittakers' place. I didn't know about Alex Bruni until Vivian Whittaker told me."

"Did you ask Devin about the missing money when you caught up with him?"

"He said he doesn't steal."

"Do you believe him?"

"I believe he's holding back." Elijah got still, his eyes half-closed on her. "But so are you."

Jo let that last comment slide over her and nodded to the box. "The key's in the lock. No reason to even have a key if you keep it in the lock."

"I'm sure A.J. will thank you for pointing that out, Jo."

She stood back from the counter and looked up at a bright red kayak hanging from the ceiling. Why not rent it for tomorrow, go out on the lake before it froze and paddle to her heart's content? Missing money, two teenagers with problems—why push herself into the middle of whatever was going on with Devin Shay, Nora Asher and the Camerons? Even Alex Bruni's death in Washington wasn't her concern.

Elijah shut the cash box. "You need to level with me. Soon."

Jo's throat felt tight. Maintaining professional distance and objectivity in her hometown was difficult. With Elijah, she didn't even know why she tried.

He returned the cash box to the back room and walked out from behind the counter. "I have a fair amount of experience with people who don't want to talk." He got very close to her. "What are you hiding from me, Jo?"

She had to tell him about his father's trip to Washington. What he'd said among the cherry blossoms about his fears for the second-born son, about his regrets. But not now. Not while Elijah was staring into her eyes. She could feel his tension and her own as she noticed a small scar on his jaw. It hadn't been there when he was nineteen. What did she know about Elijah Cameron anymore? What had made her think she knew anything?

"Jo." He tucked a finger under her chin, nothing about him less intense. "Hell."

She could have done something to break the tension between them. Smiled, laughed, kicked him, started talking about hypothermia. Anything. But she didn't, and when his mouth dipped to hers, her lips were already parted. This time it wasn't a light kiss. It was fierce, hungry, his arms going around her as he drew her hard against him. Even through his jacket she could feel his muscles, the ruggedness of him as they gave, took, fired each other with their kiss.

He caught her around the hips and lifted her, pressed her against him, and she could have stripped off every stitch on her—on him—right then and there.

But he'd had that effect on her forever, and even as she moaned with wanting him, she knew it would be madness to give in to it.

"Elijah," she said.

"I know."

He set her down, kissed her on the lips and walked out of the shop without so much as a glance back at her.

Jo ended up helping herself to a pair of wool socks after all—she'd pay for them later—and tucked them into her jacket pocket as she left the shop, locking the door on her way out.

The sky had darkened, just a hint of orange now on the western horizon. The air was still, very cold.

She didn't see her hawk.

Elijah stood on the walk with his hands shoved into the pockets of his canvas jacket. "You're a complication, Jo." There was no desire or humor in his expression now, but no bitterness or anger, either. "You always have been."

"Does that mean you'd have kicked in Devin's door if I hadn't been standing there?"

His gaze fell on her and the corners of his mouth twitched. "I was more tempted with you there."

He didn't have to explain further. Devin's room, Jo thought, had a bed. Not so cold now, she changed the subject. "It looks as if Devin's spending the night on the mountain."

"If he is, he'll need gear. He didn't have a pack on him."

"Maybe he has one in his truck. Where is it?"

"Not here—neither is Nora's car. I'll check up the road and see if they parked at any of the trailheads." He looked out across the road toward Cameron Mountain. "Camping in these conditions is a serious business. Devin's done it before. Nora hasn't."

"They could both show up back here in time for dinner—"

"A.J. will let me know if they do."

Jo gave an exaggerated shiver. "I'd be on my way by now. Just the thought of a bowl of hot beef stew in front of the fire would get me back down here. It's freezing."

With his thumb and forefinger, Elijah took hold of the zipper tab to her fleece and zipped it all the way up to her chin. "It's easier to stay warm than to warm back up." His fingers lingered along the line of her jaw. "Go find yourself that stew and fire, Jo. Whatever's going on with Devin isn't your fight."

"Stay out of your way, you mean?"

He stepped back from her and started across the frozen grass to the parking lot. "Be careful driving in the dark," he said. "There's not much ambient light up here at night. You're used to the city."

He continued on to his truck, and Jo didn't try to stop him or come up with a retort. She walked up to the lodge, and A.J., who must have been watching for her, joined her on the terrace. He had on a jacket this time, but his big shoulders were hunched against the cold—or more likely, with tension.

"You and Elijah make a good team," she said.

He shrugged. "On certain things."

She noticed a light come on in a window above the terrace. The shades were pulled, softening the effect. "Many guests tonight?"

"Six. They appreciate having the place to themselves."

"Is Lauren—"

"She's gone back to the house with the kids." He and his wife were renovating an old farmhouse at the four corners up the ridge road. But A.J. obviously hadn't joined Jo in the cold for small talk and moved right to the point. "Elijah told you about the money?"

"Finally, yes. He should have said something sooner."

"Don't blame him. I asked him not to. The lodge doesn't need that kind of publicity. We're being more careful."

"Does Lauren know?"

"No."

"You should tell her. And tell her Elijah thinks your father was murdered."

"Thank you for the unsolicited advice, Jo," A.J. said coolly. "I'll tell Lauren everything tonight when I get home. As for Elijah, he went through hell earlier this year. If he needs to ask questions, he can ask away as far as I'm concerned."

"Do you believe your father was murdered, A.J.?"

He inhaled through his nose but otherwise showed no emotion. "You're blunt, aren't you?" He didn't wait for her to answer. "He died of hypothermia, that much we know. The rest..." He looked down as he ran the toe of his boot across the stone. "I'm not used to the world you and Elijah live in, Jo. Lauren isn't, either. Our kids are little."

"Take care of your family. Let the police worry about anything else. Elijah needs to back off." She hesitated, her eyes narrowed on Cameron Mountain, a dark, forbidding presence against the blackening sky. "I'm not in Elijah's world, A.J. Your brother's a warrior and a hero. I'm neither."

Her words seemed to take A.J. by surprise, but he was a

man of supreme self-control. He raised his eyes to her. "A lot of people around here are proud of you, Jo."

"Not this week," she said with a quick, light smile to cut the tension.

"Maybe especially this week." He seemed to try to return her smile but his didn't quite take hold. "Elijah is fighting some tough demons. He could use an ally."

"You're his brother—"

"I'm not you."

A.J. spared her having to respond by muttering a good-night and heading back inside. When the door was safely shut behind him, Jo exhaled and shivered for real this time. "Yikes, it's cold," she said out loud, then bolted for her car. Time to get off Cameron land before she really lost her bearings.

As she drove out along the ridge, the centuries-old sugar maples that lined the road stood out against the still, quiet landscape. She came to what everyone in Black Falls called the four corners, where the ridge road intersected narrow, twisting Cameron Mountain Road. It was the oldest settlement in town. An early-nineteenth-century, white-steepled church stood on one corner; on the corner across from it was a cemetery marked off by a stone wall. A stately, now weathered, clapboard building once used as a tavern occupied a third corner. It was owned by an elderly couple in town, but rumor had it Sean Cameron had his eyes on it. What he'd do with the place, Jo couldn't imagine. As kids, she and her brother and sister had been convinced it was haunted.

Just past the tavern, the house A.J. and Lauren were renovating, one of the prettiest houses in Black Falls with its graceful trees and mature gardens, was lit up as dusk gave way to night. Jo could have continued a half mile farther down the ridge road to the house where she grew up, and invited herself to dinner. Her father was an experienced law enforcement officer still tapped in to the goings-on in town. She could talk to him about Drew Cameron's death, the hit-and-run in Washington that morning, Alex Bruni's ties to Black Falls, Nora Asher's impulsive camping trip, even Devin Shay and the missing money.

What she couldn't talk to her father about was Elijah Cameron.

Not now, not ever.

And having just kissed him twice in one day, Jo decided to turn off the ridge road and take the shortcut down the hill to town.

It *was* dark on the mountain roads. She hadn't forgotten.

Black Falls wasn't a hopping place on a cold November night. A popular bar owned by a longtime friend of the Cameron brothers looked busy and lively, and the library, located in a 1920s stone building on the green, was still open. A handful of cars were parked in front of the Three Sisters Café. It was closed for the day, but its lights were on.

Jo pulled in behind her younger brother Zack's truck. When she entered the café, she was greeted by the clean smell of citrus. Beth was scrubbing a table in the front window as Zack, a firefighter and the cause of numerous heartbreaks in the southern Green Mountains, stood over her, deliberately aggravating her by pointing out what spots she'd missed.

Beth finally thrust her washrag at him. "You want to do this?"

He grinned at her. He was solidly built, his hair darker than either Jo's or Beth's, his eyes more green than turquoise. And his smile was notoriously deadly. "For time and a half."

"A day-old chicken potpie."

"Sold."

From the clanging and the voices coming from out back, Jo assumed Dominique and Hannah were working in the kitchen. "I can help," she said.

Beth shook her head. "We're almost done." She reached into her bucket of sudsy water and plucked out another washrag. "We have a regular cleaning service, but we like to turn this place upside down ourselves every now and then. It hasn't been a great day. We were all looking for something to do."

"Nora hasn't been by, has she?" Jo asked.

"No sign of her." Beth seemed to make an effort to be cheerful and gestured toward the glass case. "There are two brownies left. Why don't you help yourself." Then she added, matter-of-fact, "You could bring one to Elijah."

Not one to turn down chocolate, Jo claimed one of the brownies and sat at a small square table while her brother and sister cleaned. "So," she said, breaking off a piece of the dark, smooth, gooey brownie. "Tell me about Devin Shay these days. And whatever you know about Nora Asher. While we're at it, Elijah Cameron."

Zack wrung out his washrag. "How long have you been back in town, Jo?"

"Today's my third day."

"Three days, and already trouble." He set to work on a table with his usual tireless energy. "Devin needs to get his head screwed back on. Nora's running from her problems, which just got worse. Elijah is Elijah, just with battle scars and not enough to do." Her brother paused, and his gaze bored through her. "You might keep that in mind about Elijah."

Jo pretended not to hear him. "Have you had any problems with Devin?"

"Not me, no. He's rubbed Scott the wrong way a few times—deliberately." Zack had never been one to shy away from speaking his mind. "He'll figure out Nora's just seeing what it's like on the other side of the tracks, and he'll feel even worse about himself. Then who knows what he'll do."

"Hurt her?"

"Nah. Not Devin. More like buy a bus ticket to Los Angeles."

Beth scrubbed hard, and Jo remembered her sister's discomfort that morning and dived in. "Beth, is money missing from the café?"

She dropped her rag in the bucket. "Hannah manages the café money. You can ask her."

In other words, Jo thought, yes, money was missing. "Does Scott know?"

"He can ask Hannah, too." Beth peeled off her rubber gloves. She didn't look particularly intimidated, but she said, "Jeez, Jo, I can't believe Charlie Neal had the nerve to pull a prank on you."

Their brother draped his rag over the side of the bucket. "Better get that second brownie, Jo," he said.

She turned just as Elijah came in, bringing a gust of cold air with him. He shut the door behind him and greeted Zack and Beth briefly, then said to no one in particular, "I found Nora's car at the east trailhead. That's a dry trail—it gets a fair amount of activity even this time of year. It leads to shelters. A good pick."

"Assuming she didn't park there to mislead people," Jo said, breaking off another piece of brownie. "What about Devin?"

"He wasn't back at the lodge when I left. I didn't see his truck at any of the trails I checked. No sign of him here?"

Hannah was the one to reply as she emerged from the kitchen. Strands of hair fell out of its pins as she rolled up an evergreen-colored apron into a tight ball. "Devin isn't here, and he hasn't been in touch."

From her cool, controlled tone, Jo suspected Hannah was aware her brother had gotten on the wrong side of the Camerons.

Elijah didn't look fazed. "What about Nora?"

"I haven't heard from her since she left here this morning. She and Devin are friends. I know she's upset about her stepfather, but if she's with him, then she's in good hands." Hannah was sincere, quietly determined. "Maybe Devin's just the person Nora needs right now."

But Jo noticed a fleeting uncertainty in Hannah that she doubted Elijah would miss. He stiffened visibly, and Jo jumped in. "Hannah, if there's anything—you can tell us, we're just trying to help."

She stared at her apron as she spoke. "Nora and Devin have more in common than you might think. They're both uncertain of their futures and lack direction, goals. That's normal at their age—any age, really." She shook her head suddenly. "Never mind. I shouldn't have said anything."

Jo could see that Hannah was reluctant to open up about any concerns she had about her younger brother and wasn't going to make this easy.

But neither was Elijah. He pounced. "Something's on your mind, Hannah. Spit it out."

Hannah's lips thinned—her version of throwing something at him. Jo got to her feet, ignoring Elijah and his narrowed eyes as she tried to reassure Hannah and get information out of her at the same time. "Have you noticed any change in Devin or Nora in recent days?"

Hannah looked away. "I don't want you making too much of it."

Meaning Elijah. Jo said, "Just tell us what you can."

Hannah walked over to a small table where Beth and Zack were silently pulling together their cleaning supplies and set her balled-up apron in an empty bucket. "Devin's been working hard at the lodge. He's figuring out what comes next for him. He knows losing Drew wasn't the same for him as it was for his children, but still…" She couldn't seem to finish.

"It was a tough loss," Jo finished for her.

Hannah nodded, no sign of tears in her pale eyes. "It hasn't been an easy year, but I have faith in him. Nora's only been here six weeks. I'm not sure any place could live up to the fantasies she had about life in Vermont, but she's very smart." With a sudden awkwardness, Hannah pulled out a couple of pins, more strands of hair flopping into her face. She clutched the pins in one hand and took a breath. "I noticed a change about two weeks ago. I wasn't alarmed. Nora came by one night and got on the computer with Devin. She was tense, secretive. I thought it was a passing thing."

"But it wasn't," Elijah said.

"No." Hannah raised her head and stared him down with quiet self-control. "You can take that accusing look off your face, Elijah. Whatever Nora and Devin have been up to has nothing to do with you and your family."

"Did you check Devin's computer?" Jo asked.

"It's a computer we all share—Devin, Toby and me," she said without a hint of self-righteousness. "He reset the Internet browser. He's done it every time he's been on the computer since then."

"Hannah," Elijah said, "if you have any reason to believe Nora and Devin know anything about what happened in Washington today—"

"I have no reason to believe anything of the sort." She didn't raise her voice, but she'd lost some of her color. "Forget what I said. I should know better than to open up with a Cameron present. I appreciate A.J. offering Devin a job, but he earns his paycheck. And it was Lauren, not A.J.—" But Hannah, her cheeks ashen now, stopped herself. "I'm sorry. I had no right to speak to you that way. Please forgive me."

He shrugged. "Forget it, Hannah. You didn't even draw blood."

She managed a small, embarrassed smile.

Jo ate more of her brownie. The two of them might be making nice, but she wasn't finished yet. "Did you talk to Nora or Devin about what they were up to?"

"They said they weren't up to anything and I shouldn't worry."

Jo wasn't surprised. No one liked to see Hannah worry. But she said, "Nora was in Black Falls in April when Drew Cameron died." Jo felt Elijah's stillness next to her. "Did she and Devin meet then?"

Hannah didn't hesitate. "No. They didn't."

"What about you, Hannah?" Jo asked. "Did you meet Nora?"

"I did, but I meet most people who come to town. Because of this place," she said, indicating the café. "Nora stopped by with her father."

"When? Was it before or after the search for Drew started?"

But it was Beth who answered. "After. They got here right after the storm. The search-and-rescue team was already mobilized. Jo..."

She kept her eyes on Hannah. "Were you aware Devin went up the north side of the mountain? That old logging road must have been barely passable. He was just a senior in high school. You'd think he'd have told someone what he was up to."

Hannah's impressive control didn't falter. "You were eighteen once, Jo. You must remember what it was like to want to be on your own. To live your own life."

Jo stayed cool. "Does this mean no, you didn't know Devin had decided to hike up the back side of Cameron Mountain to look for Drew?"

She thought she heard her brother inhale behind her, but Elijah remained motionless, his eyes on Hannah Shay. Hannah tossed her head back, tears shining in her eyes now. "Correct," she said stiffly. "I didn't know. Happy now, Jo?"

"Nora was here with her father that day. Did they help in the search?"

"Ask them. Or ask your brother or your sister, or Scott. Don't ask me. I didn't do a damn thing to help find Drew except keep this place open for the search teams and reporters." She took in a deep breath, tucking strands of hair behind her ears. "It was a difficult time. I'm glad you weren't here."

In her own quiet way, Hannah could slice someone to ribbons, Jo thought. The budding prosecutor. "If any of us could go back in time, Hannah, we'd put ourselves in Devin's place that day, just so that he didn't have to be the one to find Drew."

Hannah's tears spilled now. "I have to go," she mumbled as she bolted for the side door. "I promised I'd help Toby with a history paper."

"If you hear from Devin," Jo said, "let us know."

Hannah didn't respond as she retreated upstairs to her apartment.

Zack carried the cleaning bucket over from the riverside tables. "You're tough, Jo. Phew." He set the bucket on the floor next to the table with the supplies. "Remind me not to cross you."

"What? I just—"

"Hannah won't admit it," Beth said, wiping her hands on her apron, "but she really is worried about Devin. And about Nora, too."

Jo nodded, aware of Elijah silently eyeing her. "Rough day."

"Hey, Jo," her brother called to her.

She turned just as he tossed a wet rag at her, grinning. She caught it and whipped it back at him, water dripping onto the floor between them. He dodged out of the way, and the rag bounced off a chair, making her laugh, which, she knew, had been his intention.

Beth just shook her head and grumbled about having to mop.

In the meantime, Elijah had left. "I have to go," Jo said.

Zack scooped up the washrag, his blue-green eyes on the door as he addressed his older sister. "Jo—you know Elijah…"

"Special ops, shot, at a loose end."

"Still in love with you," Beth said half under her breath.

Jo pretended she didn't hear her and said good-night, heading back out to the street.

Elijah was still there, standing by his truck in the harsh light from the café. He raked an unrelenting gaze over her. "You got pretty tough on Hannah." He yanked open his truck door. "It would have been worse if it'd been coming from me."

"She's loyal to her brother. That's not a bad thing."

"She knows something. Just like he does. You, too."

"Elijah, what are you doing? Why—"

"What are you having for dinner?"

"Don't try to change the subject."

"I'm not trying. I just did change it. So, dinner?"

"I just ate a brownie."

"A scone for lunch and a brownie for dinner. What kind of buff Secret Service agent are you? You need nutrition. Getting shot in the line of duty takes something out of you."

"I was the victim of a prank," she said, then added quietly, seriously, "*You* were shot, Elijah."

He shrugged but kept his eyes on her. "All's well that ends well." His tone was unreadable. "I have leftover grilled chicken if you can come up with something to go with it."

"I can toss a salad together and bring it over to your place. I'll follow you back to the lake." She smiled at him. "Don't speed."

She decided she didn't need to remind him that her father used to nail him all the time for speeding when they were teenagers—before the army, the Secret Service. Long before his father's death on Cameron Mountain.

As she got in her car, Jo saw herself and Elijah as teenagers, walking hand in hand through the fallen leaves on the town green, and she felt a surge of tenderness for the crazy-in-love kids they'd been.

Not an image for a long, dark Vermont night.

Best just to go back to the lake and make salad.

# Twelve

"You're still a little in love with her, aren't you?"

Thomas Asher quickly clicked off his Internet connection at the desk in his first-floor study as if Melanie had just caught him watching porn videos instead of the two-minute clip of Jo Harper tackling the vice president's teenage son. It was even more entertaining than he'd expected—and just the distraction he'd needed from Alex's death and his own appalling behavior.

Jo had called and told him Nora had taken off into the mountains.

What the hell was his daughter thinking?

What had *he* been thinking that morning when he'd panicked and run from the hotel?

He swiveled in his leather desk chair. "Not even a little," he said, smiling at the woman who would become his wife in less than two months. She stood in the doorway, looking more amused than annoyed.

"Uh-huh," she said.

Thomas knew he couldn't fool her. He didn't want to. But

Melanie believed he harbored feelings for Jo Harper, and he couldn't convince her otherwise.

She entered the study and put her slim hands on his shoulders as he swiveled back to his computer. She had yet to suggest he sell his northern Virginia house after they were married. He and Carolyn had bought it together nineteen years ago, raised their daughter there. Thomas didn't know why, but he couldn't part with it—it was as if selling the house would somehow mean the Thomas Asher of the past had never existed.

Melanie kissed him on the top of his head. "I know it's been an awful day for you."

She slid her hands down his chest, her nails shining, polished a neutral color, and nodded at the blank computer screen. "Do you think Jo gave Charlie Neal what he deserved?"

"*Everyone* thinks Jo gave Charlie Neal what he deserved. She's a professional, but she's blunt by nature. Generally speaking, I'm sure that's an asset in her work."

"I like that," Melanie said. "I hate when people don't speak their minds."

She didn't know he'd run that morning. He leaned into her and wished for the thousandth time that he hadn't panicked. Now he had to live with his shame and guilt. He had nothing to hide, but fleeing the scene the way he had would look suspicious to the police. He wouldn't lie to them, but he hoped they left him alone. He couldn't bear the thought of Melanie and his daughter—even Carolyn—finding out that his only instinct when he'd realized it was Alex dead on the street was to get out of there.

Thomas's only hope now was that the police would find the driver of the car that had hit Alex—without his help.

Why hadn't the messenger reported what she'd seen?

His complicated history with Alex didn't help matters. Thomas cringed at the thought of the police suspecting him of having a role in his friend's death, but what could he do? It was no secret that Alex had betrayed their friendship by taking up with Carolyn. Everyone knew it and would assume that, regardless of how mature he'd wanted to be about the situation, he'd had moments when he'd wished Alex a bad end. He was only human, after all.

His love for Nora had forced him to step back from his hurt, his anger, his humiliation and get on with his life. Now he had Melanie—a new beginning.

She slid her hand over his and eased the mouse from his grip. "Enough," she said, shutting down the computer altogether. "You need to turn everything off."

"I don't know if I can explain. Alex and I were friends even before I'd met Carolyn. That he's gone now…" Thomas fought back tears as he stared at the blank monitor. "What's done is done. There's no going back."

"Have you talked to Nora?"

"Not since I gave her the news this morning. I wish she'd stayed put after hearing about Alex instead of going on this camping trip. Lowell and Vivian say they're not worried."

"Easy for them. Still no word of what route she took?"

"I heard from Jo a little while ago. Nora's car was located near one of the trails up Cameron Mountain. That's some help, but it's not the same as leaving her specific plans with someone. We don't know she went up that trail—she could have met friends and taken their car to some other trail."

"She's eighteen, Thomas. It's not that she's trying to be irresponsible—she just doesn't think things through." Melanie sighed softly. "I can see you're worried about her. You're a good father. You're not overreacting. Nora still needs you, even if she doesn't think so."

"Maybe I should go up there."

Melanie squeezed his hand. "If you decide that's what's best, I'll go with you. Listen, I know Jo Harper is a friend of yours, Thomas, but are you sure you should be talking to her? This thing with the vice president's son..."

"That'll blow over. It's just a silly incident that will entertain people in this town for a few days and then be replaced by someone else's misstep. Alex's death has probably wiped it out of people's minds already. I don't want Jo to do anything that will further jeopardize her career, of course, but I don't see how checking on Nora will."

"Still, Jo's got to be distracted, and she might need to be more cautious than is in your interest right now. There's a guy I know—I met him skiing in Colorado last year, and we exchanged business cards. His name's Kyle Rigby. He does private searches for people. He's very experienced, and he's discreet. I've already been in touch with him. He said he can get to Black Falls and figure out what's going on with Nora, make sure she's okay. He'll keep a low profile. And if anything's wrong, he'll know what to do."

"What is he, a private contractor?"

"Yes, exactly. Not everyone who goes missing or who has a family member who goes missing wants or needs to involve the authorities. Not that Nora's missing. You know what I mean. But she has her whole life ahead of her and doesn't need whatever she's up to getting blown all out of proportion. With Alex's death, you know the media would jump on this one."

"I hadn't thought of that."

She patted his shoulder. "You've been thinking about your daughter and your friend."

He could feel himself sinking emotionally, physically. "You're so good to me, Melanie."

"Let's just find Nora and get her back to you and her mother."

"That's all I want," Thomas whispered, latching on to Melanie's idea. "If Alex hadn't been killed this morning, I'd still be concerned about her going off winter camping with so little preparation, but not like this..." He trailed off, felt himself choke up with emotion. "She's still so young. So very young."

"Then let Kyle go up there. Jo has enough on her mind, but I'm sure she'll help him if he needs it. He'll be able to devote himself just to finding Nora. He just needs a green light to get moving. I know how upset you are, and I figured it would help if you had someone take action."

"Thank you. Yes. Go ahead. Tell him to see what he can do." Thomas blinked back tears. "I don't know what I'd do without you."

"It's okay," she said. "It'll all be okay. We can go up there ourselves tomorrow. Maybe by the time we get there, Nora will be back. It'll be awkward, I know, with Ambassador Bruni's death, but we're going to have to figure out how to move forward."

Thomas nodded wearily. "Then we might as well get started."

"Yes. We might as well. Kyle will help." Melanie hugged him. "Trust me."

Since she was still sore from her afternoon with Kyle, Melanie hadn't wanted to make love to Thomas, but that was what a good Asher wife would do. Now, lying next to him in the king-size bed he had once shared with his dull, brainy first wife, she gave a silent moan of pain. Honestly, though, how could she not have seduced her fiancé when he needed a distraction? What she was to him—and she hoped he realized this—was a woman who would put him at the center of her world.

He was a generous, thoughtful, gentle lover—not the unthinking, relentless piston Kyle was. Unlike Thomas, Kyle didn't care whether she was satisfied or not, but he liked it when she writhed and screamed…and begged.

She could hear herself a few hours ago.

*"More…more…don't…ever…stop."*

And later, when he'd awakened her from a doze with a hard, erotic slap, her moans of pain as she'd pleaded with him. *"No more…I can't take it, Kyle. Please. Stop."*

But he'd known she hadn't meant it. He'd lifted her by the hips and straddled her and took her from behind, every yell she gave for him to stop only fueling him, as if he was deliberately doing the exact opposite of what she wanted.

Except they both knew that wasn't the case. She'd made that clear months ago. She wanted every vicious thrust into every eager, hot part of her. When she and polite Thomas were married, she would be able to call upon the memories—the sensations—of those months of near-violent sex with Kyle.

There had been times when he'd gone too far. When he'd hurt her—shamed her—and made her do things she didn't want to do. To him, to herself. But that fear, pain and humiliation ended up only adding to the pleasure and intensity—the risk—of their next encounter.

Not that Kyle had ever been aware he'd gone too far or had ever apologized. That would have required a level of introspection he simply didn't possess.

That afternoon, he'd been particularly ruthless and selfish, but he'd taken a certain amount of care not to leave any visible redness, bruises or scrapes. He was aware that she was going back to Thomas.

After she and Thomas were married, Kyle would have to find someone else.

The thought of another woman crying out for him didn't sit well with Melanie at all.

He could be in Black Falls by now. Whether or not Thomas had agreed to hire him, Kyle intended to be in Vermont tonight. He had gone up there several times in the past couple of weeks since Nora had first become a problem—watching her, formulating a strategy.

Kyle was, after all, the planner.

Melanie tried to quiet her mind as Thomas snuggled closer to her and flopped an arm over her middle. She extricated herself from him and rolled closer to the edge of her side of the bed. She couldn't bear for anyone to touch her right now. After she'd returned to Thomas's house, she'd tried to relax in the library, flipping through magazines for ideas for their New Year's Eve wedding. She wanted it to be elegant and romantic.

She stared wide-eyed at the ceiling. She loved everything about her life with Thomas. It was the life she'd been meant to lead: privileged, quiet, elite, sensible. Her family was concerned that Thomas was fifteen years older than she was, but otherwise they were delighted. He was everything they'd ever wanted in a son-in-law.

They'd never met Kyle. They wouldn't. Her almost year with him had been a detour. It wasn't the real Melanie Kendall. But it had made her a stronger person; she'd be a better Mrs. Thomas Asher because of it.

She turned onto her side, her back to Thomas as he slept soundly, snoring faintly. Kyle had stayed at a roadside motel outside Black Falls in April. They'd hiked up the north side of Cameron Mountain from an old, remote logging road that was at least a ten-mile drive around the base of the mountain from the Camerons' lodge. No one had seen him before or after they'd left that old man in the cold. Kyle would have been equally careful on subsequent trips to Black Falls. If he had any concern someone would recognize him when he showed up to look for Thomas's daughter, he would plan accordingly. But Kyle understood, as Melanie did, that they had to deal with Nora Asher.

Melanie felt a prick of fear, but this time it wasn't mixed with excitement. She and Kyle couldn't fail. They *had* to deal with Nora. She wasn't just a potential problem anymore. She was a real problem.

*We'll do what we have to do.*

Thomas would miss Nora at first, but with her and the dangers she posed out of the way, Melanie could focus on her future husband and help him through his grief.

All would be well.

She closed her eyes, picturing her New Year's Eve wedding.

She smiled, relaxing again. She'd wear white. Why not? It would be her first—her only—wedding.

# *Thirteen*

When she arrived back at the lake, Jo got out her cell phone and walked up the path behind her waterfront cabin for a better signal. The only light was a single beam through the trees from Elijah's place—not enough to help her, but it was a clear night. The stars and half-moon were out, creating shadows and silhouettes on the dark, wooded hillside.

She tried Mark Francona, but he didn't pick up. She didn't leave a message and dialed Harry Watson, a friend in Washington who worked with the Bureau of Alcohol, Tobacco and Firearms. As she waited for the call to go through, she noticed eight or ten wild turkeys pecking in the low brush at the edge of the woods and tried not to scare them. They warbled and fluttered, slowly making their way toward three cabins tucked in the trees higher up the hill.

Harry answered on the second ring. "I heard you were in New Zealand," he said.

"That's the backup plan. What do you know about Ambassador Bruni?"

"Why?"

He wouldn't tell her anything if she wasn't straight with him. "His wife's ex-husband asked me to check on his step-daughter."

"The one in Vermont? Harper. You're not…"

"I'm in Black Falls. I grew up here. Nora Asher works at a café co-owned by my younger sister."

"I have frequent-flyer miles you can use for New Zealand. Call me if you need them."

He disconnected, and Jo slipped her cell phone into her jacket pocket. If Harry knew anything, he'd have told her. She shuddered against a breeze off the lake. She wanted to take a few moments to let her mind sift through the events of the day, but not out here—it was too damn cold. She'd go make her salad and head over to Elijah's.

She heard a noise behind the more secluded cabins farther up the hill and went still on the narrow footpath. The turkeys flapped their wings and scurried deeper into the woods, away from the cabins, their shuffling making it more difficult for her to identify any other sounds.

Devin? Nora?

Jo crept toward a particularly dilapidated cabin on the far edge of the clearing behind the main cabins along the lake.

A branch snapped in the darkness.

Someone—something—was up there with her.

She waited for a few minutes in the darkness, listening, peering up into the trees for any sign of movement. But animal or human, whatever was out there didn't make a sound.

Or was gone, she thought, giving up.

Without a flashlight, she didn't investigate further and walked back down to her cabin. When she opened the rickety door, she knew instantly someone had been in there. None of the cabins had decent locks and hers apparently hadn't caught when she'd left earlier in the day.

She switched on the dull overhead and scanned the room. Everything appeared to be intact. The lilies Charlie had sent her were still in the middle of the table. Her exercise clothes from her morning run were still on the bed. Her old coffee cup was still in the sink.

But she smelled...*something.* Not cologne or soap. She couldn't place it.

Then she recognized what it was. Stirred-up dust. Whoever had been there had gone into places she hadn't yet.

Bats?

She pulled open the utility closet by the kitchen area.

*No bombs.*

What was she thinking? She'd probably just interrupted some kids looking for a place to party who panicked and ran when they realized the cabin was already occupied.

Telling herself she was being thorough not paranoid, Jo grabbed a flashlight and went back outside. She squatted by the front steps and angled the beam of light under the cabin, but she didn't see signs of a hidden incendiary device or anything else that didn't belong there.

She stood up, breathing hard.

*Elijah.*

Had whoever been through her cabin gone through his place as well?

Had she heard *him* in the woods?

It had been a long, strange day, and she supposed she could have heard a stray turkey after all and no one had searched her cabin. But she didn't think so.

Another breeze gusted up from the lake and, once again,

Jo wished she had a Vermont-worthy winter coat—or even a hat and gloves. She drew her hands up into her sleeves and ignored the biting cold as best she could as she headed up the road, the gravel crunching under her fast steps.

She didn't slow her pace until she reached the top of Elijah's steep driveway. A solitary light shone in the sliding glass doors on the deck. In the months since she'd inherited her lakefront property, she hadn't been this close to her neighbor's house. It looked as sturdy and solid as the man who'd built it.

Smoke curled from the chimney. Jo could smell it in the air. Elijah had been home all of a half hour, and he already had a fire going.

She heard a noise under the deck and pointed her flashlight beam in that direction, illuminating Elijah as he walked out with an armload of cordwood. "What's up, Jo?"

She lowered her light to his feet. "Did you search my cabin?"

"Why would I do that?"

"That's not what I asked."

He moved forward with his wood. "No, Jo, I did not search your cabin."

She felt the cold now and tried not to shiver. "Someone did. It's not obvious. The place wasn't tossed."

"But you're a Secret Service agent, and you can tell."

She didn't think he was being sarcastic, but it was just a guess. Sometimes it was hard to tell with him. "Yes," she said seriously. "What about your place?"

He nodded toward the deck stairs. "Let's go up and have a look."

"You'd have noticed, wouldn't you?"

"Not necessarily. I wasn't thinking about break-ins when I got back here."

"What were you thinking about?"

His eyes settled on her. "You don't want to know."

"Did you hear anything in the woods?"

"Turkeys, but I only just got out here." He nodded toward the stairs up to the deck. "Let's go inside."

"I haven't fixed the salad—"

"Forget the salad."

He carried his armload of wood up the stairs and led her through a slider into a warm, cozy room than ran the length of the deck. The furnishings were in warm woods and earthy colors, and although he'd only been in town a few weeks and hadn't yet finished the house, it looked lived-in, as if he were at home now and meant to stay. On the back wall was a stone chimney with a Vermont Castings woodstove. Wooden spiral stairs wound up to an open-rail balcony with two doors, presumably to bedrooms.

Elijah dropped the wood into a rustic box he'd obviously constructed himself. As much as he might belong there, Jo had sensed that his presence in Black Falls wasn't permanent. He'd seemed as rootless as she was, if in a different way. Now, she wasn't so sure.

The sliders and large windows overlooked the lake, dark now with nightfall.

Jo noticed how quiet it was with the doors and windows shut—no wind, no lapping of the lake below, no night sounds. Just the popping and hissing of the fire. "Do you like being back here?" she asked abruptly.

"Sure. I don't like the way I got back." He turned from the wood box. "Anything suggest an intruder to you?"

She shook her head. "No. Not to me."

He advanced a few steps toward her. "You're an experienced Secret Service special agent who rumor has it can shoot the eyes out of a crow, and here I am worrying about you being alone in your cabin."

"You're feeling protective of me, are you?" She couldn't resist a smile. "That has to be a first."

"Not really."

He was right in front of her now. There was nothing casual about him, but nothing confrontational, either. The stiffness and tight control of earlier at the café had abated. But Jo had no illusions as his so-blue eyes settled on her with a frankness she found erotic, a little unnerving and totally irresistible. This was a dangerous man at a critical turning point in his life, and having her there, with him on the lake, wasn't necessarily good for either one of them. She had a career to save, but Elijah had lost his father and very nearly lost his own life in combat. And he'd seen friends die.

Jo motioned toward the pleasant room. "It's a nice place," she said, then attempted a smile. "Homey."

He touched her hair and smiled back at her. "Like you care about homey. You're restless, Jo. Always have been."

"I keep coming back to Black Falls."

"So you do."

But she saw that his mind wasn't on his words. He let his hand fall to her waist, and she thought she heard him say her name as his mouth found hers. His arms encircled her, and he drew her toward him. She responded eagerly, welcoming the kiss, deepening it herself as she slipped her arms around him. He hadn't worn a coat down to his woodpile. His soft sweater warmed her hands.

Even after fifteen years, he felt familiar, comfortable—as

rugged and sexy and desirable as she remembered of their days together on the lake so long ago.

How out of their minds were they?

But the question evaporated from her mind as he lowered his hands to her hips, boldly easing them under her jacket and shirt and finding her bare skin. She heard her own sharp intake of air as desire spread through her. He lifted her off her feet and into him, and she could feel that he was hard already. He pressed himself against her in just the right spot. Her head spun, and with a start, she realized he wasn't a teenager anymore. He was a man in his thirties, hard-edged and battle-scarred, literally and figuratively, in ways he hadn't been at nineteen.

Finally, he raised his mouth from hers and set her down onto the hardwood floor. He dropped his hands from her. She stood back, breathless, wanting more. But she adjusted her shirt and her jacket and cleared her throat. She was hot now and she could see he was, too. As calm and controlled as he was outwardly, she noticed the flare of his nostrils, the dark cast to his eyes. His gaze skimmed over her as if she were naked. "Hell, Jo, you're wearing me out. Takes a lot out of me to hold myself back with you. Kissing you is the easy part." He traced one finger over her lips. "It always has been."

"We're in uncharted waters here, Elijah."

"Not so uncharted."

When they were growing up, it seemed as if they had nothing in common at all. Now, after they'd both been on their own, had left their families and small town, she could see that she and Elijah had more in common than they could possibly have realized as teenagers.

Which didn't mean kissing him was smart.

"Would you like me to have a look around and tell you what I think?"

"Of what, my choice in sheets and towels?"

"As to whether or not someone searched your house," she said.

"Ah. No, that's okay. Want me to check out your cabin?"

"No." She ignored his amused, knowing smile and continued, "Let me take a rain check on dinner. The brownie I ate at the café has my head spinning."

"I don't think it's the brownie."

"Elijah…"

His eyes held hers a moment, but he didn't speak.

She did. "Your father came to see me when he was in Washington in early April."

He lifted a log from a small stack on the brick hearth and opened the top of the stove and lowered the wood onto the fire. "I didn't know he'd gone to Washington."

"He said he didn't tell anyone. He just went and let A.J. and Rose and everyone else in Black Falls think he was on a fishing trip. He wanted to see the cherry blossoms. I know that much." She stood closer to the fire, felt its heat. "He told me he'd had a premonition that something bad was going to happen to you."

"Anxiety about the dangers I faced isn't the same as a premonition. He knew I was in Afghanistan." Elijah adjusted the dampers on the woodstove. "It's just a coincidence that I was wounded in April."

"Maybe so. Drew was dealing with some guilt about us." Jo didn't go into detail. "We had a pleasant afternoon together. The cherry blossoms were particularly beautiful this year, and it was a gorgeous day. It's a good memory, Elijah."

He glanced back at her. "I'm glad for that, Jo."

"I wish you'd been the one walking among the cherry blossoms with your father. I'm sorry it wasn't."

"Don't be sorry." He turned from the fire. "I want you to have a good memory of my father."

"I never hated him," she said quietly.

"I know. I didn't, either."

"He loved you, Elijah. He knew you butted heads with him as much as you did because you were both so much alike. And he didn't drive us apart. If we'd been meant to be together, we'd have found a way. We were kids. We weren't ready for what we thought we wanted."

He kissed her on the forehead. "I still broke your heart, sweet pea."

He didn't wait for her response—not that she could have mustered one—and crossed the dark wood floor to the slider. He opened it and walked out onto the deck. "A half-moon tonight," he said.

Jo joined him in the cold night air. "It'll still be dark up on the mountain."

"Maybe one night up there will give Nora her taste of winter camping and get her over the initial shock of her stepfather's death, and she'll head back in the morning." He glanced sideways at her. "Her father asked you to look in on her. That's it, right?"

"That's it."

"You didn't know Ambassador Bruni well?"

She shook her head.

"And he and Thomas Asher didn't hate each other?"

"I gather they tried to stay friends or at least get along for Nora's sake. Thomas was concerned about her even before her stepfather was killed, because she'd dropped out of Dartmouth."

"If she was afraid, would she go to him?"

Jo leaned against the railing. "Why would you ask that?"

"Because it's a common-sense, routine question."

"No." She paused. "Something's bothering you."

"Coincidences," he said. "Lots of coincidences."

"You just said—"

"That was about my father thinking he knew I'd be shot. He was in Washington two weeks before he died—two weeks before Thomas Asher and his daughter happen to show up in Black Falls for a visit. Then Nora drops out of college, moves to Black Falls and takes up with a local boy. Now money's gone missing, and her ambassador stepfather's dead in a suspicious hit-and-run." Elijah's eyes were black in the night air as he faced Jo. "And you turn up."

"Want to throw the wild turkeys into the mix, too?"

He gave her a sudden, quick smile. "Maybe." But he gestured toward the deck stairs. "You should leave or I might kiss you again just to get that scowl off your face. You look like you want to arrest someone."

"Elijah—"

He cut her off. "I need time, Jo," he said quietly. "The thought of you and my father among the cherry blossoms…" He didn't finish.

She nodded. "I'll see you in the morning, unless the bogeyman comes in the middle of the night and you need a federal agent."

"Right, Jo." The sardonic smile was back. "I'll scream for help."

"Because you wouldn't have any illegal firearms left over from your military career, now, would you?"

"Who says my military career is over?"

"No one around here. You're the subject of lively rumors."

"To be expected, I suppose. Make yourself that salad, Jo. I'll open up a can of green beans to go with my chicken. Dinner another time."

She got out of there, appreciating the cold air after being around Elijah. Her cabin was freezing. It was barely winterized—the propane heater couldn't keep up. She sat on the ratty couch and wrapped herself in a fleece throw that a colleague had bought as a thank-you gift, or for self-preservation, in October.

*Had* someone been through the place?

It wasn't the sort of call she planned to make to her boss. *Gee, Mark, I got suspicious after the turkeys went nuts in the woods….*

Truly, she thought, selling the cabins and the land to the Camerons made sense.

But that wasn't what Drew Cameron necessarily had wanted.

*"You'll do the right thing…I know you will, Jo."*

He'd apologized, with a quiet emotion she'd never seen in him, for driving her and Elijah apart and told her he'd been seeing them out on the lake with the children they would never have.

*"Because of me."*

She'd tried to tell him that it wasn't because of him. Elijah had made his choices, too.

So had she.

The image of her and Elijah and kids on the lake wasn't one Jo wanted on a cold November night.

She threw off the fleece, jumped up, grabbed her flashlight again and charged back outside, following the footpath and checking the rest of the cabins one by one for an intruder or any sign of one. But she only ran into spiders and heard an owl nearby.

The turkeys had wandered off.

She got a decent cell signal and stood on an exposed pine root and tried her boss again. This time he picked up. "Don't you have a duty assignment in some back-elbow place I could take?" she asked him.

"You're in a back-elbow place."

"What if I told you Ambassador Bruni's stepdaughter decided to go camping in the mountains after hearing about his death?"

Silence—yet Francona didn't hang up. Finally, he said, "I thought you were canoeing."

"Can't. It's dark."

"You and the stepdaughter should go canoeing together. Safer. Let me know if you see any loons."

And that was enough for Jo. He'd made his point without being direct: If she found out anything useful, that was a good thing.

If she got herself into trouble, she'd swing for it. Alone.

Elijah listened to Grit's report while the fire crackled in his woodstove and he tried not to think about kissing Jo, because if he thought about it, Grit would figure it out and come up there and shoot him for sheer stupidity. He'd wanted to do things his way and be unencumbered by a federal agent next door, and what had he done? Kissed her. More than once. Grit might know even without being told. He was tuned in to people in a way Elijah had never seen in anyone before. It was almost spooky. It'd gotten worse—sharper, weirder—since the firefight that had taken his leg and Michael Ferrerra, known far and wide as Moose, a legend even among SEALs and Grit's best friend.

"The police found a car in a public garage a couple of blocks from the scene. It looks to be the one that struck Bruni." Grit spoke briskly but without emotion. "Police dropped a net around the area once they got the 911 call about the accident—or whatever it was—but the driver slipped through. They're not saying much. They'll comb the car for evidence, but I'm guessing they won't find anything."

"Witnesses?"

"None yet. You'd think everyone at that hotel shut their eyes just as Bruni got hit."

Grit had obviously worked on the scenario. "You have friends in the D.C. police department?"

"No."

"You could make some."

Grit was silent.

"Grit?"

"I've got a reporter I'm talking to. Myrtle Smith. She's like a hundred and twelve or something, but she knows everything that's gone on in this town since the Lincoln assassination."

"Her name's Myrtle?"

"Yeah. Like crape myrtle. That's a flowering tree originally from Southeast Asia, but there are dozens of American hybrids. They love the heat."

"A Southern thing," Elijah said.

"That's right. You're a dyed-in-the-wool Yankee mountain man, Cameron. You wouldn't know about Southern things."

Grit was from the Florida Panhandle. He was a mix of Creek Indian and Scots Irish—and eccentric if not crazy. Elijah wasn't entirely sure if Grit accepted that Moose was dead. Now he had a new friend. But even Grit wouldn't make up a reporter named Myrtle. "Grit...you're not serious about the Lincoln assassination, right? Myrtle—she's one of us?"

"Yeah, yeah." No irritation. "Myrtle feels guilty because of all the crap she's written about the military over the past two hundred years. Figuratively. Not literally. Look her up, Elijah."

"I don't have to."

"Let me see what I can get out of her. By the way, Moose says hi. He says you need a dog."

Elijah had learned not to tell Grit that Moose was dead.

"Jo Harper is here with me."

"The Secret Service agent you cut out on when you were kids? Great, Cameron. Lucky you. Now you can get yourself arrested on top of having gotten shot."

"My father went to see her in Washington in early April before he died. Can you find out what all she's been up to since then?"

"Maybe," Grit said and hung up.

Elijah looked at his woodstove hearth. He'd thought about getting a dog upon his return home.

Two minutes later his phone rang again. "Grit—"

"Grit? Oh. The SEAL from your firefight on the Pakistan-Afghanistan border in April. No, it's not Grit. It's Charles Neal."

Elijah took a moment before responding. The military chain of command didn't include the vice president or his sixteen-year-old son, but Elijah couldn't imagine any officer he'd ever served under wanting him on this call. He pictured Charlie's red face in the video as Jo had grabbed him by the ear. "How'd you get this number, Charlie? And how do you know Grit?"

"I don't know Grit. I know of him. Getting your number was easy. Seriously, it's on the Internet. It's getting Jo's number that's hard. Special Agent Harper, I mean. Is she there?"

"No. She likes her flowers. Did you know lilies are her favorite?"

"I found out. Mr. Cameron—is it okay to call you Mister, or should I call you Sergeant?"

The kid was something. "Elijah will be fine, Charlie."

"Please give Special Agent Harper a message." He paused, and when Elijah didn't say anything, proceeded. "Tell her that I have reason to believe that Ambassador Bruni was the target of a team of international assassins who are also responsible for the deaths of at least four prominent Americans in the past six months."

"And you're telling me this why?"

"Because you have access to people in a way that I don't. You're one of them. The people who'd know things, I mean. Not the killers. I'll report more details as soon—"

"No, you won't," Elijah said in his best drill-sergeant voice. "You'll get your butt to school tomorrow and do what the Secret Service tells you to do. Got that, Mr. Neal?"

"Yeah, yeah. Sure." The kid was unruffled. "You'll tell Jo, though, right?"

"Stay out of this thing before you screw up someone else's career or get yourself into a bigger mess than an airsoft firefight."

"You're an American hero, Sergeant Cameron. Thank you for your service."

The kid was gone.

Elijah considered his options. Odds were, if Charlie knew about assassins and unsolved murders, he'd found the information on the Internet, which everyone else could read, too. Law enforcement could have made the same connections he had—if any connections were to be made.

He called Grit, filled him in. They'd known each other for

several years, but Grit was navy, Elijah was army—it wasn't until the firefight in April that they'd become friends for life. Elijah would give his life for Grit. He knew Grit would do the same for him.

"We're talking about the irresponsible, genius son of the vice president of the United States," Grit said. "Right, Elijah?"

"Yeah. I like this kid. He called me an American hero."

Grit burst out laughing and hung up.

Elijah resisted marching down to Jo's cabin in the dark. The Secret Service had their eye on Charlie Neal. They probably kept track of what he was up to on the Internet. Then again, the kid was a genius. Probably he could outwit the Secret Service if he put his mind to it.

The wonder, Elijah thought, wasn't that Jo had gotten him by the ear or said what she'd said to him. The wonder was she hadn't strangled Charles Preston Neal with her bare hands.

# *Fourteen*

Nora unrolled her sleeping bag in the pitch-dark of her small dome tent. She had a flashlight but didn't want to use it and risk someone finding her. She felt safer that way. But she hadn't considered how dark it would be. Even with the half-moon, it was a black night. She'd set up her tent on a level spot off the falls trail—Beth Harper had once described it to her. She and her sister used to camp up here as kids. It was located on the saddle that connected Cameron Mountain to an unnamed peak that had few trails and wasn't popular with hikers. Devin had told her about a kind of pathway along the saddle, off the main trails, around to the north side of the mountain.

That was her ultimate destination. She could have driven out to the old logging road over there, but then it'd be obvious to anyone who found her car where she was headed.

She wanted to see the spot where Devin had found Drew Cameron.

She hadn't known Devin then, but she believed the horror of that day was key to whatever was going on with him.

Maybe if she could understand, she could help him—even if he had stolen money from her.

"Which he didn't," she whispered aloud, getting on her hands and knees and smoothing out her sleeping bag as best she could. She'd been lucky to find the campsite before nightfall. She could have hiked longer, but she hadn't wanted to trip over a rock or a root in the dark and break something. Then what would she do?

Pitching her tent hadn't taken her as long as it might have if she hadn't practiced after she bought it for her class with Elijah. The poles were color coded, which had made things easier. She'd eaten up daylight trekking from where she'd left her car. Everyone would think she was on the east trail—it was one of the easiest and most popular—but she'd cut off onto a seldom-used spur that intersected the falls trail. And she hadn't stayed on it, either. Going off trail was a huge risk, but she didn't want anyone to stumble on to her—including Devin, she thought, feeling guilty at her disloyalty.

She'd started up the mountain too late in the day to get to the north side before nightfall. Even at a moderate pace, she could cover *maybe* a mile an hour hiking in the rugged terrain, but her heavy pack and the conflation of a thousand different emotions—fear, grief, shock, everything—had slowed her down.

She sniffled, crawling back to the head of her sleeping bag. She'd taken off her boots, but her feet were dry and warm in her socks—wool with a moisture-wicking liner. The tent was tight quarters, but Elijah had explained how a smaller space was easier to warm up and keep warm. He'd emphasized all the ways not to freeze to death.

*Like his father did.*

Nora pulled off her gloves—she'd put them and a hat on once she'd gotten up on the mountain—and tucked them back in her pack, her teeth chattering, although not from the cold. It was her jumble of thoughts and all the different scenarios that her mind kept throwing out to her of what was going on.

She wished she could just stop *thinking.*

There was, mercifully, no wind where she was, although supposedly her tent could withstand high winds. She could hear the rush of the waterfall straight down from her campsite and an owl in the nearby spruce tree, its rhythmic hoot eerie but not scary. It was as if it were calling to her, trying to reassure her that all would be well.

Fully clothed except for her hiking boots, Nora slid deep into her mummy-style sleeping bag. It was rated to keep her warm in temperatures as cold as minus twenty. It'd be cold tonight, but not *that* cold. She'd be fine. She'd eaten a couple of energy bars and drunk plenty of water; Elijah had pounded in the importance of staying hydrated.

She lay on her back, not feeling as claustrophobic as she'd expected. She adjusted the sleeping bag's hood up over her head, another way to prevent heat loss.

Shutting her eyes was the same as keeping them open. Everything was black. Her tent had a little mesh stargazing window that she could open, but she thought looking up at the night sky would only make her feel smaller, more alone.

*Alex is dead...Melanie hates me...Mom doesn't care about me...*

"Don't think," she whispered, wriggling inside her sleeping bag. She hoped she didn't have to go to the bathroom in the middle of the night. She'd dug a cat-hole outside her tent, but she hated—*hated*—the idea of having to use it, especially in the dark. Such niceties wouldn't faze Devin.

Maybe she should have trusted him.

She clutched the silky sleeping bag from the inside.

*You're in shock.*

She wished Alex hadn't been killed, but she didn't delude herself. She'd never loved him and resented how he had treated her father. Ever since her mother and Alex got together, Nora had tried to be neutral about him. Devin didn't understand why she'd bothered. "My father was a total cretin, but he'd never have done something like that—steal his best friend's wife," he'd said. "That's really disgusting."

But who were they to judge? Nora just wanted her mother to be happy. That was what her father had told her, too. "I just want your mother to be happy."

Except it wasn't that easy. Maybe, with Alex's death, her father would dump Melanie and go back to her mother.

Just so long as no one thought *he'd* run over Alex. Her father had never shown any anger or sense of betrayal, but he wouldn't. He was restrained that way—*emotionally repressed,* her mother would say.

A branch snapped down toward the trail, and Nora bolted upright and stifled a scream.

Dead leaves crunched nearby—she couldn't tell how close.

She could feel her heart thumping as she took small, shallow breaths.

The owl had stopped hooting, but she could hear the rush of the falls down the mountain. She sat as still and as quiet as possible.

But she didn't hear anything more.

*A bear, maybe.*

Making as little noise as possible, she eased deep into her sleeping bag. It was funny, she thought sarcastically—right now she'd rather have a bear find her tent than anyone she knew in Black Falls. Even Beth, Dominique and Hannah. Even Elijah. What did she know, really, about any of them? And why should they care about her?

Nora stared wide-eyed into the darkness and told herself over and over again not to think.

*Don't think, don't think, don't think.*

As if it was a mantra that could block out any intrusive thoughts and fears, and keep her safe.

# *Fifteen*

Grit decided Myrtle Smith could drink him under the table without even putting her mind to it. It'd come automatically, effortlessly. She was a hard-nosed warhorse Washington reporter. He was a SEAL.

He didn't stand a chance.

It was late at the bar in the hotel where Alexander Bruni had been run over by a black car, now in the hands of law enforcement.

"You know the natural result of banning smoking in bars?" Myrtle asked out of the blue. She was like that, Grit had figured out; her mind pinged around like a pinball machine.

He set down his scotch. "Less cancer?"

"More drunks. You wait, someone will do a study and discover those of us who smoke aren't quitting—we're just having an extra scotch or two when we're trapped in a bar without our cigarettes."

"You should quit."

"Some politician will kill me in my sleep long before I die

of lung cancer. But I did quit, you little snot. Two years, seventy-seven days, ten hours ago. The 'us' was in solidarity with smokers. I hate seeing smokers treated like criminals."

"I don't think I've been called a 'little snot' since I was four."

"'Little' as in you're younger than I am. 'Snot' as in—well, you know. You're a SEAL. All that humility and professionalism is just your way of saying you're better than the rest of us without being obnoxious."

"How'd you know I'm in the military?"

"I'd like to say I have a nose for Navy SEALs, but I don't. I checked you out with a source. Silver Star. Badly wounded in Afghanistan in April. Lost a friend."

Moose gave a low whistle next to Grit. *"She cuts to the chase, doesn't she?"* Grit ignored his comment.

"I'm sorry," Myrtle said simply.

"Yeah. Thanks." Grit appreciated how succinct she was.

She leaned forward, her eyes darkening to purple in the dim bar light. "Life sucks. So, want to get on with it?"

"Okay. What do you know about Ambassador Bruni's enemies?"

"Nothing no one else doesn't know. He was tough, smart and arrogant. Ambitious. Important. He divorced his first wife to marry the wife of his best friend. According to my sources, he had enemies but no active threats against him."

"Then there's no reason to think the hit-and-run was a professional job," Grit said.

Myrtle leaned back, eyed him. "Are you suggesting there is?"

"How would I know? Anything on where he was headed when he was hit?"

"Most likely a breakfast meeting that wasn't on his calendar. No reservation in his name. No one left waiting in the restaurant, checking his watch for him—at least no one who stuck around after he got run over."

"Maybe whoever it was didn't hear the commotion outside and thought Bruni blew off their meeting."

"I suppose it's possible, but the news is out now."

"Would you come forward, or would you fade quietly into the woodwork?"

"I'm not the fading-into-the-woodwork type."

"If you were," Grit said.

"I don't know. Doesn't matter what I'd do. The FBI and Washington PD are conducting a joint investigation." Myrtle sat back, her eyes catching more of the light and turning back to lavender. "But it's not like the hotel has a sign-up sheet for people who walk in off the street. A hotel guest would get asked his room number, but that's a dead end so far. Interesting, isn't it? My take—whoever was meeting Bruni doesn't want to come forward."

"Could be for political, personal or professional reasons—someone who wants to keep a low profile." Grit sipped some of his scotch. He was careful about booze. It'd be too easy to dive into a bottle, even with Moose right there. Maybe especially with Moose right there. "There are endless possibilities. What if it wasn't a breakfast meeting? What if the breakfast was a setup? There was no one waiting—it was just to get him here at a particular time so the car could be there and bounce him into oblivion."

"You've got a twisted mind, Petty Officer Taylor."

Grit shrugged. "I'm not a pro. The cops will have a dozen other possibilities by now." He swirled the ice and booze in his glass. "What if he was going to someone's hotel room?"

Myrtle slanted a sharp look at him. "A woman?"

Grit shrugged, noncommittal. "I suppose it's possible."

"But a long shot, even if his wife was out of the country. They seemed happy together."

"What about the ex-wife?"

"She moved to Seattle. They have two grown sons out there."

"The new wife's ex-husband?" Grit asked, just to see how Myrtle would respond.

"They've stayed friends—they're 'evolved.' It's easier on the daughter."

"How's she taking the news, do you know?"

Myrtle gave him an openly suspicious look. "No. Why? Is there something I should know?" She leaned forward again, her eyes like purple-tinted onyx now. "There is, isn't there?"

"It's a good thing you're on our side."

"I'm not on anyone's side. I just want to know what's going on. I've kept quiet in the interest of national security from time to time. Depends. For instance, if I'd had a tip about what you special-ops types were doing when you got your leg blown off, I wouldn't have told the world. If I found out it was illegal or nefarious, then I'd have had to make a judgment call."

"Nefarious?" Grit couldn't hold back a grin. "Come on. Nefarious?"

"Now you're making me sound like one of those pompous reporters."

"You *are* one of those pompous reporters. And I don't know anything."

"You're a good liar, but I'm good at seeing through liars. What's on your mind, soldier?"

"Not soldier. Technically—"

"I know. Sailor. Don't start with me on the SEAL thing. Sea, land, air. Navy. I know. I was just trying to be nice."

"No, you weren't, but whatever. Is there a chance Bruni's death is connected to any other hits?"

Myrtle tapped her fingers on the table. "Ah. You do have your ways, Petty Officer Taylor."

"You know, just because you found out I'm a SEAL doesn't mean you have to get formal. Grit's fine."

"All right, Grit. What do you know? Some of your old SEAL pals are HRT, counterterrorism, spooks, right?"

He didn't answer.

"How come you're not?"

He shrugged and didn't answer.

"The leg?"

Moose gave another low whistle next to him. *"She doesn't let up. If she were thirty years younger, you'd be in love."*

Grit sighed. "Just shut up, will you?" But Myrtle's eyebrows went up, and he smiled at her. "Not you."

Her expression softened. "Human frailty can be hard to take, but we all bump up against it at some point. I'm dying with my boots on. I have friends on Captiva Island, friends in Puerto Vallarta, one very good friend in Nova Scotia. Not me. I'm staying right here in Washington until I say the big good-night."

"You've a flare for drama."

"Not when it comes to my work. Then I give it straight. Always have, Grit. I don't play games, and I don't let my politics infect my reporting. I'm not introspective and don't overthink these things, but that much I do get." She gave a matter-of-fact shrug. "In my world, everyone's fair game."

"Ms. Smith," Grit said, lifting his scotch and eyeing her over the rim of his glass, "who are you working for?"

A kind of pain crossed her face. "No one," she said. "Bastard."

"Did you have a thing for Bruni?"

"Not my type. Stick to what you're doing and never mind me."

"Know anything about assassins on the loose, Ms. Smith?"

"Myrtle. Okay? Just Myrtle. As for assassins—" She grabbed the check, but Grit could tell he'd struck a nerve. "I'm going to take a chance and say something I know I shouldn't. It's not a gray thing—I'm clear I should keep my mouth shut because you're a SEAL and you probably can put me away."

"Let me help you. Bruni isn't the first hit you've looked into recently."

"I've done some research. I don't know if I'm on to anything or not. I've got a list of suspicious deaths over the past year. Prominent people—not necessarily headline grabbers, though. The methods of death are all different. Sniper shot. Fire. Hit-and-run. Poison. They all involve a noticeable lack of passion—there's no crazy lover, no deranged psychotic hearing voices. They've all been in the news. No one's hushed them up. But to make any connection among them…" Myrtle shrugged. "That'd be a stretch for authorities."

"Anyone investigating?"

"Me." She clutched the bill in her small hand. "So, who're you working for, Grit?"

"Just passing the time between PT appointments." He reached across the table, took the check by his fingertips and pried it away from her. "I'll pay for our drinks."

"I'm rich, Grit. Allow me."

He didn't.

She looked at him as he got up. "I have a niece in her twenties."

"She look like you?"

"Same eyes. That's it."

Moose chuckled in that knowing way he had, but Grit said, "Your eyes aren't bad, Myrtle. Maybe I'll give your niece a call someday."

He thought she might have blushed. She must have been something in her day. Hell, she was something now.

"I think I'll stay for another drink," she said. "You okay getting home?"

He realized she was serious and grinned. "Yeah. I can get home." He glanced down at her. "And the leg. It didn't get blown off. It had to be amputated."

"In the field?"

He nodded.

"It was that or die?"

He could hear Moose that night. "Live, Grit. Come on, *live.*"

He left Myrtle to order another scotch. On his way out, he thought about what she'd said. He did have friends in positions that could put them in the know when it came to assassins on the loose.

He splurged and took a cab back to his apartment in a bad part of town. It was in a square brown-brick building with four other apartments. His was on the ground floor overlooking the street.

He shared the sidewalk in front of the entrance with a fat rat.

*"That fella's so ugly, he's almost cute,"* Moose said.

Grit ignored him and unlocked his apartment door. When he flipped on the light in the entry, a half-dozen roaches scurried across the cheap wooden floor.

*"Nothing cute about a cockroach."* Moose wasn't letting up, obviously. *"Man, Grit. Why don't you find a better place to live?"*

Grit didn't care about rats and roaches so long as he didn't find one in bed with him. And there was no point paying for a better place when he didn't give a damn where he lived.

It wasn't something he needed to explain to Moose—Moose knew.

But he was gone. He'd never cared for cockroaches.

# *Sixteen*

Her cabin got so cold overnight, Jo wouldn't have been surprised if she'd had to chip ice off herself when she crawled out of bed. She pulled on her new wool socks and headed to the shower. The ancient propane heater was trying, but the place wasn't even remotely warm. At least no one had slipped in overnight and stolen food out of her refrigerator or attacked her in the dark.

"Always a positive when waking up," she muttered, turning on the water in the shower. She waited until it was steaming before she stripped and got in.

She was toweling off when she heard a knock on the door, which just helped her hurry into her clothes that much faster. She figured she'd be up on the mountain today and put her new wool socks back on, the one pair of wool pants she'd brought up to Vermont with her and, for layering, a moisture-wicking exercise shirt and a wool pullover sweater.

When she yanked open the door, she expected to see Elijah, but instead, a short-haired, broad-shouldered man in expensive cold-weather hiking attire greeted her politely. "Special

Agent Harper? My name's Kyle Rigby. Thomas Asher asked me to stop by and let you know I'll be checking on his daughter and getting her back to Washington."

"You're…what? A friend?"

He gave a small smile. "Mr. Asher and I have never met. He hired me." The smile disappeared. "Feel free to check with him yourself. He appreciates your efforts, but he doesn't want to impose on your friendship or put you in an awkward position—he didn't expect Nora to take off this way."

"No one did." Jo stepped out onto the front step in her stocking feet, letting the door swing shut behind her; she didn't want any heat to escape. She eyed the big man in front of her. His parka was unzipped, and he wasn't wearing a hat or gloves. She didn't see a backpack but suspected he would have everything he needed for a November hike. She asked, "Are you familiar with the area, Mr. Rigby?"

"Kyle," he said. "And you're Jo, right?" When she didn't answer, he continued in the same clipped, professional tone. "Mr. Asher doesn't like the idea of Nora being out on the mountains by herself, especially given the shock she's had. He prefers to keep the situation private. Involving you, given your job…" Rigby didn't shift his gaze from her. "It's simpler to hire me."

"Do you have search-and-rescue experience?"

"I know what I'm doing."

"Are you working with a team?"

"Like I said, I know what I'm doing. I'm here to get Nora Asher safely back to her family. That's it. I don't doubt everyone here will cooperate to make sure that happens."

"Did Thomas give you any update on the investigation into Ambassador Bruni's death?"

"No, but that's not why I'm here. Sorry, I don't have a lot of time. Sunset's around 4:00 p.m. and the forecast calls for a fair amount of snow at higher elevations in the next couple of days. Nora's inexperienced and very upset. It'd be good to find her." He dipped a big hand inside his jacket, withdrew a business card and handed it to Jo. "Call me on my cell phone if anything comes up. Leave me a message if I'm out of range."

"I'll do that. Where are you staying?"

"The second apartment in the Whittakers' guesthouse. They insisted through Mr. Asher that I stay there. It's decent of them."

"Were you there last night?"

He shook his head. "I dumped my stuff off before I drove out here. I'd hoped Nora had come back during the night." He shrugged. "But she didn't."

"What's your plan now?"

He ignored her question and walked back to his car. Jo remained on her step and watched him drive off down the dirt road, the sun higher now, glistening on the lake. Then she directed her attention to the trees behind the next cabin, where she'd noticed a slight movement.

Elijah stepped out from behind a hemlock with a .30-06 rifle balanced comfortably on one shoulder. "Off the case, are you?"

"There is no case. Thomas has a right to hire someone if he wants to." Jo crossed her arms to keep herself warm. "Elijah, is that a freaking machine gun?"

"Rifle. You know the difference, Ms. Secret Agent."

"Secret Service agent. Which you know."

"It's almost deer season. I was cleaning my hunting rifle."

"You've never gone deer hunting in your life."

"Once. I was thirteen." He stayed close to the woods, the

morning sun glinting on the rust-colored oak leaves behind him. "I went up on the mountain with my father, and I got a buck in my sights—a big guy."

"You didn't fire," Jo said. "I'd have heard the story if you had. Why didn't you?"

"I don't know. My father didn't understand, either, but I never took to hunting. That was years before he left you this property."

"So it was."

"He was a good man, but he never gave people something for nothing." Elijah's eyes, with their piercing Cameron blue, settled on her. "I figured he owed you."

"If he did, it was in his own mind, not mine."

"Maybe so."

Jo wasn't about to tell him about his father's vision of the children they'd never have; that part of their conversation was between her and Drew. But she couldn't help wondering how much her response to Elijah last night—the taste of him, the feel of his body hard against hers—had to do with her visit with his father. For the past seven months, she'd been thinking about Elijah in a way she hadn't before Drew Cameron had turned up at her Washington apartment.

But such thinking wasn't going to get her anywhere, and she dropped her arms from her chest. "Take your rifle and go home, Elijah. I need to get back inside. My hair's turning to icicles."

"Cold morning for a shower in a barely heated cabin."

"At least there is a shower, although sometimes it'd be nice to have a tub."

"I have one at my place if you ever—"

"Thanks." She cut him off quickly. Today, she'd promised herself, would be different. Her life was complicated enough right now without kissing her neighbor and one-time lover. "I'll keep that in mind."

"You could always borrow my bathrobe if you didn't bring one with you."

"No way do you have a bathrobe, Elijah."

He looked amused. "You don't think so?"

She opened the cabin door, sorry she'd brought up the subject. But he didn't move, just stood there with his rifle still on his shoulder. She frowned at him. "What are you doing?"

"Picturing what kind of bathrobe you have."

"I don't own a bathrobe."

It was the wrong answer. He grinned at her. "Even better."

"Go drink a gallon of coffee, Elijah. You need it."

But his grin faded, and he said seriously, "Put a pot on. I'll be back in ten. I need to talk to you about your new best friend in Washington."

"My new…" Jo took a breath. "Charlie Neal? Elijah—"

"He's fine. Has a hell of an imagination. Coffee, okay?"

He headed back through the trees to his house, and she shut the door hard behind her, wishing she weren't even a little attracted to him. But she was a lot attracted, not so much a shock as a pointed reminder of why she should have resisted coming back to Black Falls.

Assassins.

*Only Charlie.*

Jo shook her head over coffee with Elijah in her cabin. They sat at the table with the vase of lilies Charlie had sent her. "He has an active imagination. He reads, plays video games and has fantasy airsoft firefights. He doesn't sit in on White House briefings."

Elijah gave her a steady, measured look that reminded her he was an experienced Special Forces soldier. "So, you don't know anything about assassins?"

"If I knew anything about an assassination team at work in Washington or Black Falls or anywhere else, I wouldn't be sitting here having coffee with you and talking about a sixteen-year-old kid—even if he is the son of the vice president. Charlie doesn't believe his father or any of his father's friends are targets, does he?"

"We didn't get into it."

"Elijah..." She got up with her coffee mug. The cabin felt warmer, but she doubted it was. "Does he think I'm here undercover?"

"He didn't say."

"Anything's possible with Charlie. He's manipulative and very smart."

"He's not so smart that he didn't talk himself out of that airsoft prank, but he's smart enough to have sent you flowers."

"It'll take more than flowers for me to warm back up to him."

"Nah. You like that kid. You're a soft touch, Agent Harper." But as he rose to his feet, Elijah's tight expression suggested that Charlie Neal had gotten to him, too. "Thanks for the coffee."

"Where are you going?"

"Out the front door. The only door, I should say."

"You're familiar with search-and-rescue protocols. If you plan to find Nora and Devin, the best starting point is to figure out where they were last seen and to interview the people who've talked to them most recently—friends, family, co-workers. Charging into the mountains willy-nilly by yourself isn't the smartest course of action."

"Willy-nilly?" He grinned as he headed for the door. "I

don't know as I've ever heard anyone use *willy-nilly* in a sentence. See you, Jo."

After he left, Jo waited until his truck passed by her cabin before she put on her fleece jacket over her sweater and headed outside. The sun sparkled on the lake and frosty grass, a picturesque scene, if different from the blazing colors of early October or the rich greens of summer. She did a quick check of the cabins in daylight, but they all looked fine—no sign of intruders, campers, picnickers or even wild turkeys.

She thrashed through the woods over to the trail up to the lodge and dialed Mark Francona from a rock with a particularly beautiful view of the lake. He picked up on the first ring. "Too cold this morning for canoeing?"

"I can see the breath in front of my face, if you consider that cold."

"I do." He gave an audible sigh. There was no humor in his voice now. "Washington PD got an anonymous tip about a possible eyewitness yesterday. A bicycle messenger. Woman."

"That's a solid lead, then. Mark..." Jo hesitated, then plunged in. "Is it possible that an assassination team targeted Ambassador Bruni?"

A half beat's pause. "Who've you been talking to?"

"Just overheard idle talk at the watercooler."

"I've heard about your place in Vermont, Harper." The Francona wit had returned. "You're lucky to have flush toilets, let alone watercoolers."

"Does that mean there are no assassins on the loose?"

"There are always assassins on the loose," he said and hung up.

Jo dialed him again and got his voice mail. She didn't

leave a message. She could call Charlie out of class at his private school in northern Virginia and ask him to clarify what he'd said to Elijah, but Charlie would have covered his tracks and would deny the conversation—he was resourceful, intelligent, bored and under the close watch of her colleagues in the Secret Service.

So it was drama, and Charlie manipulating her, and she shouldn't bite and end up the victim of another of his pranks.

She continued up the three-quarter-mile trail to Black Falls Lodge, but there was no marker—no fence, no mean dogs—that indicated when she'd crossed onto Cameron land. The trail ended at the far corner of the meadow below the lodge. Out in the open, the air was even colder. She slipped as she crossed the frost-dampened grass to the walk, following it up to the stone terrace.

She found A.J. taking down umbrellas at the tables, hatless, working without gloves. He acknowledged her presence with a curt nod. "Cold morning for a hike," he said.

Jo couldn't argue. "I thought I might find Nora and Devin sitting by the fire. I was hoping they'd come down off the mountain looking for pancakes and hot maple syrup."

"No such luck."

She looked out at the wide sloping meadow from which she'd just come, the mountains blue and gray out across from the ridge. "It's a beautiful spot. Easy to forget when you're not here."

"It's easy for some people never to notice even when they are here."

Jo thought he might be making a gibe at her youthful self but let it pass. "A.J., did your father have much to do with Ambassador Bruni when he was up here?"

"It's possible. Pop did his own thing." A.J. laid a tall, rust-colored umbrella against a table with three others. He stood up straight, the wind catching the ends of his hair as he studied her. "Where are you going with this, Jo?"

"Nowhere. I'm just spitting in the ocean. It's not the best way to do things, I know, but—"

"You're at a loose end right now. Don't go looking for things that aren't there just because you're bored or need a distraction." He turned abruptly and tackled another umbrella. "Elijah's had a rough year. You might keep that in mind."

Her breath caught at his words, but she tried to smile. "Since when have you started looking after your baby brother? You used to have apple fights—didn't one of you end up with stitches?"

"Sean did. Third man in." A.J. abandoned his umbrella and gave her a faint smile, his blue eyes unreadable in the bright morning light. "You were one of us growing up, Jo, whether you want to admit it or not."

"Just don't say that where my father can hear you. What did you plan to do with the lakefront property?"

"Doesn't matter now."

"It belonged to a Harper for most of the past century—"

"Lauren says maybe that land wasn't meant for us. People don't really come here for the lake. They can rent a kayak, but they want the mountains. Hiking, biking, skiing, the views, the quiet, the waterfall. We're doing fine."

"I'm glad, A.J."

But he looked troubled as he squinted out toward the mountains. "People get lost out here from time to time, but it's rare for someone to actually die. Pop..." He trailed off, then seemed to make an effort to be conversational. "How's the cabin?"

"It has bats. Don't tell Elijah. I think he's afraid of bats."

A.J. gave her one of his glimmers of a smile. "Stay here and look at the view to your heart's content."

"You wouldn't be trying to stall me again, would you, A.J.?"

"I'd never stall the law two days in a row."

Wishing she had Kyle Rigby's parka, Jo left A.J. to his work and walked out to the topographical-map sign on the edge of the parking lot, which, she hoped, would help jog her memory. She was rusty. She'd repressed a lot of memories of hiking in the area, since most of them involved Elijah. With the impressive network of recreational trails, Nora could go for miles—days—if she had the supplies, the energy, the will. Assuming she had, in fact, started up the east trail at midday yesterday, she could be almost anywhere by now.

Jo was joined by Lauren Cameron, no toddlers at her side now. She had an athletic build and a striking beauty that, according to town gossip, A.J. had barely noticed at first, so preoccupied had he been with work six years ago. She'd come to Black Falls Lodge to escape an abusive relationship and ended up staying.

"If you're wondering where Devin found Drew," she said, "I can point out the exact spot to you."

"It's okay. I know," Jo said quietly, sensing Lauren's pain. "Drew was so proud of little Baylee and Jim. He showed me pictures of them when I saw him last."

Lauren studied her a moment, then said, "I had a feeling he saw you on that trip of his in April. A.J. always envisioned our kids growing up with cousins close by, but I guess that's one of the prices he pays as the eldest. Elijah, Sean and Rose haven't met their soul mates yet, or if they have, they haven't figured it out."

"Their time will come."

"They might need someone to hit them over the head with a two-by-four to figure things out." Lauren gave a quick laugh that lit up her hazel eyes. "The Camerons can be thick."

"What a shock," Jo said with a smile.

Lauren nodded to the map. "We looked everywhere for Drew once we realized he was missing. It was awful, Jo. Then finding out about Elijah." She shook her head. "Rose in particular had a hard time. She's been pushing herself nonstop since then. Now Elijah's back…"

Jo frowned at her. "Lauren?"

She sighed. "He's looking for answers that he just might never get."

"About Drew, you mean."

She didn't respond, just inclined her head toward the mountain. "Elijah's up there. He found Devin's truck near the falls trail." She hesitated, then said, "Jo, maybe you should be up there, too."

"A.J. *did* stall me."

Lauren managed a quick smile. "He'll consider that a small victory."

# *Seventeen*

Elijah noted three chickadees darting among the spruce trees just below the falls but didn't pause to enjoy them. He'd done the hike up from where he'd just located Devin's beat-up truck in forty minutes. Normally it took an hour. The trail was steep, rough and rocky. He hadn't taken the time to enjoy the view. He figured Jo was down there, though, and decided he should have just wrestled her gun off her and thrown her in his truck with him.

She was a capable, experienced federal agent. He liked the idea of knowing where she was.

Devin had pulled onto an old lane and left his truck hidden among pine trees. Elijah had found it because he was looking for it, and because he'd been trying to think like an eighteen-year-old kid butting heads with his family and friends over a girl he couldn't have.

It wasn't that hard to do.

The falls trail started closer to the lodge, which allowed guests to get to it on foot without a long trek along the ridge road. The lane where Devin had parked was farther down the road, but the trail up to the falls was shorter. Also more difficult, though Elijah didn't mind that part.

The chickadees danced off into the wilderness as he came to the falls trail. He followed it around a level curve, hearing the water rushing down off the mountain.

The air wasn't that cold. He was warm enough in his fleece without resorting to the extra layers in his pack.

He ducked under the low branches of a red oak and made his way to a ledge above the falls. Water swirled below him in an endless cascade that smoothed and shaped the wall of gray granite.

He remembered holding hands with Jo under this same oak as she told him she wanted to marry him at the falls. It was just like her not to wait to be asked. She'd been so full of dreams, so eager to leave Vermont and their small hometown. He'd been clueless about anything beyond his desire to get Jo Harper into bed.

"Some things don't change," he muttered, and warned himself to focus on the task at hand.

Find Devin, find Nora. Go from there.

In his winter-camping class, Nora Asher had been dedicated and self-conscious—a perfectionist who didn't want to be the yahoo Ivy Leaguer who got lost in the woods and had to be rescued. She hated, she'd said during their afternoon break, the idea of a bunch of Vermonters searching for her and thinking here was another dumb-assed flatlander in a self-inflicted mess.

Not that anyone would think that, but that was how Nora saw the world.

She'd also wanted to prove she was tough. In Elijah's experience, that was as sure a way into trouble as being an idiot was. But it didn't matter.

"Forget your pride if you get in a jam and ask for help," he'd told her. "Just get home alive."

She'd given him the sort of look that he'd become accustomed to—the one that said she knew she couldn't imagine the brushes with death he'd had and wasn't sure she wanted to.

As he turned back toward the trail, he caught a movement just below him, on the other side of the falls. Devin emerged from a cluster of hemlocks and stared up at Elijah, then spun back around on his heels.

Seeing the danger, Elijah called to him. "Devin—don't run."

But he paid no attention and bolted toward the cover of the evergreens, losing his footing on the wet ground and going down hard on one knee. Unable to get himself back under control, he slid, flailing, yelling, down the slippery rock outcropping, finally stopping just short of a deep coppery pool.

Elijah was already moving. He ran up through the trees to the stream that fed the falls and leaped onto a dry boulder in the middle of the shallow, sparkling water, then jumped to the opposite bank. The ground was soft, covered with freshly fallen maple and birch leaves. Avoiding slippery rocks, he ducked among the hemlocks and made his way quickly down the steep hill to Devin. As he got closer to the falls, Elijah could hear the whoosh of the tumbling water and Devin's uninhibited swearing.

"Hang on," Elijah said. "Don't move."

"I can't move. I'm stuck." He sounded more frustrated than panicked.

Elijah eased out from behind a hemlock. "Hit your head?"

Devin grimaced. "No—I just slid under this damn rock."

"Ribs?"

"I'm okay." He gulped in a breath and sank back against the steep rock incline. He had on a canvas vest over a hooded sweatshirt. And jeans. But he didn't look cold. He squeezed his eyes shut in pain. "Just go on. I don't need you to rescue me."

"It'd be easier on you if I did."

Devin swore at him, but Elijah squatted in the muck to get a better look at the situation. Devin's momentum had shoved his lower right leg down into the muck and under a basketball-size boulder, dislodging the boulder and trapping him from midcalf down. If not for the spongy ground, he probably would have broken his leg.

"Not smart," Elijah said. "Running from me. Slipping like that. You're used to being up here."

"Go to hell."

"I can get you out of here."

"I don't need your help."

"It'll be faster, easier with my help. Where's Nora?"

"Who the hell cares?"

So that was it. Elijah shrugged off his pack and set it on dry leaves. He had a first-aid kit, but Devin didn't appear to be more than scraped, bruised and distressed about his predicament. "I found your truck. You spent the night up here?"

He didn't answer, but his breathing was calmer. And he'd stopped swearing.

"There's a spot up above the falls where we all used to camp as kids," Elijah said. "Did A.J. tell you about it?"

"He didn't have to. I already know." Devin gritted his teeth and groaned as he grasped his right knee with both hands. "Just get me out."

"Did you tell Nora about it?"

"Beth Harper did." He hissed through his teeth. "Elijah, hurry up, will you?"

"I don't want to make a wrong move and end up crushing your leg."

"That'd be bad." He sniffed and looked up at the sky, streaked now with high clouds. "I wanted to make sure Nora was okay. I didn't bug her. I just— I keep a daypack with a bivy sac in my truck. I slept under the stars a little ways down some from where she camped."

"Did she know?" Elijah asked as he inspected every inch he could get to of the boulder that had Devin pinned.

"Probably. I think so. I tried not to scare her. She left at first light, while I was still asleep." He blinked back tears, embarrassed, angry. "I would never hurt her, Elijah, and I'm not a thief."

"Are you dehydrated? Cold?"

"No. I'm fine. Just get me out."

Elijah paused and looked at Devin. "You'll talk to me?"

"Yeah. Whatever."

"Where's your pack?"

"It's up in the trees. My walking stick, too. I set them down when I heard something. I thought it might be Nora."

"You got me instead. No wonder you went ass over teakettle."

Devin attempted a smile, but he made a face and groaned. "Crap. Not her."

*Jo.* Elijah followed Devin's gaze and, sure enough, there she was under the oak tree he had just vacated on the other side of the falls. She gave them a critical look, then disappeared back through the trees. Elijah stood up and eyed Devin, who probably would have shrunk himself to slug size and slithered under the boulder if he could have. Elijah couldn't blame him. "Two minutes until the law arrives," he said. "Anything you want to tell me in the meantime?"

"I'm sorry I ran."

"Yeah." Elijah saw Jo already charging down toward them and thought of her smile at eighteen—the hope, love and promises it held—then shifted back to Devin. "Sometimes it's just easier to run."

"I bet you never run."

"We all run, Devin. At some point in our lives," he said, squatting back down, "we all run. Let's get you out of here."

Jo arrived and immediately assessed the situation with an air of authority and competence that didn't surprise Elijah. "What happened?" she asked.

"I slipped," Devin said. "It was an accident. Elijah startled me."

"Let's get him unstuck," Elijah said. "Then we can sort out the rest."

Jo got down into the muck to help but kept up with the questions. "Did you see any other hikers?"

Devin winced. "I'm in pain, Jo."

She narrowed her eyes on him. "You don't want to lie to me, Devin."

"Jo." Elijah kept his voice even, but he decided he'd been indulging in too many fantasies and regrets. She wasn't eighteen anymore. She wasn't in love with him anymore. She was a federal agent who could hold her own when it came to shooting and fighting. "You want to help, or you want to interrogate him?"

She bit off a sigh. "All right. You're the expert. Tell me what you need me to do."

"Stand there and look pretty."

She glared at him.

He grinned, then turned back to Devin, who wasn't so far gone he was going to say anything provocative in front of a Secret Service agent. He didn't even let out a curse.

Jo got behind Devin and tucked her hands under his arms.

"Devin," Elijah said, "I need to make sure your leg isn't broken."

"It's fine—just some scrapes. I can wiggle my toes and everything. I could get out of here on my own."

"How?" Jo asked. "By carving off your leg with a jackknife?"

"If I had to. I've got one in my back pocket."

"I could throw you both off the mountain," Elijah said. "Devin, when I pick up this rock, Jo's going to pull you up. Go with the momentum. Don't fight her. But don't do more than you can manage."

He nodded. "Okay. Come on. Let's just hurry."

Elijah ignored him and positioned his arms under the boulder. As he lifted, Jo moved fast, helping Devin get his lower leg free. He yelled and swore, pounding the muck with his fists, which Elijah interpreted as his way of getting over a rush of pain.

"Does he need an ambulance?" Jo asked.

"Nah. He's fine." Elijah bent over him. "You going to be okay, Dev?"

He grabbed a fistful of muck and hurled it into the water.

Elijah shrugged at Jo. "I'm taking that as a yes."

Devin rolled onto his back and hissed through clenched teeth. "Damn, that hurt. Jo, what kind of fingernails do you have? They're like finishing nails or something. I think you took a chunk out of my underarms."

She showed him her hands. "No fingernails to speak of."

"Well, it was your fingertips digging into me, then." He sat up, breathing hard, sweat creating streaks on his dirty face. "I can get myself back to the lodge."

"I'm taking you back," Elijah said.

Devin looked at Jo, then nodded, obviously concluding that Elijah was a better bet than a no-nonsense Secret Service agent.

Elijah turned to Jo. "You can go on and finish your hike."

"I'm not hiking." She settled her federal-agent gaze on Devin. "Did you spend the night up here? With Nora?"

He wiped his forehead with the back of his wrist, smearing dirt and sweat. "Why? She hasn't done anything to upset the Secret Service, has she?"

"Have you seen her?"

"No."

"Yes, you have."

"Technically, no, I haven't. And it doesn't matter. She wants to be alone." Devin got unsteadily to his feet, groaning in pain, but shaking off any help from Elijah. "She didn't tell me that. As I said, I never saw her. But she's okay. She's just getting away from everyone. Me, included."

"How do you know if you didn't speak to her?" Jo asked sharply.

"I just do." Devin stared at the water and shivered once. "I followed her last night and camped nearby. I'm not sure she even knew I was there. She was gone when I woke up."

"Then you weren't invited—"

"I'm getting out of here. I don't have to answer any more of your questions."

He took a couple of steps up the hillside, limping. Elijah hoisted his backpack on his shoulder. "Let's get your pack," he said, falling in behind Devin.

"I'll get it later." He stumbled and yelled, swearing, then continued up the hill.

"He's hurt," Jo said tightly behind Elijah. "And he's got attitude."

Elijah glanced down at her, noted her mix of concern and irritation. "Pain will do that," he said. "I'll find out what I can. Meantime, you should come with me back to the lodge. You don't need to be out here alone and run the risk of having to be rescued yourself."

If she wanted to argue with him, she didn't. "I'll check the campsite and see if I can pick up Nora's trail." She scrutinized him a moment. "I'm not missing anything, am I? You didn't come up here last night, did you?"

"Nope." He adjusted his pack. "I stayed in my toasty-warm bed thinking about you a couple hundred yards away in your toasty-warm bed."

"My bed wasn't warm." But she obviously regretted her words as soon as they were out of her mouth. "Never mind. Can you get Devin back to the lodge by yourself?"

"Yes, but I'd rather you came with us."

"Don't worry about me."

"What about Rigby? Any idea what he's up to?"

"None. He could be on a different mountain altogether, or sitting in town drinking coffee. I'll have a look around and meet you back at the lodge. I have my cell phone, Elijah. It should work out here. I'm wasting time."

He didn't know why he felt such a protective impulse toward her. It'd happened that morning, too, when he'd spotted Rigby at her place.

It wasn't as if Jo Harper couldn't take care of herself.

"Suit yourself," he said, and fell in beside Devin.

* * *

When they reached his truck, Elijah yanked open the passenger door, grabbed Devin around the waist and heaved him up onto the seat. Not that he appreciated the help. "I could have done it," he said, sullen now.

Elijah ignored him and went around to the driver's side. Devin had managed the few easier stretches of the trail down to the lane with little difficulty. On the steeper sections, he moaned, swore, complained—as if that gave him energy—and yet refused any assistance. When he stumbled, Elijah steadied him as best he could and let go.

"I can drive my own truck."

"You're not driving your truck," Elijah said.

Five minutes later, he pulled into the lodge and parked as close to the shop as he could. Devin was out of the truck, stumbling for the walk, before Elijah had a chance to get the key out of the ignition.

The kid was getting on his nerves.

"If A.J. sees you," he said, catching up with him, "he might just call the police. You know that, right?"

"Yeah. Let him. I haven't done anything wrong."

Devin limped to the front door of the shop, dug a key out of his jeans pocket and, his hands shaking now, fumbled around with it before managing to get it in the lock.

"You're a mess, Devin," Elijah said.

"I guess you should have left well enough alone and worked on your house today, then, huh?"

Devin pushed open the door and went inside, heading straight for the stairs. He hung on to the railing all the way up. Elijah spotted him, but he managed to get into his room and collapse on his unmade bed, his legs hanging off the end.

Elijah glanced around the messy room but saw nothing to indicate Devin had lied about spending the night as Nora Asher's personal Musketeer. A large multi-day pack was leaned up against the side of his dresser.

He turned back to Devin. "You should elevate your leg."

"It's fine."

"Devin…"

"All right. I'll elevate my damn leg." He scooted backward, pulling his legs up onto the bed, and tucked a pillow under his injured leg. "There. Happy?"

"Do you hurt anywhere else?"

He rolled his eyes. "No. You saw what happened. I just slipped."

"On purpose?"

"Why would I bust myself up on purpose?"

"A diversion. So I'd find you and be forced to help you, and Nora would have a chance to get a head start."

"Why would she want a head start, especially if she knew it was you? You're her idol. She has a big crush on you."

"She took off by herself yesterday. You'd think if she had a crush on me, she'd have come to me after she got the bad news about her stepfather." Then again, Elijah figured he wasn't one to be trying to make sense of how Nora Asher thought. "Sure you're not helping her avoid people?"

Devin's expression gave Elijah his answer. The kid was tortured by whatever was going on with Nora, and he was completely at a loss as to what to do. He hadn't given her a head start.

"You don't trust anyone, do you? Here's the thing." Elijah went very still and gave Devin a moment to absorb his tone, his body language, and understand how serious he was. "I know you haven't told us everything about April. I also know you don't steal." He paused, but Devin didn't speak or meet his eye. "And I know you're worried about Nora."

Devin just took in a breath and stared out the window.

"You were worried before her stepfather was killed. What's going on, Devin?"

"Nothing."

"You want to help her, don't you? Then talk to me. I'm not the law. I'm not family."

"Okay, yeah, I'm worried about her. A lot's going on. Nora doesn't like her father's fiancée. Her stepfather just got run over like a bug. I'm being framed for stealing money."

"Are you suggesting they're all connected?"

"I'm not suggesting anything. I'm just saying."

"Does Nora have a specific reason for not liking Melanie?"

"Instincts. I don't know. For one thing, she's a lot younger than Nora's father."

"Gold digger?"

"I don't think that's it. She has her own business. Nora's father comes from an old-money family, and he's a Washington insider. I'm guessing Melanie wants that world."

For eighteen, Devin had keen insight into people. "So Nora's afraid that Melanie's using her father?"

"Yeah."

Elijah eyed him skeptically. "It's more than that, isn't it?"

Devin squirmed, uncomfortable with the question.

"Devin?"

He glanced at Elijah. "I'm not some enemy combatant you pulled out of a cave." But he slumped immediately after the words were out. "Sorry. That was a real jackass thing to say."

Elijah didn't respond.

"You've been on my case since you got back here. I'm

sorry about your father. As sorry as anyone. I know you feel guilty because you were hardly ever around, but I saw him all the time." Tears spilled down his cheeks, but he brushed them angrily with the back of one hand. "Think I *wanted* to find him frozen up on the mountain like a dead porcupine? Think that made me feel good? He treated me like his own son."

"It must have been rough." Elijah didn't react openly to Devin's emotion. "I'm sorry for that. I wish it had been me in your place."

"Yeah. I know. Sorry, too." He sniffled, more under control. "Getting shot—it was bad?"

"Not great."

"Makes sliding under a stupid boulder seem like nothing." He gritted his teeth and leaned forward, pulling up his muddy pant leg. "My ankle's seizing up. I need some ice—"

"I'll get some from the lodge," Elijah said. "Don't move. When I get back, I want to hear everything that you and Nora are up to. Start to finish. Understood?"

"Okay. I'll stay put. Just get me the ice. You and Jo Harper—hell, Elijah." Devin gave a weak laugh. "The military and the law on my case. But I'll tell you everything."

Elijah stopped at the door. "Including why you were on the north side of the mountain in April."

Devin looked away and sank deeper into his pillow. "I miss your dad," he said quietly.

"I do, too, kid."

Elijah left, barely aware of the cold as he went up the walk. He climbed onto the terrace and slipped into the dining room. No one was around. He ducked back to the kitchen and helped himself to ice from the freezer and a couple of dish towels from the sink. A.J. had fancy ice packs somewhere, but Elijah was satisfied with ice cubes and towels.

He headed back outside. The wind had picked up. He thought of Jo up on the mountain by herself. They were violating basic hiking protocols, but at least it kept them occupied. He didn't think he could stand just kissing her again. It would lead to something else, and that was probably dumber than hiking in the cold alone.

It would be best if Nora decided one night in the wilderness was enough, but Elijah didn't think that would happen.

A.J. intercepted him halfway back to the shop. "You wanted to talk, Elijah? What's up? I got your message."

Elijah frowned. "What message?"

"Didn't you call? The front-desk clerk said you did, and I should find you. I was tied up with the kids, or I'd have gotten out here sooner."

*Hell.*

Elijah ran back to the shop and took the stairs three at a time, but he was too late. Devin was gone. So was his multi-day pack.

He charged back outside. A.J. gave him a tense look. Elijah sighed, calming himself. "We need to talk," he said, and gave his brother the rundown of what had happened up at the falls.

"If Devin's injured—"

"He's not so injured he couldn't sneak off." Elijah felt his thigh tingle and blamed the scar tissue from the bullet he took in April. He breathed, willing his muscles to relax. "He probably ducked into the woods. I can try to find him, but he's a kid, A.J. I'm not going to hunt him down."

"Here comes the law," A.J. said, nodding up toward the road. Jo was walking toward the lodge at a brisk pace with Kyle Rigby right behind her.

Devin could have spotted them from the window in his room and decided to bolt. Had he run into Rigby on the mountain? Or was he just seizing the moment and never meant to talk? Either way, Elijah didn't like the situation.

A.J. sighed. "I can't help it," he said. "I guess it's because I haven't been around her all that much lately, but it's still hard for me to think of Jo as a Secret Service agent."

Elijah blew out a breath. "Tell me about it."

"Probably hard for her to think of you as a Special Forces soldier."

"Probably."

"Elijah?"

"I'm doomed, A.J."

His brother nodded grimly, still watching Jo and Rigby. "You always have been when it comes to her."

"Pop—"

"He knew. He understood. Why do you think he left her the lakefront property? It wasn't to stick it to us, Elijah." Just the slightest spark of humor crept into A.J.'s eyes. "It was to put her next door to you."

"Conniving old bastard," Elijah said with affection.

"Yep. That he was."

"A.J., Devin hasn't told us everything. Maybe what he's holding back doesn't matter, but he needs to tell us."

"For his sake," A.J. said.

Elijah nodded and gritted his teeth as he noticed Hannah Shay's heap of a car coming up the road.

# *Eighteen*

Jo hooked Devin's daypack on one shoulder as Kyle Rigby veered off toward the map sign. He'd parked at the lodge and walked over to the east trailhead, where Nora had left her car. As far as Jo could tell, he was killing time and just waiting for Nora to turn up on her own. He could collect his check from Thomas and go home. She'd run into him on her way back from the falls. She'd found Devin's pack in the trees where he'd slipped, and decided to skip checking the campsite. There was no point. Nora would be on her way by now. Instead, Jo had taken the shortcut trail down from the falls. It ended in a quiet lane, where she'd discovered Devin's truck, which explained both his and Elijah's presence at the falls. The lane was almost a mile down the ridge road, but an easy, reasonably level walk back to the lodge.

As she approached the shop, Jo noticed Hannah Shay standing toe-to-toe with A.J. and Elijah, her arms crossed on her chest as she spoke to them in her steady, determined manner. "I'm not afraid of you Camerons," she said. "I never have been. If you have any complaints about Devin, you can call the police and tell them. I believe in my brother."

A.J. was impassive. "Go home, Hannah."

She didn't back down. "Devin isn't obsessed with Nora Asher, and he didn't cause your father's death. That was a horrible tragedy, and I'm sorry. Devin actually did you all a favor by finding him." Her control faltered slightly. "And he doesn't steal. We grew up poor, but that didn't turn us into criminals."

But A.J. was just as tightly controlled as she was and looked at her in that uncompromising way he had. "Money's missing from the café, isn't it?"

Hannah dropped her arms to her sides. "That's none of your business, A.J."

"Come on," Elijah said gently, easing in between her and his older brother. "I'll walk you back to your car."

"I'm perfectly capable of walking back on my own."

He raised his eyebrows. "Prickly, Hannah."

"I'm sorry." She drew in a breath and spoke directly to Elijah, ignoring A.J. "I believe in my brother. Period. There's nothing else to say."

Elijah started to speak, but Hannah spun around and headed back toward her car.

Jo jumped in front of the Cameron brothers before either one could move. "Let me talk to her, okay?"

"I'll be at the lodge," A.J. said tightly. "Elijah?"

He didn't respond immediately, then gave a curt nod and joined A.J.

Jo caught up with Hannah at the edge of the parking lot. "Hannah," she said, "have you talked with Devin?"

"Are you asking as a friend, Jo, or are you going to show me your badge?"

"I'm sorry I was hard on you last night," Jo said simply.

"I can take it." But she softened slightly. "I've left a couple of messages on Devin's cell phone. I don't know if he's gotten them. I haven't heard from him. Elijah said he wasn't hurt badly. That's true, isn't it? Elijah wouldn't not tell me if something was seriously wrong, right?"

"Right. Devin's not hurt badly. He has some scrapes and bruises, that's all." Jo frowned suddenly. "Isn't he here?"

"He took off on Elijah."

No wonder he and A.J. were in rotten moods. Jo asked, "When?"

"Just before I got here. Apparently Elijah had gone to get some ice. Devin hasn't done anything wrong. A.J. and Elijah can't just hunt him like he's a rabid dog."

Hannah was a gentle soul, but she was proud—and she wasn't afraid of anyone, especially when it came to defending her two younger brothers. Jo had to admire Hannah's belief in Devin and her grit in standing up to the Cameron brothers.

"A.J. and Elijah are still here," Jo pointed out. "They haven't gone after anyone."

Hannah looked out toward the mountain. "Nora wasn't thinking clearly yesterday, obviously, after the shock of her stepfather's death. I'm sure Devin's just trying to be a friend to her. That other business I mentioned last night. Whatever they're up to, I'm sure it's innocent."

"Do you have any idea where they could be?" Jo asked.

Hannah tightened her unzipped jacket around her, hesitated a split second, then, without a word, returned to the walk and headed straight up to the map sign. Jo followed, noticing that Rigby was now at the lodge's main entrance, talking with A.J. and Elijah.

Hannah pointed to the section of the map marking the remote north side of Cameron Mountain. "Devin found Drew's body in this area here," she said, calm and serious. "Native Vermonter that I am, I'm not much on wilderness hiking. Day hikes are fine, but I don't need to spend days tramping through the woods. Devin's a lot like the Camerons. I think that's why he and Drew got along so well."

"I'm glad they did, Hannah. Is that why Devin was able to find Drew in April?"

Crossing her arms on her chest, Hannah stared at the whirl of lines on the map. "Devin helped Drew with something up on the north side of the mountain last fall. Apparently it's where the Camerons first settled when they came to Vermont. Most of the land was cleared back then. Devin didn't tell me exactly what he did. He said he really doesn't know what Drew was up to."

"He didn't tell the police about this project after Drew died?"

"He answered all their questions truthfully. Drew asked Devin not to tell anyone. Whatever he was up to was meant as a surprise."

A lawyerlike response, Jo thought. "How long have you known?"

"A few weeks. He'd gotten pulled over for a broken taillight. This was right after a fight he had outside the café one night. A couple of guys were picking on Toby, and Devin let them have it. He fell apart later and finally told me about Drew. He felt guilty—as if he'd violated Drew's trust. I promised I wouldn't say anything. Now…that might have been a mistake."

"You all have a lot to deal with," Jo said.

Hannah faced her without a hint self-pity. "I never tried to pretend I was anything but Devin and Toby's older sister. We're a family, but I'm well aware that my brothers grew up without a mother and father."

So had Hannah, when it came down to it. Jo handed her Devin's daypack. "You might want to hang on to this. He dropped it when he fell. Does Nora know about his and Drew's project?"

"No one does that I'm aware of. It's a haul up there."

"But that's why Devin was on the north side of the mountain in April. That's why he was able to find Drew."

"He said it never occurred to him Drew would go up there at that time of year. He was so sure he was wrong. Otherwise he would have told the search teams."

Jo thought of her own unsettling conversation with Drew two weeks earlier and understood.

"It hasn't been good since then," Hannah said quietly.

"Have you talked to this Rigby guy?" Jo asked, nodding to him as he edged their way.

"Yes, briefly, earlier this morning." Hannah tightened her jacket around her. "I didn't tell him about Drew's project. I haven't told the Camerons, either. No one, Jo, except you."

Jo acknowledged the statement with a nod.

"Look, I should go," Hannah said. "I'll let you know if I hear from Devin. I have nothing to hide." She glared back toward the lodge.

"Something happened to that money, Hannah. Do you think Nora—"

"No, I don't. I don't know what happened to it."

Hannah headed off briskly, in the opposite the direction of

Rigby. Jo studied the map with its detailed designations of trails, streams, knolls, gullies, sags and peaks. The north side of Cameron Mountain bled into a remote wilderness area with few recreational trails. It wouldn't be a good place for an inexperienced hiker like Nora Asher to get lost.

"It's beautiful country up here," Rigby said as he approached the map. "I'll say that. I'm guessing, based on this morning's festivities, that Nora is sticking close by. Hannah Shay have any idea where her brother took off to?"

Jo shook her head. "There's no reason to think he's a danger to Nora."

"Maybe not, but if anything happens to her, he'll be the first one police will want to talk to." He squinted out toward the mountain. "It could be a tad warmer for my tastes. I'll grab my pack out of my car and get moving. From what I've been able to learn about her, Nora's emotional, but if she set up camp and got through the night, she's got her act together. That's a good sign."

"If you need assistance, or if you feel she's in trouble—"

"I know what to do. Keep me posted, Agent Harper."

She let him go and returned to the lodge, scooping herself a bowl of piping-hot chili bubbling in an iron pot in the dining room. A month ago, at the height of foliage season, the lodge would have been bustling with guests. Now the place was almost empty, just a handful of diners enjoying a late lunch and the views.

She took her chili out to the fireplace in the lobby, where Elijah and A.J. were on their feet and still looking aggravated. She gave an exaggerated shiver. "Brr. I forget how cold it is here in November."

"You should come back to Black Falls more often," A.J. said.

"I should. Your wife and I could become best friends and give you Cameron boys a hard time."

"What is it you want, Jo?"

A barrel of laughs A.J. was. But Jo didn't blame him for his mood. "Answers," she said. "The three of us need to work together. We're on the same side."

A.J.'s eyes narrowed, reminding her of his father. "Are we?"

She debated a moment, then relayed what Hannah had told her about Drew's enlisting Devin's help with some project on the north side of Cameron Mountain. Elijah and A.J. listened without interruption. When she finished, she added, "I'll bet your father finally found that old cellar hole he'd been looking for all these years. Or some old cellar hole."

"Devin should have given that information to the police," A.J. said.

Or at least to Drew's children, Jo thought. But she said diplomatically, "I imagine it's been hard for him to have this on his mind. Provided he didn't actually lie, he's in the clear as far as the police are concerned. Hannah says he told the truth."

"He just left out what in hell Pop was doing up there. Do you know how many times I've asked myself—" A.J. broke off. "Never mind. He had his chance to tell us, too, and he didn't."

"Hannah says he wanted whatever he was doing to be a surprise."

Elijah's eyes darkened and he looked at his brother. "I'm leaving. A.J.?"

"I'll let you know if Devin or Nora show up."

Short of finding a pair of handcuffs or shooting him, there wasn't much Jo could do to stop Elijah. So she plopped down on a warm, comfortable chair in front of the fire and dipped a spoon into her chili. "You're thinking I should go back to the lake and clean the cobwebs out of my cabins, aren't you, A.J.?"

"I imagine your boss back in Washington would approve."

He had a point there. But A.J. abandoned her, too, with a curt goodbye.

Jo set her chili onto a rustic oak table arranged with brochures, guidebooks and a cheerful autumnal display of pumpkins, mums and little figurines of wild turkeys. Lauren's doing, again. A.J. would have left a stack of kindling there.

With her feet as close to the flames as she could get them without sliding out of her chair or setting herself on fire, Jo called Thomas Asher's cell number. "Why'd you hire Kyle Rigby?" she asked when Thomas picked up. "And who is he?"

"He's an objective professional—"

"A licensed investigator?"

"He's acting as a friend."

"Is he a friend? You're paying him, aren't you?"

"Jo, why are you so defensive? I thought you'd appreciate not having to take on Nora as your responsibility. Melanie and I are on our way. We're at the airport now—"

"D.C. or up here?"

"We're at Reagan National. We'll be in Black Falls after dark. The Whittakers have invited us to stay with them. Alex and Carolyn loved it there. I…" His voice caught, reminding Jo that he'd lost a friend, never mind his and Alex Bruni's complicated history. "Carolyn's on her way home. I can't imagine what she must be going through right now. For Nora to act out—" He broke off, then said more calmly, "I don't approve of her solo camping trip, of course, but Kyle has assured me there's no reason to sound the alarm."

"How did you find him?"

"Melanie recommended him. They met skiing in Colorado last winter and exchanged business cards. It's strange how that can happen. Serendipity, she calls it."

"Then you've never met him?"

Thomas didn't answer.

"You haven't," Jo said.

"He can handle the Vermont terrain and find my daughter. That's all I care about. Not that I don't trust you, Jo, but you're not objective. You're from Black Falls. You have preconceived ideas about the people there."

Jo leaned forward in her chair, the flames hot on her face. "Thomas, do you suspect someone up here was involved with Ambassador Bruni's death?"

"No. Good heavens, Jo. Listen, our flight's boarding. I have to go."

Jo decided not to tell him about Devin and the missing money, his friendship with Nora, taking off on Elijah. Let Rigby tell him what he knew. She wasn't working for either one of them.

She finished her chili and returned her empty bowl to the dining room, then headed back outside and checked down at the shop. But it was closed and locked, and there was no sign of Devin. No sign of anything.

Had Elijah let Devin give him the slip and get away with it? Where was Devin going?

And what was Nora's plan?

Were she and Devin together? Planning to meet somewhere? Avoiding each other?

Jo hoped they both would hike down the mountain before Thomas arrived in Vermont later tonight.

In fact, maybe they were on their way down now. But she didn't think so.

* * *

An hour later, after hiking back down to her cabin for her car, Jo stood in the kitchen of her childhood, watching her father cut up apples—northern spies, a late variety that kept well—into a bubbling pot on the stove. Her mother was spending the day at the outlets in Manchester. Her grandmother was reading a book in the front room.

The smell of cooking apples filled the air, as it had every autumn in the rambling old Harper farmhouse for as long as Jo remembered.

Retirement seemed to agree with her father, but she knew he was still tapped into the goings-on in town. She seldom discussed her work with him. But Alex Bruni's likely murder yesterday and his stepdaughter's flight—or whatever it was—onto Cameron Mountain had nothing to do with her work.

Charlie Neal's talk of assassins did, but only peripherally, because he was trying to get back into her good graces after his prank. What he didn't understand was that he didn't need to be in her good graces. He just needed to be safe.

She grabbed a paring knife and an extra cutting board and lifted an apple out of the sink. As she cut it into pieces, she ran everything past her father—except the part about kissing Elijah Cameron. That, she decided, wasn't anything Wes Harper, former town chief of police, needed to know. Whether he could guess on his own or not was another question.

He listened without interruption, then batted ideas around with her, asked her questions, examined her options. But he offered no advice.

Finally, he put down his knife and leaned back against the counter. His hair was almost white now, but he was still the vibrant, strong man she'd loved—and battled—her entire life.

Neither of her parents had wanted her to move away. No matter how many visits she made back to Black Falls, she wasn't down the road like Beth or Zack. They'd hated her postings in faraway places and had been relieved at her assignment to Washington eighteen months ago.

She'd never told them about Drew's visit in April.

She told her father now, because somehow, she thought, it was a part of what was happening.

"I can't help you with that one," he said. "Drew didn't tell me about his comings and goings."

"The investigation into his death—"

"I wasn't a part of it."

"But you heard things," she said.

"There's a difference between something that raises the hairs on the back of your neck and something you can prove." His deep green eyes settled on her. "Drew Cameron regretted what he did fifteen years ago—the way he did it, anyway. He knew he had to draw the line with Elijah, but he was sorry he hurt you in the process."

"Drew wasn't the one who hurt me," she said.

"He embarrassed you. I'd have handled things differently, but it might have been worse. I don't know. I remember I couldn't think straight. I had you and Elijah on your way to Las Vegas. Not Drew—he knew you were sticking close to Black Falls."

"Elijah and I just weren't meant to be."

"That's for you two to decide. It always was, even back then." He set his knife on top of a stack of apple peels and lowered the heat under the pot. "Elijah's disciplined, and in my book, he's a hero. But I don't know if he'll find a place for himself back here the way he always thought he would.

Sometimes it's hard to come back home. His experiences might have changed Black Falls forever for him."

Jo nodded, dropping her apples into the pot. "Maybe so."

"But don't be fooled," her father said. "There's a lot of the old Elijah left."

Good, she thought, remembering how much she'd loved the old Elijah—his energy, his stubbornness, his sense of loyalty and justice. His courage. Drew and her father had focused on his youth and inability to make a living—and her oft-stated desire to get out of Black Falls.

But it was never just that they were afraid of him ruining her life. They were also afraid of her ruining his.

"Even before the military, Elijah was mission oriented," her father said. "He set his sights on something, and he got it. He has questions about his father's death, Jo. He'll find the answers."

On her way out, Jo thanked her father and extracted a promise that he'd save her a jar of applesauce. She stopped in the doorway. "Do you trust Elijah, Dad?" she asked.

"With my life." He reached for a pot holder. "With your life."

Unspoken was her father's worry—an old worry—that he didn't know how far Elijah would go, how many rules he would break, to get his answers.

# Nineteen

"*You're playing with fire,*" Moose said in that way he had—direct, sardonic, insightful. He stood next to Grit on a narrow, curving Georgetown side street. It was another warm, gloomy November afternoon inside the Beltway of the nation's capital.

Grit nodded. "I know. My left shoe feels like it's on too tight. The right one—the one with a real foot in it—feels fine. I fell in the shower this morning. I have 877 PT appointments coming up. Myrtle's right. Life sucks."

"*One day at a time, my friend.*"

"Scares me when you're nice. It must mean I'm even more pathetic than I think I am."

"*Long day.*"

"Yeah. And it's only half over."

Grit had been talking to people who didn't necessarily like to be talked to. He'd gotten kicked out of a few offices and buildings, but he didn't really care.

When he glanced to his left again, a compact, buff man with classic good looks had taken Moose's place on the Georgetown street. Early forties, Grit decided. Fed of some kind. Just a question of which kind. Probably Secret Service, since one of the places Grit had been that morning was Jo Harper's office. He'd been politely kicked out.

His cell phone trilled.

The fed gave a slight incline of his head. "Go ahead. Answer it."

Grit did, and a kid's voice said, "Ask Myrtle Smith about the Russian diplomat killed in London in August. He was poisoned."

It had to be Charlie Neal. "How did—"

"I can't talk. I have to take a calculus test in a few minutes. I know you and Ms. Smith are investigating Ambassador Bruni's murder."

"And you know this how?"

"Sergeant Cameron told me."

"Bet he didn't. And my cell-phone number? How did you get it?"

"My sister Marissa was almost killed two months ago," Charlie said in a near whisper. "Jo saved her life. Special Agent Harper, I mean."

Grit was very aware of the armed, ass-kicking federal agent standing next to him. "I haven't heard about—"

"You wouldn't," Charlie said knowledgeably, then added, "Supposedly it was an accident. I don't think so."

"You're not a detective, are you?"

"The Russian, though. That was flat-out murder."

"Hang up. Go take your test and relax. Let people do their jobs. Got it?"

"Sure, sure. You'll ask Myrtle?"

Charlie Neal hung up before Grit could answer. He flipped his cell phone shut and smiled innocently at the fed next to him. "All done."

"I'm Deputy Special Agent in Charge Mark Francona," the fed said. "Jo Harper's boss. This is the building where she lives. Who are you?"

Grit could tell Francona already knew. "Her boyfriend."

"Wrong."

"I'm too cute for her?"

Francona waited.

"Ryan Taylor, sir."

"You talked to some of my people earlier, Petty Officer Taylor."

"I've been given an impossible mission."

"You SEALs thrive on impossible missions." Francona nodded to the ivy-covered brick building. "She has the ground-level apartment. She objects if anyone says it's the basement. I guess there's a difference. An old guy from her hometown stopped by to see her in the spring. They went and looked at the cherry blossoms together."

"Must be something. The cherry blossoms."

"You've never seen them?"

"No, sir. I arrived here after they'd bloomed."

Francona's expression tightened. "I'm sorry about your leg, Petty Officer Taylor. And I'm sorry about Petty Officer Ferrerra." He spoke crisply, with sincerity but no pity. "I want to thank you for your service."

"A privilege to serve, sir." Grit had to work at keeping any sorrow and self-pity out of his voice. It'd be easier if his leg didn't hurt. If Moose would quit bugging him. If Charlie Neal hadn't called and Alexander Bruni hadn't been killed and Myrtle was being straight with him. And if it wasn't November in Washington. "Drew Cameron was the name of the old guy. But you know that, right?"

"He died two weeks later on a mountain in Vermont."

"Ever been to Vermont?"

Irritation flickered across Francona's face. "No."

"Me, neither. I'm a Southern boy. My family makes the best tupelo honey—"

"Drew Cameron's son Elijah is a decorated Green Beret. Master sergeant. He was almost killed in April." A half beat's pause for the fed's eyes to narrow. "So were you."

"He's army. I'm navy." Grit kept his voice even. "We did some stuff together. Went through a bad night together. That's it. It's got nothing to do with why you and I are standing here."

"You, Elijah Cameron and Special Agent Harper want to know if there's a connection between the death of Elijah's father in April and the hit-and-run that killed Alexander Bruni yesterday."

"Is there?"

Francona didn't answer, instead nodded to Harper's apartment. "You'd think a Vermonter would have greenery in her window, wouldn't you?" He glanced at Grit. "What's Jo to Elijah Cameron?"

Jo this time. Not Special Agent Harper. "The girl who got away. He has amends to make to her. He knows it, and so does she."

"Does she have amends to make to anyone?"

"Herself."

"For not following him into the army," Francona said.

"That's in her file, or are you guessing?"

"I don't guess. I also don't believe anything happens because it's meant to. I believe in cause and effect."

"You wouldn't want to tell me what went on with Marissa Neal two months ago, would you?" Grit knew it was the sort of statement that could get him thrown behind bars somewhere, but he didn't care.

Francona regarded him through half-closed eyes. "People tell you things, don't they, Petty Officer Taylor?"

"You're not. I checked out Marissa on the Internet after I saw Special Agent Harper's video. Think she would go to a movie with a sailor?"

Francona didn't seem to consider that funny. "Going to tell me who called you just now?"

Grit figured Charlie wouldn't make it through calculus class if he ratted him out, and he had a test to take. "No."

"Stay in touch," Francona said, and walked away.

Thirty minutes later, Grit met Myrtle at a popular restaurant near the White House. He sat across from her in a dark wood booth with comfortable red-cushioned seats. She'd called right after Francona had left saying she had a hankering for crab cakes. She already had a glass of iced tea in front of her and had put in her order, but she clearly wasn't in a good mood. "I've been turning over rocks all over town. You didn't tell me Bruni's stepdaughter is in the same town where Jo Harper is from," she said. "Harper's there now. Did you see her video?"

"Kid's lucky she didn't shoot him for real."

"Is she in Vermont because of Bruni's murder?"

"He was killed after she arrived."

"If she's undercover—"

"She'd have found an easier way to get sent home besides getting shot in the ass by a hundred airsoft pellets, never mind what she said about the veep's kid." He wasn't getting into his or Elijah's conversations with Charlie Neal. Myrtle was still a reporter, and Grit figured she was on a need-to-know basis.

She picked up her tea. It didn't look as if it had alcohol in it, but Grit couldn't know for sure. "Fair point," she said, "but if there's anything going on in Black Falls, Harper will run into it. She's the type. She's the one who got you involved in this?"

"I've never met her."

There was a moment's silence as Myrtle drank some of her tea and set the glass down as a waiter appeared. "What do you want to eat?" she asked Grit.

"Nothing."

She looked at the waiter. "Bring him some crab cakes." He retreated, obviously wanting to please Myrtle more than Grit, and she tapped two fingers on the table. "I can waste time scratching the itch, Grit, or you can just tell me. Who has you looking into the death of a prominent ambassador?"

He thought of about twenty things he could to do shut her up, then said, "A friend of mine. You're going to want a name, aren't you?"

"Not 'going to.' Do."

Grit debated. He didn't need Myrtle spinning her wheels figuring out Elijah's name. "Elijah Cameron. This is off the record."

"What'll he do if I print his name, hunt me down?"

It was Grit's turn to be silent.

Myrtle sighed. "You guys. Harper and Cameron?"

"Love-hate thing since preschool."

"Yin-yang. Okay. Anything going on up there?"

"Alex Bruni's stepdaughter took off into the mountains after she learned about her stepfather's death."

"I don't like that," Myrtle said.

"You got kids?"

"Why are you asking, Grit?"

"I just wondered if you and the dead Russian in London got it on—"

"You bastard." She didn't raise her voice. "I'm a split second from throwing my drink in your face."

"Question asked and answered. Want to tell me about him?"

"No."

"He had enemies?"

Her crab cakes arrived. Grit's would be a minute. Myrtle dug in, ignoring him.

He settled back against the comfortable booth. "We all have enemies, Myrtle, but not all of us have enemies willing to hire assassins to poison our soup."

"It was his toothpaste," she said. "The poison was in his toothpaste."

"He didn't notice?"

"He didn't have a chance. It was a fast death." She snapped her fingers. "Just like that. I don't know what kind of poison. Getting anything out of the Brits is next to impossible."

Grit considered a half-dozen options for a fast death by poisoned toothpaste. Most were ones Myrtle probably had considered herself by now. "So your interest in Bruni's murder isn't professional."

"No, Grit. It's not. I don't give a flying rip if I ever write this story or get paid for uncovering whoever these assassins are. I'm freelancing these days. I don't answer to anyone but myself. If there are paid killers out there, I want them found. That's it. Then I'm done."

The waiter brought Grit's crab cakes. He wasn't hungry, but Myrtle stuck her fork out at him and told him to eat up.

He saw that she'd cleaned her plate. "Like those crab cakes, do you?"

"I didn't even taste them."

"You can have mine."

She shook her head. "No. Eat. Your pants hang on your ass. You need to put on some weight."

Grit knew he wasn't getting out of there alive if he didn't eat. He picked up his fork and had a bite. "Ever have tupelo honey, Myrtle?"

"Honey's honey."

"No, it isn't. True tupelo honey is the only honey that doesn't crystallize. It's produced from the tupelo gum tree that grows in the river swamps of northwest Florida." He set down his fork. Half a crab cake would have to satisfy her. "Come on. Walk with me to the White House. Tell me what it was like when it was being built. You remember, right?"

"You're a jerk, Grit."

Moose materialized next to him and laughed. *"Old Myrtle's got your number."*

Grit ignored him and walked out into the late-autumn gloom of Washington. He wanted to take off his fake leg and climb into bed with a fifth of scotch, but Myrtle paid their tab and joined him.

"Let's go," she said without looking at him.

Moose blew out a breath. *"She's hurting in ways you don't understand and don't want to know."*

"Aren't we all?"

Grit walked easily, his prosthetic giving him no trouble. Not that walking was the same as before that bad night in April. Not that anything was the same.

He stood with Myrtle at the tall, black-iron fence on Pennsylvania Avenue and looked out at the White House and its still lush green lawn. He thought about assassins and high-profile targets like Ambassador Alexander Bruni, and he remembered Elijah, covered in blood, those piercing blue eyes of his connecting with Grit's just for an instant as he'd said, "If I don't make it, tell Jo it wasn't her fault." He'd tied on his tourniquet. "Tell her I loved her."

Jo Harper.

Definitely the girl who got away.

*"The girl Cameron let get away,"* Moose said.

"Yeah," Grit said. "Well. Those things happen."

Myrtle looked at him, the lashes of her lavender eyes glistening with tears, but she said nothing.

# *Twenty*

Elijah climbed over an old stone wall that early farmers had built when they'd cleared the land to till, and thrashed through a thirty-yard strip of woods to the pond by the Whittaker guesthouse. No cars were parked in the small turnaround, but he'd driven past it and left his truck around a curve just down the road.

Best not to draw attention to his presence, given what he had in mind.

The mallards weren't on the still, gray water. Elijah supposed they could have headed south.

He hadn't been home for a full winter in Vermont in a lot of years. He used to dream about snowshoeing, cross-country skiing, working on his house, reading by the fire. Now that he was healed, he had options available to him, in and out of the military, that used his particular skills.

His family had ideas about what he should do. A.J. had invited him to work at the lodge. All four siblings were owners, but A.J. had always handled the day-to-day operations. Black Falls Lodge was his baby.

Rose wanted him to train a search dog.

Sean wanted him out in California—that was where the money was, he'd said.

None of his options would matter, Elijah thought, if he spent a chunk of the coming winter in jail awaiting trial for breaking and entering.

His cell phone vibrated. He checked the readout, and answered.

"Where are you?" Grit asked.

"Looking at ducks and avoiding arrest. You?"

"White House. I wasn't invited in."

"Just a matter of time."

"Charlie has my phone number," Grit said bluntly. "Jo's boss is on high alert. Myrtle's Russian lover had his toothpaste poisoned. And Jo saved Marissa Neal's life two months ago. Hang on."

Elijah gripped the phone, impatient.

Grit was back. "It occurred to me the Secret Service agents on the other side of the fence read my lips when I said M-a-r-i-" Grit started to spell out Marissa's name.

Elijah cut him off. "If you get locked up, Grit, let's see if we can share a jail cell. I'll bring paper, and we can write a book on what not to do after you get chewed up in battle. How did Jo save Charlie's big sister?"

"She and friends borrowed a cottage in the Shenandoah Mountains for a weekend getaway. Marissa is a history teacher at Charlie's private school, by the way."

"What happened at the cottage?" Elijah asked.

"The gas stove blew up. Our Jo dived into the flames, basically, although she wasn't burned, and saved Marissa from certain maiming or even death. Risked her life."

"Was Charlie there?"

"No."

"Is the incident under investigation?"

"You know, I'm brave, honorable and true, but I don't walk up to Secret Service agents and ask them if an unreported fire I'm not supposed to know about that nearly killed the eldest daughter of the vice president is under investigation."

"You SEALs are just so damn smart."

"We're missing something," Grit said.

"Yes—"

Grit had already hung up.

Elijah tried the front door of the guesthouse and wasn't surprised to find it unlocked. A small entry with a cold slate floor had a door to the left and a door to the right. He tried both. One was locked, one wasn't. He'd bet real money that the teenager with the romantic view of Vermont had left her door unlocked and the humorless meat her father had hired to look for her had locked his.

An unlocked door wasn't a defense against a charge of breaking and entering, but Elijah figured Nora would either never know or never press charges.

Either way, he went in.

The apartment was decorated with cottage-style furnishings in light green, brown, rust. He couldn't remember if Vivian had said she'd done up the place, but since nothing looked cheap, either she had or Nora had received more financial help from her family than she'd let on. She'd added her own laptop, a flat-screen television and DVDs that included collections of Jane Austen PBS movies, *Dr. Who,* Steve McQueen and Humphrey Bogart. Elijah remembered Nora telling him that she wanted to major in film, but both parents were opposed, on the grounds that she'd only become another Hollywood failure.

"They said I'd just end up as a waitress who could name obscure facts about obscure movies," she'd said with a little laugh that had struck Elijah as entirely fake.

He checked the laptop, but it was password protected. He'd only go so far in his search and decided to move on to the bedroom, its windows offering a view of the duck pond and the woods from which he'd just come. A well-worn stuffed penguin looked forlorn and downright lonely on the pillow of the made bed; it was a reminder of just how young Nora was. Emotionally if not legally, she was straddling childhood and adulthood. She had to negotiate her own expectations with those of her successful parents, navigate the dynamics of a complicated family.

Elijah figured his own father had simplified that age for him by kicking him out.

A couple of skirts and tops on hangers in the closet. Expensive-looking shoes. A dressy coat. He checked the dresser drawers—no hiking clothes left behind.

He returned to the living room and headed to the kitchen at the back of the apartment. He took a quick look around. Milk and eggs in the refrigerator. Dishes clean in the dishwasher. Nothing suggested Nora planned to be gone for more than a few days.

Nothing on Melanie Kendall, the fiancée.

He found a flower-covered notebook journal on the kitchen table. He debated, but he wasn't ready to go so far as to intrude that deeply on Nora's privacy. He'd check the date of the last entry and go from there. But he immediately saw that the journal contained graceful entries of poems and quotes she'd copied, all positive and uplifting. She'd apparently created her own book of inspiration for dark days.

Elijah shut the journal. He'd never been one for inspirational quotes. Reading that stuff made him focus on why he needed uplifting. Easier just to focus on what he needed to do.

He found Nora's cell phone next to her toaster. She could have forgotten it, but he didn't think so. There wasn't much, if any, service in the backcountry, but there was some. He'd explained to his wilderness-skills class how a cell phone could sometimes help searchers find a lost hiker. Nora could have decided not to rely on anything but her own skills.

On the other hand, she could have wanted to make sure no one found her.

Or she could simply not want to talk to anyone.

Elijah checked the screen and saw she had a half-dozen voice messages.

He left the cell phone by the toaster. Whatever Nora's reasoning, if she did get in trouble in the mountains, she'd have to find other ways to save herself. He thought back to what he'd told the class.

Not enough.

He took a key off a hook next to the refrigerator, walked back out to the entry and tried the door to the second apartment, where Rigby was staying. Sure enough, Nora's key worked on that door, too. Elijah went into the combined living room and kitchen done in a style similar to Nora's apartment.

Before he could get started, he heard a car outside and checked a side window. Rigby had pulled into the turnaround. Elijah watched him get out of his car and start up the stone path. Big guy. But Elijah wasn't worried. He continued his check of the small apartment, but he found nothing of interest—no weapons, no notebook filled with detailed plans, not even a laptop.

He found a change of clothes, shaving gear, a pair of new wool socks.

In other words, zip.

He finished up and walked back outside, by which point Rigby was on the stone walk. "I locked the door on my way out," Elijah said, trotting down the porch steps. "Locked Nora's door, too. I'm sure she wouldn't mind if you borrowed her copy of *Pride and Prejudice.*"

"You're a piece of work, aren't you? I've heard a lot about you Camerons."

"All good, I trust. What are you doing back here?"

"I'm running out of daylight. I could search in the dark if I had a credible lead or if I believed Nora was in serious trouble. I went back up the falls trail after I saw you at the lodge. I located Nora's probable campsite—Devin Shay's, too, just down the hill from hers."

"Did you get lost?" Elijah asked with only a trace of sarcasm.

"No. I don't get lost." He nodded to the guesthouse, less combative. "I appreciate your caution. In your place, I'd do the same."

Elijah brushed past him and started back for the duck pond, but not soon enough. Jo pulled into the turnaround and got out of her car, looking like the Secret Service agent she was. She eased over to the stone walk. "What're you boys up to?" she asked coolly.

Rigby shrugged. "Cameron here was just leaving. I gave him my update on Nora Asher. Apparently she's spending another night in the woods." He paused, then said, "Devin Shay, too."

Jo slanted a look at him. "Thomas and his fiancée are on

their way. He said Melanie recommended you. I got the impression you don't know each other that well. Is that accurate?"

"We ended up on the same ski trail in Colorado. I told her to give me a call if she ever needed a hand."

"No contact with her since then?"

"None," Rigby said. "I'm in close touch with Mr. Asher. He and Ms. Kendall are arriving soon. I offered to pick them up, but he's renting a car. It's a long drive from the airport. I guess it'd be hard to put an airport in around here, since there's not much flat land."

"A storm's on the way," Jo said. "Higher elevations could get a good dump of snow. It's not supposed to start until later in the day, but there's a chance it could start earlier."

"I've seen the forecast. Snow should get Nora's attention."

He headed inside, and as soon as the door shut, Jo swooped around at Elijah, her turquoise eyes hot and suspicious. "You just broke into the guesthouse, didn't you?"

"Who says I wasn't invited or didn't hear someone in imminent danger?"

"I do. I know what you've been up to."

"You can be sanctimonious, you know that?"

He tried to make it a joke—a tease—but it must not have worked, because she grabbed his arm. "Did you search my cabin last night, too? Was that you—"

"I expect it was Rigby. You might want to drop the third degree, Jo, and unless you want some real trouble, you'll let go of my arm. That's twice in two days. Yesterday I kissed you. Not without your cooperation, I might add. Today—"

She dropped his arm as if it'd caught fire, and he figured she'd seen something in his eyes that reminded her that not all that much, really, had changed in fifteen years. The pure sexual energy that had always been a problem between them was still there. Well, not always a problem. A *fact* between them.

He smiled. "Thought you'd see the light."

"I should call the damn police on you."

"Go ahead. Your future brother-in-law the state trooper likes me. Call him."

"Scott's not necessarily... Never mind." She breathed out, looked down at the placid water, the ducks visible again, floating under the low-hanging willows. "I don't know why I bite every time you try to tweak me."

"Now, there's an image."

She almost smiled but instead gestured back toward the guesthouse. "Find anything interesting?"

"Nora's cell phone, an old stuffed penguin and Tao quotes—"

"If you saw anything that suggested she was a danger to herself or in danger from someone else, you'd tell the police."

"Without question."

She nodded. "I know, it's tricky figuring out what to do."

"Relax, Jo. I haven't been in the back of a police cruiser in years."

"You took a big risk," she said. "Not just because you entered a private residence without permission. What if Rigby had caught you in his living room?"

Elijah rocked back on his heels, amused. "Worried about me, Jo?"

"Never mind. I give up. What about Devin? Has he been in touch?"

"No. I assume he's back on the mountain trying to work things out with Nora."

Her eyes sparked with just the slightest touch of humor. "You let a bruised, scraped, scared eighteen-year-old kid get the better of you?"

"He wasn't that bruised or scraped. It was all a big act."

"One you fell for," she said.

"Running off was a dumb move on his part. I trusted him, and he threw that trust back in my face."

She went very still, her eyes half-closed now. "Not a fun position to be in, is it?"

He looked at her dead-on and said, "No."

"He made a promise. You took him at his word. Maybe he was sincere when he made the promise, and something changed."

"You and Rigby were on your way back to the lodge when Devin took off. Maybe he saw you and decided to bolt."

"Maybe." Jo walked down to the edge of the pond. "Where's your truck?"

"Through the woods," he said, following her.

She shoved her hands into the pockets of her fleece and stared at the still, gray water. "You're having trouble adjusting to being back here, aren't you, Elijah?"

"No, I'm fine with being back here."

She glanced sideways at him. "You just broke into a guesthouse."

"Show me the evidence—"

"You're a rule breaker, Elijah. You always have been. Assuming it wasn't you last night, going to break into my place next?"

"Nope. I did that first."

He could tell she didn't know if he was serious or not.

He grinned suddenly. "I swear, Jo, if I weren't afraid of being attacked by wild ducks, I'd kiss you right now."

"Elijah…" She licked her lips, which, in his mind, meant she was thinking about him kissing her, too. But she gestured to someone behind him, and he turned and saw the Whittakers ambling down the lawn. "You should go."

"I don't want to leave you—"

"Ten to one they invite us to tea."

He gave a mock shudder. "Save me, Agent Harper."

This time, she smiled all the way. "I'll see you back at the lake."

He got out of there, cutting through the woods back to the stone wall and his truck. He arrived back at his place above the lake just in time to answer his phone.

"Grab a pencil, Sergeant Cameron," Charlie Neal said, then added, "please."

# Twenty-One

Nora dumped her backpack against a rotting fallen tree and collapsed onto her knees in tears of frustration. It was dusk, and she didn't know where she was—not that she was lost, exactly. She knew she was on a knoll on the north side of Cameron Mountain in the general vicinity of where Devin had found Drew's body. But she'd never find the exact spot, and now she didn't want to, because it was getting dark and she didn't need any more reminders of death, especially with the gray sky and the eerie shadows—and the silence.

She hadn't considered what it would really be like to spend the night up here by herself. She sat back on her heels, sobbing. She'd sunk into a bed of wet pine needles. She could hear Elijah telling her to get up or put a tarp down or sit on her pack. Stay dry. Stay warm. Prevent hypothermia.

But she didn't get up. She looked around at the endless woods. It was hard to believe police and rescue workers had been up in this wilderness just seven months ago. In the snow. Scott Thorne and Zack Harper had been among them. But they'd never talked to Nora about what they'd seen.

Drew had just gone to sleep and died in the cold.

She could see now how it'd happened. The shivering, numbness and pain of mild hypothermia giving way to more severe symptoms—confusion, slurred speech, clumsiness. Then unconsciousness, death.

If she didn't want to die of hypothermia herself, she needed to find a spot to pitch her tent soon—and never mind being creeped out. She'd operated on instinct yesterday. *Get out, get out.* Now she wondered if she'd actually panicked and should have gone to someone when she'd had the chance.

*Devin.*

She willed back her guilt at having sneaked out on Devin before first light. After deciding he couldn't possibly have stolen her hundred dollars, she still hadn't trusted him enough to go to him. She'd been irritated, she realized, that he thought he had to be protective of her. And why hadn't he just *told* her he was out there?

*Because you treated him like crap yesterday, that's why.*

She'd put on clothes that blended with her gray environment and made her harder to spot and had stayed off the trails—not that anyone was up on the mountain. She hadn't seen a soul all day.

She didn't know what she'd expected. A flag marking the spot where Drew Cameron had died? A gravestone? All she'd seen were trees, rocks, birds, squirrels and chipmunks—and three deer. She'd paused to watch the deer leap through the trees, unaware of her presence. One of the few nice moments in the past two days.

But she gulped back a sob and went rock still, convinced she'd heard a noise below her in the woods. Not a deer. Her heart pounded. *What was it?*

"Nora? It's me…Devin."

"Devin!" She called to him without hesitation and leaped up, sniffling with relief. She'd been feeling guilty about leaving him, not trusting him, and now here he was. "I'm here!"

She started to run, following the rustling and crunching sounds of him making his way through fallen leaves and branches, until they found each other partway down the knoll.

He was panting and sweating and gave her a feeble smile. "Hey, Nora."

"Oh, Dev. I'm sorry I ever doubted you. How did you find me?"

"I knew you wanted to see where Drew died. I figured you'd head this way. Then I heard you crying." He coughed, shrugging his pack off his shoulders. "I know all the shortcuts, but I still had to hump it. I just want to be sure you're okay."

Nora saw his wince of pain, his scraped hands, dirty face. "What happened? Dev, you're hurt—"

He held up a hand, still catching his breath. "I fell and hurt my leg. It's not bad." He used his thumb to wipe a tear on her cheek. "How 'bout you?"

She attempted a smile. "I'm better now that you're here. I should never have come up here alone. It was crazy. But I— The money, then Alex and Melanie…"

"I know. It's okay. I understand."

She almost cried again. "Dev."

"I'm being framed for stealing," he said without drama. "There's the money you're missing, and there's money missing from the lodge. Probably the café, too."

"Who would do such a thing?"

"I don't know."

But Nora suspected he was just trying to spare her.

"Melanie. She hates me. She must have figured out we're onto her lies, and she wants to discredit you."

"We have no proof—"

"I don't need proof."

"Just because you don't like her doesn't mean she's some crazy evildoer."

Nora didn't want to argue with him. He had an almost scary ability to penetrate a current situation with clarity. He could look at the facts without going off on a million different tangents the way she would.

"Can you show me the spot where you found Drew?" she asked.

"Yeah. We're close. Let me carry your pack."

She shook her head. "I've got it. But you were right—it's really heavy. I thought I was in better shape."

"You've got a lot on your mind. It drags you down."

He was matter-of-fact in his sincerity. Nora said nothing and followed him as he led her through the trees, moving with an assurance and familiarity with the difficult terrain that she didn't have.

"Devin," she said behind him, "have you ever considered if Drew's death wasn't just an awful accident?"

He glanced back at her. He was wearing only a sweatshirt, vest and jeans, but he didn't look cold at all. "Don't start thinking like that."

He wasn't one to jump from A to Z without going carefully through all the letters in between. She'd seen that in how he was helping her look into Melanie's background.

So far they'd found out that she came from a middle-class Long Island family and had a degree from the State University of New York at Binghamton. She'd worked for several different high-end furniture stores in New York before moving to Washington, D.C., two years ago to set up her own one-woman interior-decorating firm.

They'd checked out her Web site, which she hadn't updated lately, and had filled out the form for more information, but never got anything back. Devin was figuring out how to approach her as a would-be client and ask for references. Nora had written down all the different places she could think of that Melanie had traveled to since April. She hadn't liked Melanie from the beginning, but she'd kept hoping her father would dump her.

Now they were engaged.

Nora ducked under the sharp, dead lower branches of a pine.

"It's almost dark, Dev," she said. "We need to figure out where to camp soon."

"Not a problem."

"I don't know if I want to sleep right on top of where a man died."

"Yeah." He stopped next to a huge boulder and turned to her, a light breeze floating almost peacefully through the trees. He seemed quiet, as if he'd gone into some deep part of himself. "I don't, either."

"I'm sorry. I don't mean to sound callous."

"You don't. It's okay." He tilted his head back at the darkening sky. "Drew was my friend is all."

Nora slipped off her pack. "It'll be cathartic for you to be back up here again, but if you don't want to go to the exact spot, I'll understand."

He dropped his gaze back to her. "No. I'll go. It's not a big deal."

"How much farther is it? It's getting dark."

"Not far."

She hoisted up her pack again. "I keep thinking about Alex," she said, hating herself for how meek she sounded.

Devin nodded. "I know."

"You do, don't you?"

He'd already started back through the woods and didn't hear her. Nora tripped along behind him. Her legs were rubbery and her back ached from her heavy pack, but she didn't have any blisters. "What if Melanie's some kind of madam?" she called to him almost cheerfully. "Maybe she's running high-class call girls to Washington politicians."

"Whoa, Nora." Devin glanced back at her with a grin. "I'm lost. Call girls? How'd you come up with call girls?"

It made her feel good to see him smile. "I'm just saying what if Melanie has secrets that she doesn't want anyone to discover, and she knows we're after those secrets?"

"What if she really loves your father?"

"*And* has secrets?"

"Yeah."

Nora was thoughtful a moment. "She has to be honest with him."

"Maybe he knows already and doesn't care."

"You could be a cop, Devin. You don't jump ahead. But right now, I need you to jump ahead just a little. Okay? Because I'm really tired, and I'm scared, and I hate this woman. It's not all drama. Melanie doesn't love my father. I know she doesn't. She just wants him because of his status."

Devin stopped suddenly and removed his pack, leaning it against a boulder. They were on the flat top of a knoll, but it sloped downward sharply just ahead. "I guess I'll never be so important I'll have to worry about women falling for me because of my status."

His tone was self-deprecating, but the humor was underlined with a touch of bitterness that irritated Nora. "You shouldn't put yourself down."

"What? I wasn't."

He seemed oblivious, which didn't surprise her really. "When this is over," she said, "I can talk to my dad—or you can talk to him yourself. He can help you if you want. He's a good guy. He's just caught up with Melanie right now."

Nora could feel her own resolve faltering. She was so tired from hiking, from the cold—from crying. Alex's horrible death had undermined some of the cocky self-confidence she'd had earlier in the week. "I'm scared, Devin. I have all these bad vibes. If Melanie really does have something awful to hide, she could fight back. We're threatening to ruin her life."

"If she's as smart and as conniving as you think she is, she won't bother with you—she won't waste her time on revenge. She'll just focus on saving her own skin."

Nora didn't argue. She knew she was freaked out and cold and maybe not acting rationally, but she was determined now to see through what she'd started. And up on the mountain, at least she could think. She didn't have to worry about anything or anyone.

But she realized Devin hadn't continued. Her heart pounded. "Dev?"

"This is the spot," he said simply, pointing off to his left. "The trail down to the logging road is just over there."

"How did you ever manage to find him? Now that I'm here..." She shivered from a breeze that created shifting, spooky shadows, as if Drew Cameron was there, trying to tell them something. But she shoved that thought aside before she really freaked out. "It's nothing but trees and more trees."

"I had an idea where to look." He sounded tired and resigned more than depressed. "He had me help him bring stuff up here and dump it off on the trail. Beams, plywood, two-by-fours, tools."

"You never said—" Nora contained her shock. "He was building something?"

"I guess."

"You don't *know?*"

"He wouldn't tell me. He said it was a surprise." Devin stared down at his hands. "He said he knew he didn't have long to live and he wanted to do this one last thing."

Nora bit back tears. "Dev. My God."

"It was easier just to not say anything. I didn't lie to anyone."

"Devin, what could he have been building up here in the middle of nowhere? It's a *mountain.* It's the *wilderness.*"

"The Camerons first settled out here. It wasn't as remote back then." He cleared his throat and stuffed his hands in his pockets. "Whatever. Doesn't matter now. He's gone."

Nora reached a hand out and brushed his arm with her fingertips. "I guess it never sunk in until now..." She bit back tears. "You miss him a lot, don't you?"

"Yeah." Devin nodded toward the trail. "There's a level spot over there where I used to leave Drew's supplies. You can set up your tent there. I have my—"

"My tent will sleep two people easily."

He looked awkward. "You're sure? I promise...you know." He turned bright red.

Nora smiled. He was so innocent sometimes. "Damn straight, Dev. We're both filthy." But when he didn't move off, she realized there was more bothering him. "What is it?"

"I didn't want to worry you, but you should know." He

hesitated only a fraction of a second before he continued. "Hannah left a message on my cell phone. I listened to it while Elijah was getting ice for my leg. A big guy's up here looking for you. Your father hired him, but it was Melanie's idea. She knows him."

"A big guy? Who?"

"His name's Kyle Rigby."

Nora suddenly felt very cold. "Devin. I don't want this Kyle Rigby to find me. Reassure me. Please, tell me I can trust you."

"You can trust me. Maybe you should talk to Elijah. Maybe we both should. He's tough, and he won't back off. You trust him. I do, too, even if he thinks I'm responsible for his father's death."

"He doesn't think that," Nora said.

"I took off on him today. I lied to him. I pretended to be hurt worse than I was."

"Devin…"

"And I broke my word to him. He'll drop-kick me off a ledge when he catches up with me—that's the way he is. Jo Harper, too. But I don't care. Nora, whatever's going on, we can't do this ourselves. We need help. I can't get a cell signal out here, but—"

Nora shook her head, stifling a surge of panic as everything rushed at her—her father marrying this woman he hardly knew and the police thinking he had something to do with Alex's death because Alex stole her mother from him and her mother being so sad because Alex was dead—and now this man Melanie had asked to search for her.

"No, Devin. Don't. Please." Nora's voice was just a croak as she pictured Alex's death for the hundredth time, at least. "Let's just get through tonight and think. I hate Melanie. I don't trust her."

"I know, Nora. It'll be okay." Devin started off painfully, clearly more hurt than he wanted to admit.

Nora pulled herself out of her jumble of crazy thoughts. The woods were so quiet at dusk. So beautiful. "I'm really sorry about Drew," she whispered.

"He wasn't easy, but he was a good guy."

"I don't have anyone in my life like that. Everyone I know has an agenda—nothing unconditional. It wasn't that way with you and Drew."

"Your folks love you, Nora. Don't give up on them, okay?"

She tried to smile, but couldn't. "You spend time up here, and you begin to realize how insignificant we all really are. It doesn't matter if we're alive or dead. The world keeps spinning. I thought of Alex this morning. He's gone, and the sun came up just like always. The birds twittered. The squirrels chattered. Nothing changed because of his death. Nothing that matters, anyway."

"Let's get your tent out."

She set her pack down and unzipped the main compartment, but her fingers were frozen now. She slipped on her gloves. She wanted to see her mother—she wanted to cry with her about Alex.

"I didn't hate him," she said.

"Alex?"

"I keep telling myself I did, because I think it'll make losing him easier, but I didn't. He could be a real prick and everything, but lately..." She cried openly now, tears streaming down her cheeks, raw already from the cold and wind. "I want my mom, Dev. I want to see her."

"You will."

"If something happened to me—she couldn't stand it, on top of Alex."

"Nothing's going to happen to you." Devin took out her tent and unrolled it on the ground, steady, competent. He gave a low whistle. "Look at that. Your tent poles are color coded. That's the coolest thing ever."

Nora smiled through her tears. He was totally in his element out here. She felt better just having him with her. "You're my best friend, Dev." She sniffled, not crying so much now. "It's so quiet. It'll be just us and the owls up here."

"I don't know. I saw a big bull moose—"

"You did not."

"And a bear, a coyote, a fox and about a dozen snakes."

She laughed. "Thank you, Devin. Thank you."

He got up stiffly, with a little wince of pain, and hugged her, more of a reassuring, brotherly hug than anything romantic. "We'll figure this out. Now, let's just pitch this fancy tent of yours."

# Twenty-Two

Jo wasn't in the mood to let Elijah out of her sight, but he'd slipped back through the trees just as the Whittakers arrived at the guesthouse and invited her up for tea. She went with them, Vivian chatting breezily about leaf raking and getting the place ready for the winter, Lowell making the occasional amiable comment as they entered their farmhouse through a side door. Vivian pulled off her barn jacket and hung it on a hook. She had on just a short-sleeved polo shirt underneath but looked warm enough. Lowell stayed bundled up in a zip-front charcoal sweater. Jo removed her fleece but kept it with her—she didn't plan on staying long.

The interior of their farmhouse wasn't what she had expected. There was no cozy decor or pictures of cows and fall foliage. The walls were stark white, the wood floors shining, the furnishings bright and modern, the artwork abstract and striking. The Whittakers took her back to a sunroom that looked out on a garden and an open field that stretched down to the river.

Vivian carried in a tray from the kitchen and set it on the

glass table. "I know Nora's a capable young woman but she shouldn't hike by herself, particularly at this time of year, with or without the shocking news of poor Alex. If Devin Shay is with her…" She hesitated, lifting a white pottery teapot off the tray and placing it on a thick fiery-red pot holder. "He knows the mountains, of course, and he's an experienced hiker, but I think Nora's concerned he's too obsessed with her."

"She told you this?" Jo asked.

"Not in as many words."

"What did she say, then? Can you remember her exact words?"

Lowell reached for a white plate of an array of cookies obviously from Three Sisters Café and pushed it more toward Jo's side of the table. "We're not trying to get anyone into trouble," he said. "We certainly don't believe Devin is stalking Nora."

"He's changed," Vivian said, briskly setting out cups and saucers. "We knew him before Drew Cameron's death—not well, but enough to see that finding Drew, losing him, affected Devin deeply. Before that he struck us as a happy-go-lucky teenager who didn't have a clue what he'd do after graduation." She picked up the teapot and filled Jo's cup, her expression pained, regretful. "You're from here, Jo. You must have heard that Devin's had his struggles."

Jo helped herself to a chocolate-chip cookie. "He hasn't been arrested for anything, has he?"

"Oh, heavens, no." Vivian poured her husband tea, not even the slightest tremble to her hands. She filled her cup next, then sat down. "I shouldn't have said anything. We like Devin very much, and Nora's a delight. I remember being very confused at that age myself."

"What about Kyle Rigby?" Jo asked, taking a bite of her cookie. "Do you know anything about him?"

"No, nothing," Lowell said. "We only met him this morning."

Vivian picked up her teacup. "He seems quite competent." She sipped some of her tea. "He'll be discreet, too. It'd be best for everyone if he finds Nora quietly, without any fanfare, or she comes back on her own. It's good that Thomas and Melanie are on their way here." She held her cup in both hands and stared out the window. "We love this place, but I don't know. Some days…"

"We're all worried," Lowell said, addressing Jo. "And we're grieving for Alex. He and Nora had their problems, but he cared about her. I think she was coming to see that in recent weeks. He started out with a deficit with her because of his friendship with her father. He was aware that she had to feel betrayed—torn by her love for both parents."

Vivian set her cup down and reached for an oatmeal cookie. "We thought it would help that Thomas and Melanie found each other and fell in love. Nora just wants both her parents to be happy. Now…I have a hard time believing Alex is dead." Her eyes shone with sudden tears. She broke off a piece of cookie. "It's a difficult situation, isn't it?"

"Yes, it is," Jo said. "Were you here in April when Drew Cameron went missing? I understand that Thomas and Nora stayed at the guesthouse then."

"We came up for the weekend," Lowell said. "Drew had just disappeared. The state police had launched a search. We weren't actually in Black Falls when he was found."

"It was our first time here in April," Vivian said. "I couldn't believe it *snowed*. Our daffodils got covered. They were just coming up. They bounced right back once the snow melted, but I don't think Vermont's where I want to be in April."

Lowell set his teacup down with a clatter and smiled awkwardly, obviously embarrassed by his wife's callous remark. "We didn't care about the daffodils, of course, but the snow caught us by surprise. We weren't involved in the search for Drew. There was nothing we could do except stay out of the way." Lowell got abruptly to his feet. "It's a tragedy Drew and Alex are both gone now. Jo, we don't want to keep you, but if you'd care to sit here a while, please feel free to stay as long as you wish. I have some work to do in the yard before dark."

Jo seized the opening and left, noting when she got outside that it already *was* dark. All her trekking up and down Cameron Mountain had consumed what little daylight a mid-November Vermont day offered.

When she got back to her cabin, she found Elijah in the doorway with a screwdriver in hand, a Red Sox cap tipped back on his head. He stood back and pointed the end of his screwdriver toward a shiny new dead-bolt lock. "Took two seconds and half the cash in my pocket." He tucked the screwdriver into his jacket pocket. "You always used to say you wanted a guy who's handy."

"It's a lousy cover for searching my place, Elijah."

"I'm on a roll. You didn't bring much up with you from Washington."

"That's because I'm an optimist and plan to get back to work soon. Elijah, you can't just walk into other people's houses. Not that this is a house, but you know what I mean."

"Then arrest me."

She sighed. "Thank you for the new lock. You could have stayed for tea with the Whittakers, and we could have put the lock on together."

"I don't like tea. Turns my stomach to even think about it."

She doubted much turned Elijah's stomach.

"Get anything out of the Whittakers?" he asked casually.

"They think Thomas is overreacting about Nora's camping trip on the one hand, but, on the other, that Devin could be obsessed with Nora."

"Devin's obsessed with being eighteen."

Elijah stood back from the door, and Jo went past him inside, feeling the old floor sagging under her. And this was the good cabin. "It's not worth it to put new locks on the rest of the cabins." She blew out a breath and spun around. "You know I don't have the slightest clue what to do with this place, don't you? The property taxes on the thirty acres alone are a killer."

"Pop got to you in April, didn't he?"

"I'm sorry," Jo said. "I'm being incredibly ungrateful. I'm glad he came to see me."

Elijah stepped up into the cabin. "He didn't think things through. What you'd do with thirty acres and a bunch of rundown cabins in Vermont."

"I don't know. Maybe he did think things through, and this is what he wanted." She pictured him among the cherry blossoms, his fear and guilt and regret—and love—palpable. But it wasn't an image she needed to share with Elijah, and she smiled, looking around at her one-room temporary home. "Remember when he found us here?"

"A good thing he didn't come armed," Elijah said dryly.

"If it'd been my father—"

"It wasn't. It was mine. But it doesn't matter. What I did after Pop kicked me out of the house was my choice. I didn't discuss it with him or anyone else."

"And you have no regrets," she said.

His eyes held hers, unreadable under the brim of his cap, but he broke off and winked at her. "I'm having fun being around you again. I forgot how much pent-up energy you have. You're like a top that keeps spinning at high speed."

Jo went with his change of subject. She didn't want to delve too deep into the past, either. Not now, not here. "What were you looking for?" she asked.

"Intruders."

"Ah. I can take care of myself, you know."

"You always could. Not the point. You're used to working with a team and high-tech gadgetry. You're alone up here."

"Not that alone," she said.

But he just gave her a teasing smile. "Relax. I didn't go through your private things." He picked up an ivory-colored petal that had fallen onto the table from one of the lilies Charlie Neal had sent her. "Anything else you're up to, Jo, besides lying low?"

"No. I'm here because of Charlie and that video. I know my presence is provocative because of what I do, but Ambassador Bruni wasn't under Secret Service protection—or any protection, for that matter. If I'd known anything about a threat against him that traced back here, I wouldn't have been hanging out at the café and canoeing out on the lake."

"You don't own a canoe."

"By the way, Beth and I borrowed yours the other day."

"So I saw. Anytime. Happy to share. Lake'll freeze soon, though."

"Not before I'm back in Washington." She ripped open her refrigerator, realizing he was right about her pent-up energy, even if he didn't understand all the reasons for it. Neither did she. "I don't know why I'm looking in here. I'm not even hungry." She shut the door again. "I think I'll go over and search your place."

He shrugged. "Go ahead."

She called his bluff and headed outside and up their shared road, paying no attention to how dark it was. Elijah followed at an easy pace, probably considering whether or not he had any illegal weaponry or pictures of girlfriends on his dresser.

She took the steps up to his deck two at a time and left the slider door open for him when she went in.

She started her search downstairs with a back bedroom and bath, which he obviously used, then charged through the small kitchen and headed up the spiral stairs to two unfinished bedrooms and a shared bath. She didn't do a thorough job. She did just enough to prove her point, although she wasn't sure just what her point was. That she could give as good as she got? That Drew Cameron had been an old man filled with fears and regrets when he'd come to see her, and his talk of the children she and Elijah had never had was just that—talk? Not a premonition. Not some unfulfilled promise of something that had been meant to be.

When she finished looking around, she returned to the front room, a little out of breath. Elijah picked up a box of wooden matches and opened up the woodstove. Jo pointed toward the back of the house. "You didn't make your bed this morning."

"I don't make it most mornings."

"And your windows need washing. There are fingerprints all over them."

"A.J.'s kids were here raising hell the day before you showed up in town. I figured I'd worry about keeping them alive and never mind the windows."

She smiled, imagining little Baylee and Jim Cameron racing through the sturdy house and running circles around their Green Beret uncle. "Probably a good idea, seeing how they're Camerons."

Elijah struck a match and set the flame to the edge of a rolled-up newspaper. "They're a couple of live wires."

"Elijah…" She dropped onto the edge of a sectional sofa and pulled herself together. "I don't want to screw up your life. If I'd known you were here—"

"You'd have bought a plane ticket to Paris?"

"New Zealand," she admitted. "Maybe Australia while I was at it."

He shut the stove lid, and behind the glass front the kindling quickly caught fire, sparking, crackling. "Maybe Nora wishes her father was marrying you instead of his fiancée, and she's staged this little drama to throw the two of you together."

"That's not what's going on."

"I don't like Rigby," Elijah said.

"Neither do I, but Thomas is self-protective. I can see he might want someone up here who answers only to him. I have conflicts that someone private doesn't."

"I think you should stay here tonight."

"Why, are you afraid to be here alone?"

"Shaking in my boots, if that's what it'll take. I know you're a tough federal agent and all that, but I still don't like the idea of you being alone out here."

Jo settled into the sofa and glanced around at the comfortable room. It would have good views of the trees and lake during daylight, a perfect spot for a man fresh back from war—for Elijah, who'd always loved Black Falls.

He adjusted the dampers on the stove. "Fetch your toothbrush, Jo. You're not staying alone, and this place has better heat than your cabin. I'm not into freezing body parts."

She studied him, noting the serious—even professional—look that had come over him, reminding her that he wasn't an aimless nineteen-year-old any longer. For most of the past fifteen years, he'd been doing the important, multifaceted work of a Special Forces soldier.

Finally she said, "There's more, something you're not telling me." She watched him lift a log from his rustic woodbox. "Elijah, has Charlie Neal called again?"

He set the log upright on the brick hearth in front of the stove. "He has names."

"Names—" Jo stopped herself. "I can't hear this."

Elijah ignored her. "Charlie combed the Internet for unsolved homicides that appear to be out-of-the-blue hits with no obvious motive. Two names struck him as being of particular interest. An arson investigator in southern California named Jasper Vanderhorn was killed in a fire in June. In August, a Russian diplomat named Andrei Petrov was poisoned in London."

Jo gritted her teeth. *Charlie, Charlie.*

"Charlie says he has other names pending. The victims aren't connected that he's been able to figure out so far—it's the manner of their deaths that got them on his list."

"That's not enough to suggest there's an assassination network involved."

"It's enough for Charlie and my friend in Washington."

"Is your friend a conspiracy nut?"

Elijah didn't hesitate. "No."

"Military?" Jo asked.

"SEAL."

"One of the ones from April?"

He didn't answer, but his expression—a mix of regret, resolve and pain—took the wind out of her. But it didn't last. It was there, almost imperceptible, then gone again.

He opened the lid on the stove again, picked up the log from the hearth and dropped it on the fire.

"Elijah, if you ever want to talk about what happened—"

"I don't." He turned to her, his eyes the color of midnight now. "Marissa Neal."

Jo didn't react. "She's in good hands. She's fine."

"You saved her life."

"Whatever I did or didn't do was my job. Charlie needs to stay out of this, Elijah. He's smart, but he's still a sixteen-year-old kid. The police won't jump to conclusions about Ambassador Bruni's death. They can't. They'll follow the evidence."

"I'm not the police."

The log caught fire, the flames hissing. Jo got to her feet. "You and Charlie and your SEAL friend in D.C. need to back off."

"And you, Jo? What do you need to do?"

She didn't respond, just started for the sliders.

Not that Elijah had given up. He tossed her a flashlight. "Don't forget your toothbrush."

She didn't mention there was only one bed in the place. Obviously he already knew. She just switched on the flashlight, went out onto the deck and shivered in the sudden cold.

But it wasn't just the cold.

The brisk wind helped clear Jo's head while she walked back to her cabin. She was listening to an owl out across the lake when she saw car headlights down the road, and in another minute, a sedan stopped in front of her cabin.

The headlights went off, and Thomas Asher got out on the driver's side. "Jo," he said, his voice croaking with emotion as she lowered her flashlight. "It's good to see you. I'm sorry it's not under better circumstances."

Before Jo had a chance to answer, a pretty, black-haired woman climbed out on the passenger side, walked around the hood of the car and stood next to Thomas. "I'm Melanie," she said, shivering even as she smiled pleasantly. "I've heard so much about you, Special Agent Harper. It's a pleasure to meet you, finally."

"Same here," Jo said automatically. "Thomas, good to see you, although I'm sorry about the circumstances. We can go inside, if you'd like."

Thomas shook his head. He was wearing just a sweater and looked cold, and clearly distraught. "We can't stay. Lowell and Vivian have dinner waiting. We're staying with them. I just wanted to stop by and thank you for your help. But Nora? There's nothing new?"

"She's apparently spending another night on the mountain." Jo decided to let Kyle Rigby provide a more detailed update. "We're expecting snow tomorrow."

"I heard."

Melanie rubbed her arms. "Gosh, I forgot how dark it is up here without the city lights. Nora's got more guts than I ever did at her age. Even now. I have no desire to camp in this cold. If not for poor Alex's death, we'd probably have never known Nora had decided to do this trip. She might have told us after she got back, but she's such a good kid. She wouldn't want us to worry."

"I'm reluctant to notify local authorities at this point," Thomas said. "They have enough to do without launching a search when Nora's technically not really unaccounted for. If we go ahead with a search prematurely—" He broke off, looking pained at the thought. "Nora has her entire future ahead of her. Dropping out of Dartmouth for a year is enough of a hurdle to overcome without causing a scene here."

"That's why we brought in Kyle," Melanie said.

Jo kept her expression neutral. "Nora's safety is all anyone cares about."

Thomas stepped back toward his car. "I'm sure she's fine and won't appreciate all our fretting. She'll think we don't respect her abilities." He looked out at the dark lake. "Alex's death has us all on edge. It's an awful thing. I just hope…well, I hate to think of her up there alone, grieving."

Jo could see he was grieving himself.

"Jo—you don't mind if I call you Jo, do you?" Melanie gestured toward the cabin and didn't wait for an answer. "May I use your bathroom?"

"Of course."

"I can't see. You have a flashlight. Do you mind?"

Thomas smiled indulgently at her, then turned to Jo. "I'll wait out here."

He walked down to the lake by himself, picking his way through the trees in the dark, while Melanie hurried into the cabin across the weedy yard. Jo debated going down to the lake with Thomas, at least giving him her flashlight, but she followed Melanie instead.

Melanie shut the cabin door quickly behind her. "I wanted to talk to you alone," she said. "Thomas is so upset about Alex it's clouding his thinking. He can't see what's going on clearly. It's obvious Nora just needs some space after what happened yesterday. She'd been planning this camping trip, and Alex's death got her to pull the trigger on it and go. It gives her a sense of control over her own life."

"Did you talk to her?"

"No, but I know her pretty well. I know how she thinks. Alex was very hard on Nora. He didn't mean to be, but she wanted to prove herself to him."

"A cold-weather camping trip would do it?"

"Yes. Exactly. She wanted to show him and her mother—Thomas, too, I'm sure—that she has the skills and the courage to handle these conditions. When she heard about Alex, I can just see her deciding to do this for him, for herself. It'd be awful now if we interfere and hover over her. It's hard for Thomas to balance worry with the need to let go—to let his daughter make her own mistakes."

"You're the one who suggested Kyle Rigby," Jo said.

"Not to escalate the situation, to keep things calm. He's solid—he knows what he's doing. He'll be straight with Thomas. If we're wrong and Nora *is* in trouble for whatever reason—lost, hurt—then Kyle will speak up. He'll put her safety first."

"Fair enough."

Melanie slipped back outside without using the bathroom, and she waved to Thomas as he walked up from the lake. "We should come out here in better weather. It's beautiful."

As he approached their rented car, Jo saw that he looked drawn and tired, and worried about his daughter. He kissed her on the cheek. "Thanks for everything, Jo," he said quietly. "I'll see you tomorrow."

After they left, Jo went back inside. Her propane heater was sputtering. It'd be another cold night.

She grabbed her toothbrush. "Are you out of your mind?" she whispered to herself.

She got halfway back to Elijah's house before she came to her senses and climbed up onto the hill and called Mark Francona instead. "Anything else on the potential witness—the messenger?"

"No."

"Any way you can find out if Drew Cameron went to see Ambassador Bruni in April? Drew was—"

"Andrew James Cameron. He left you your Vermont property. He died of hypothermia two weeks after you took him for a walk among the cherry blossoms."

"Sometimes you scare me."

"Good. And yes, I'll let you know."

"In the meantime," she said, "watch out for my friend the airsoft buff. He sees things other people miss. He's the youngest of five, he has a high IQ and has grown up in a savvy political family. His brain's on overdrive all the time. He wants to make amends to me. He sent me flowers—"

"Flowers? You?"

"Yeah. Lilies. I love flowers. He doesn't owe me, but after his little prank, he's focused on me." And after Marissa's brush with death, Jo realized. Charlie must have been more upset than he'd let on.

She told Francona about Charlie's assassins theory and gave him the names of the alleged victims.

When she finished, her boss blew out a long, pained breath. "How's Vermont? Any snow up there yet? I gave up on downhill skiing, but I could do cross-country, I think. You?"

"Real Vermonters don't ski."

She hung up. She did ski. She'd just let him get on her nerves, but she'd also delivered her message. It wasn't the job of the Secret Service to run Charlie's life or be his nanny—

or his parents—but he had no business digging around on the Internet for unsolved murders.

She found some bath salts the wife of one of her Secret Service friends had left and headed back over to Elijah's place.

"Calm down, Sergeant Cameron," she told him as she entered his warm, cozy front room. "It's your bathtub I'm after."

He grinned. "Help yourself."

# Twenty-Three

Elijah sat on his favorite chair in front of the fire while Jo was in the tub, probably, he decided, not contemplating her options for the night so much as thinking about assassins. He took her choice of the bathroom just off his bedroom as a sign of where she meant to sleep.

She'd warned him not to peek while she was in the tub. Since she'd come with toothbrush, bath salts and her Sig, Elijah was heeding the warning.

He dialed Grit's number. When Grit answered, Elijah gave him what he had on Melanie Kendall, Kyle Rigby and Thomas Asher.

"Bruni could have been hit by some senator late for a hair appointment," Grit said.

"What about your reporter friend?"

"She has a personal stake in whatever's going on. Something with her and the Russian, this Andrei Petrov your new friend told you about." Grit spoke as he always did, without a lot of fanfare or emotion. "But I think Myrtle's one of the good guys."

"Or?"

"Or she's the one running the thing and she's just playing me. Moose is no help. He likes her."

Elijah made no comment.

"Whatever Myrtle's agenda is," Grit said, "she's crusty and knows how to find the right rocks to turn over."

And Grit would turn them over. He was single-minded, and he needed a mission. "We're not law enforcement," Elijah said. "We don't have to worry about building a case."

"Jo Harper? She's a federal agent."

"I'll handle her."

"Ah."

"There's no 'ah,' Grit." But there was, and Elijah knew Grit was already onto him.

"If the veep's kid doesn't ruin her career, you could."

"Not my problem."

He heard the bathroom door open. In two seconds, Jo was there in an oversize red-plaid flannel nightshirt his grand-mother had given him for Christmas one year. He'd stuffed it in the linen closet and forgotten about it.

"Cameron?"

"Jo just got out of the tub."

"Uh-oh."

"She looks like a female version of Paul Bunyan."

"Just your type, mountain man," Grit said and hung up.

Elijah got to his feet and didn't bother with niceties. "Jo, if I don't make love to you soon—"

"That's what I was thinking in the tub."

He kissed her softly, then scooped her up as he had so long ago and carried her back to his bedroom. It was cooler in there, away from the woodstove.

She draped her arms over his shoulders. "I can't fall in love with you again," she whispered, not taking her eyes from him. "Except I've never been out of love with you. Elijah…"

"Shh," he said, and lowered her onto his bed. "Let's love each other right now."

His mouth found hers again, and he held her and closed his eyes, pretending for a moment that the past fifteen years hadn't happened and he was nineteen again and loving her, making promises that he'd keep. He skimmed his hands over her slim body, remembering all her curves, the places she liked to be touched.

She went still, then held his face in her hands and lifted his mouth from hers. "Open your eyes, Elijah."

He did so and smiled. "Jo. Damn. It's worth opening my eyes just to look at you."

But she wasn't buying it. "We're not teenagers anymore, and you've never been one to go backward."

"I would if I could. Just not to hurt you." He kissed her nose, her forehead, her cheeks, wanting nothing more than to love her. "Ms. Secret Agent," he whispered, trailing more feathery kisses along her jaw as her hands slid down to his upper arms and dug into his flesh. "You're something else."

"Elijah."

There was a little catch in her voice that he liked. A tightening of her grip on his arms. He kissed her throat, even as he eased his hands up under her nightshirt along the bare, smooth skin of her thighs. She squirmed beneath him in just the right way.

And he said her name again and again as he had in countless dreams.

How had he let her go?

He felt the quickening of his pulse and hers as he curved

his palms up along her hips and stomach to her breasts and caught a nipple between his fingertips. He'd been her first love, remembered her cry of pain and ecstasy as he'd plunged into her, trying to be careful, trying to hold back for fear of really hurting her. But she'd urged him on, tears flowing as she'd promised to love him forever.

A long time ago.

His hands skimmed back down along her sides and over her hips, feeling the last of the airsoft welts. She was strong and fit, and she'd been loved by other men—she'd gone on with her life as he had with his.

He'd left her no other choice.

He felt the tremble in her fingers as she eased them down his arms and over the tops of his hands and held on, raising herself up just a little from the bed. "Elijah. I can't…wait." Her turquoise eyes held his with an intensity, a fire he'd long thought he'd never see again. "I've been hiking up and down these damn hills for two days. I can't— Can you please take your clothes off? And get this nightshirt off me while you're at it?"

He laughed. "With pleasure."

"Good, because I…" She gave a sexy little shudder. "I need to conserve my energy."

"I'll get your nightshirt off first," he said with a wicked smile.

"I thought you might."

It was only a matter of whisking the nightshirt over her head and casting it onto the floor. But he couldn't jump right into disrobing himself. He gazed at her, his throat tight with want and emotion and a need that reached right to his soul.

"Jo," he whispered, kissing her, soaking in the taste and the feel of her. "You're beautiful."

She slid her arms around his neck and drew him onto her, deepening their kiss, writhing erotically under him. But she wouldn't be distracted. "You're still clothed," she said, her voice ragged, her body hot and soft.

"So I am."

He dealt with that problem in seconds, flinging his clothes onto the floor, floor lamps—wherever—he didn't care. When he rejoined her, she was breathless, eyes wide open as she took in the sight of him.

"Your scar," she said. "Are you okay now? A femoral artery injury is dangerous."

"It didn't affect anything vital."

She raised an eyebrow. "Just your blood supply."

"There was that. But I lived," he said, pushing back a sudden image of that night. He paused, staring at her, and repeated himself. "I lived."

He settled himself on top of her, figuring the feel of what mattered would distract her from his scars, and she responded with a small cry of surprise, delight—memory.

"I'm glad you lived," she said. "Elijah, I don't know what I'd have done if I'd lost you. You've always been out there, indestructible…"

"No one's indestructible."

"I love you." She parted her legs, settled down into the soft bed. "I always have."

"I know."

"The rest—"

"Shh."

"Love me now, Elijah. No more waiting." She lifted herself up and clutched his shoulders. "You won't hurt me."

"Good," he said, "because…damn, Jo…"

He entered her, slowly at first, trying to savor the feel of being inside her again, but she fell back and wrapped her thighs around him, and pulled him in hard and fast and deep. He responded, driving himself into the depths of her. She cried out and threw her hands behind her head, giving herself up to her own heat and need. He could see the desire in her eyes, and it fueled him. He didn't relent and let the sweet ache he'd known only with her take him to the edge.

All this time—all these years. There'd only been one Jo.

She clasped his hips and held him inside her, caught her breath as their bodies fused even more tightly together, until finally she wriggled her hips and that was it. He peeled her hands off him and pinned them to her sides as he thrust into her over and over, faster and faster, until he felt her release—and then his own.

When he collapsed next to her, she drew the covers up over them. "The heat here's better than in my cabin, but it's not great." Her voice was ragged, her body still slick and hot from their lovemaking. "I don't want you to get chilled after you cool off."

He propped his head up on one arm. "Who says I'll have a chance to cool off?"

She smiled. "There's that," she said, easing in close to him, lifting his arm over her shoulders. "I hear an owl."

He kissed her hair. "Maybe it's a son or daughter of the one we heard fifteen years ago."

"Or a grandchild," she said, and was quiet for a while before turning to him and touching his right thigh where he'd been shot. "Your father feared for your life, and maybe he had a premonition of the danger you were in. But that's not why he died."

"Jo..."

"If he built his own cabin on that old cellar hole, he had shelter. Good shelter. Better than trash bags. He could have survived the storm." She eased her fingertips gently along Elijah's scars, as if trying to imagine the pain, the blood, how close he'd come to death. "He didn't go up the mountain with a storm on the way to die. He knew what he was doing."

Elijah didn't speak.

"Someone killed him, Elijah."

He slid his arms around her and drew her to him. "I know."

# *Twenty-Four*

Melanie felt exhilarated and nervous at the same time, relished the tension between the two emotions as she pulled the shades in Kyle's bedroom in the Whittakers' guesthouse. She was tingly with wanting him. She'd told Thomas she needed air after their flight and the long drive from the airport. He'd worried about the dark, but she'd assured him there was plenty of light from the house—and there was.

But Kyle wasn't in a good mood.

"It's a beautiful place, isn't it?" She sat on the edge of his bed. "Although I'm not sure I'd want a second home in Vermont. It's too cold here most of the time. Thomas loves it, though."

"The way things are going, you'll be lucky your new home's not a prison cell."

"Don't be so pessimistic." She chided him with a smile—no point in annoying him—but he always saw the downside to the situation, and she always saw the upside.

"The police are looking for the messenger you were worried about," he said.

"You're the one who said not to worry."

"Who do you think called in the tip?"

Her stomach twisted. *Thomas.* "I have no idea, and I don't care."

"The people we work for don't like screwups. I dealt with one before you came on board. It wasn't pretty."

"We're not screwups."

"*I'm* not."

But he was her partner. He'd recruited her. If their employers were unhappy with her because of Nora Asher and her snooping into Melanie's background, Kyle would be held responsible, too. He looked concerned, which wasn't like him, but he got nervous when he had to think on his feet. He wasn't good at it. She was, and when she wanted something, she put her mind to it and got it.

More than once on her trip up from Washington she'd realized she might end up having to kill him. Let him take the fall for Nora, both with the police and with their employers. Melanie wanted Kyle's plan to work and Nora to die up on the mountain because of the cold, Devin Shay's obsession with her, her own out-of-control emotions. Drew Cameron's death seven months ago would actually work to their advantage and provide more substance, even poignancy, to the deaths of the two teenagers.

It was a good plan, but Melanie was prepared to take matters into her own hands. Blaming Kyle. Painting herself as one of his victims—vulnerable, innocent.

Thomas was up at the Whittaker farmhouse in front of a roaring fire in their living room. Melanie liked Lowell and Vivian. Thomas was handling himself with such grace under pressure. Melanie looked forward to tapping into his network of friends once they were married. A shame Alex Bruni wasn't in the picture anymore, given his prestige as an ambassador, but that hadn't been Melanie's call to make. She'd driven the car—but she wasn't the one who'd decided to kill him.

When she and Thomas had arrived at the Whittakers' farmhouse from Jo Harper's wreck of a cabin, Kyle had reported on his actions on Nora's behalf. Mostly lies, of course, but Thomas was obviously impressed and relieved to have Kyle involved. Melanie had felt good for arranging for Thomas to hire him.

She'd thought about what it would be like to sneak down to the guesthouse in the middle of the night and have Kyle make love to her, with Thomas and the Whittakers none the wiser. But Kyle had barely acknowledged her existence. He was obviously in no mood for her risk taking. He could be like that.

Kyle had recommended that Thomas inform local and state authorities of his concerns, especially with bad weather coming in—and the talk he'd heard about Devin. The Whittakers had heard the talk, too, which helped. But that was all Kyle's doing. He'd been setting up Devin even before Alex Bruni's death.

The planner.

But then he'd given Melanie a nod that told her he wanted to speak with her in private.

Kyle unbuckled his belt and ripped it off his pants. "Jo Harper and Elijah Cameron are a problem."

"Then deal with them," Melanie said.

He dropped the belt onto a chair. "Did Nora or Devin ever see us together?"

"No. Impossible." She shook her head, as much to reassure herself. "We're safe."

"What about your would-be client who came to a bad end?"

"We've been through that, Kyle. There's no way to connect him to me. You'd never have taken me on as a partner if there had been. Nora and Devin don't know anything. They're just looking for something to break Thomas and me apart."

"You should never have invited Nora's scrutiny by getting involved with her father."

"Spilled milk, Kyle."

She felt a sudden chill. She'd never liked the cold—she certainly hadn't wanted to hike up that stupid mountain in April. Kyle had insisted. They'd been instructed to make Drew's death look like an accident, an old man who'd miscalculated the elements and went to sleep in the snow.

Kyle unbuttoned his pants. She didn't know, really, if he wanted a quick round of sex or just wanted to go to bed. "Why did we kill Drew Cameron?" she asked in a low voice.

"You're asking for trouble with that kind of question. We do a job. We don't get to know who wanted it done or why." He stepped out of his pants and folded them onto the chair. "You're caught up in a fantasy. You think you're two different people, but you're not. Your life this past year was for real. You can't erase it. You did what you did."

"I'm not in denial. I'm moving on."

"I never should have let you get involved in my business. It was a mistake."

"You needed a partner. Even with what I got paid, you earned far more these past eight months than you would have on your own. Don't you have hopes and dreams, Kyle?"

"Yeah. Living through this mess we're in up here."

But Melanie could see he had a level of calm that indicated he believed he had a solid plan. "You'll miss me when we've gotten through this mess."

"No, I won't, Melanie."

He continued to stare at her. She shivered, not with the cold—with fear, with excitement. "What?"

"We have to get this right or we'll be on the list for one of our colleagues. We'll be a liability."

"Drew and Bruni got too close to our people, didn't they?"

"I know as much as you do. You have to stop, Melanie. Just stop."

He pulled off his shirt and laid it neatly on top of his pants, then took off his socks. There was nothing erotic about his movements.

"If you got an assignment to kill me," Melanie said, "you'd tell me, wouldn't you?"

His eyes were slits on her. "Would you tell me?"

"I just want to be Mrs. Thomas Asher."

He stood in front of her and took her hand, pressed it against his crotch. "Do you?"

"Yes." But she cupped him, stroked him. "I do."

"Then help me make sure his daughter doesn't get off that mountain. We have to deal with Elijah Cameron and Jo Harper. You're a rookie compared to them. You have no idea." Kyle shook his head, even as he thrust himself against her hand. "You've never gone up against real professionals."

"They just want to find two kids in over their heads and get them safely down off the mountain."

"I searched Harper's cabins last night. If the feds are onto us and sent her up here undercover, she's doing a good job hiding it."

"If she'd caught you—"

"She didn't." He lowered his boxers and threaded his fingers into her hair. "I couldn't get into Elijah Cameron's place. No time. But he suspects his father had help dying up on that mountain."

"He can suspect all he wants. It won't do him any good." She raised her eyes to him. "We just have to deal with Nora and Devin."

"I could go up there in the dark and look for them, but I need rest. I need to give the snow a chance to develop."

"What do you want me to do?"

He cupped the back of her head with his hands and produced a nasty smile. "You know what to do."

"I mean tomorrow. More deaths on Cameron Mountain will be hard to explain."

"That's where planning comes in."

It was a dig at her, but she shrugged it off and moved her mouth closer to his erection. "Was this planned?"

Her sarcasm was ill timed. He'd retaliate for her snottiness, and she'd have no satisfaction tonight. She'd service Kyle and be sent on her way, back out into the cold night. Thomas awaited her, but it wasn't the same.

"I feel like the wicked stepmother in a fairy tale," she said when he didn't answer.

"It's not a fairy tale. You're the real deal."

"There'll be a happy ending for me."

"You're something else, Melanie. I wish I'd never met you."

She raised her eyes to him. "If you're getting squeamish, walk away. I'll take care of everything."

"There's no walking away." Kyle's grip on her head eased. "You need to forget Thomas. Once we're finished here, you Dear John him. Say you didn't bargain for all this tragedy."

"You don't tell me what to do, Kyle."

He gave her a supercilious smirk. "Sure."

But even as she opened her mouth and did his bidding, she knew the power she had over him. She and Thomas were getting married. She was walking away from her life with Kyle stronger, better. He would remain a work-for-hire killer.

Of course, he had power over her, too. He could ruin her.

Or kill her. She didn't want to end up on his list of targets.

He moaned, threading his thick fingers into her hair, and she smiled to herself. She could kill him, but Kyle could never hurt her.

All would be well.

When she arrived back at the farmhouse, Melanie decided she'd absolutely have to talk Thomas out of a Vermont wedding. It would be frigid on New Year's Eve. It was cold *now.*

She sat next to him on the couch in front of the fire, welcoming the warmth, the elegance of the beautifully decorated room. As wealthy and well-connected as Vivian and Lowell Whittaker were, Melanie wasn't sure if she and Thomas would want to maintain a friendship with them after Nora and Devin were dead. It would be just too awkward.

No one seemed the least bit curious about how long she'd been gone. She'd been right, Kyle had refused to satisfy her. She was still all tingly with wanting him. But he'd been adamant—cruel, even. He'd taken her out to his car and given her a gun, a 9-millimeter Browning that she rather liked.

"Be prepared to cut your losses," he'd told her.

She'd tucked the Browning into her handbag. Thomas was too much of a gentleman ever to paw through any of her things without her permission. She would do what she had to do to protect herself.

But so would Kyle. How much hadn't he told her? She couldn't count on his loyalty. If he had a client who'd pay him to do it, Kyle would kill his own mother. An apt cliché in his case.

Melanie trusted her own instincts. She had succeeded in her violent work this past year not just because she enjoyed it and understood her strengths and weaknesses, but also because she didn't defer to Kyle or anyone else. She had her own mind. Her own plans.

Melanie snuggled closer to Thomas in front of the fire. She sensed his worry and grief—and guilt—and held his hand. Lowell Whittaker offered her a brandy, but she didn't dare accept. Alcohol in her hyperalert state would be dangerous.

Lowell and Vivian told a funny story about Alex almost falling into the duck pond on a visit to Vermont, and Thomas managed a smile. Melanie nudged him. "Tell us what he was like in law school," she said. "I can just imagine what you two were like then."

It took a bit more prodding, but Thomas finally reminisced about his and his dead friend's days together at Yale. Melanie mumbled a few appropriate comments, but mostly listened sympathetically. He was still in shock, the poor thing. She hated to think what he'd be like after his daughter was dead, too, but nothing to be done about that now. They might have to postpone their wedding. Never mind the cold, New Year's Eve might be too soon.

Melanie felt her heartbeat quicken with irritation at the position Nora had put her in. She deserved to die—and to suffer before she gave up her last breath. Kyle never concerned himself with making a target suffer. Get in, get out. Do the job. That was his philosophy. Melanie wasn't that noble.

Maybe a Valentine's Day wedding would work. It could be fun. More fun, even, than New Year's Eve.

She smiled inwardly, already visualizing venues and decorations.

# *Twenty-Five*

Elijah was loading his backpack on the kitchen counter when Jo got up and eased onto a stool at the breakfast bar. It wasn't quite light out, and it was cold. He wasn't much on keeping the thermostat up and hadn't yet lit a fire in his efficient little woodstove.

He had the look of a man with a mission.

She'd slipped his nightshirt back on but was barefoot, her toes already cold. "You could hand me over a pair of your wool socks," she said.

"Top drawer of my dresser. All the socks you need."

He hadn't even looked up from his array of supplies. He was fully dressed—wool pants, fleece pullover atop an army-green undergarment of some kind. Not cotton, Jo thought. Cotton was a poor insulator when wet, dried slowly, and therefore tended to promote hypothermia.

He'd made coffee. She'd smelled it while she lay snug under his soft wool blanket and down comforter, warm and loose from their night of lovemaking. She'd heard him get up, run the shower, dress and head to the kitchen, and she'd debated whether it would be better to get up herself and go find out what he was up to, or if it was better that she didn't.

He had food, water, a tent, extra clothes, a sleeping bag that would keep him warm on Mount Everest. Snowshoes. Basic rescue equipment. If he had to spend the night in the elements, he'd be fine. If he had to dig a snow cave, he could.

"Only thing missing there is a mule," she said lightly.

He didn't answer. His hair was still a little tousled from last night. She remembered coursing her fingers through it as he'd spun her into orgasmic ecstasy.

"Where are you going?" she asked him.

He tucked a couple of protein bars into an outer pocket on his pack and zipped it up. "To find Devin and Nora or meet them coming down off the mountain. Out. Doesn't matter."

"Your route?"

"I can handle myself."

"Elijah."

He lifted the pack onto one shoulder, grabbed his coat off the back of the bar stool next to hers and finally looked at her, his eyes resigned, as if he'd known he wouldn't get out of there without having to deal with her. She hadn't disappeared in a *poof* with the coming of dawn. "I'll start on the falls trail and take it from there," he said. "I'll probably end up taking the saddle around to the back side of the mountain. Ten to one that's the route Nora and Devin took."

"To where your father died."

"Correct."

He headed out of the kitchen and down the short hall to the front room. Jo jumped off her stool, grimaced at the feel of the cold wood floor on her bare feet and went after him.

The view down the hill through the trees and out across the

lake was, indeed, breathtaking. Mist rose up from the water, and frost clung to the rust and burgundy oak leaves as the sun burned through in places, sparkling.

But Elijah didn't seem to notice. He shoved open a slider and stepped onto the deck, looking back at her with a harshness she hadn't experienced last night and knew had nothing to do with her. "Devin should have told us that Pop had cooked up something with him."

Jo's heart broke at the way he said "Pop." Drew had been a commanding force in the lives of his four children—in the lives of the people of Black Falls—and now he was gone. Elijah, in particular, had never had a chance to say goodbye.

But she nodded to the milky sky. "The weather isn't going to be good today."

"More reason to get moving."

She crossed her arms against the draft. "I can go with you."

"You're not dressed, and I'm not waiting."

"All right. I'll meet you."

Some of his intensity eased, and she thought she saw a spark in his very blue eyes. "Bring your own sleeping bag." But he sighed as he eased the door shut a little ways. "You need to go back to your life. You don't belong here, Jo. You never did."

"Nothing like waking up with regrets."

"I didn't say I had regrets. Jo—we're not right for each other. We weren't right fifteen years ago and we're not right now. Let's not break each other's hearts again."

"I didn't break your heart, Elijah." She moved right up to the slider screen and focused on the man in front of her and the old hurt deep inside her. "I'd have followed you to the army. Leaving me behind made it possible for you to do what you wanted to do."

"Saved me from your father having me thrown in jail."

"That, too. Elijah…I'm sorry." Jo saw it now, what needed to be said. "I should have let you go. I shouldn't have held on the way I did."

"Jo, Jo, Jo. Sweet pea. You didn't do anything that needs forgiving, including falling for me."

"Did you get my letters?"

She saw the muscles in his jaw tense and knew he hadn't expected her question.

Then his gaze softened, and he said, "Every one of them."

He shut the slider and headed down the deck stairs, his mind, she knew, back on his mission of the day. She shivered in the draft, thinking back to herself at eighteen, sitting on a boulder on the lakeshore and pouring out her soul in letter after letter in those first weeks after he'd left Black Falls for the army.

She hadn't let go easily.

She returned to the kitchen, splashed more coffee in her mug and sat at the breakfast bar as she debated her options, none of which involved leaving Elijah Cameron to his own devices.

Everyone in Black Falls had always known he would end up back there.

Everyone except Elijah—he had never expected to come home alive.

That was what Drew had tried to make her understand on their walk among the cherry blossoms. Elijah didn't court death. He wasn't reckless or pessimistic. He was forward looking and had a strong, positive mental attitude.

"But he's a realist," Drew had said. "He understands the dangers. He's looked death in the eye, and he knows if he makes it home, it's a bonus. It's not something he counts on."

Jo let the coffee warm her insides and soothe her soul.

Bad boy Elijah Cameron and good girl Jo Harper… She'd been a little bad last night. And he'd been good.

So good, she thought with a smile.

His phone rang, and she picked up the extension on the counter next to her.

"I'd like to speak to Sergeant Cameron, please," a male voice said.

She frowned. "Who is this?"

A gasp of shock. "Special Agent Harper?"

*Charlie Neal.* Jo almost knocked over her coffee. "Charlie, what are you doing?"

"Uh. Just checking on the flowers I sent. Were they pretty?"

"Very. Thank you." She spoke crisply, noting the time—just after 7:00 a.m.—and figuring Charlie was at, or almost at, school. "I know you've been in touch with Elijah. How did you find out his name, rank and home phone number?"

He ignored her question. "The stove fire. With Marissa. Was it the work of these assassins? Are you trying to protect us by not telling us?"

"Listen to me. Don't—"

"Marissa said it was just an accident."

Jo heard the fear in his voice. "You need to stop this, Charlie. Just stop."

"I have to go. I have play practice. Conor and I are on the production crew. In fact, we *are* the production crew."

Conor Neal was Charlie's first cousin, the second of the four children of the vice president's older brother, and, Jo suspected, a coconspirator in the airsoft prank and the source of the incriminating video.

Charlie disconnected quickly, and Jo immediately dialed

her boss. "You all are watching my young friend in D.C. like hawks, aren't you?"

Francona didn't answer right away. "Maybe he has a crush on you. If he were fifteen years older, you two could have a Rose Garden wedding."

"He didn't call me. He called a friend of mine up here in the cold."

"It's seven o'clock in the morning, Harper. Do I want to know where you are?"

She looked down at her nightshirt and her cold feet and thought of last night. "No."

"I didn't think so," Francona said, then blew out a breath. "By the way, your young friend got a sixty-eight on a calculus test yesterday. That's the kind of grade I'd get. He always aces his tests. Doesn't matter what subject. He doesn't get D's."

"Did someone ask him about it?"

"Yeah. He said it was a D-plus."

Francona disconnected, and Jo poured herself more coffee and headed for Elijah's bedroom and a pair of his socks. But his phone rang again. She snatched it up and said a tight hello, expecting her boss or Charlie on the other end.

"Elijah isn't answering his cell phone," a man with an easy Southern accent said. "Special Agent Harper, I presume?"

"And you would be—"

"Elijah's friend Grit."

She eased back onto the bar stool with her coffee. "The SEAL."

"Yes, ma'am. I saw your Internet video. You're as cute now as you were at seventeen."

"How would you know?"

But he'd hung up.

Jo slipped back into her clothes, grabbed her Sig, left her bath salts and got out of Elijah's house before she gave in to temptation and looked for old pictures of them together. Not only would it be a violation of trust, she didn't want to know. What would be worse, finding out he'd carried her picture off to war, or finding out he hadn't thought twice about her after he'd left Black Falls?

She had to remind herself she wasn't that hurt teenager anymore.

Maybe his SEAL friend had just decided to have a little fun with her and didn't have a clue what she'd looked like at seventeen.

She returned to her cabin, which was much colder than Elijah's house, and took a quick shower, got dressed and pondered whether she should have regrets about last night. She decided she shouldn't. It had been inevitable, she and Elijah in bed together. She'd known it would happen, on some level, the moment she'd spotted him walking down the road with Charlie's lilies.

On her way up to the ridge road above the lake, she listened to the forecast on her car radio. Snow was expected to start by midday and continue on and off through the night. It wouldn't be a huge storm by northern New England standards, but higher elevations could get up to a foot of snow.

Black Falls Lodge was quiet, just a few cars in the parking lot. Jo recognized Thomas and Melanie's rental. She pulled in next to Elijah's truck and climbed out. The air was close with the drop in pressure and rise in moisture, signaling the approaching storm. Skiers and snowshoers would welcome the snow. Devin—and Elijah—wouldn't care one way or the other. Jo wasn't as sure about Nora. Did she even know a storm was on the way?

As she crossed the lot to the lodge, she noticed A.J. out on the stone terrace. He gave her a curt wave and walked down to meet her. He had a mug of coffee with him and wore a canvas jacket, but no hat or gloves. "Thomas Asher and his fiancée just took off for the falls trail," he said.

"Everyone's up and at it, I see. Rigby?"

"He left early. Said he'd try up by the falls first. He's convinced Nora won't want to get too far out from the lodge."

"A lot of nervous people, A.J."

He cupped his mug in his hands and glanced across the road at the mountain, blue-gray under the clouds. "Elijah's gone up there."

"I know."

Just the barest smile from Elijah's older brother. "I thought you might."

"A.J.…your father…"

His gaze darkened. "Whatever happened up there in April, it had nothing to do with my brother living or dying in that firefight."

A.J. obviously wasn't looking for moral support from her, but Jo nodded anyway. "Agreed."

He frowned at her. "You'll need gear if you're going after Elijah. Go see Lauren. She's down at the shop. Help yourself."

"Thanks, A.J."

He dumped the dregs of his coffee in the dirt. "I called Scott Thorne, just in case. He's on his way up here."

Jo nodded and said nothing.

"Stay safe," A.J. said, and headed back inside.

# Twenty-Six

Nora knew she needed to calm down and keep herself from sweating in order to retain body heat, but she couldn't help herself. She broke into a run, her heart pounding with excitement. For the first time since she'd started up the mountain, she didn't care about the weight of her backpack. She'd found it—she'd discovered what Drew Cameron had been up to on the north side of Cameron Mountain.

It made sense now…why he'd asked for Devin's help, why he'd come up here in April.

She made herself stop running and hold her breath to the count of three, then exhaled slowly as she crept up the last few yards to a small cabin—a tiny little house, really. It was obviously new, not quite finished, built on what appeared to be an old foundation. If she imagined the land cleared and a well and some roads and maybe a neighbor closer than there were any now, the location, on level ground just beyond a quiet, beautiful cluster of tall evergreens, was perfect.

With the dense woods and all the contours on that side of the mountain—the dips and sags and knolls and gullies—

Nora could see why no one had come upon the cabin in April. Devin had found Drew's body at least two hundred yards through the trees near the trail down to the old logging road. It might as well have been a million miles.

Forcing herself to breathe normally, she pushed open the solid wood door and entered the cabin. It was small, smaller, even, than her room at home. The interior smelled of fresh wood. It had brand-new glass windows on one side of the front door and on each of the side walls and the back wall, but the walls themselves were unfinished. Open beams crisscrossed in the ceiling, and there was a second door on the back wall.

Nora looked around for nests—mice, bats, squirrels—but didn't see any. There was no insulation, no wiring, no generator—no outhouse, even. A simple black woodstove stood against the windowless wall, but it wasn't hooked up yet. Lengths of round metal stovepipe for a metal chimney were stacked neatly next to the stove, and Nora wondered if Drew had been on his way up here in April to install it.

Why hadn't he ducked in here for shelter? She couldn't imagine him getting lost, even in the snow. She hadn't really known him, but he'd struck her as a man as rugged and competent as his sons, just older.

"I can't wait to tell Devin," she whispered.

He was searching in another spot on the other side of the evergreens. They'd agreed to take a look around for what Drew had been building, then go on back down the mountain and talk to Jo and Elijah—one or both of them—about Melanie. Nora had obsessed all night and finally came to her senses. Her concerns about Melanie were real, she'd decided, but she had to keep them in perspective.

And of *course* her father wasn't involved in Alex's death.

Alex had often warned her against speculating ahead of the facts.

He was right. Searching for what Drew had been building up on the mountain and knowing Devin was there and they had a plan had helped her feel less out of control. She'd awakened before dawn and smashed Devin's cell phone in a panic at the prospect of someone tracking them. It seemed crazy now.

When she'd spotted the cabin, she'd spiraled right up again, not panicked and crazed this time but excited. She'd have something to show for her two nights on Cameron Mountain. She'd be able to give Drew's children some closure on what had happened to their father. He hadn't just wandered up here. He'd had a purpose.

She set her pack on the plywood floor. She was dirty and smelled, and she wanted hot water, hot food, a hot fire. But she could see snow falling in fine, tiny flakes and wasn't sure now that she and Devin should risk descending the mountain in the middle of a storm. They could take the trail down to the old logging road, but it wouldn't do them any good; they'd still have to trek miles to get to civilization. If one of them had left a vehicle there, that would have been a sensible option. On foot, they'd get to warmth, electricity and running water faster if they headed back to the lodge the way they'd come.

And now that she'd smashed Devin's phone, they couldn't just get to a spot where there was service and call for help. Not that there was one close by, anyway.

*We could sit out the storm,* Nora thought, surveying the dry, cozy cabin.

She and Devin had enough supplies to last at least another day, and maybe he could figure out how to install the chimney and get the woodstove working.

Nora liked the idea that no one else would be able to find the cabin, either. They'd be safe there.

She'd get Devin, and tell him her idea.

As she started back for the door, she heard someone moving fast in the evergreens out in front of the cabin and went still, stifling a startled scream.

"Nora!"

*Devin.*

"Run, Nora, run! Hide!"

He was yelling frantically, and she could hear the terror in his voice. Her heart jumped, a painful jolt of adrenaline surging through her as she gulped in air. She didn't know what to do. She didn't have a weapon or know how to fight or *anything.*

"Stay away from her!"

*Devin, Devin, Devin.*

Nora bolted for the cabin's back door, tore it open and scrambled outside, over scrap lumber and an old tarp slick with snow. She dived into the trees and crouched down low, snow whipping into her face and down her neck, sharp branches clawing at her.

*My backpack…*

She'd left it in the cabin. She had on her hat and gloves, but her tent, her sleeping bag—all her supplies were in her pack. She couldn't turn back, and she moved fast down a short incline into a steep, shallow gully.

The leaves were wet and slippery under the snow. One wrong step, and she could fall and break an ankle, knock herself out on a rock. Even if she was able to get right up again, she didn't want to lose her head start.

*Devin, where are you?*

She kept moving. She didn't call him, didn't say a word. She tried to make as little noise as possible as she descended the short, very steep hill into the crevice of the gully. She couldn't hear the sounds of running anymore—just her own panting, and, she swore, her thumping heart.

The sky seemed to disappear, become a part of the endless trees towering over her. The snow came down nonstop. She looked up at it and felt as if she were in the middle of an all-white kaleidoscope that just kept whirling and wouldn't let her out.

Choking back tears, too frightened to cry, she stumbled and fell onto one knee. The deep, sopping leaves and evergreen needles immediately soaked through her pants. She got up, shaking now.

Rotting fallen trees and huge boulders, some taller than she, littered the crevice, offering places to hide. Nora knew she had to stop, or whoever was chasing Devin would hear her, see her, follow her footprints…find her.

*I need to help Dev.*

But what could she do? She was defenseless, helpless. She didn't know where he was. Who was after him.

*Maybe it was just a bear chasing him, and he'll be all right.*

She dropped behind a massive boulder, into snow and brown, wet leaves. She sank as low as she could, squeezing herself between the cold granite behind her and the gnarly roots and trunk of a tall evergreen in front of her. She curled herself into a tight ball, trying to make herself as invisible and as hard to find as possible.

She knew it wasn't a bear chasing Devin.

She realized her hat had come off and pulled up her hood, which she should have done sooner to keep the snow from going down her neck. She thought of Elijah explaining how to trap body heat. Wind and cold, wet conditions were the enemy.

And here she was, tucked against cold, wet rock and sitting on cold, wet ground, both of which would suck the warmth out of her and send the cold straight in.

It was snowing. Hard.

*At least I'm out of the worst of the wind.*

Without her pack, with her pants already wet…

She started to cry, but she could hear Elijah warning the class not to waste energy and body heat panicking.

And she didn't want whoever was out there to find her.

She drew her knees up under her chin and watched the snow collect on the spruce needles and dead leaves.

Now she knew how Drew Cameron had died up here.

*He was murdered.*

*Just like Alex.*

She strained to hear even the slightest sound out above the gully, but all she heard was the howl of the wind whipping through the trees.

*Don't think.*

Nora squeezed her eyes shut tight and silently repeated her mantra.

*Don't think, don't think, don't think…*

# *Twenty-Seven*

Three hours after he'd left the lodge, Elijah was well onto the north side of the mountain and figured Jo was probably fifteen minutes behind him. He'd spotted her a while back. She'd catch up with him eventually. She was fit as hell.

He remembered the feel of those strong legs of hers last night.

How to mess with a man's situational awareness. He refocused on the steep, rough trail. Light, wet snow clung to the evergreens around him and slickened a stretch of exposed rock, but the storm was just starting. It would get worse. He'd be spending the night out in it.

He'd made good time and hadn't run into anyone or seen any sign of anyone on the mountain. If Devin and Nora had taken another route and gone back to the lodge, all the better. Elijah figured he and Jo could have a snowball fight and heat up cocoa over a hot fire.

Given the conditions, he estimated he was still a half hour out from where his father had died. They'd come this way dozens of times when Elijah was a boy. Day hikes, overnight camping trips. His father could hike for hours without a break and could sleep anywhere—on rocks, roots, pine needles, in the middle of ferns, on the side of a mountain. Elijah had inherited—or learned—those same abilities, which had come in handy during his years of military service.

The trail leveled off and narrowed even further as it curved sharply along the base of a rock-faced knoll. With a near-vertical wall of granite to his right and a sharp drop to his left, Elijah decided to stop thinking about Jo's legs and focus on not falling off the damn mountain.

He heard a scraping sound directly above him and then a hissing as small stones and dirt let loose and cascaded down onto him. He put up an arm, deflecting a baseball-size rock, and jumped back, maintaining his footing on the slippery ground.

More rock and dirt piled onto the trail in front of him.

He quickly retraced his steps back to where the trail had leveled off, then charged up through dense spruces to the top of the knoll. The mini landslide hadn't started spontaneously, when he happened to be on a tricky section of the trail. One wrong move, and he'd have gone right off the trail—at least a forty-foot drop.

But Elijah didn't see anyone, didn't hear anyone over the sound of the wind. The falling dirt and rock and the noise of his own running through fallen leaves and evergreen needles had covered any sound his attacker had made in retreat.

He stepped over a decaying, moss-covered oak stump to the edge of the rock face where the rock-and-dirt slide had started and saw footprints—almost certainly from a man's boots—fast disappearing in the accumulating snow.

He squinted out into the trees and falling snow, which

was coming down faster, more heavily. Even in the storm, it was a hell of a view out across the mountain peaks from up here—and a perfect spot to lie in wait for someone down on the trail.

His hand stung where he'd bloodied his knuckles dodging the mini landslide. Served him right, he thought, for not wearing his gloves. He focused his attention on the scene and noticed a walking stick on the ground, partway beneath a knee-high boulder that, obviously, someone had tried to dislodge, setting off the rock-and-dirt slide.

Elijah picked up the walking stick. It was Devin's—had to be. Had that skinny little bastard just tried to knock him off the mountain? But Elijah didn't think so. He clutched the thick walking stick. Devin had left it behind before his tumble at the falls yesterday. Jo had just fetched his pack back to the lodge.

Pushing back a spark of fear for the teenager, Elijah concentrated on the immediate problem. The main purpose of the attack hadn't been to kill or disable him—there were more efficient ways to accomplish either one—but, more likely, to interrupt him, delay him, slow him down.

And, possibly, to implicate Devin at the same time.

A diversion.

From what?

Elijah debated tracking his attacker, but only for a half second. Jo was right behind him, and she needed to know what was going on.

The snow was several inches deep as he headed back to the trail. He dropped down onto it just as Jo came around the curve. He felt a dangerous rush of emotion. He had no regrets about last night, he decided. Not one. But that didn't mean it had been sane to make love to her.

She fastened her turquoise eyes on him. "What happened to you?"

"Someone tried to play King of the Hill with me."

"You were attacked?"

"That sums it up." As he eased his pack off his shoulders and set it down in front of him he gave her a quick rundown of what had transpired.

"You don't know who it was?" she asked.

"Nope."

"Have you seen anyone else out here since you started up the mountain?"

He shook his head. "Just me and the chickadees. And you, of course. Didn't like being left behind, did you?"

She ignored him. "I haven't seen anyone, either. Let me look at your hand. Do you have a first-aid kit?"

"Yes, but all my hand needs is a glove. It's damn cold out here."

"Elijah—"

He interrupted her. "The storm's moving in fast. We're already up here. Let's just find Nora and Devin." He unzipped his pack's main compartment and got out his gloves, noting that Jo was decked out in high-end hiking gear and clothing—A.J., he thought. "You have a price tag hanging from your spanking-new backpack."

"I'll cut it off later."

"We can go our separate ways, or we can stay together." He put on his gloves, ignoring the sting of his knuckles. "Which?"

"We stay together," she said without hesitation.

"You armed?"

Jo gave him a tight look that reminded Elijah she was a federal agent.

"Because I am," he said.

He lifted his pack and shrugged it back on as he walked up through the trees onto the knoll, in order to bypass the pile of rock and dirt that now blocked the trail. He thought he heard Jo mutter something about Camerons and rules, but when he glanced back, she was right behind him. "I'm not letting you out of my sight," she said.

"Same here, sweet pea."

She fell in beside him. "It wasn't Nora or Devin who set off that landslide. You know it wasn't. A.J. said Rigby was checking up at the falls, but I didn't see him. There's cell phone coverage back there. I tried him a few times. No answer. I don't trust him, Elijah."

"Whoever attacked me knows he has company up here."

"He knows who it is, too," Jo said. "The storm's getting worse. If he's smart, he's beating a path off the mountain and out of Black Falls. But I never count on bad guys being smart. We need to find Nora and Devin before he does."

Elijah didn't respond. He knew he didn't need to.

Jo moved with assurance, gripping the front straps of her pack as she ducked around the low branches of a hemlock. She'd been hiking for hours and her pack had to be heavy, but she looked tireless, determined. That was the Jo Harper he'd always known. How the hell had she ended up protecting the vice president's kids?

How had he ever let her go?

But he had, and there was no going back.

They intersected the trail about a quarter-mile out beyond the knoll and took it uphill—no sign of footprints. Both the wind and snow picked up, reducing visibility. Elijah had snowshoes, but Jo didn't. Luckily, conditions were still fine for boots.

They were close now to where his father's body had been found by the teenager he'd befriended.

"Elijah."

Jo touched his arm and slowed her pace, but he'd heard it, too—a moan, a shuffling sound up ahead. He took off his pack, unzipping the outer compartment to locate his weapon, a .45-caliber Smith & Wesson. Her Sig, he'd already observed, was in a belt holster on her waist, under her new jacket.

He heard another moan, this time mixed with a sob, but left his gun where it was in his pack when he saw Devin stagger out from behind a snow-covered balsam fir. He tried to speak. "Nora..." He was ashen and in obvious pain as he clamped one arm to his middle. "He's after her."

Elijah heard Jo's quick intake of breath, but he was closer to Devin and caught him as he fell forward, shutting his eyes, grimacing. He sank against Elijah's chest. "You're all right now, Devin. I've got you. Who's after Nora?"

"That big bastard..."

"Rigby?" Jo asked sharply. "Where is he now?"

"I don't know. Nora..." Devin's eyes flickered open, and Elijah could see the fear shoot through the teenager as he tried to pull away. "I have to go to her."

Jo wasn't having it. "Not a chance." She shrugged off her pack and set it on a gnarled, snow-covered tree root. "You're hurt, and you need to be straight with us, so that we can help."

Elijah got Devin down onto the ground, his clothes already soaked. He moaned, near tears, shivering in pain as snow collected on his bare head.

"What happened?" Elijah asked.

"I spotted Rigby just past this grove of spruce trees. He didn't see me at first. Nora and I had split up. He was heading straight for where I was supposed to meet her. I pretended to be her—to distract him—and he came after me." Coughing, sobbing, Devin squeezed his eyes shut again, just for a moment, before he collected himself. "Once he figured out I wasn't Nora, I tried to warn her and give her time to hide. I was running like hell myself. He whacked me in the side and I went flying, got the wind knocked out of me. I thought he'd come and finish me off. But he didn't."

"You're not his priority," Jo said with brutal clarity.

Devin stared straight at her. "Nora was right. She said not to trust anyone."

"Where is she, Devin?" Elijah asked.

"I don't know. I tried to distract Rigby and lead him away from her. I yelled for her to run."

"He nailed you with your walking stick?"

"Yeah. I think so. I dropped it when I fell yesterday."

Elijah studied Devin a moment. The kid was a mess. His pack was gone, and he was injured, wet and cold. Even if Nora was better outfitted and uninjured, she, too, was in danger of hypothermia. Rigby didn't need to stick around. The treacherous conditions would do his work for him. Hence the mini landslide. Distract, delay, divert. Implicate Devin. Then let time, the cold, the wind and the snow take their toll. Make it look as if two teenagers with a flair for drama, at odds with each other, had come to a bad end on Cameron Mountain.

And make Devin look responsible—desperate for money, desperate to impress wealthy Nora Asher, refusing to take no for an answer.

But would Rigby get out of the storm, or would he make sure his work up here was finished?

Either way, Elijah knew they needed to get Devin warm and find Nora.

Fast.

He became aware of Jo peering at him, but she said nothing as she turned her attention back to Devin. "How long ago were you attacked?" she asked.

Devin's teeth started to chatter, and he seemed to shrink into the arm he held to his middle, as if to control waves of pain. "I don't know." He moaned, shivered. "Half hour? Maybe more."

Jo unzipped her pack and dug inside. "You helped Drew haul building materials up here last fall. Did you and Nora figure out what he did with them?"

He didn't answer and went very still, his jaw visibly tensed as he tried to keep his teeth from chattering. Elijah sensed his fear—his terror that he might say or do something that would worsen Nora's situation. It was what he and Jo needed to penetrate. "We're out of time, Devin," he said. "You need to tell us what you know. What if Rigby was up here in April and killed my father? What do you think he'll do to Nora?"

Devin pounded his fists into Elijah's chest, but he didn't have the strength to do any damage. Then he buried his face in his bloodied, bruised hands and cried. "I shouldn't have left her."

"Left her where, Devin?" Elijah asked.

He took his hands from his face and pointed up the hill into the trees. "There's a flat section up there. You go through spruce trees. On the other side—Nora found a cabin. We were both looking, figuring Drew must have built something up here."

Jo produced a dry fleece pullover from her pack. "You hadn't searched before?"

"No. I…" Tears streamed down his cheeks. "I couldn't."

"I understand," Jo said. "Did Nora go into the cabin?"

"Yeah. I think so. We were going to look around for a little while, then meet up and hike back down to the lodge and find you. The storm, though…" He looked at Elijah, then Jo, his fear and regret palpable now. "I have to find her. I have to help her."

Jo shook her head. "Elijah will go," she said firmly. "He knows these woods better than either of us. You and I will do what we can."

They would be taking a risk by splitting up, but Elijah knew—as Jo obviously did, too—that it was the only way they stood a chance of finding Nora before either Rigby or the conditions got to her.

Elijah rose, adjusted his pack. "You know what to do, Jo?" he asked, only half-serious, because, of course, she did. "Stay in the cover of the trees. Don't expose—"

"Yeah." There was just a hint of amusement in her eyes. "Go. I'll get Devin to the cabin and meet you there."

Elijah blew her a kiss and winked at her. "See you soon, sweet pea."

Color rose in her cheeks, and Devin managed a weak smile at her. "Sweet pea?"

A gust of wind rattled through the trees, and Elijah pushed off in the direction Devin had indicated. He thought of the countless times he'd been up here as a kid with his father, searching for that damn cellar hole.

# *Twenty-Eight*

Nora huddled against her boulder. She didn't know how long she'd been there. She was still in a tight ball, but she was shivering uncontrollably, her teeth chattering as she tried to stay quiet and out of sight. She needed to go to Devin, help him. Something terrible had happened to him. She just knew it. He'd sacrificed himself for her, but she felt paralyzed—what could she do to help him? She didn't want to make his situation worse, and she didn't want to get killed.

*Help me, someone. Please, help me.*

She didn't dare speak the words out loud. She wasn't sure she could, anyway, but she didn't want to make a sound.

*I'm so cold.*

She heard the crack of a branch somewhere behind her, maybe above her, and felt a painful surge of adrenaline. Tears poured down her raw cheeks and into her mouth. Her nose ran. She stiffened, trying to keep her teeth from chattering, in case whoever was out there could hear her.

*Mom...Dad...I'm so sorry, I'm so sorry...*

"Nora. It's Elijah."

She sniffled, thinking she'd imagined his voice.

"I'm here to help you, okay?"

His voice was so gentle, yet strong, confident. She pictured him in front of the class and remembered his so-blue eyes when he'd looked at her and asked her why she'd wanted to go winter camping. She'd given him some dumb answer. The truth was that she'd wanted Alex and her parents not to think of her as a wimp anymore. She'd wanted them to be proud of her.

*I am a wimp.*

"Call to me, Nora. Throw some snow up into the air. Anything."

Elijah sounded close. Her tears were flooding down her face now, snot running, her entire body shaking with relief and self-disgust and terror.

"Devin's okay. He's with Jo Harper. I'll keep you safe, Nora. Trust me."

*Devin, Devin—oh, God! Thank you! Thank you, thank you!*

Nora tried to speak, but she started to cry, and her body convulsed into shivers. She was so tired and tensed up, she couldn't even pry her arms apart to grab snow. Instead, she sat back hard against the boulder and managed to kick a foot out, causing snow to drop off the lower branches of the tree in front of her. A clump of it fell onto her nose. She couldn't even feel the cold.

She kicked again, and more snow fell, and then she couldn't do anything but shiver and cry and pray.

"Hey, kid."

Elijah eased in close to her. He was covered in snow but so strong and warm, and she suddenly imagined him bleeding in combat and felt horrible for how condescending she'd been about his military service.

"I'm sorry," she whispered. "I'm so sorry."

He got down low in front of her. His hat was covered in snow. His shoulders. Nora squinted, trying to focus. How much snow had fallen? She didn't even know.

"Nora. Look at me." His voice was quiet and reassuring, but firm. "Let me keep you safe, okay? Will you do that for me?"

She couldn't stop shivering. She thought she nodded, but she wasn't sure, and she hated him seeing her like this, crying and scared and shivering.

"I'm not going to let anything happen to you." He put a snowy, gloved hand toward her. "Can you stand?"

"I—I don't know. I did everything I could to stay warm and dry." Her words sounded strangled, unintelligible. Her mind felt fuzzy. Fresh tears flowed down her face. "Rigby found us. He had to have known about your dad's cabin."

She thought she saw Elijah falter, but she couldn't imagine such a thing. He was so strong. She'd never known anyone that strong. But he said, "Let's get you warm. Then we can go from there."

"I think I have mild hypothermia. I can't—stop—shivering...."

"I'm going to pick you up and carry you, okay?" He just scooped her up, as if she weighed no more than her stuffed penguin. She sobbed into his chest and for a second thought she'd throw up all over him, but she didn't.

"If he's still out there—" She got a death grip on his jacket and raised herself off his chest. "How did you find me?"

"Footprints, but they weren't easy to spot. I spotted his, too, but they lead down off the mountain." Elijah spoke calmly, clinically, as if he were discussing tracking a rabbit. "The weather's our ally right now. It's making us harder to find."

"Devin warned me..."

"He's hurt, but Jo's taking good care of him."

Elijah walked over the rough ground, not even straining under the weight of her and his backpack. He carried her up the steep hill onto the flat area where his father had built his cabin, where the Camerons had first settled in Vermont.

"There," Nora whispered. Her teeth still chattered, but she wasn't shivering as much as she absorbed some of his warmth and pointed. "Up by those evergreens."

"Spruces," he said, and she heard a smile in his voice.

She sank into his arms, vaguely aware of his movements and the howl of the wind, then the creak of a door and the smell of the cabin's fresh wood as he set her on the floor. She didn't want to be out of the protective cocoon of his arms, but she saw Devin curled up in a sleeping bag near the cold woodstove and almost screamed. He looked so awful. She crawled over to him, shivering and crying. "Dev, Dev. You saved my life. You did." But he was half-asleep and didn't respond, and she turned back to Elijah. "What can I do to help?"

Jo Harper answered. "Talk to him," she said as she grabbed Nora's backpack and got her sleeping bag and handed it to her. "Reassure him that you're fine. And get yourself warm and stay warm."

"I can do that."

Her eyes stayed on Nora. "And tell me what happened."

Jo was scarily focused, but pretty, Nora thought, fighting back tears. "I wish my dad were marrying you instead of Melanie."

Jo looked shocked for a split second, then was back under control. Elijah didn't comment, just went to the back of the cabin and checked the rear door while she got dry clothes out of her own pack and handed them to Nora. "Put these on. Can you manage on your own?"

"I think so." The thought of Jo or Elijah helping her made her feel self-conscious. "Yes. I can do it."

The wind picked up, whistling, beating fiercely against the cabin. But Nora decided the walls had to be solid, because any man who'd fathered Elijah would have insisted on building a structure that could withstand a Vermont storm.

She sniffled. "I shouldn't have come up here." Her fingers stiff inside her gloves, she unzipped her sleeping bag. Somehow she'd use it to create a little privacy as she changed, although she knew she had to be careful with her wet clothes. *I'm such a dope.* She sniffled again and said half to herself, "I didn't mean to cause problems for everyone. Just help Devin. Please."

"I'll help both of you," Jo said, "but I need your cooperation."

Startled by Jo's tone, Nora realized that in her own way Jo was just as big a hard-ass as Elijah.

He returned from checking the back door and touched Jo's arm. "Rigby's either waiting out the storm, or he's already cut his losses and gotten out of here. Either way, it's near-zero visibility out there right now. We're not going anywhere."

Nora saw something between them. A spark, a look. She wasn't quite sure, but what it meant was obvious to her. Jo was falling for Elijah—and he for her.

"Elijah," Jo said, "if Rigby comes back and tries anything, you know you can defend yourself, don't you?"

He grinned at her. "Yeah, Agent Harper, I know."

Nora got closer to Devin. "Avert your eyes while I change."

He smiled weakly at her. "Sure, Nora."

"Dev…you saved my life."

"We'll be okay," he said. "Promise."

She suddenly felt warmer, safer. Jo and Elijah would protect her and Devin.

They'd all be okay.

# Twenty-Nine

The storm had forced Melanie and Thomas back to the lodge. She washed her hands with Vermont-made goat's milk soap in the ladies' room. Thomas was getting on her nerves. He was so preoccupied with his daughter, never mind how irresponsibly she'd behaved. Melanie knew she needed to be understanding, but she hated Nora for all her dramatics.

She hadn't thrown up. That would come later. Right now, she knew she needed to push her fury down deep and focus on making sure Kyle had a chance to execute his plan for her almost-stepdaughter and her no-account boyfriend. Melanie had her instructions. Kyle had found her before he went up on the mountain. She felt a familiar jolt of excitement mixed with panic at the prospect of doing her part to make everything work out.

"Mislead any search teams, Melanie," Kyle had told her early that morning. He'd been so grave and humorless with all his misgivings about their situation. "Pick a spot and send them there. Anywhere but the north side of the mountain."

He'd been so confident that was where Devin and Nora

would be. Melanie had argued that they'd have to explain the lie to A.J. Cameron and any search teams once Nora's and Devin's bodies were discovered.

But Kyle had an answer for that, too. "We blame Devin for the misinformation. Leave that part to me." He'd paused, then added, "He and Nora aren't making it down the mountain."

Melanie still had misgivings. The more she thought about why she and Kyle had been dispatched to kill both Drew Cameron in April and Alex Bruni yesterday, the more she didn't like it. Drew had never made any sense—he didn't fit the profile of anyone else she and Kyle had killed. Who was he? As far as she knew, he was just an old Vermonter with no serious connections.

Except, she thought, to Alex Bruni, a repeat guest at Black Falls Lodge.

What if the person—or people—who dispatched killers like her and Kyle, paid them and kept them from knowing too much about their targets, had decided Drew and Alex were threats to *them?* To their network of paid assassins?

That made screwing up that much more complicated and dangerous.

And if she suspected she and Kyle had been hired to kill Drew Cameron and Alex Bruni to protect one of their own, then Kyle suspected it, too.

No wonder he was so serious.

Melanie dried her hands. She liked the soap. It had a clean, soft scent. Roses, maybe? She didn't know. She inhaled the scent, calming herself, and returned to the dining room. It was almost dusk now. Scott Thorne, the Vermont State Police trooper, had left after interviewing both her and Thomas, every indication suggesting an official search for Nora and

Devin would be launched before long. Melanie had done everything possible to make sure that wouldn't happen.

The handful of guests staying at the lodge seemed to enjoy being there during a storm. Three or four inches of snow had accumulated, enough to whiten the landscape. Conditions were worse at higher elevations. She wanted to go sit in front of the fire, but Thomas was still rooted to his chair at a table near the windows overlooking the terrace and the meadow. Lauren Cameron had brought them hot cocoa. She was so beautiful, and from a good family, too. Melanie imagined Lauren and A.J. having her and Thomas up to their house for dinner, becoming friends with them. But with Drew Cameron's death, and now a series of deaths about to happen, Black Falls would be reeling for a while. Melanie wasn't sure she and Thomas would want to spend much time there. Maybe they should put this experience behind them and make their own friends.

She pulled out a chair at the table and sat down, irritated when Thomas didn't even look at her. He stared blankly out at the snow. A.J. had dropped into a chair across from him. A.J. looked serious and hard-bitten, but from what Melanie had gathered, he usually did.

"I just heard from Kyle," she said with just the right touch of both relief and caution. "He got through to me on my cell phone just before his died. I could hardly hear him, but Nora's fine. He ran into her above the falls. She didn't have a clue anyone was worried about her."

"Oh, thank God." Thomas flopped back in his chair and almost cried. "Thank God."

Melanie liked giving him the good news. He grabbed her hand and squeezed it, and she let her eyes fill with tears. "I know it's a hard time for you, darling," she said.

"Did he say anything about Jo and Elijah?" A.J. asked.

She shook her head. "No, but he only had a few seconds, really, before his cell phone died."

A.J. said nothing, and Melanie sensed his skepticism. The Camerons were all so damn tough. The police could check her cell-phone records for proof that Kyle had called her, but they'd have to have a reason. She wouldn't give them one, and if she did, she'd get out, flee. She didn't want it to come to that, but she was prepared. She had money stashed. So did Kyle. They could disappear for a couple of years. Let things cool off. Then resurface.

Thomas pushed his cocoa aside and shot to his feet, and she bit back her irritation with A.J. His question had clearly spoiled Thomas's sense of relief. "Then Jo and Elijah are looking in the wrong place," he said. "They're stuck in the storm now, too. What about Devin?"

A.J.'s eyes darkened, but he left the dining room without another word.

Melanie stood next to Thomas and hooked her arm through his. "You're so warm," she said, leaning into his shoulder.

"The snow's piling up. The wind, especially up on the mountain…" He was clearly too distressed to go on.

Melanie slipped his arm around her waist and snuggled into him even closer. He was a little soft in the waist. Not hard everywhere like Kyle. But that was okay. "Kyle's with Nora. He'll do what he can for Devin. And Jo and Elijah—"

"I'm not worried about them. They're both Black Falls natives who know these mountains better than anyone." Thomas seemed to struggle to make himself sound optimistic. "They'll do fine up there."

Melanie felt a sharp prick of fear.

Then she thought—*this could be good.*

It could work to her advantage if Kyle didn't come off the mountain, either.

Whatever happened, she'd do what she had to do. Kill Nora. Kill Devin. Kill Kyle, too, if she had to. Jo, Elijah. Thomas.

All of them.

But that was crazy thinking, an overreaction to her circumstances, although she relished how it made her feel, how it relieved her fear and her tension to picture herself killing all the people who threatened her and her happiness with Thomas.

He kissed her on the top of the head. "What would I do without you?"

Melanie squeezed him gently. Everything would work out. She and Kyle had yet to fail, and they understood what they were up against. They'd do what they had to, and that would be that.

Kyle would find a new partner, and she would marry Thomas.

They just had to get through the long night ahead.

# Thirty

Grit had spent the day shaking every tree in Washington, and he found his way to the attractive suburban street where Thomas Asher lived just as the sun went down. He'd had to do a combination of bus, cab and walking to get there.

The house was a Dutch Colonial with mature gardens and shade trees. Nice place even in the November gray, Grit thought. Earlier in the day he'd been to the Bruni house in Georgetown. It was smaller but more expensive, more elegant. Law enforcement had already done their thing there, and it was quiet when Grit went by. But he figured it was probably still under surveillance and his presence had been duly noted.

Just like now, he thought as he headed up the brick walkway.

The front door of the Asher house opened, and a woman who looked to be in her early forties stumbled out and ran down the steps. She stopped abruptly and stared down at pink and white impatiens drooping at her feet along the edge of the walkway.

Grit started to introduce himself, but without acknowledging him, without even looking at him, she said, "I played hopscotch with my daughter out here when she was three. I can see her now. She was such a sweet little girl. I remember one day when Thomas came home early and joined us. We laughed and laughed. Such a simple thing." Tears shone in her eyes as she finally focused on Grit. "We were a happy family. I don't care what anyone else thinks."

"You shouldn't," Grit said.

"You're one of Thomas's friends?"

"No, ma'am. My name's Ryan Taylor. I know Elijah Cameron—"

"Elijah?" She seemed confused. "From Vermont?"

"That'd be the one."

She took in a breath through her nose and collected herself. Carolyn Asher Bruni, Grit had learned, was successful in her own right, even compared to her second husband. But she held all that in check right now, clearly exhausted and grief stricken despite her self-control. "I only know Elijah by reputation," she said. "I've met his brother A.J. and his sister, Rose. They're lovely people. I'm sorry. I'm not myself. You're not from Vermont, though, are you?"

"No, ma'am, I live here in Washington."

She glanced back at her former house. "I threw away a good life, Mr. Taylor. I didn't expect to come out here, but here I am. Do you know what I want right now more than anything else? Just to go back in time—to be here, playing hopscotch with my daughter."

Unspoken was what was going on in Vermont. What had happened a few miles away in Washington. "If anyone can keep Nora safe," Grit said, "it's Elijah. I don't know Jo Harper—"

But Carolyn Bruni wasn't listening. "I stayed home with Nora the first few years. Thomas and I never had other children. We got caught up with other things."

"I guess that happens."

"Alex was so ambitious, so driven. I loved that about him. Thomas is more laid-back. I thought being here..." She took a step forward, her shoulders back as if she were steeling herself against a hard wind. "It doesn't matter now. Alex is gone, and Thomas is no longer part of my life."

"He's still your daughter's father."

"Nora's barely a part of my life anymore, either," she said with a trace of regret, maybe bitterness, too. "She's eighteen. She's taking a break from school right now, but she'll go back."

"I'm sorry for your loss," Grit said simply.

"You want to know if I have a clue as to who killed my husband." She got combative and raised her chin at Grit. "If *I* killed him. Isn't that what everyone wants to know? I don't, and I didn't."

"Mrs. Bruni—"

"Some days I wondered who *wouldn't* want to kill Alex. I don't mean that as an insult. He could be very intense, exacting, tough. He didn't demand of anyone what he wouldn't demand of himself." She shook her head, some of the fight going out of her. "I'm so jet-lagged, and upset, obviously. I barely know what day it is. Maybe it'll all turn out to be just a terrible accident." She narrowed her tired eyes on him. "Why are you here?"

He wasn't all that sure himself. "Just trying to help. Your daughter—"

"Nora knows what she's doing. She's very capable. She's young, but she'll find her way."

"You're not worried about her going off on this camping trip by herself?"

"I'm concerned about how she's handling Alex's death, but

no, I'm not that concerned about her camping in Vermont. She's very levelheaded. She and Alex got along all right, but they didn't see that much of each other. If you're wondering if she hired someone to kill him, that's ridiculous. She wouldn't know the first thing about how to do such a thing."

"You just said she's capable."

"In the woods, not with hired killers." Her cheeks reddened suddenly, but she remained under control. "I should go. I don't normally pour out my soul to a perfect stranger."

"Melanie Kendall went up to Vermont with your ex-husband," Grit said. So far, his turning-over-of-rocks and shaking-of-trees hadn't turned up much on the fiancée and future stepmother.

Carolyn Bruni's gaze steadied on him. "Good for her."

"Nora get along with her?"

"I have no idea. We haven't discussed Melanie. She has absolutely nothing to do with me. Good to meet you, Mr. Taylor." Carolyn Bruni paused and gave him a cool, superior smile. "Perhaps you and Elijah Cameron should mind your own business."

She marched past Grit, got into a little BMW parked on the side of the road and sped off.

Moose fell in next to Grit on the walkway. *"The mother's conflicted,"* Moose said.

"Well, I guess she is. She's also a Type A control freak who thinks her daughter hates her and she deserves to be hated."

*"She has regrets. Big regrets. It's tough living with big regrets."*

Grit breathed out. "Yeah. It is."

He noted a surprising lack of security at the Asher house. He could have gotten inside in seconds. Instead, he walked down to a dark sedan parked a half block from the spot that Carolyn Bruni had just vacated. His leg wasn't hurting much today. He liked walking.

A window rolled down, and Grit said to the beanpole of an FBI agent behind the wheel, "I'll save you the trouble of trying to figure out who I am and what I'm up to. I just need a ride back to town. I took the bus, and my leg—"

"Get in the car."

He climbed into the backseat. Up front next to the beanpole FBI agent was a very cute female FBI agent who turned a little in her seat and gave Grit a steel-melting look. "You've been talking to a lot of people today, Petty Officer Taylor."

"You know my name? I'm flattered. You're—"

"We're the ones driving you back to Washington."

"Guess you don't need directions to my place, do you?"

Not even a twitch of a smile. "You were outside the vice president's residence today," she said.

Grit didn't respond. The street he'd been on was a public street, and they all knew it. He'd begun to wonder if maybe the assassins theory was just the product of a bored genius kid with an Internet connection, but that didn't feel right to Grit, mostly because of Myrtle and the Russian and the poisoned toothpaste. Myrtle didn't get bored. She didn't make up stuff.

"We appreciate your service," the cute FBI agent said when they finally pulled up to his dump of a building. "Now mind your own business."

"Mrs. Bruni said the same thing, except she didn't add the platitude—"

"It's not a platitude." She seemed chagrined.

"You don't want to know my assassins theory, do you?"

"No. Good night, Petty Officer Taylor."

One thing about his military service, Grit thought dispassionately, was how good it had made him at detecting when people were hiding things. Even those people who were good at hiding things.

The two FBI agents already knew about assassins.

The beanpole glanced in his rearview mirror at Grit's reflection. "You okay back there? Your leg…"

Grit opened the door and got out. He wasn't getting into the nuances of transtibial amputations with the guy. Besides, he'd spotted Myrtle hiding behind a sick cedar tree on the corner of his building and figured she wouldn't really want to talk to the FBI.

After they left, she stepped out onto the street and shuddered. "Holy moley. I just saw a rat the size of a raccoon."

"Ah. Little fella."

"Why do you live like this?"

"Like what?"

"Never mind. I'd go in, but for all I know, you have pets, and I can only just imagine." She nodded at the retreating car. "Feds?"

"I caved and gave you up after the girl fed batted her eyes at me."

"Are you ever serious? Don't answer—I know. You're a man of action. Words mean nothing, so you might as well be irreverent." Her lavender eyes stayed on him a fraction longer than he would have preferred. "I did more research on you, Grit. It wasn't easy. You and your friend Elijah Cameron are a couple of ghosts, but you're both bona fide, indestructible American heroes."

He thought of Moose, who really was a hero. "No one's indestructible."

"Figure of speech," Myrtle said. "You know what I mean.

Let me buy you a cup of coffee. We can talk about the vice president's son, a dead ambassador, his best friend, his stepdaughter and assassins."

"And Drew Cameron," Grit said.

Reporter that she was, she pounced. "Who?"

"Coffee first."

"Not here. We'll take my car," she said, eyeing the cedar tree. "I don't do well with rats."

# *Thirty-One*

Staying low, Jo crept to the back window of the cabin. Elijah was checking the window on the side wall. Weapons drawn, they'd taken turns on watch overnight. It was first light, and the storm was over, leaving behind eight or ten inches of wet snow. The branches of the spruce trees surrounding the cabin drooped under the weight of the snow, but the cabin itself had remained dry. Even the worst of the winds hadn't penetrated its weather-tight walls.

Leave it to a Cameron, Jo thought as she noticed Nora stir. Devin was already awake, just not talking. He'd slept little and had tried several different positions before he'd found one that was the least painful, propping himself against the wood-stove. He hadn't moved since.

Nora sat up, her sleeping bag twisted around her, and tried to smile. "I wish the woodstove was hooked up and we could build a fire."

"A fire would confirm to Kyle that we're here and you and Devin survived," Jo said. "Are you warm enough?"

Nora nodded, then gave Devin a worried look. "You okay, Dev?"

"Yeah." His lips barely moved as he spoke. Any movement seemed to cause him pain. He was clearly miserable, but he said, "I'm fine."

As the storm had raged around them, Nora had quietly related how she and Devin had been conducting their own background check of her father's fiancée. Both Jo and Elijah had forbidden the use of flashlights, and with the storm, there was no moonlight or starlight to help ease the darkness on the mountain. She'd heard the pain, grief and loneliness in Nora's voice as she'd told her story.

"I've made a mess of things," she'd said, almost tonelessly. "I'm sorry."

Elijah had spoken up at that point. "Sorry for what?"

"For putting you all in this position."

"Did you hit Devin? Did you chase yourself into that gully? You're not the enemy here, Nora. You're a kid. If you made mistakes—hell, why should you be exempt? Put them behind you. Focus on what you can do right now."

"I can't do anything. I'm useless."

"You can stay warm and dry and get some rest." When he'd paused, Jo had felt his smile as he teased. "I'll have all I can do to carry Jo down this mountain."

Of course she had protested, and Nora had sniffled and laughed, at least a little, Elijah's comment providing the distraction it was meant to.

He and Jo both checked on Devin regularly through the long night.

A.J. knew his brother had hiked out to the north side of the mountain, and that Jo had followed him. When they didn't turn up, he wouldn't sit around for long. Neither would his family. Her paramedic sister, her firefighter brother—and her father, the former police chief. They'd all be raising hell by now.

Then there was Beth's trooper boyfriend. Jo smiled to herself as she stayed to one side of the window and peered out at the snowy landscape. Scott Thorne would just love to rescue a Secret Service agent and Special Forces soldier.

But she knew that wasn't exactly true, either. Scott would want what they all did—a good outcome. Kyle Rigby in custody, explaining himself. Devin and Nora safe. Jo and Elijah back on the lake.

"Everyone down!"

It was Elijah, intense. Jo dropped, even as a sharp crack shattered the silence and, simultaneously, the front window splintered and shards of glass crashed onto the cabin floor.

Another shot went through the same window as the first and struck the solid wood beam above the back wall of the cabin.

Staying low, Jo dived for Nora and Devin. Nora had already thrown herself onto Devin and was half dragging him, half rolling with him across the plywood floor around to the back of the woodstove.

She looked up, her eyes wide with terror. "What's happening?"

"We're getting shot at." Jo shoved the backpacks toward them. Devin stirred, white-faced as he caught the strap of Nora's pack and pushed it at her. "Use the packs for cover. Stay behind the woodstove. Understood?"

Devin barely reacted, the pain of his injuries evident in every breath he took. Nora nodded, recoiling as a third round hit the same window, and the report of the heavy-caliber weapon boomed and echoed on their quiet hillside.

Elijah pulled the slide on his .45. He'd already raced to the front of the cabin and was positioned in the corner by the shot-out window.

He aimed and fired one round.

Crouched down, Jo ran to him, ignoring the glass shards as Elijah fired again.

Two more shots in quick succession smacked into the sturdy wood door.

Jo knew she didn't need to tell Elijah it was a heavy-caliber weapon firing at them: an assault rifle. And she didn't have to tell him it was Kyle Rigby.

He probably had a thirty-round clip. A lot of bullets.

When he used them up, he'd reload.

"He's using the trees my father cut down as cover. Right by the spruce trees." Elijah didn't take his eyes off the spot. "I'm going after him."

"I'll keep him from moving," Jo said. "He wants us all dead, Elijah."

"I can tell from the bullets." He looked at her, his gaze steady. "We're past negotiations, Jo."

"Yeah. Go." Her breath caught. "Stay safe."

He winked at her. "Be good, sweet pea."

Moving fast, he crossed to the back of the cabin. Snow blew in as he went out the back door, shutting it silently behind him.

Nora and Devin stayed quiet and still behind the woodstove, huddled among the backpacks, as protected as possible with a madman shooting at them.

Not a madman, Jo thought. Rigby had examined his

options and picked the one he'd considered most likely to get the job done. He knew what he was up against. He'd counted on Nora and Devin freezing to death up here, and when he'd realized that wasn't going to happen, he'd come up with a new plan.

The all-or-nothing approach.

She fired toward the fallen trees before he could get off another shot, ducked low and fired again from another angle. She wanted to provide cover fire and keep Rigby pinned down and guessing. He was aware he was dealing with two shooters. Let him think both she and Elijah were still in the cabin.

"Rigby, I know it's you out there," she yelled. "Let's talk."

"No talking. You're all dead."

"Let's figure something out." She moved to another spot on the window and fired again. "You're not in a good situation. I'm armed, I've got food and water and I'm warm. Bet you're frostbitten."

Another shot.

Not frostbitten enough not to be able to shoot.

Then she heard three quick shots of a .45.

*Elijah.*

She waited, poised to shoot again if necessary.

But there was silence. Finally Elijah called to her. "He's down, Jo. No sign of another shooter."

She turned to Nora and Devin, who still hadn't moved. "I have to go out there. I'll be back in two minutes. Stay put."

She raced out the front door and into the snow, wet and deep as it sparkled in the bright rising sun. She pushed through the tiny clearing in front of the cabin and slowed her pace as she ducked behind the felled trees and entered the spruce grove.

Elijah had picked up Rigby's assault rifle—not that there

was any chance Rigby would be able to use it. But it was what Jo would have done.

She knew Elijah had checked Rigby but she felt compelled to do so herself. He was dead.

"I'm sure you gave him a chance to put down his weapon," she said.

"Ten chances."

Rigby had fired ten rounds.

"Don't touch anything. The police need to get here."

There was just a hint of humor in his very blue eyes. "Sure, Jo."

She heard a cry of pure anguish up by the cabin and turned just as Nora leaped out the front door into the snow and ran, tearing off back toward the gully where Elijah had found her.

Jo went after her, post-holing her way through the deep snow. "Nora, stop," she called sharply. "You don't have the energy or the equipment to go far. Neither do I. You're safe now."

But she kept running.

"*Stop.* Now, Nora."

She fell onto her knees in the snow. "It's all my fault," she sobbed, covering her head with her hands. "It's all my fault. I should have left well enough alone."

Jo caught up with her and crouched next to her. She said gently, "It's okay, Nora. Come on, kiddo. We're safe. Let's go back into the cabin. Storm's over. We can get out of here."

She dug her fingers into her hair and seemed to try to rip it out as she cried. "I want my mom, but she doesn't care about me." She raised her head, dropping her arms as tears flowed down her pale cheeks and she shook uncontrollably. "I'm so scared. My dad—what if he's involved in whatever's going on? He's so caught up in Melanie."

"First things first, Nora."

She glared up at Jo. "What if he did something stupid, and now he's ruined his life? What if he's being blackmailed?"

There was no way Jo was going into all that right now. "We'll get everything sorted out. You knew something was wrong, and you were right. You trusted your instincts."

"I never thought anyone wanted to kill me. I wouldn't have come up here. I'm so stupid." As she spoke, she started shivering. "I'm so cold. Jo…"

"You survived. You did what you had to do."

"Don't patronize me." With a sudden burst of anger, Nora shook off Jo's offer of a hand and stalked back toward the cabin. But she stopped short of the front door, lurched toward a felled tree and vomited in the snow.

Jo hung back and said nothing. When Nora finished, she just silently returned to the cabin.

Elijah stepped out from the spruce trees and stood next to Jo. "Rigby had his chance to get out of here and disappear. Interesting that he didn't."

Jo nodded grimly. "He knew he had to succeed up here. Failure wasn't an option."

"Yeah."

"We need to get these kids off this mountain. How much time do you figure before the cavalry arrives?"

"My guess is they're close enough to have heard the shots."

"I can go down the trail and meet them."

"No." Elijah shook his head and brushed a knuckle across her cheek. "We stick together."

# *Thirty-Two*

Grit stood outside the revolving doors of the hotel where Ambassador Bruni had been killed and watched the passersby. It was almost noon and cloudy, but other people seemed to be enjoying themselves. Last night, Myrtle had said to meet her there. She'd added a little something to her coffee and was in a maudlin mood when they'd parted, the kind that indicated she had layers and secrets and dark corners that she didn't like to look in.

He had a bad feeling about Myrtle.

Just down the street a fair, buff teenage boy in a navy Georgetown University cap, hooded sweatshirt and tan chinos was staring at the spot where Bruni was hit.

The pants were neatly pressed.

Well, well, Grit thought, and eased in next to the kid. "Hello, Charlie."

He looked startled. "That's not my name."

"Sure it is. You know a friend of a friend of mine. Jo Harper."

"The Secret Service agent in the video?"

All innocent. Grit narrowed his eyes. "What're you doing here, Charlie?"

"What makes you—"

"Prep-school pants. And the hat and the sweatshirt both Georgetown? Come on."

He reddened some, but not much. "I have a trombone lesson around the corner."

"You don't play trombone."

The kid stared at the asphalt and said calmly, "A doctor's appointment would have worked better?"

"No," Grit said.

"Who I am is none of your business."

"I'm a caring citizen." But Grit figured Charlie Neal, being a genius as well as sixteen, already knew who he was. "There are no Secret Service agents strong-arming me right now, so that means you gave them the slip somehow. What did you do, hide yourself in a suitcase?"

He shrugged. "I didn't do anything. You obviously have me confused with someone else. I'm just a kid."

Grit studied him thoughtfully and considered his research into the life and times of Charles Preston Neal, the only son and youngest child of the current vice president of the United States. "Your cousin," he said finally, "Conor Neal. You two are the same age. You both look like Prince Harry did at sixteen."

"Prince Harry?"

"You and the cousin switched places. Create a little bedlam, and next thing, he's you and you're him. Conor doesn't have a Secret Service detail. You do." Grit thought it through and figured that was it. "It's sort of like *The Prince and the Pauper.* Ever read that book?"

Charlie didn't answer, but his ears got red under the lower edge of his Georgetown cap.

"Must be refreshing," Grit said with some sympathy, "just to be normal."

Big roll of the eyes. "That's not the point." Charlie turned his head and glared at Grit. "You're Petty Officer Taylor, right? You and Petty Officer Michael Ferrerra, also a Navy SEAL, were each awarded a Silver Star last year. It's for gallantry in action—"

"I know what it's for."

"I keep track of Silver Star recipients. I figure it's the least I can do." Charlie stuffed his hands into the front pocket of his oversize sweatshirt and kept his blue Prince Harry eyes on Grit. "Petty Officer Ferrerra died in April. He saved your life."

"Photographic memory?"

"I just pay attention, Petty Officer Taylor."

"Just Grit is fine. And not because you're the vice president's son." He nodded to the spot where Bruni was hit. "Was Ambassador Bruni meeting you the other morning?"

Charlie's shoulders slumped, and he shook his head but didn't speak.

"Why are you here, Charlie?" Grit asked.

"I don't want to get anyone into trouble."

"You want to keep yourself out of trouble, too, don't you?"

That gave him his spine back. "I don't care about that. What're they going to do? Just watch me even closer than they do now. The people who are supposed to keep an eye on me will get in trouble, though. And that's not fair."

"It's also not your problem."

Charlie glanced behind them at the revolving doors, then shifted back to the street. "I followed him here," he said. "I wanted to talk to him about Agent Harper. My sister Marissa told me they're friends. Agent Harper has lots of friends in various federal law enforcement agencies, but I didn't want to go to them. You know. Risk getting them in trouble."

"Risk having them recognize you and haul your ass back to school. Who's 'him'? Who'd you follow?"

"It doesn't matter. Marissa misinterpreted their friendship. It's not as close as I thought."

Grit realized Charlie wasn't talking about Bruni, but he said, "Is Marissa like you, smart and doesn't mind her own business?"

"She's not as smart as me. I'm not bragging. I'm just..."

"You're just stating the facts," Grit finished for him.

Charlie hunched his shoulders and said quietly, "I wanted to figure out how I could make amends."

"Ah." Grit got it now. "You're talking about Thomas Asher."

The kid was silent.

Grit figured it was pretty much like holding a live grenade, having the veep's kid right next to him with no Secret Service protection. "All right," he said. "Let's go."

"Go? Go where?" Charlie straightened, his cockiness back in full force. "I have to get to school. I have another calculus test today. I can't miss it. I'm down to a B-plus average as it is. My cousin took this one test for me, and he isn't great at math—"

"Too bad."

"You can't just kidnap me."

Grit scratched the side of his mouth. Now what? He'd tried calling Elijah first thing that morning but got no answer. It was lousy weather up north. Snow, ice, wind. He could always try to reach Agent Harper, but Grit had a feeling she was onto Charlie herself. And she was up north in the same storm as Elijah and probably in his back pocket wherever he was.

"The Secret Service will have egg on its collective face," Charlie said, "if it gets out that my cousin and I switched identities."

There was that. "Tell me about Thomas Asher."

Charlie debated a moment, his lips compressed in a manner that suggested he was accustomed to being called onto the carpet. He nodded back toward the hotel entrance. "He went in through the revolving doors and entered the restaurant and waited at his table for a while. I hung around. I figured I'd talk to him after he finished breakfast. I assumed he was meeting someone, but I kept checking and no one ever came. Then there was this big commotion out here."

"Where exactly were you?"

"In the lobby outside the restaurant. I didn't see Ambassador Bruni get hit."

"Asher?"

"No. Impossible." Charlie shook his head, adamant. "He ran out into the lobby to see what all the commotion was about. Then he left."

"How'd he look?"

"Shocked. Upset. Terrified—but under control. He was in self-protection mode."

"Witnesses?"

Charlie adjusted his cap, a hunk of blond hair falling down on his forehead. "That's why I came here today. I hoped it would help me remember."

"Did it?"

"There was a messenger on a bicycle. A woman. I saw her. I heard about the tip the police received. I didn't realize she'd witnessed what happened."

Grit waited, then said, "And?"

The kid obviously didn't want to go on. Finally he answered. "Mr. Asher spoke to her."

"Can you describe her? The tip didn't have details. If Thomas phoned it in, he might have been too upset to remember specifics and—"

"Fleet of Pedal is the name of the messenger service."

Grit waited again. "Charlie. You have to tell the police."

"It doesn't have to be me." Charlie turned to him. "You could tell them."

"I wasn't here," Grit said. But he could tell the FBI or even Myrtle, let her work her wonders and get Charlie's tidbit to the police without putting him into the middle of a media firestorm.

In the meantime, Grit wasn't about to leave the only son and youngest child of the vice president of the United States—a smart, troubled, sixteen-year-old kid with assassins on the mind—out on the streets.

He jerked a thumb at Charlie. "Let's go."

"Are you kidnapping me?"

"I'm taking you back to school."

Except he didn't have a car. Where the hell was Myrtle?

Ten seconds later, as if he'd conjured her up, she pulled next to the curb in a fancy little car, her window rolled down. "Sorry I'm late." She frowned at Charlie. "Who are you?" She swallowed, obviously recognizing him. "Oh. You do have some interesting friends, Petty Officer."

They got in her car, Grit in back with Charlie, and Myrtle drove them out to the rolling northern Virginia campus of a very private school. Grit's high school in the Florida panhandle had been a series of trailers. Charles Preston Neal was good-looking, smart, athletic—and surprisingly invisible. It was tough to stand out when you were good at everything and were handed everything. He wanted to matter.

Not your problem, Grit reminded himself. "How does your cousin explain where he's been when you're off following people and hunting bad guys?"

"We're careful. Except for that one time during calculus, we switch during play practice. It's intensive, total immersion into the play. We're doing *A Midsummer Night's Dream.* Conor and I work production. We switch off, so it's easy—he can be himself and me. Neither of us is missing that way. No one notices when one of us isn't there."

"You've pushed it. He took a test for you. Ever take one for him?"

"He was going to fail trig. He has this awful, obtuse teacher—"

"Conor sounds like he's as big a pain in the ass as you."

"I have four sisters," Charlie said quickly. "They're all pretty. If you don't rat me out, I can arrange a date with one of them. Come on. Cut me some slack."

The kid wasn't exactly begging, but Grit said, "I've got enough problems without dating one of your sisters. Go on. Get to class. Myrtle and I will keep your secret." He glanced up front. "Won't we, Myrtle?"

"Sure." She smiled into her rearview mirror. "You've got that look, Grit. I'll agree to anything you say. I don't want you killing me in my sleep."

Drama. He reached across Charlie and opened his door, then sat back again. "You and your cousin are not to pull this stunt again. Understood?"

Charlie nodded, then hesitated, his skin losing some of its color. "I don't care what happens to me," he said quietly.

"These assassins. They're not done. There's a network of them out there. They're ruthless, Petty Officer Taylor. I don't know if it's all about money or what. There has to be a middleman who hires killers on behalf of different clients. It's so clear to me."

"Fair enough. Any theories about who ordered Alex Bruni killed?"

The kid hesitated, then said, "What if he knew Drew Cameron's death in April wasn't an accident? What if he was killed by these assassins? Alex Bruni was a prominent ambassador. He probably had enemies who'd be willing to pay someone to kill him—who'd be able to figure out how to get in touch with such people. But he also knew Drew Cameron, and…" Charlie didn't go on.

Grit finished for him. "Cameron was just a guy from the mountains. He doesn't fit with the other victims. Bruni does, but since Cameron and Bruni both have connections to Black Falls, it's a problem."

"Yeah," Charlie said. "It's a problem."

"That's why we have cops. Anything you haven't told me? Your father—"

"He's not in danger that I know of. Absolutely not." Charlie blinked back sudden tears, his breathing rapid and shallow now.

Up front, Myrtle didn't say a word. Grit stayed very still. "Charlie?"

"I told you. Marissa was almost killed in September. Agent Harper saved her life. Jo could have died. Marissa could have died."

"According to my sources, that fire was an accident."

"What if it wasn't? I don't want anyone dying for me. The airsoft prank…I don't know what I was thinking."

"On some level, that prank made the risks Jo and her colleagues take feel less real to you."

"Yeah."

"And it was funny," Grit said.

"Jo got sent to Vermont. I didn't realize that's where Nora Asher moved after she dropped out of Dartmouth. If her father's mixed up in this network…if Drew Cameron and Alex Bruni were among its latest victims…if it's connected to Black Falls somehow—"

"Whoa. Slow down. How do you know about Nora Asher?"

He rolled his eyes. "Facebook. Come on. That was so easy."

Charlie noticed everyone and everything. Couldn't be an easy way to live.

A stunning, fair-haired young woman appeared on the walkway down from Myrtle's car. She was flanked by Secret Service agents. Charlie pulled his sweatshirt hood up over his cap and sank low in his seat. "That's Marissa. She teaches history here. I told you, didn't I?"

Very pretty, Grit had to admit. Even prettier than the pictures of her he'd found on the Internet.

Charlie slipped out of the car and ran, as if he were just a regular kid.

Moose slid into the seat Charlie had vacated. *"Wow. She's a knockout. The FBI agent, now the veep's daughter. Myrtle's not bad, either. Not so sorry you lived after all, are you?"*

"Don't speak too soon," Grit said. "The Secret Service is running Myrtle's tags right now."

"Not mine," Myrtle said. "It's my mother's car. And who the hell are you talking to?"

Grit grinned at her. "Your mother's still alive? She must have been born during the War of 1812."

"Revolutionary War." Myrtle sighed at him. "Don't you have PT exercises to do for your leg?"

"Did them. You going to tell me what's going on?"

"No. My problem. I'll deal with it."

"You and the dead Russian?"

"Go to hell, Grit."

Charlie's seat was empty again, and Grit pictured Moose bleeding, screaming at him to let the Special Forces medic cut off his leg. He said, "Been there."

# Thirty-Three

Jo took her mug of coffee and followed Melanie Kendall onto the terrace. The snow—half as much as up on the mountain—spread smooth and untouched down across the meadow and into the trees. The sky was clear now, a heart-stopping shade of blue. The police were still processing the scene on Cameron Mountain. As Elijah had anticipated, a search-and-rescue team had arrived soon after Rigby's first shots into the cabin. They'd heard them on their way up the mountain.

Jo's sister had been part of that first team to reach them and had treated Devin and helped transport him down to the old logging road and then to the hospital by ambulance. Beth had hardly spoken, but her expression had said everything. Words weren't necessary to convey just how close she knew Jo, Elijah and the two teenagers had come to getting killed early that morning.

There was much work to do to re-create Kyle Rigby's activities since arriving in Black Falls.

And even before then, Jo thought as she looked out at the beautiful view. She didn't see her hawk and wondered if he knew, by instinct, that it had been a bad day in his mountains. Elijah was in the dining room with A.J. and a couple of local police officers. A.J. hadn't believed what Rigby had told Melanie Kendall in his call to her.

Thomas was inside by the fire with his daughter.

Melanie shivered as a gust of wind blew across the meadow, whipping her black hair into her face. She wore a putty-colored shearling jacket but was hatless, her nose red, her eyes sunken. "I'm sick," she said as she stared at the view. "Just sick. That awful man wormed his way into my life. Then I *invited* him into Thomas's life. He used us all."

"He told me you two met in December," Jo said.

Melanie nodded. "Yes, in Colorado. I've been through all the details with the police. He told me he was an experienced, private search-and-rescue expert. That's why I thought of him when Nora took off after Alex's death. I didn't think anything of calling him. I was drawn to his certainty, his clarity, his decisiveness."

With her free hand, Jo scooped up snow from the top of a wooden table and, ignoring the cold on her bare fingers, formed it into a small ball as she flashed on countless snowball fights she'd had with the Camerons. Drew would often participate. He'd loved the snow.

She tossed her snowball off the end of the terrace and watched it plop into the fresh snow and disappear.

"You met Thomas in Black Falls in April," Jo said. "Had you been here before?"

Melanie shook her head. "No, never. It was my first visit." She turned, shoving her hands into her jacket pockets as she faced Jo. "Why?"

Jo didn't answer her. "Did you know anyone from here?"

"No." She smiled. "Agent Harper, please. Just tell me what's on your mind. I can see something's bothering you."

"I want to know how you ended up in Black Falls four months after you ran into Kyle Rigby in Colorado. Did you pick it at random? Did you know someone who'd been here?" Jo paused. "Did Rigby suggest Black Falls?"

"Oh, I see where you're headed." Melanie frowned and returned her gaze to the sparkling, endless view. "Kyle mentioned Vermont, but I can't remember if he said anything specifically about Black Falls. He told me he'd hiked here often and loved it."

"He knew where Drew's cabin was," Jo said, watching Melanie.

She seemed surprised. "Really? Are you sure?"

Jo didn't give her a direct answer. "The police are already checking with local inns and motels to find out if Rigby was in the area in April when Drew died."

Melanie gasped. "I could throw up. Do you think he followed me here?" She shuddered, tucking her bare hands up into the sleeves of her jacket. "I realize now that he was a horrible, manipulative man. I don't understand any of this. I just feel so guilty, but I suppose that's natural. Victims often blame themselves."

"You still haven't told me how you picked Black Falls."

"I was working night and day and needed a break, and I started looking on the Internet. I saw good reviews of Black Falls Lodge. I made a reservation."

"Had you been in touch with Rigby, or he with you, since December?"

"No. I'd filed his card under people who could be good to know and didn't think of him again until Nora went camping after Alex's death. Thomas was so upset. It just made sense to call Rigby."

"Then he shows up here and ends up nearly killing four people out of the blue? I don't buy it. I don't think you do, either."

"He engineered this whole thing. He obviously lied, manipulated—I don't know why. I'm not a detective. Maybe he was just a crazy killer who seized the moment." Melanie was defensive now, even angry. "I'm cold. I'm going back inside."

Jo didn't stop her, instead followed her into the dining room—no sign now of the two Cameron brothers and their cop pals—and down the hall to the lobby, where Thomas was in a wingback chair in front of the massive stone fireplace. He had Nora in his lap, holding her as if she were five again.

Obviously at a loss, Thomas barely acknowledged Melanie and Jo as he hugged his traumatized daughter. "I can't believe this," he said, his voice cracking with emotion. "Oh, Nora. Sweetheart. We'll get through this ordeal together. I promise."

Nora lifted her eyes to Melanie. "What about her?"

"She wants to help."

"No, she doesn't."

Thomas looked pained, almost stricken. "Nora." There was just the slightest edge to his tone. "I wish I knew what to say."

Melanie's mouth thinned, but she smiled cheerfully as she plopped down onto the sofa across from them. "Hey, guys. You're the smart ones, staying here where it's warm."

Nora slid off her father's lap and moved to another chair, and pulled her knees up under her chin, curling herself into a tight ball. Jo had learned from Lauren that Carolyn Asher Bruni would be arriving in Black Falls soon. Nora had indicated overnight in the cabin just how much she dreaded seeing her mother. Then she'd have to confront the reality of Alex's death and the days ahead. A funeral, an investigation, her mother's grief—and her own. Alex Bruni had been a strong force in Nora's life.

Thomas, ashen now, blinked helplessly at Melanie. "I'm sorry," he whispered.

She gave a little shake of the head. "Don't worry. Please. Nora's been through an awful, awful time."

Jo left the three of them by the fire and headed back to the dining room. No one was around—Camerons, cops, guests. She felt her own emotions well up, her fatigue gnawing at her. And questions, she thought. So many unanswered questions.

A.J. and Elijah emerged from the kitchen, A.J. carrying a golden-crusted pie, Elijah plates and forks. They set them on the first table they came to.

"Over here, Jo," A.J. said. "You never could resist apple pie. I picked the apples myself."

"You did not."

He smiled at her. "It's good to have you back home."

She approached the table, steam rising out of the pie and the smell of apples and cinnamon filling the air. "A.J., could Kyle Rigby have stolen the money from the shop's petty cash box? To frame Devin. It would have been easy to get the money out of Nora's kitchen, and even the café. Could he—"

A.J. was having none of it and shook his head. "I don't want to think about that son of a bitch crawling around here, near my family, our guests." His Cameron blue eyes held hers for an instant, his anger and his fierce love for his wife, his kids, his life in Black Falls radiating out of him. "Later, Jo."

She nodded. He cut three thick, warm slices of pie and set them on plates.

Elijah stood next to Jo and slid an arm around her waist. "Sit before you drop."

She shivered, not with cold this time, but with the awareness that she'd done it to herself again. Or maybe just had let herself reawaken what had been there all along, buried deep, dormant. Dangerous, even.

She loved Elijah Cameron, and she had since she was a girl.

# *Thirty-Four*

Myrtle dropped Grit back at the hotel where she'd picked up him and Charlie and took off again. The only reason he'd let her go was that he'd spotted his new FBI pals, and he thought he might need their help after all. As he walked toward their black sedan, he hit the redial button on his cell phone. This time, Elijah answered. "Storm over?" Grit asked.

"Long night. What do you have?"

Grit gave him the news. "Alexander Bruni was on his way to meet Thomas Asher for breakfast. Asher must have phoned in the tip about the messenger. They now have more specifics on her identity."

"How do you know?"

"I have my ways." Best not to tell Elijah about Charlie and his cousin switching places. Grit didn't want to put Elijah in the position of having to lie to his Secret Service-agent girlfriend. "I'm about to get into a car with a couple of FBI agents. I could be a while. If you don't hear from me in six months, come find me."

"Will do," Elijah said without hesitation, and Grit knew he meant it.

"What're you up to, anyway?"

"I'll fill you in later. Right now I'm eating apple pie."

"Vermont," Grit said and disconnected.

The back door of the FBI car opened, and he climbed in, ignoring a sudden tightness in his left foot. The cute female agent was driving this time. She glanced in the rearview mirror at his reflection. "Who were you just on the phone with?"

"Elijah Cameron."

From the narrowing of her eyes, Grit guessed she hadn't expected a straight answer, but she got her FBI face back on fast—just not fast enough. Whatever had been going on in Vermont while Elijah was *incommunicado,* she knew about it.

"Let's go see Myrtle Smith," Grit said, snapping on his seat belt. "She just dropped me off. But I figured I might need your help. You know where she lives, right?"

"Where have you been?" the beanpole agent asked him.

"Parking with Myrtle. She's a doll, isn't she? Those lavender eyes."

The female agent wasn't in the mood. "Start talking, Petty Officer Taylor."

"That reminds me. What are your names?"

They pretended not to hear him and drove out past Embassy Row and onto a shaded cul-de-sac of tidy Craftsman-style houses.

Flames were coming out of the front window of a cream-colored stucco two-story.

The two FBI agents swore under their breath, but before their car came to a full stop, Grit had the door open and was on his way, racing across the lawn in long, even strides, arms pumping, his mind focused on one thing and one thing only: Myrtle. She lay crumpled in her doorway as black smoke poured out of the house and swirled around her.

Grit heard popping, hissing and cracking sounds from inside as he ran up the front steps. He grabbed Myrtle up in his arms, turned and charged back out across the grass and all the way to the side of the road.

The beanpole FBI agent was on the radio, calling in the world.

Myrtle coughed, spat black gunk and sat up. "I knew you were on my tail," she told Grit.

He grinned at her. "You hoped I was."

The female agent beelined for them. "Ma'am, are you all right?"

"Just ducky."

Grit could see Myrtle was shaken, but he said, "You should have told me you were getting threats."

The female agent's brow furrowed, but she kept quiet.

Myrtle wiped a shaking hand across her mouth, smearing soot. "Hindsight. I get people warning me to back off all the time. I guess these bastards meant business."

"The Russian?"

She coughed, then nodded. "Andrei was a good man with bad enemies."

"You two—"

"Doesn't matter anymore." Her lavender eyes were red rimmed and watery. "One of his enemies hired our assassins to kill him."

"Proof?"

"My damn house burning down does it for me." She looked back at the flames and smoke, sirens already sounding in the distance. “At least I don’t have a cat. I’d have hated to have a cat killed in a fire.”

“Ever have a cat?” Grit asked her.

She spat some more and shifted her gaze to him. “Why? Do I strike you as the type?”

“Yeah.”

Tears welled in those big eyes of hers. “Lefty. I had to say goodbye to him a year ago. He was eighteen. Life sucks, Grit.”

“Sometimes.”

“We’re dealing with ruthless, dangerous people.”

“Yeah, Myrtle, we are.”

The beanpole FBI agent joined them, and his partner looked up at him and said, “The fire trucks are on the way. In the meantime, Myrtle and Grit here are going to talk to us about assassins.”

# *Thirty-Five*

Thomas took in a sharp breath when he saw Jo walking toward him from the dining room. He could tell she knew about his breakfast meeting with Alex, and he wanted to die on the spot. "Melanie. Please."

"Thomas—what is it? What can I do?"

He summoned his last shreds of dignity as he got to his feet, the fire crackling behind him, hot on his back; he felt flushed, sick to his stomach. He couldn't look at Nora. "Take Nora back to the Whittakers'."

Melanie took his hand. "What's wrong?"

"Just do as I ask. Please."

She nodded. "Of course."

Finally he turned to his daughter and spoke firmly. "Nora, I want you to go with Melanie. Lowell and Vivian are expecting you. They have a guestroom set up for you, since the police might still be at the guesthouse."

"Dad—"

"Your mother is on her way there."

He didn't wait for Nora to respond and extricated himself

from Melanie, who obviously sensed his distress. But he couldn't think about that now. He hurried down the hall toward Jo, intercepting her before she could say anything in front of his daughter and fiancée. "I panicked," he told her. "I panicked, and I ran. I'm sorry. I don't know what else to say."

"You need to talk to the police." Her tone was crisp, professional. "Scott Thorne just got here with my sister. I'll introduce you to him. You two can talk."

Thomas held back a surge of defensiveness. "The meeting was Alex's idea. He wanted to talk to me about Nora—he was worried about her. There was something else on his mind, too, but he didn't go into detail. He was late. I waited. Then when he was hit by that car…" Thomas pictured his friend's briefcase, the crease in his pants. "I don't know anything, Jo. I swear. I talked to a messenger who said she was a witness. I gave the police everything I could remember when I called in the tip. That's all."

"Who else knew about your breakfast with Ambassador Bruni?"

"No one that I know of. We wanted to be discreet, because of our personal situation. I just don't understand. Why kill Alex?" Thomas repeated the question, stunned, as if it would help him make sense of everything that had happened. "Who would want to harm him? He was my friend. He fell in love with the woman I married, but Carolyn and I weren't meant to be a match forever."

"As far as you know, she didn't know about your breakfast?"

"There was no reason for me to tell her, and I doubt Alex did. She was in Hong Kong, on an entirely different schedule. But he might have told her. I certainly don't know either way."

"What about Melanie?"

"No, I didn't mention anything to her, but I didn't hide anything from her, either."

Jo gave a curt nod. "Talk to Trooper Thorne. He's in the dining room with A.J. and Elijah."

"Jo—"

But she stayed focused. "I'll bring you to him."

Melanie resisted an impulse to get Nora by the hair and drag her across the parking lot. One more frosty look or moan of fatigue or whine about Devin and how scared she'd been, and Melanie wouldn't be able to resist smacking her. Thanks to the little bitch and Kyle's idiotic assault on Elijah Cameron and Jo Harper, Melanie realized that her life as she knew it was over.

"Just a few more steps," she said sweetly. "I know you're tired, sweetie."

Nora gave her a sullen look and didn't pick up her pace a fraction.

Melanie resisted an impulse to slap her across her sorry, tear-stained face. What did that little bitch have to worry about? Her life would go on. She had her mother and her father and her trust fund. She could go back to Dartmouth. So, Alex was dead. So, she'd been scared. Melanie thought of all *she* was in danger of giving up thanks to Nora and her lack of trust, her inability to let her father fall in love again. She realized she was losing Thomas. The police must have been provided with some new bit of information about Alex's death—someone who'd seen Thomas at the hotel. He'd looked guilt stricken when he'd seen Jo coming down the hall, but also maybe a little relieved, as if he'd been waiting for the moment when everyone would finally discover what a weasel he'd been.

Not that it mattered. As the day had worn on and Kyle's death had penetrated her psyche, Melanie had recognized that Kyle's stupidity left her no choice but to deal with Nora Asher herself.

*Damn you, Kyle.* She went around to the passenger side of her rented car and opened the door. He must have known that Elijah and Jo were armed. They weren't the cold-blooded killer Kyle was, but they were more than capable of taking him down.

He hadn't committed suicide. Not intentionally. Knowing him as well she did, Melanie was convinced he'd thought he could make his plan work. He just wasn't that good at thinking on his feet.

But she was.

"Here," she said, opening the front passenger door. "Do you need help getting in or are you—"

"I'm fine," Nora said, stepping past Melanie and flopping down onto the car seat.

Melanie kept her mouth shut and ignored the twitch in her fingers. It would be so easy to reach into the car and choke Nora to death right here, right now. But Kyle had warned her countless times to control her impulses and not let the thrill of doing the unexpected get ahead of her thinking and her self-interest.

She went around to the driver's side of the car and got in behind the wheel. Very calmly she reached inside her shearling jacket and withdrew the pistol that Kyle had given her last night. She slipped it into her right outer pocket and looked at Nora with a small, satisfied smile. "You're in trouble, my darling daughter."

"I'm not your daughter," Nora said, "and I hate you."

"Fine by me." Melanie stuck the key in the ignition.

"Where are you taking me?"

"To a cold and lonely place where you'll die a cold and lonely death, just like Drew Cameron did. The cold will make you sleepy after a while. You'll stop shivering. You'll go to sleep. It'll be nice. I'll tell police that you went to meet Devin. They'll believe me."

"You're Kyle Rigby's partner."

"Kyle's dead. I'm marrying your father on Valentine's Day."

"No, you'll die a horrible death and suffer for all eternity in the fires of hell."

Something about her tone—her moral certainty—made Melanie frightened for the first time in years. But her fear didn't last. She would take Nora to an isolated spot in the mountains. With the weather, the location, the approach of nightfall, there was virtually no chance anyone would find her in time.

After she turned Thomas over to Scott Thorne, Jo walked back down to the stone fireplace and took a call from Mark Francona. She'd been expecting one. He didn't ask her about the shooting. "The police received another tip. They've located their messenger." He spoke without any hint of relief. "She said she didn't come forward because she assumed there were other witnesses."

"She saw the driver?"

"A woman. Blond hair—probably a wig."

"Rigby had a partner."

"We're assuming he was involved in Bruni's death."

"He was." Jo paused. "Mark, Thomas Asher's fiancée recommended he hire Rigby."

"Where is she now?"

"With Nora. I have to go."

She dropped her phone and drew her weapon as she ran out the door, not surprised, somehow, when Elijah fell in beside her.

"It's Melanie," Jo said.

"I'll find Nora."

"Elijah—"

He shot ahead of her, charging out to the parking lot toward Melanie's car. Jo ran behind him, leveling her Sig at the driver's side. The window whirred down. Melanie looked shocked. "What on earth—"

"Hands up where I can see them," Jo ordered.

"Why? What—"

"Hands up. Now."

Melanie's hands went up. "Good heavens. Relax."

On the other side of the car, Elijah ripped open the passenger side and grabbed Nora, even as she screamed, "Melanie's got a gun!"

He half carried, half dragged Nora behind his truck and told her to stay down.

Melanie sighed at Jo. "Nora's talking nonsense. Where would I get a gun? I'm just taking her back to the Whittakers' house. I know she's upset, but to be this irresponsible and inconsiderate is beyond the pale."

"Keep your hands where I can see them," Jo said. "No sudden moves."

"Why are you treating me like a criminal?"

Jo kept her weapon on her. "The police have a witness who can place you behind the wheel of the car that killed Alexander Bruni. You're in a tough situation, Melanie. Your partner's dead. He took us on because he knew he had no choice. It was kill or be killed by his own people. You need to cooperate."

Her eyes shone with tears. "Please. Stop. I have no idea what you're talking about."

"You and Rigby have failed, Melanie. I'm guessing the people you work for don't like failure. The police are combing Drew's cabin for evidence. If you left behind so much as an eyelash when you and your buddy Rigby killed Drew Cameron, they'll find it."

Melanie didn't move, but a kind of calm came over her. She leveled her gaze on Jo with a bloodlust that was soul deep. "Drew died believing he'd exchanged his life for his son's."

"That's not what happened," Elijah said, cold, controlled.

"It is what happened," Melanie said, addressing Jo, clearly taking pleasure from whatever image she had of that day. "He'd had a premonition. He knew his son was in mortal danger. He died and Elijah lived."

"He was onto you and Rigby," Jo said. "That's why you and Rigby killed him."

Elijah stayed in front of Nora by his truck, but Jo could feel how much he wanted to go after Melanie. "I'd already been wounded," he said. "Maybe my father was tuned in to my pain and maybe he wasn't. You and Rigby killed him for reasons that didn't have a damn thing to do with his fears for me."

As he spoke, Jo took a step toward the car. She was about fifty feet away.

Melanie was still enjoying herself. "The moment Drew saw Kyle and me, he knew he was dead and there was nothing he could do."

"You had guns," Elijah said. "He didn't. Never mind his fears, any connection he had with me. You killed him. You got his pack off him and made sure he'd freeze to death up there."

Jo didn't go any closer to the car. "Open the door, Melanie. Step out of the car. Do *exactly* as I say."

Fear sparked in her eyes. "If I cooperate—"

With no warning, the car erupted into flames and smoke. Jo felt herself being blown backward, off her feet, as a heavy double thump ignited the gas tank, sucking the air out of the immediate area. The car jerked off the ground and then slammed back down hard in a flaming heap.

She felt the ground hard under her, then became aware of Elijah leaping toward her as she fought for air, her chest tight. She rolled onto her stomach, shoving her bare hands into the snow up to her wrists. The shock of the cold helped revive her, and she jumped up.

Elijah was there now, and he grabbed her. "There's nothing we can do. She's gone."

"Elijah, what the hell—"

"It was a remote-controlled device. Not on a timer. Maybe a cell phone."

She nodded, the acrid smoke filling her nostrils, clogging her throat. "Then someone's close enough to have set it off. We need to get moving."

A.J., Scott Thorne and Beth ran out of the lodge with fire extinguishers. But they, too, quickly saw there was no hope for Melanie Kendall. The explosive device had very clearly been set near—probably under—the driver's seat. She hadn't stood a chance.

"Her own people killed her," Jo said.

Elijah nodded grimly.

Thomas Asher walked tentatively out the main entrance of the lodge. He hesitated as he took in the scene, then descended the steps and pushed his way past A.J. and Scott, breaking into a run as he yelled not for his fiancée but for his daughter.

Elijah grabbed him and brought him over to Nora, who was curled up, not moving. Her father dropped to his knees and held her, sobbing. "Nora, thank God. My baby."

"We need to see if we can locate whoever set this thing off," Jo said to Scott Thorne.

He was already on his radio, calling in a fresh surge of state troopers. Jo fell in beside Elijah. A.J. was there, too. But she could tell from their expressions that they all knew what she did: they wouldn't find the paid assassin who had just set off a remote-controlled explosive device and killed one of their own.

# *Thirty-Six*

Grit entered Myrtle's favorite D.C. bar, which had pale pink walls and a lot of pictures of movie stars from before his time. He found her in an ornately carved wooden booth with a lit votive candle in the middle of the table. She was drinking Perrier with lime and obviously hating it. "Hey, Myrtle," he said. "Got a place to stay tonight?"

She shrugged. "Here. The owners like me. I can sleep under the table."

"Bet you booked yourself a room at the Four Seasons."

"Not me. I hate spending money on fancy hotels. But I'm not sleeping on your sofa, so don't invite me. I couldn't take the rats." She tipped back her glass and took a big swallow of her water, then set it down and stared at it as if it had answers. "The arson investigator says the fire started in my office. Probably electrical."

"It wasn't an accident."

"No, but killing me wasn't the main goal. A bonus, maybe." She peeled the little lime off its toothpick and dropped it back into her water. "I had a lot of source material that went up in flames. I think I just got too close to these bastards."

"What do the police say?"

"Nothing. Your FBI friends aren't talking, either."

"Everyone's tight-lipped on this one," Grit said. "This network's been flying under the radar. It could be a guy in his basement with a computer, hiring killers on behalf of people who want someone killed."

"Like Andrei," Myrtle said.

"Yeah. You and Petrov were an item?"

"I loved him. He loved me. We weren't ever going to be together. I'm not the marrying type, and he was a worse workaholic than me." She looked away, her pretty eyes shining but tearless. "Paid killers aren't easy to find. There's no connection to the victim. No passion. No *reason*. It's all about money. Sometimes I don't know which I detest more—the killer for hire or the one who hired him."

"I'm sorry about Petrov," Grit said simply.

"Yeah. Thanks." She cleared her throat and turned back to her water. "I have a feeling Drew Cameron and Alex Bruni were killed for the same reason my house got torched. I think they got too close to these bastards. This network of assassins."

Grit considered her words a moment, then said, "I think you're right."

But she didn't respond, and a slim, pretty waitress in an outfit a slightly darker pink than the walls came for Grit's order. Scotch. No water for him. When she left, Myrtle rolled her eyes. "What is it with you and women?"

He paid no attention. "You know, Myrtle," he said, "you could have been killed today."

"They teach you that in SEAL school—that a fire can kill someone?"

"It's not called—"

"Don't start with me. You know what I mean. I wasn't killed today. Neither were you." She raised her eyes, a dark purple in the dim light. "You weren't killed in April, either."

"Should have been."

She reached down to her side and produced a printout of a color photograph, which she pushed across the table at him. "That's Moose Ferrerra's baby boy. Ryan Cameron Ferrerra. Three months old. Adorable, isn't he? His mother named him after two men who fought with his father in his last hours in this life. Two men who were also badly wounded and could have died that same night."

Grit didn't look at the picture. "Don't turn Elijah, Moose and me into a human-interest story."

Myrtle squeezed her lime into her water. "His widow chose the name for their son after his father was killed. Not before, Grit. Give me a break, okay? You know what I'm saying. This baby carries the names of three good men."

"April shouldn't have turned out the way it did. Moose had a family. I didn't."

"Elijah Cameron doesn't have a family."

"He does," Grit said. "Just different. And he wasn't a SEAL, and he wasn't supposed to die. I was."

"You still are a SEAL, Grit. And Moose's widow doesn't think that way. You think that way."

Grit's drink arrived. He flirted with the waitress and pretended Myrtle wasn't there. But the waitress had to go back to work, and Myrtle was hard to ignore.

She said, "Elijah set up a trust fund for Moose's two kids—

a two-year-old boy and this little guy. Contribute to it. Be there for those boys when they want to know what their dad was like."

"You need to stop, Myrtle."

She didn't. "Let Moose go. Let him be at peace."

Grit drank some of his scotch and wondered about the tragedies in her life, what ghosts she'd had to face. The dead Russian. Others.

"Come on." She took one more sip of her water and shoved the glass to the middle of the table. "Let's walk over to the Lincoln Memorial."

"Did you know Lincoln?"

"Is Cameron as big a pain in the neck as you?"

"Yeah."

"Fun, because after we talk to Lincoln, we're going to Vermont. You're a one-legged SEAL and I'm a lonely reporter with cat pictures in her wallet. Let's go see that other ghost you're friends with—Cameron—and talk assassins."

"I like Vermont maple syrup," Grit said. "That's about it."

He had to slow down for her on the walk to the memorial, then a couple of times up the steps to the massive statue. It wasn't a lack of fitness on her part, he knew. It was the fire at her house. The Russian. Assassins. Maybe Charlie Neal.

He was on the top step when he felt Moose ease in next to him, but when Grit turned to say something, his friend and teammate—the man who'd saved his life—was gone.

# *Thirty-Seven*

Jo found Nora on the floor in front of the stone fireplace with her knees tucked up under her chin as she stared, motionless, at the flames. Lowell Whittaker had just called A.J. to let him know that Nora's mother had arrived in Black Falls and he and Vivian were driving her up to the lodge.

With his fiancée and best friend dead on top of not mentioning his breakfast with Alex Bruni, Thomas was still with the police. Dozens of law enforcement vehicles stretched down the ridge road. The local police, the Vermont State Police, the FBI, ATF, federal prosecutors, state prosecutors—they were all there.

So was Wes Harper, the recently retired Black Falls police chief.

"Mind if I join you?" Jo asked Nora and, without waiting for an answer, sat on the floor next to her. The fire was roaring. Everyone who passed it seemed to toss on a log. "I could sleep here, I think. Have you had anything to eat?"

"Some cocoa."

"Me, too. It's good, isn't it?"

"I guess. Devin… How is he?"

"He's back home with his sister and brother. He's banged up, but he'll be okay."

She sniffled, but her eyes never left the fire. "He saved my life. I wish I'd saved his instead." Fat tears rolled down her cheeks. "I wish I'd done something."

"You did. You trusted your instincts, and you ran after Alex's death." Jo spoke quietly but firmly, believing every word she said. She was aware of Elijah behind them, close enough to hear, far enough not to intrude. "Drew Cameron came to Washington in April two weeks before you and your father were up here."

Nora didn't respond. She seemed unaware of the tears streaming down her face, over her mouth and chin, onto her knees.

"Did you see him?" Jo asked.

This time Nora answered. "He stopped by Alex's office. We'd just had this big, awful fight about colleges. Dad hadn't met Melanie yet. Drew walked in—I'd seen him in Black Falls but didn't really know him. He looked like…" She sucked in a breath, her nose running now, too. "I thought he looked like such a hick."

Jo smiled. "He'd like it that you thought that."

"Really?"

"Trust me. Drew would have hated anyone to think he actually belonged in Washington. Did he say anything?"

"Just that he wanted to talk to Alex. Alex wasn't very nice but let him in."

"You weren't very nice, either?"

If possible, Nora sank her chin deeper into her knees, her guilt and regret palpable. "He told me that when I was his age, I'd know that the people I loved and who loved me would matter to me more than a fight over which college to attend. I made fun of him." She buried her face in her knees and said, her voice muffled, "He was about to die, and I made fun of him."

Behind them, Elijah said nothing. Jo felt the heat of the fire and her own fatigue, her own regrets. "Drew was also a wise man, and he'd have understood that you were eighteen and trying to figure out your life. He had a lot on his mind, more even than I realized. He didn't tell me everything. It's clear now that he'd figured out something that posed a threat to some very dangerous people."

Nora raised her head off her knees, but still didn't look at Jo. "He asked for Alex's help. I don't know about what—I didn't hear any specifics. But Alex was mad at me, and he took it out on Drew. Now they're both dead."

"I guarantee that the reasons they're dead have nothing to do with you or your behavior that day."

Elijah finally came closer, and he got down next to Nora, tucked one finger under her chin and raised her eyes to him. "Listen to me. Okay?" He waited until she nodded, then dropped his hand and continued. "My father didn't die because of you. He and then Alex died because they got too close to a network of paid killers. Melanie and Kyle were a part of that network. We don't know all the particulars yet. We might never know."

"Melanie…"

"Her own people killed her. She screwed up by getting involved with your father. That complicated things for them."

"Because Devin and I started checking her out—"

Jo broke in. "No, Nora. Because Melanie was who she was. If she'd just been an interior decorator, she wouldn't have cared all that much about what you and Devin were up to."

Nora didn't respond right away. Then she sat cross-legged, her fatigue and distress evident in the dark circles under her eyes, in the tremble of her lower lip. She addressed Elijah, speaking quietly. "If Alex and I hadn't had that fight, maybe he'd have listened to your dad. Maybe they could have stopped these guys."

"If my father had known he was onto a bunch of paid assassins," Elijah said, "he'd have gone to the police, not to your stepfather. Whatever he knew got them nervous enough to kill him."

"That awful woman…Melanie…" Nora paled when she spoke the name of her father's dead fiancée. "What she said about your dad…"

"There's no question in my mind that my father would have exchanged his life for mine without hesitation. It's not what happened, but I hope he died believing his death meant I would live. I hope he had that consolation."

"He was a good man. My mum and dad…"

"They've made their mistakes. Right now, your father, especially."

"I don't want to go to Alex's funeral."

"Go," Elijah said bluntly. "Give yourself that chance to say goodbye."

# *Thirty-Eight*

Elijah entered the Harper kitchen for the first time in more than a decade, but it hadn't changed. He wasn't surprised. Wes Harper had a dozen canning jars of applesauce lined up on the round oak table. He'd let Elijah come in. Elijah took that as a positive sign. It was five days since his ordeal on Cameron Mountain with Jo, Nora and Devin.

Most of the reporters who'd descended on Black Falls in the first twenty-four hours after Kyle Rigby and Melanie Kendall had died on Cameron land had departed.

There'd been no official mention of paid killers at work.

Jo was still on the lake, running every morning, consulting with her law enforcement colleagues. Her Secret Service boss had flown in and out again in one day. Mark Francona had struck Elijah as a serious hard-ass. Elijah had offered him use of his canoe, in case Francona and Jo wanted to paddle across the lake before it froze solid. Francona didn't seem to think that was funny.

Grit Taylor and Myrtle Smith had arrived the morning after the storm and showed no sign of leaving anytime soon.

Grit had set up in the most isolated and removed of Jo's run-down cabins. Myrtle had checked in to the best room at Black Falls Lodge. Her presence was just the distraction A.J. and Lauren needed—Myrtle loved the idea of a luxury spa at the lodge.

The younger Cameron siblings had returned home. A.J., Elijah, Sean and Rose had sat up last night in front of the fire at the lodge and talked until dawn.

When he'd left for the lake, Elijah had known what he had to do. He didn't care that Jo had been back in his life for just days. In a way, she'd always been there, for as long as he could remember.

"I'd like to talk to you, sir," he said to Jo's father.

Wes Harper had a black permanent marker in one hand. "Drew was right," he said as he wrote the date on the cap of one of the applesauce jars. "I never cut you a single break."

"Because of Jo."

"Yeah." He looked up at Elijah with eyes that were darker than his daughter's but still bore a resemblance. "I didn't make up reasons to get in your face, but I was harder on you than I ever was on anyone else, before or since. Maybe you'll be the father of a teenage girl one day and be able to forgive me."

Elijah shrugged. "I forgave you a long time ago. You probably saved my life. You probably made it possible for me to ask your daughter to marry me."

Harper's hand stopped in midair.

Elijah didn't falter. Not this time, he thought. Not ever again where his love for Jo was concerned. "I'd like your support."

Harper set the marker on the table and steadied his cop gaze on Elijah. "It would be an honor to have you as a son-in-law—if Jo's crazy enough to have you." Still, he didn't smile. "If she won't, Elijah, then that's it. Never again. Let her go for good this time."

"She'll have me."

"Yeah." Harper almost smiled. "I know."

"I realize we haven't been together that long."

"Fifteen years, Elijah. Longer. She had her first crush on you when she was six. Hopeless." But Wes Harper wasn't a man for a lot of talk, especially about matters of the heart, and he grabbed up his marker again and said, "Those two killers—Rigby and Kendall. There are more where they came from."

It wasn't a question, but Elijah nodded. "Yes."

"Jo?"

"She won't tell me, but I think she's working the investigation."

Her father sighed. "I don't mind telling you this whole business scares the hell out of me. To have a daughter in the Secret Service..."

Elijah recognized the fear of a father for a child. "Jo's a chip off the old block, Chief Harper. She doesn't cut anyone slack, either."

Harper gave a satisfied smile. "Good." Then he added, "And it's Wes, son. Just Wes."

It was cleaning night at the Three Sisters Café. Jo had scrubbed the stainless steel sink in the kitchen and was about to start on the counters, but then quiet, lovely Dominique pulled a tray of scones out of the oven and that was it. "Time for a break," Jo said, and she, Beth and Scott grabbed scones, plates, silverware and small pots of butter and jam and took them out to the dining room.

Hannah and even tireless Dominique promised to join them in a few minutes. For the first time in days, their lives weren't centered on the close call on Cameron Mountain. Even Devin, recovering rapidly from his injuries, had taken Toby to a movie, an act of normalcy that their older sister obviously welcomed.

But as Jo broke off a piece of scone, her cell phone rang. She winced at the intrusion and expected it was Mark Francona, who had sentenced her—his words—to a few more weeks, at least, in Vermont. Francona didn't care about her getting Charlie Neal by the ear anymore. He was more interested in finding assassins. He had seized on her presence in Black Falls and figured it was meant to be, a product of his intuition and brilliance. "Buy a snow shovel," he'd told her. "You're going to be in the frozen north for a while."

But it wasn't Francona's voice she heard on the other end of the connection. "Special Agent Harper?"

Jo sat up straight, recognizing the deep male voice. "Yes, sir."

"This is Preston Neal. Charlie and Marissa's dad. I just want to say…" Clearly emotional, the vice president paused for a moment, then gave a little cough and continued. "Thank you, Jo. Thank you for what you did for both of them."

"Just doing my job, sir."

"You saved Marissa's life. And Charlie. I need to spend more time with him. It's amazing how fast the years pass by. He's sixteen…"

"He's a great kid."

"Thank you. His mother and I think so, too."

Jo was aware of Scott Thorne glowering at her from across the table, as if he could guess whatever she was up to was about to complicate his life. Beth sat next to him. She glanced at Jo, then distracted her trooper boyfriend by putting a dot of butter on the end of his nose. Scott laughed, probably for the first time since he had trekked up the north side of Cameron Mountain after the season's first snowstorm. The investigation into Kyle Rigby and Melanie Kendall and their murderous network had only just begun. It would be long, thorough and painstaking.

So far, it looked as if Charlie Neal had been dead-on.

But not about everything.

The vice president took a breath. "Jo?"

"Sir," she said finally, "your son needs to understand that what happened to his sister was an accident. It had nothing to do with this other business."

"This network of assassins," Preston Neal said. "Charlie helped?"

"Yes. He has a sharp eye, but he's a kid. He should be playing lacrosse and acing calculus tests."

"The challenge for Charlie is that he can do those things *and* stick his nose in other people's business." The vice president spoke with a father's mix of love, pride and pure frustration. "But you're okay, Jo? You've done so much for my family. Don't forget to live your own life."

She thought of Elijah. She'd heard his truck out on the road in front of her cabin at dawn as he'd headed back from what she'd known had been a long night with his sister and two brothers. Jo was already up stretching for her run. The night before, Grit Taylor had decided to join her, saying he could keep up with a girl Secret Service agent, no sweat. He'd told her to be ready at sunup. Since he was the type to dump her out of bed, Jo had been ready. He'd teased her some more as they'd set off. He had kept up with her, too. When they returned to the cabins, Elijah was out skipping stones into the lake.

"The difference between Cameron and me is this," Grit had said quietly, unusually serious. "I lived and wished I hadn't. Elijah never thought he'd live, but he's glad he did. Because of you."

Then he'd gone inside, leaving Jo to her cold cabin.

Preston Neal went on, as if he could read her mind, "I understand there's a certain Special Forces solider…"

"We grew up together."

"Sergeant Cameron is a hero in my book. So is his friend Ryan Taylor. And so are you, Jo. Please. You all be careful."

"We will, and thank you, Mr.—" She stopped herself, aware of the people around her. "I appreciate the call."

After she hung up, Jo avoided the questioning looks of her tablemates and finished her scone as she experienced a jolt of reality. What had she been thinking? Life could never be normal for her again in her hometown. She'd left at eighteen, and she now had a job to do. Even if everyone suspected that she'd been given a role in the investigation, she had no illusions. She didn't belong in Black Falls.

Then her sister kicked her under the table. "Smile, Jo. Lighten up. You'll catch the bad guys. The good guys didn't do so bad this round."

"If we'd managed to take either one of them alive…"

Scott shook his head. "You know better than to second-guess yourself that way, Jo. Rigby had 120 rounds on him. You and Elijah had no other choice. As for Kendall—" Scott shrugged. "She was playing with a rough crowd."

Beth leaned forward over the small table. "Jo, if you and Elijah hadn't acted, Nora wouldn't have survived."

Jo understood. Her sister had been the first of the medical personnel on the scene after the explosion and had witnessed what it had done to Melanie Kendall. Investigators had concluded that a simple pipe bomb constructed of smokeless gunpowder, black powder, two thin strands of copper wire and a cell phone had been placed under Melanie's front seat. Someone had called the cell phone, and the electricity from the call was just enough to ignite the lethal charge.

Nora had gone back to the Georgetown home that her mother had shared with her second husband. Thomas was cooperating with police. Detectives were going through Nora and Devin's research into her father's fiancée and had already discovered that one of her potential interior decorating clients had turned up murdered. They had travel records to investigate. DNA results would be coming back on both her and her partner in killing. They'd test everything they'd collected in Drew's cabin for a match.

Jo grabbed her scone and rose, realizing she'd just reminded everyone of what they'd been trying to forget, at least for a few hours. "I should go."

But Scott pointed at her. "Sit down. Finish your scone." He smiled. "Some tough Secret Service agent you are, eating scones." He reached over and slung his arm across the back of Beth's chair; she settled against him. His smile faded, his eyes still on Jo. "Come on. Sit. We all need to talk. Why should you be any different?"

Hannah and Dominique joined them from the kitchen, and Jo returned to her seat. Beth dived into her second scone without any hint of guilt. Hannah took a tiny nibble of her scone and offered up her theory. "These killers went to a lot of trouble to try to make it look like two kids got in over their heads with each other and died on the mountain."

"That's more or less what they did with Drew," Beth said quietly.

"Do you know what that tells me?" Hannah looked out the window, although it had been dark several hours. "Whoever hired them didn't want attention focused on Black Falls."

Scott gave a low whistle. "You'll make a hell of a prosecutor, Hannah."

She turned to him with a small smile. "I'll take that as a compliment. I hope I'm wrong. Either way," she added, "those of you in law enforcement have your work cut out for you."

Jo didn't comment. Dominique shuddered, and they continued in that vein for a long time, until the entire tray of fresh scones was gone. By the time Jo drove back to the lake, she figured she'd have to run a marathon in the morning to burn off her share of the scones.

It was a crisp, clear, late-autumn evening, quiet and downright cold in her cabin. She tried twice to get a call out on her cell phone, but it just wasn't going to work. Finally she gave up, grabbed her flashlight and walked out the road to Elijah's house in the woods.

She saw him up on his deck and called to him. "There's a bat in my cabin."

He ambled down to her in his canvas jacket and baseball cap. It was bad, she thought. Even the way he walked struck her as sexy. He said, "I warned you about the bats."

"You're handy. Think of something."

He smiled. "Already have."

Of course, there was no bat. When they got to her cabin,

he didn't bother to look for one, just grabbed her in his arms and fell onto the old iron bed with her. They tore at each other's clothes—coats, sweaters, wool socks, everything going, tossed onto the floor. Jo felt as if she was eighteen again, bursting with the need for him, wanting nothing more than to make love to bad boy Elijah. But the air was colder than those hot June days and nights fifteen years ago, and she wasn't eighteen or twenty-five or even thirty—but it didn't matter. He skimmed his palms over her bare skin, setting it on fire, and she knew she was as in love with him as ever.

"I should have answered your letters," he whispered between kisses. "Jo. I'm sorry."

"I shouldn't have written. I should have let you go."

"No." He gave her a long, tender kiss, even as one hand drifted over her hip. "I kept the picture you sent me of us together here on the lake."

Her heart almost stopped. "Elijah…"

"Maybe it wasn't smart, hanging on to a picture of an old girlfriend, but I kept thinking it was bad luck to throw it out." He raised himself up, his eyes locking with hers in the dim light. "I'd have died without you. I know it."

She held back tears. "I'm glad you didn't die."

She draped her arms around his neck and pulled herself up, their mouths meeting as she lowered her head back against the pillow. His hand eased over her hip, and she parted her legs for him, arching toward him as his fingertips, then his fingers, worked an erotic magic on her. She slipped a hand between them and touched him, stroked him, matching the rhythm of his fingers inside her.

"Jo." There was a catch of pure desire in his voice. "Ah, Jo."

And she guided him into her, welcoming the feel of him

as she eased both arms around his back and smoothed her palms up his hard muscles. He thrust deeply into her, and she responded, moving with him, not holding back even a little as she abandoned herself to the heat pulsing through her, the sweet ache of wanting him.

Then she couldn't think anymore. Every fiber of her mind and body—her soul—was caught up in the feel of him, his powerful strokes, the way he drove her to the edge, then pulled her back again.

She'd never wanted a man as much. She'd never loved a man as much.

She buried her face in his shoulder when the spasms started. He didn't relent, and she didn't want him to, and when she cried out, she heard him say her name, over and over, and realized they were in unison, their timing perfect as they spun into a long, almost endless release.

"Jo," he said softly again when it was over, as he lay next to her.

She smiled. "I like hearing you say my name." And she propped up her head on one hand and looked down at him. "Elijah, Elijah, Elijah."

"You couldn't even talk there a minute ago."

They both laughed, and they got dressed again, drawn, as if by an invisible force, back outside and down to the lake. The air was still but very cold, and the water sparkled in the moonlight. Jo's eyes adjusted quickly to the dark. She didn't miss the city lights.

Elijah stood very close to her, their toes almost in the water. "Right here or at the falls. My deck. The lodge. Washington. I don't care." He turned and brushed a knuckle gently across her cheek. "I love you, Jo."

She grabbed his hand into hers and took a breath, and she tried to speak but couldn't get any words out.

He kissed her hand. "I want to love and cherish you for the rest of our lives."

"Elijah…"

"The rest doesn't matter. What we'll do, where we'll live—it doesn't matter, so long as we're together. Jo, I'm asking you to marry me."

She couldn't get a decent breath.

He smiled. "Speechless, are you?" With his free hand, he dug into his jacket pocket, producing a diamond ring. He held it between his thumb and forefinger. "I don't know what happened to the little box it came in. Maybe there wasn't one."

"You've been chasing bad guys, Elijah. When have you had time—"

"I bought this ring for you the day you graduated from high school. I helped old Pete Harper cut cordwood out here to earn the money. I didn't buy it in town. I knew your father would shoot me if he knew. It's not expensive, but I thought for now…"

"Forever." It was all she could think to say. "It's perfect."

"I'm sorry I hurt you, Jo. I'm sorry I never answered your letters."

She blinked back tears. "I'm sorry I hung on. Elijah…" Finally, she laughed, squeezing his hand. "Nothing's changed after all, has it? I love you. I always have. I've never stopped. I never will stop."

He slipped the ring onto her finger and put his arm around her, pulling her close to him as he kissed the top of her head. "Can you picture it, Jo? Our kids. Out here. I can see them now." He laughed as if he could, indeed, see them. "We'll have our hands full."

"We will," Jo said.

Elijah's arm tightened around her as a breeze stirred, floating down from Cameron Mountain and across the moonlit lake, and she leaned against the man she'd loved for as long as she could remember.